The Twilight Club

Annabel West

Bella
BOOKS

2011

Bella Books, Inc.
P.O. Box 10543
Tallahassee, FL 32302

Printed in the United States of America on acid-free paper
First published 2011

Editor: Medora MacDougall
Cover Designer: Judy Fellows

ISBN 13: 978-1-59493-257-1

For Helen

About The Author

Annabel West lives in Melbourne, Australia, with her partner and, as often as time allows, enjoys traveling throughout Asia. The histories, cultures, vibrancy and mystery of the Orient are a constant source of fascination.

CHAPTER ONE

It was that breathless time just before sunset when the heat of the day pulsed from white-hot concrete and baked tiled roofs. The road in front of the old Peranakan Hotel snaked along the river's edge and rippled in a heat haze. On the riverbank the squeals of playful children were fading. Down in the street market, voices had dropped to a low murmur.

Overlooking the river, and beyond it the sea, Angelique relaxed on the shady hotel verandah. Droplets of water from the hotel's pool trickled from her short dark hair. The bleached sky showed traces of gold in the west; the cooler relief of darkness would come soon.

Angelique removed her sunglasses, dropped them onto the cane table. She took a sip of her iced tea. In the distance, beyond the faded façades of houses, she glimpsed the tumbledown buildings lining the old port. The rusty iron roofs of warehouses were buckled, the once grand red-tiled roofs of the customs offices blackened with age and relentless sun. She imagined them teeming with ghosts who dreamed of the days when the wharves had groaned under the weight of precious spices, silks and gold. Wealth and opportunity had brought princes and emperors from India and Siam, and the first immigrants from China. But strategic trading had moved elsewhere long ago. Nowadays Malacca was a sleepy old town that Angelique loved and made a point to visit at least once each year.

It was Wednesday, the last day of her week's holiday. After a difficult three-month-long job in Jakarta she had needed a break before returning home to Singapore. As a freelance business consultant she assisted Asian companies seeking foreign investment partners and Westerners—mostly Australians—planning expansion into Asian markets. The Jakarta job had been for an Australian company setting up a software manufacturing business. It was satisfying that more than a hundred new jobs had been created. A resurgence in business activity had kept her busy, but in a few regions of southeast Asia lax government regulations and people keen on making up losses had lured more than a few sharks looking for easy money.

The sun's yellow tentacles crept onto the verandah and curled around the outstretched claws of the dragon carved into the balustrade. The heat was sweltering, yet there was a gentleness in that buttery sun. Not like the sun she had grown up with. Australian summer sun seared. It sliced the world into colors so bright they hurt your eyes. You couldn't look at anything white except through tears. Earth and walls and nerves cracked. At sunset, the sun wouldn't be sliding like melting butter across a dinner-plate sky. It would be sizzling, blood-red, the sky gashed and bloodstained. Australia's sun went down screaming.

Seven years ago, at age twenty-eight, Angelique had landed a job with an international aid agency. She had left her hometown of Melbourne and been based in Jakarta. Her work as a financial administrator had taken her to the agency's long-term projects in Papua New Guinea, Vietnam, parts of Malaysia and Indonesia. As she met with field managers working in villages battling the aftermath of flood or drought or war, her job was to assess expenditure and allocate budgets. But like many of the field staff, Angelique had grown increasingly frustrated with the agency's narrow and lofty vision. It tended to favor grandiose schemes at the expense of practical, grassroots assistance. Angelique believed that, with money to start or regenerate businesses and the provision of modern farming technology, people could be eased off the handouts and resume normal lives. Parents would actually send their children to the lovely, empty schools the agency provided once they no longer had to keep them at home to help the family scratch out a living. After four years of this Angelique had grown disillusioned and restless.

Then a chance opportunity had led her to quit her aid job and return to the business world. Bianca, a friend and old associate in Melbourne, had phoned to ask Angelique's help for an acquaintance wanting to set up a clothing factory in Malaysia. Angelique discovered that, with her knowledge of Asian cultures and regulations, she had specialist skills. The satisfied manufacturer had paid her a generous fee, and her business, East West Connections, was born.

Ice swished as she plucked the slice of lime from her glass and nibbled it. The brief twilight had arrived. A sudden breeze drifted from the sea, carrying the smoky, spicy aroma of cooking in the street market. She had always assumed she would return home at some stage, yet she hadn't even visited in the past five years. Home seemed so distant now. Her father died long before she left, and her mother had returned to her native Mauritius. There was a time when she had felt unable to return. A love affair that had shattered within a year of her departure for Asia had kept her a painful distance away. Except for Bianca, Angelique's connections with Melbourne were mere memories.

It would be winter there now. Winter memories were sketchy, but sun-drenched summer ones were stacked in warm layers in her mind. She had grown up in a seaside town outside Melbourne, in a big airy house clinging to a cliff overlooking the ocean. The sun was always pouring through the French doors and the polished floor glistened like it was coated in honey. Early in the mornings she would roam the beach with her mother.

While Angelique peered into rock pools of shell houses and seaweed gardens, Mama gazed out to sea. A sarong knotted at her breasts, her bare feet brown against the yellow sand, her eyes seemed focused beyond the horizon.

Suddenly, there was shouting from the street. Getting up and looking over the balustrade, Angelique scanned the marketplace. Under striped awnings, stalls displayed clothing, kitchenware, and spices. In the shade of tall royal palms, women in bright floral headscarves sat on grass mats amid stacked mangoes, red chilies, cabbages and snake beans. Through a gap in the gaggle of onlookers, Angelique saw a woman waving her arms around. In Bahasa Malay, she was yelling furiously at a man at a nearby stall. His flimsy satay barbecue had tipped over, spilled hot charcoal onto her mat. "Ma'af! ma'af!" the man shouted in apology. The onlookers began to laugh, and Angelique chuckled as the man comically sank to his knees. With his bare hands he began gingerly retrieving his lumps of smoking charcoal.

Dimly, Angelique became aware of the thin shrill bleeps coming from her mobile phone inside her room. She crossed the verandah, pushed open the plantation shutters. The room was dim. The late sun, squeezing through the louvers, lay in yellow wedges across the wooden floor. The ceiling fan turned slowly. She pulled off her damp sarong, tossed it over a teak chair and picked up the phone from the coffee table. "Angelique Devine."

"Hello, Ms. Devine. My name's Bettina Chan. I'm personal assistant to Andrew Nolan, managing director of Pacific Holdings Australasia."

"Oh, yes?" Angelique hadn't heard of the company.

"It's an Australian company. I'm based in our Singapore office."

"Uh-huh."

"Mr. Nolan's flying in from Melbourne tonight and he'd like to meet with you tomorrow if possible."

Angelique's flight was leaving for Singapore at ten o'clock the next morning. Including the taxi trip from Changi Airport, she'd be home by midday, and her appointment book was empty. "I'm sure I can find some time in the afternoon. Do you know what Mr. Nolan plans to discuss?"

"We're in commodities, but looking for new opportunities." Angelique detected a smile warming Bettina's cool, precise voice. "You have an excellent reputation, Ms. Devine, for facilitating exciting and profitable ventures. Mr. Nolan's very keen to work with you."

Angelique smiled. "Please tell Mr. Nolan I'll be happy to meet with him." Bettina gave her the office address and they fixed an appointment for two o'clock.

It was suddenly dark. Angelique switched on a lamp and glanced at her watch on the bedside table. Seven o'clock. She grabbed jeans and a tank top off the end of the bed and headed for the bathroom. After a quick shower she would stroll into town for a last dinner at her favorite restaurant, where they served the best curry laksa in the world.

At little after noon the next day, Angelique's taxi drew up outside her home in the leafy suburb of Katong. It was a two-story house in a terraced row. The tall front hedge of wild cinnamon had come into bloom during her long absence. White flowers mingled with blue-black berries. Rising above the hedge, heavy with flowers, the branches of the jacaranda tree in the tiny front courtyard threw dappled shade over the shutters of her upstairs study. The driver took her two suitcases to the door while Angelique grabbed her briefcase and laptop.

Putting her key into the lock, she glanced at the small octagonal mirror above the door. Her friend, Siow Lian, had hung it there when Angelique first took a lease on the house three years ago. It was essential, Siow Lian said, to prevent bad spirits from entering the house. So far, it seemed to have worked.

The house was blissfully cool. Angelique dragged her luggage inside, then kicked off her shoes. The chill of the terra-cotta tiles was heavenly. She pulled off her sunglasses and blinked in the shuttered dimness. On the rosewood sideboard she was surprised to see a vase brimming with mauve and white Singapore orchids. There was a note beside the vase:

Welcome home, honey.

Don't forget our Twilight Club dinner on Saturday night! Pick me up on the way at seven thirty. Can't wait!
Love, S.L.

Angelique smiled. She had missed Siow Lian. She recalled buying the sideboard at an antique market in Chinatown and inviting Siow Lian around to see it.

Angelique had positioned it like a partition, creating an entrance foyer in an otherwise completely open living room. Siow Lian had been impressed. She nodded approvingly while Angelique pointed out the intricate carving on the drawers and around the mirror. "Good feng shui," Siow Lian finally pronounced firmly. "Right in front of the door, too. Excellent."

Angelique was confused. "But I thought the mirror outside took care of bad spirits."

Siow Lian gave an impatient sigh. "The sideboard forms a barrier," she said. "It replaces the wall that the Peranakans would've originally had here. Some Brit would've knocked it out. It'll stop good luck from running straight out the front door!"

Angelique crossed the living room and opened the shuttered doors to the central courtyard. Yellow water lilies perched in the pond nestled in a grove of ferns. No doubt Siow Lian, who had been keeping an eye on the house, had fed the goldfish. Opposite her, the doors to the kitchen baked in the midday sun. The high brick wall adjoining the neighboring house dripped with pink bougainvillea. The courtyard was completely private, and unless it was raining heavily she always kept the shutters open.

She headed around to the kitchen. The fridge was humming. Siow Lian had switched it on, filled it with Coke and fruit juice, and a couple of bottles of wine too. But Angelique was craving jasmine tea. She filled the kettle, then threw open the doors. The sweet scent of magnolia rushed in.

She peeled off her jeans and top and dropped them onto the floor. A gentle breeze brushed her skin. She watched a gecko lizard scoot up the trunk of the magnolia, then pause, swaying in a beam of sunshine. It was good to be home. In recent years her wanderlust had diminished considerably.

The kettle boiled. She spooned some tea into the teapot, poured in the water and savored the perfumed steam. She filled a cup and sat on a high stool at the counter.

She was looking forward to Saturday night. The Twilight dinner had been planned for months. During her years of aid work she had made four close friends, including Siow Lian. In various capacities they had worked for different agencies. Like Angelique they had all quit, disillusioned, and moved on to other careers. They were spread around the world these days. Yet they had never lost their interest in aid. In particular, they shared a passion for the small business assistance that the agencies were reluctant to bother with. So, a couple of years ago, at one of their regular dinners, they had come up with a scheme to bypass official channels and provide this financial assistance to people in aid-dependent villages. They opened a bank account into which they all put some money. Jeremy and Lucy, both wealthy and generous, had put in the most. Plus, they'd squeezed some money out of a few wealthy contacts. Then they began operating a loan scheme. Charging nominal interest to cover costs, they channeled money, discreetly, to where it was needed. The conduit was a friend and old colleague from the aid agency where Angelique had worked. Danni advised them of suitable projects and distributed the funds through her field staff. Usually the tiny loans were repaid, sometimes they weren't. It was a rewarding part-time interest, and they called themselves The Twilight Club.

Angelique glanced at her watch. Twelve forty-five. It was time to get ready for her meeting with Pacific Holdings Australasia. No wonder this Andrew Nolan was looking around for new business. The financial crisis had made some commodities risky. Maybe Pacific Holdings would be interested in branching into retailing, and manufacturing. At dinner on Saturday night she would ask Mason if he knew anything about the company. The only other Australian among the Twilights, and from a well-connected family, Mason seemed to know everyone.

At close to two o'clock Angelique's taxi pulled into the rank outside the Orchid Central shopping complex in Orchard Road. From there it was a short walk to Pacific Holdings' office. Stepping out of the cool car she gasped as the air wrapped around her body like a hot moist towel. As always, Orchard Road was bustling. She merged into the surging stream and found her pace among the business suits and chirping mobile phones. Brightly dressed tourists clutching shopping bags and cameras hurtled along the street like candy wrappers blowing in a gale. On benches under Tamalan trees, old people sat fanning their faces. Just ahead, the revolving doors of the Chanel store glittered like crystal in the hot sun. The office of Pacific Holdings Australasia was in the steel and glass tower next door. Angelique veered out of the throng.

The automatic glass doors whispered open. Glossy black granite stretched out before her in the immense foyer. Her high heels clacked sharply as she strode over to the elevator bank. A uniformed security guard behind an inquiry desk looked up.

"Pacific Holdings?" Angelique asked.

"Tenth floor, madam."

The elevator opened before double glass doors sporting the words "Pacific Holdings Australasia" in bold gold letters. Angelique approached a polished wood reception desk. It was beautiful mahogany. The receptionist invited Angelique to take a seat while she advised Mr. Nolan's assistant of her arrival.

Angelique sank down on one of the leather sofas beside a tinted full-length window. On the large glass coffee table, magazines and a copy of Singapore's major daily paper, the *Straits Times*, were laid out neatly. At one end of the table stood an exquisite wooden carving about a foot tall. It was a statue of a woman. Her head was thrown back, her eyes half-closed as if in ecstasy. Her arms raised, her hands were clasped behind her head. Her slender body was dark, her robes brightly painted in turquoise, red and gold. She seemed to represent a deity, but unlike any that Angelique had seen before.

"Ms. Devine." A woman in a navy blue business suit was smiling at her. "I'm Bettina Chan."

She led Angelique down a short corridor, then knocked on a door before opening it. "Mr. Nolan? Ms. Devine has arrived." Bettina ushered Angelique into the office.

Andrew Nolan rose from behind a big mahogany desk. Clad in a light gray linen suit, he was tall, and well-built. Beaming, he strode across the room to her. "Terrific to meet you," he said, his deep voice resonating within the smoky-blue walls. "I'll call you Angelique, will I?"

Angelique smiled. "Of course." They shook hands.

"Coffee, thanks, Bettina," he said, barely tossing his assistant a glance. Bettina lowered her eyes, nodding almost imperceptibly as she closed the door. With a grand gesture, Nolan indicated the sitting area at the window end of the room. "Take a seat, Angelique."

The office was spacious and cool. Angelique glanced through the window at Orchard Road below, simmering in the afternoon heat. She placed her briefcase on the floor beside her, and crossed her legs. Nolan sat on a matching sofa opposite her. Smiling, sifting his blue silk tie slowly through his fingers, he looked her over. In his mid-thirties, he displayed a self-confidence teetering on the edge of cockiness. Angelique guessed he was accustomed to having women respond positively to him.

She shifted her gaze to take in the room. A portrait of Nolan hung on the wall behind his desk painted in oils of rich greens and blues. Its heavy timber frame was glossy with black lacquer. It had probably cost a fortune, yet it had the bright, flat look of the paintings that were knocked out by the old Buddhist monks in the Chinatown market for fifty bucks a throw. The low oak coffee table between them was Japanese, possibly antique. "Nice office," she said. "Great location."

"Yeah, well, I've got to have somewhere impressive to meet Asian clients. Especially the Japanese." He grinned. "Wouldn't want to be out in the Little India area or something." Angelique gave a polite smile. "Mind you, it's starting to feel a bit expensive these days. Cash isn't flowing like it was." He loosened his tie slightly, relaxed back in his seat. "I'm in timber. Forestry. It's been a dream until recently."

"Where? Malaysia?"

"No. I started out there. But ten years ago I discovered a little treasure. Seragana."

It was an obscure island country in the South China Sea where Angelique's work, both in aid and business, had never taken her. "I haven't heard of anyone doing business there. Pretty undeveloped, isn't it?"

"That's the beauty of it. It's virtually untouched. Britain had a go at it late in the eighteen hundreds, but it wasn't much use to them. It's very mountainous, so opening it up was too hard. Plus, the main island's surrounded by tiny islands and atolls, so they couldn't establish a deep-sea port. They put in some plantations, you know, coffee, spices. But it wasn't worth the effort and expense, so they took off after about fifty years."

Reaching over to the coffee table he opened a red lacquered box filled with gold-tipped cigarettes. He offered them to Angelique. She shook her head. He carefully placed a cigarette in the corner of his mouth. A gold ring on the little finger of his left hand glittered with a large diamond. He lit the cigarette.

"Left a nice little town behind, though. Ngali, the capital. Overlooks Victoria Harbor. Pretty place. I've got a house there." He shifted in his seat, exhaling a stream of smoke. "Anyway, fortunately for me, Seragana remained an independent kingdom. When I got a whisper about the place, I thought I'd take a look." He gave a satisfied sigh. "I found this big island, sparsely populated and two-thirds covered in old-growth rainforest, including enormous reserves of mahogany. I struck up a nice deal with the old king and started taking it out."

Angelique felt a chill of warning in the pit of her stomach. Of all the companies she had ever declined work with, most had mining or logging interests. In her experience, foreign companies got away with as much as they possibly could. Much of her aid work had been in places like Bougainville in New Guinea that had been ecologically and socially devastated by careless exploitation of natural resources. Unless Nolan could convince her that his company's practices were exceptional, she would leave this meeting without his business.

There was a knock at the door. Bettina came in with a tray of coffee that she set down on the table. Ignoring her, Nolan tapped his ash into the crystal ashtray. Catching Bettina's eye, Angelique smiled. "Thanks," she said. Bettina returned the smile and quickly left the room. Charming and elegant, Bettina was at least ten years Nolan's senior. The dismissive manner he showed her was puzzling. Keeping her tone light, Angelique said, "You must rely very much on Bettina when you're back in Melbourne. She'd handle a lot of important business on your behalf, I would imagine."

He beamed. That broad handsome smile he could serve up in a flash would be like money in the bank. "Oh, yeah, Bettina's a good girl. A real honey."

Angelique groaned inwardly. Arrogant and sexist. She and this rich Aussie boy were not going to hit it off.

He poured the coffee and handed her a cup. "Anyway, I was getting excellent returns from Seragana until things recently got difficult."

Angelique stirred some sugar into her coffee. "Cash is beginning to flow again. I'm sure if you could hold tight for a while, your customers will begin spending again."

He shook his head. "The business slowdown is a secondary problem. I could ride that out. The real problem's in Seragana itself. The king died last year, and his niece has waltzed over from England and taken over. She won't honor the arrangement I had with her uncle."

Angelique's waning interest sharpened a little. "What's her problem, exactly?"

He drew on his cigarette. "She says I should've put in some infrastructure. You know, roads, drainage. Claims erosion is silting up the rivers." He leaned forward for emphasis, his elbows on his knees. "I told her I'm a businessman, right? Not the Salvation bloody Army! That little country's lucky I'm there. My company gives people jobs in the forest and the mills. I pay royalties for the timber, taxes too. Less than I'd have to pay anywhere else, of course, which is why it's a great business that I don't want to see jeopardized. If the place is as backward as hell, it's down to her uncle. It's just too bad if the rat-bag old king gambled it all away."

"But surely your original agreement with the ruler included

infrastructure considerations. Perhaps his niece just wants to re-negotiate the terms. As for the rivers, aren't you working within their environmental laws?"

"Environmental laws..." he muttered in a tired tone. "Thankfully, Seragana wasn't big on ridiculous regulations that strangle enterprises like mine. Not till she showed up, anyway. The old king didn't interfere in my company's activities. He let me get on with my affairs, and he got on with his." He dragged a hand impatiently through his thick brown hair. "His niece doesn't know what she's talking about. Of course I never poured money into village access roads through the logging areas. They wouldn't benefit my business, and they're not my concern. And I won't limit the logging, either. That's just plain uneconomic." He leaned back in his seat and eyed Angelique, his expression a touch defensive. "What do you know about the logging game?"

"Not a lot."

He nodded. "I told you this place is mountainous," he said evenly. "Steep as hell. You get in wherever you can. You cut a swath through this rainforest all the way down to the nearest river or estuary. You have teams of men, bulldozers, chains dragging the trees out and pushing them down the mountain to the river. They get rafted to the mill on the coast. Of course a bit of dirt gets in the river," he snapped. "I think this princess expects the logs to grow wings and fly out of the forest." Picking up the coffeepot, he topped up their cups.

Angelique smiled to herself. "What's her name?"

Nolan sloshed some milk into his coffee and stirred it. "Kira Na Murgha." He shook his head. "She's making business very bloody difficult. Got her customs people holding up my vessels at the wharf, got her lackeys—the Royal Guards—wandering around the mill bitching about workers' conditions. She's made it perfectly clear she wants my company out of there altogether." He gulped down his coffee. "But I'm not going anywhere. I own half that island, and I can do what I like on my own land."

Out of nowhere, an icy breath seemed to brush Angelique's skin. "You own it?" she asked incredulously.

"Freehold." He smiled. "The king was very cooperative. He liked the sound of the money I'd bring in and agreed to my buying the land. It was a token price, of course, but ownership gave me security. Didn't want him getting any ideas about doing deals with opposition companies."

"Competition," she said dryly. "Heaven forbid."

He nodded, oblivious to her sarcasm. "Gave me honorary citizenship too after a couple of years." He shrugged. "Anyway, she won't last. In due course someone else'll take control, then we can get back to full production. She's having a lovely time playing princess in that big palace, but no doubt she'll tire of it and slink off back to London. Or she could be given a push. She's got relatives on her mother's side who've been itching to take over since the Brits left." He gave a knowing half-smile. "One of them, her cousin, Mbulo, is an acquaintance of mine. He's a businessman too. Lives here in Singapore. I could work with him. In the meantime, I need something else to keep up the cash flow. That's where you come in."

Angelique watched him stir his coffee. It was time to tell him she wasn't interested. Perhaps another consultant would be happy to assist him with the financial leverage he needed in his standoff with the princess. But it was hard to walk away suspecting that Kira Na Murgha stood little chance of survival. Her negotiating position was hopelessly weakened by Nolan's ownership of the land. And her getting rid of him altogether was probably impossible. Perhaps if she arranged a meeting with the princess, got her perspective, some kind of resolution could be found.

Nolan was watching her. "So, do you have a proposition in mind?"

Angelique put down her cup. "Well, I know of some basic retail ventures in Malaysia that might interest you. Partnerships, going-concerns with a quick turnover. The businesses are relatively cheap." Nolan was nodding. "I'll put together a few specific proposals for you and an estimate of my fees."

"Terrific."

"But I can't help thinking that your problems in Seragana could be overcome. With some give-and-take, your relationship with the government could be mutually very beneficial."

Nolan tugged at his tie. "It's already beneficial," he snapped.

"I've no intention of allowing her demands to ruin my business. It'll be thirty years or more before those forests come anywhere near depletion. It's a huge resource. She should just relax."

"I'd like to discuss the situation with her just the same."

Nolan delivered one of his smiles. "Get her to see reason, you mean." He shrugged. "I've offered her more money. She doesn't want it. But sure, give it a go. It can't hurt."

Angelique grabbed her briefcase and stood up. "Leave it with me, Andrew. I'll get back to you within a fortnight."

"Great." He showed her to the door. "Call me in Melbourne. I'll be back there by then. Bettina will give you the details." They shook hands. "I look forward to hearing from you."

CHAPTER TWO

The cold wind howled around Stephanie's car as she drove down Beach Road along the Port Melbourne foreshore. The long fronds of the date palms lining the road streamed like bunting in the wind. Rounding a curve, she passed a plantation thick with tea-tree scrub and creamy papery-trunked melaleucas. The grand beachfront homes slipped from view, and she arrived at an expanse of sandy wasteland. Half a dozen police cars lined the curb. Stephanie parked her seventies-model Jaguar coupé behind them. It was eight o'clock on Friday morning.

The wasteland extended down to the water's edge. Across a stretch of leaden, churning sea, the rear of the cargo wharves loomed. Near the water, a dozen or so officers hovered outside the bright yellow tape sectioning off the crime scene. Hugging their navy blue greatcoats around their bodies, puffing clouds of steam, they stamped their feet against the cold. Getting out of the car, Stephanie shuddered as an icy wind gust sliced through her. She dragged her long tweed overcoat from the passenger seat and quickly slipped it on. Gazing out to sea, she took a pair of black leather gloves from the pocket of her pinstriped pants. Wind blew her long dark hair over her face. At the horizon, the mouth of the Yarra River yawned into the bay. Through the fog she could just make out a few tall masts of yachts moored at the wharf on the river. Low purple clouds drizzled a fine cold mist.

A white station wagon was moving away from the crime scene and heading up to the road. A coroner's vehicle transporting the tiny victim to the morgue. The driver paused at the curb, waiting for a break in the traffic. Dr. Eliza Jones gave Stephanie a little wave from the passenger seat. Stephanie nodded a greeting.

Drawing a deep breath, she strode down toward the scene. Seagulls screeched overhead. The wind carried the scent of rotting seaweed and the sound of someone crying. She shoved her hands deep into her pockets and pushed against the wind.

No one noticed her approach. One of her detectives, Senior Sergeant Dave Ryan, was talking with a sergeant from Fingerprints. Constable Jenny Saunders, the youngest in Stephanie's team, was standing with a young constable from the uniform branch.

"So who the hell are we waiting for now?" the uniformed constable whined.

"Detective Inspector Tyler," Jenny replied in a rather superior tone. Stephanie smiled.

"Well, I wish she'd bloody hurry up. I'm freezing my arse off out here!"

Overhearing the constable's remark, Dave Ryan swung around looking furious. He was clearly ready to bite the young man's head off. Then, catching sight of Stephanie standing right behind the constable, he hesitated.

"I'm sorry to keep you waiting, Constable," Stephanie said quietly.

He jumped and turned to her, his face reddening. "Aah...yes, ma'am, I mean, sorry, ma'am," he stuttered.

Stephanie glanced at Jenny. "Morning, Jenny."

Jenny smiled warmly. "Good morning, ma'am."

Stephanie headed over to the tape surrounding a battered orange Ford Escort.

"Be right with you," Dave said to her, marching over to the constable. Looking at the car, Stephanie listened to Dave bellowing behind her. "Would getting your arse kicked warm it up for you, Constable?"

"Yes, sir! I mean, no, sir! Sorry, sir!"

"You'd reckon that a baby would pick a more convenient time to die, wouldn't you, Constable? Very bloody thoughtless dragging us all out here on such a cold morning."

"Sir! Sorry, sir!"

Stephanie raked her hair back from her face. The car doors were open, the interior smudged with sooty fingerprint powder. On the backseat an infant seat contained a pink bunny rug and a small blue teddy bear. At a sudden outburst of crying, Stephanie glanced up. Beside a squad car several meters away, under the watchful eye of a woman police constable, the mother of the dead baby, fifteen-year-old Kylie Burzomi, was weeping on the shoulder of her seventeen-year-old sister, Andrea.

"Little smart-arse," Dave muttered, appearing at her side. "I'll be having a word about him with his sergeant later." Snorting indignant clouds of steam, he tugged his coat collar around his throat. "Barely out of the bloody academy and he wants to know why we're keeping him waiting." Stephanie grinned and shook her head. "By the way, I saw you on the news last night. You didn't mention you had an interview coming up."

"Didn't know anything about it till I switched on the TV. I nearly fainted. It was part of an interview I did for TVQ a while ago. You know, the gay community TV station. It was used last night without my permission."

"Shit! I thought it was a bit, you know...well, laid-back, to say the least." Dave gave a short embarrassed laugh. "Houlihan'll go ballistic, won't he?"

"To say the least." She slid her hands into her coat pockets. "So, what's the update on this situation?"

"Well, the coroner's first impression is that the baby died of exposure. Would've only taken a few hours in this weather, she said. I let them take the body. Fingerprints might get some fresh dabs that'll tell us who dumped the car here with the baby in it. But I was waiting for you before I had a proper poke around in the vehicle."

"Have the Burzomi girls added anything to their story?"

Dave dug into his trouser pocket and took out a pack of chewing gum. "Nope. They're sticking with what they told the local police last night. Kylie maintains that around eleven thirty last night she parked her car in the shopping center car park to race into the supermarket to buy something for the baby." He shook his head. "Fifteen, she is! What the hell's she doing driving, anyway? Three years underage!"

Stephanie shrugged. "Kylie's a Burzomi. Her dad would've been teaching her to drive while her friends were in kindergarten. It's George's car. I guess they figure that while their father's doing time, they might as well use it."

"Right, well, when this investigation's over, I'll get the damn thing impounded before they mow some poor bastard down with it." Dave paused for a thoughtful chew. "Anyway, Kylie reckons that when she was heading back to the car park, she saw some young bloke getting into her car. Before she could get near it, he took off. Only got a glimpse, she says, but she's sure it was that arsehole, Don Williams. She'd left the key in the ignition, of course! Her two-month-old baby was in the back." He ran a hand through his thin sandy hair. "Poor little thing. Seems she wasn't touched at all."

"Do you believe Kylie's story?"

"No reason not to at this stage," Dave said. "We're out looking for Williams now. He wasn't home when we went round to his place last night or this morning."

"The girls wouldn't be overly fond of him, remember," Stephanie cautioned him. "There was some trouble, I believe, between Williams and their father last year."

"That's right. Williams was dealing on George's patch. Got a bit ugly. But he's a thieving idiot, Williams. I can see him doing something this stupid, no problem."

Stephanie lifted the yellow tape and stepped over to the car.

"Haven't known him to bother with cars since he was a kid. Dealing and doing over warehouses keeps him pretty busy."

"Keeps us pretty busy too! You know as well as I do that he's involved in all these break-ins we've been having lately."

Stephanie bent down and peered inside. "Pinning those jobs on him is proving difficult, though. I don't want to see us jumping at a chance to pull him in if we're on the wrong track." She heard Dave give an impatient little sniff. "If he was going to snatch a car, why pick one with a baby in the back?" She straightened up and turned to him.

Dave shrugged. "He wouldn't give a stuff about the baby. The key was winking at him. It was easy. Maybe he took it for a quick drug delivery or to move some stolen gear. Maybe he didn't even notice the baby at first, then dumped the car when she started crying or something." His eyes suddenly lit up with inspiration. "Could've just wanted to give the Burzomis a bit of grief."

"How tall is Williams?"

"A streak! About six foot four."

Stephanie pointed at the driver's seat. "Either he likes driving with his knees up under his chin, or he thoughtfully put the seat back the way he found it." It was positioned all the way forward, perfect for five-foot-nothing Kylie. Dave rubbed his stubbly chin. Stephanie reached down to an open shelf below the dashboard and picked up a near-full pack of cigarettes. "Smokes, does he?" Dave nodded. "You'd think he would've slipped these into his pocket." Replacing the pack, she nudged a matchbox with her gloved finger. It rattled oddly. She picked it up and opened it. "What are these, do you think?" The matchbox was filled with pink pills.

Dave shook his head. "Nothing I've seen before." He pulled a small plastic bag from his top pocket. "I'll get them checked out." Stephanie dropped the box into the bag. "They'll belong to Williams, I'll bet my arse," Dave added.

The gusty wind tugged at Stephanie's coat. She pulled it around herself more tightly. "Or the Burzomi girls are following in their daddy's footsteps. Turned to dealing. I can't see Williams forgetting those, can you?"

Dave looked over at Kylie and Andrea. "Jesus..."

"I'll head off to the station," Stephanie said. "I'll tell the girls they can go. We can talk to them again later."

Her hands in her coat pockets, Stephanie strode over to them. Andrea was watching Stephanie's approach through narrowed eyes. Shivering in a thin, oversized khaki sweater, she gave her chin a slow rub on a bony shoulder. Kylie was dabbing her eyes with a tissue. At five feet nine, Stephanie towered over her. "I'm sorry about your baby, Kylie," Stephanie said gently. Kylie averted her eyes.

"She doesn't know nothin' else," Andrea snapped. "She already told 'em what happened. And when do we get our car back?" Andrea's thin face was red and pinched with cold.

"You got a job yet?" Stephanie asked. Andrea gave an insolent shrug. "What happened with that video store job? I put in a good word for you. You promised me that after your last bit of trouble you were going to turn over a new leaf."

"Yeah? Well, that smart-arse manager starts askin' me about all the stuff I done. Pinching stuff and that. So I told him to stick his job! Whatcha tell him about all that for?"

"I had to tell him the truth. He's a decent guy, actually. He's given other kids a chance. And he was prepared to give you a chance too."

"Well, I don't have to take that shit from the likes of him. You could fix things for me properly." Her eyes flashed. She crossed her arms, jutted out her chin. "A bloody inspector! You can make people do things. And you're a dyke! You should look after your own."

Kylie was staring at Stephanie wide-eyed, biting her lip. The uniformed constable nearby gazed off into the distance, her face impassive.

Stephanie held Andrea's cold gaze. "Has your mother come back?" she asked quietly.

Andrea shook her head. "Haven't seen her for three months."

"Who's looking after you two and your younger brothers?"

"I fuckin' am! Like I have most of me life. We don't need no one, all right?"

Stephanie raked her hair back from her face. Kylie was shaking, her eyes welling with tears. "This officer will drive you home now. We'll have some more questions in a day or two."

Andrea sighed. "Kylie already told 'em everything. It was that bastard, Don Williams."

"They tell me you didn't get a clear look at him, Kylie."

Tears trickled down Kylie's cheeks. "Think it was him…" she murmured. Andrea was staring at the ground, kicking at a piece of broken brick.

Stephanie turned to the officer. "Constable?"

"Yes, ma'am." She opened the back door of the car. As the girls climbed inside Stephanie headed back up to the road to her car.

It took twenty minutes through the peak-hour traffic to make the short trip to police headquarters on the edge of the central business district. In her office in criminal investigations, Stephanie took off her coat, pulled off her gloves. Glancing across at her desk she saw a sheet of paper lying in wait for her. She went over and sat down, tugged up the sleeves of her black sweater and picked up the memo. It was from her boss, Superintendent Houlihan.

"…Questions at the most senior level are being asked about your unauthorized TV interview. Public concern has brought the matter to the attention of the Minister of Police. I have been ordered to provide a report on the incident to the Chief Commissioner. I require your written report on how this unprofessional public announcement concerning GALPA took place. I want to see you with your report in my office on Monday at six thirty p.m…"

"Christ," she muttered. GALPA was the gay and lesbian police association that she, along with a few other senior cops, had recently initiated. It provided support for officers, particularly the younger ones, who often suffered from a persistent culture of homophobia in the force, kept alive by a die-hard minority who chose to live in the past. GALPA had been given official sanction due to Stephanie's seniority and, importantly, a trust in her good judgment.

A sharp knock on her door made her jump. It was her friend, Jan, a senior sergeant in the uniform branch.

"What's going on, Steph?" Jan looked anxious. "The whole station's talking about your TV appearance." She plopped down in the chair on the other side of Stephanie's desk and loosened her shirt collar.

Stephanie slid the memo across the desk for Jan to read. "I think we can assume I'm in a bit of trouble."

Jan snatched it up. "Bloody hell..." she breathed. "How did it happen?"

Stephanie sighed and swiveled her chair halfway around to gaze through the large window behind her. It was raining. The broad tree-lined boulevard leading into the city was choked with traffic. On silver tracks, green trams whirred down its spine. "I couldn't believe my eyes. I immediately rang Sage Jaspar, the program manager down at TVQ. You've come across her, haven't you?"

Jan took a pack of cigarettes from the breast pocket of her shirt. "Oh, yeah. Always starting up angry little protest groups about one thing or another. Makes sure whenever she sees me to mention the dope plants she's got growing in her backyard. I think she'd love to be arrested just so she could scream her head off about police harassment."

"Well, she sent the interview I did with them a while back to a journo friend at Channel Ten." Jan's eyes widened in amazement. "She said they wanted something personal about me to add to my profile." Stephanie swung her chair back and planted her elbows on the desk. "It's all because of the news conference I did recently about this spate of violent break-ins we've had. My first public statement since becoming D.I." She grinned. "Young and female, I'm a novelty."

"So Sage thought an interview about gay matters was appropriate?" Jan lit a cigarette. "Open the window, will you, hon?"

Stephanie reached around, flicked up the latch and shoved the window open. No wonder the air-conditioning system was always playing up. Half the people in the building seemed to spend their time hanging out the windows smoking. A gust of cold air stung her face.

Jan tapped some ash into the rubbish bin. "Upstairs," she raised her eyes to the ceiling, "they're pretty comfortable with GALPA. It shows a modern management attitude that respects equal rights. So I don't know what point she thought she was making."

Stephanie picked up a pencil and began doodling on the corner of the memo. "And upstairs, they like control over their public image and announcements. They wouldn't have liked seeing one of their inspectors sitting on prime-time TV in old jeans and a T-shirt, calmly chatting away about problems in the force." She tossed down the pencil and sighed. "What I said was for a selective audience. They left out the part where I praised management for sanctioning GALPA. The clip only showed me complaining. I should never have done the original interview."

Jan shook her head. "I'm sure Houlihan will understand you were hijacked."

"What about that business last year?" Stephanie stole a quick glance at Jan, then averted her eyes. "They'd be remembering that now."

"Oh, come on, hon." Jan stubbed out her cigarette on the side of the metal bin. Stephanie quickly pulled the window closed. "Just being human isn't something they can hold against you. This job drags us all down sooner or later. You'd been through an especially rough patch. It got on top of you for a while, that's all."

There was another knock on the door. It was Jenny Saunders.

"Excuse me, ma'am. I've got the fingerprint report for the car." She handed it to Stephanie.

Stephanie scanned the report. "So Williams's prints weren't there, huh?"

"No, but the sarge reckons he could've been wearing gloves. For the cold, you know." Jenny gave a little shrug.

Stephanie smiled. "Well, that's true. Thanks, Jenny. Tell Dave I'll come and have a chat with him about it later."

"It's really sad about that baby," Jan said after Jenny left. "The press will have a field day with that one."

Stephanie nodded. It was another miserable chapter in the lives of the Burzomis. And she had a niggling feeling that there was something Andrea wasn't telling her.

"Charlotte coming down for the weekend?" Jan asked.

"Yeah, and I hope it's more fun than last weekend. We haven't been getting on all that well lately. We've talked on the phone, of course. But it's hard to get things straight when you only spend a few days together each week."

"I thought you liked that part, not being together all the time."

Stephanie shrugged. "I do. It suits me, and I thought it suited Charlotte too. But things are changing between us, becoming complicated." She glanced at Jan to catch her reaction. "Charlotte wants to transfer from the Sydney office to the bank's headquarters down here. She wants us to tie the knot, so to speak."

"Oh," Jan said flatly, averting her eyes and busying herself picking at a bit of fluff on her pants.

"You've never liked her much, have you?"

Jan shifted uncomfortably in her chair. "Oh, you know. I was just put off her a bit last year when you had to take that time out from the job. She didn't...I mean, it's not really for me to say, but she wasn't very supportive."

"Did you expect her to take leave from her job to sit and hold my hand?"

Jan gave Stephanie a long silent look before scratching again at her navy blue polyester.

Stephanie got up and stood at the window, gazing down at the street. Rain spattered the window. Crystal droplets clung to the glass, shivering in the wind. She slid her hands into her pockets. "Yeah, well..." she began softly, "I don't think she was too impressed with my crybaby routine." She gave a dry laugh. "She goes for the strong, in-control type. She was very relieved once I was back to my old self."

"Sometimes we all need someone else to be in control. Even you, Steph."

A red Alfa Spyder suddenly tore down the tram tracks. Water sprayed up behind it like silvery wings. Cutting into the traffic, it slithered and swerved, just avoiding a collision with a black cab before straightening up. "Idiot," Stephanie muttered. "Aren't there any cops out on the roads today?"

"What?"

A police siren suddenly sounded. The raindrops on the window shimmered blue for an instant as a police car whizzed past, lights flashing. "It's okay. Got him." Stephanie sank back down onto her chair, swiveling it slightly from side to side. "I'm happy to leave things with Charlotte the way they are. When she's not pushing for more, everything's great. But it's been about a year now and she thinks we've got to move on to the next stage. There has to be a next stage, apparently, where you make a total commitment and buy a damn house."

Jan gave a little shrug. "I remember a time when you wanted that more than anyone."

Stephanie fidgeted with the memo, folding over the corners. "Yeah, a long time ago. That was different. She was different." She sighed. "Came to nothing, though, didn't it? So what's the point?"

"Well, you made your choices then, like you've made choices now. Sometimes they're hard to live with." Jan gave a wry smile. "Still, Charlotte's got her positive points. She's a pretty cool-headed, practical person—"

"And pretty." Stephanie grinned.

"And she's worked out what she wants. She'll dig in her heels, I reckon."

It was true that Charlotte was tenacious, but she was reasonable too. In many ways they viewed the world from opposing angles, but they worked around their differences. No doubt they would resolve their present rough patch in time.

Jan glanced at her watch. "I've got to get going. I'm due on patrol in five minutes." She grabbed her cigarettes off the desk and popped them back into her pocket. "Maybe Charlotte's just feeling insecure. Get her some flowers, make a fuss of her."

Stephanie chuckled. "Thanks for the tip."

Jan made for the door. "And good luck with Houlihan on Monday. Let me know if there's anything I can do."

CHAPTER THREE

Angelique opened her bedroom shutters, closed all day against the sun. It was Saturday evening, and the room was washed in gold by the setting sun. A lone song thrush was perched on top of the high brick wall above the bougainvillea, its complex melody overlaying the simple rhythms of the blues track wafting upstairs from the CD player. Jeremy had phoned that morning to say he'd booked a table at the Somerset Maugham Hotel for their Twilight dinner. They were meeting in the Writers Bar at eight.

Angelique first met Jeremy and Lucy five years ago at an international aid conference in Fiji. Jeremy was the public relations director for a British aid agency. During one of the breaks in the endless round of speakers, Angelique heard an aristocratic English voice ring out above the sedate chatter. "Frightfully bloody hot, isn't it, darling?" Glancing over the shoulder of a delegate from France who was explaining why French aid procedures were superior to everyone else's, Angelique saw a tall fair-haired man in a pure-white linen suit madly fanning his face with a large red silk fan. She caught his eye, they exchanged a smile. Before long they were talking, laughing together like old friends. The son and heir of Lord Walthorpe, Jeremy now worked as a barrister in the family's law firm in London.

Lucy had been a high-profile fund-raiser for an American agency. She made herself instantly appealing when she took to the podium. Wearing a short black skirt and silver high heels, she impatiently tossed her long mane of black curly hair. "Well, I gotta tell you!" she began in her you'd-better-fucking-pay-attention-to-me New York twang. "I think all you people are talking through your goddamn asses!"

Since quitting her aid job, Lucy had become a perpetual student of anything from sociology to astrology. She rarely finished her courses, though, her interest always drifting to something new. Her overly interfering parents also seemed to take up much of her time and energy.

Angelique's colleagues at the time, Siow Lian and Mason, were also at the conference, and the group of five had become a clique. These days Mason lived with his Italian wife, Gina, in a small provincial town outside Milan and made his living as an independent stock market trader.

Angelique fastened the buttons at the side of her emerald-green cheongsam. She loved the body-hugging fit and simple elegance of the traditional Chinese dress. She added a jade bead choker and bracelet. Stepping into black stilettos, she glanced at the clock on the bedside table. Just after seven, it was time to leave and collect Siow Lian. The taxi beeped as she descended the stairs.

Twenty minutes later the taxi pulled into the driveway of Siow Lian's apartment block in Dragon View Park.

Mei-mei, Siow Lian's younger sister, answered the door. She

hugged Angelique. "It's been so long," she said. "Siow Lian?" she called over her shoulder, taking Angelique's hand and tugging her inside.

With a crackle, a curtain of tiny wooden beads over the living room doorway parted, and Siow Lian appeared. She let out a low whistle. "Sexy dress, honey."

They hugged and kissed each other. "Sexy yourself," Angelique said, smiling. Siow Lian's outfit, a tailored black suit with a white shirt, was an elegant respite from her normal uniform of jeans and T-shirt.

Grinning, Siow Lian self-consciously ran a hand over her short, spiky hair. "Thought I should dress up a bit, you know."

When they first met Siow Lian was studying for her master's degree in economics. Fluent in Mandarin, Indonesian and Bahasa Malay, she had worked part-time as an interpreter at the aid agency's Singapore office. When her widowed mother died a few years ago, Siow Lian had inherited the family's profitable coffee shop business. With her sister she had also inherited the family apartment and along with it, responsibility for their grandmother.

"Siow Lian!" Grandmother suddenly barked from behind the beaded curtain.

"Yah?" Siow Lian called back.

"Bùyào wàngjì nDde fùmÔbài."

Siow Lian rolled her eyes. "She's grumpy tonight," she whispered. "Yah, yah, okay," she called back. "Jesus," she muttered, stepping over to the little shrine on top of a sideboard in the entrance foyer. Photos of her mother and father in elaborate gilded frames glowed in a soft red electric light. She picked up two joss sticks and turned to Angelique with a mischievous grin. "She's complaining that I haven't shown respect to my parents all day. Says I'm always forgetting. I have to light these before I go out or she'll go crazy." Mei-mei giggled. The acrid smell of the joss sticks filled the air. Siow Lian placed them into gold holders in front of the photos. Then she returned to the living room doorway. The beads shivered as she poked her head through. "Okay, Gran? I'm going now." There was a grunted reply. "You get some study done for a change," she said to her sister. Mei-mei playfully pulled a face. Angelique kissed her, and she and Siow Lian left.

"I had a call from Robyn a few days ago," Siow Lian said as the taxi sped off to the city. "She's glad to be home but says she misses you. I think she's pining for you, honey."

Angelique groaned. She had met Robyn at a women's business club in Chinatown. Their affair had lasted six months. Robyn's tenure teaching English literature at Singapore University had only been for one year, and she was due to return home to San Francisco at around the same time Angelique was to leave for her Jakarta job. For their last night together, Angelique had planned a special dinner to mark the end of an affair she had always considered casual and temporary. She was shocked to discover Robyn had seen their relationship very differently and had thought the evening would be devoted to their making future plans.

"I made a mess of that," Angelique murmured.

Siow Lian shrugged. "It depends, you know. If it was only lust, she'll get over it, and you'll be friends again some day." She gave a world-weary sigh. "But love lingers on and on. After a while, they hate you. Eventually, they're indifferent. Couldn't care less."

Angelique threw her a sidelong glance. "Thanks, sweetie. I feel so much better now."

Fifteen minutes later they arrived at the hotel. The grand old three-story Victorian building was lit up by floodlights. Patchy, desperate repairs in the white-painted stucco barely concealed the ravages of more than a century of tropical climate. Like an aged, overly made-up whore, the once-beautiful building exuded an aura of seediness that somehow added to its mystique. Majestic palm trees dotted the lawns. The air was heavy with the scent of gardenias brimming from the garden beds, their pure-white flowers luminous.

The Writers Bar was packed. Voices buzzed at a high even pitch, punctuated by glassy peals of laughter. The strains of low-key jazz played by a quartet was discernable under the voices. Tall, graceful arched windows offered a view of the palms in the garden. At the bar people sat shoulder to shoulder. Cane tables and chairs were grouped around the room. In cozy nooks, sofas were clustered around coffee tables. The lights were low.

A waiter greeted them and led them to their table. Angelique felt the breeze on her shoulders from flat rattan paddles on the ceiling, swinging back and forth, fanning the air.

Lucy, Jeremy and Mason were already seated on armchairs in a corner by a window. Jeremy saw them first. He jumped to his feet.

"Here they are!" he exclaimed, brandishing a cigarette in a gold cigarette holder. "Luscious Little Lotus Flower and the Delectable Dyke from Down Under!"

The others got up, smiling. Angelique hugged Jeremy.

"Great to see you, darling," Lucy planted a glossy red kiss on Angelique's mouth.

Mason kissed her cheek, then flicked back his long blond hair. "How've you been, mate? All right?"

The waiter stood by patiently. Jeremy gave him a charming smile. "A round of Singapore Slings, I think." The waiter nodded and left them as they all sat down.

"How's Gina and the baby?" Angelique asked Mason. He had said in an e-mail that Gina hadn't wanted to make the trip to Singapore with their newborn.

"Oh, great. Gina sends her love." He dug into the breast pocket of his lightweight pinstriped suit and pulled out a photograph. "She's unreal," he said in a low, reverent tone, handing Angelique the photo of Melissa. He shook his head, looking slightly incredulous. "Perfect. Like her mum."

Angelique and Siow Lian examined the photo. "She's beautiful," Angelique said. "You must've felt bad about leaving them behind."

"Yeah." Mason grinned. "But a Twilight meeting's a pretty big deal, isn't it?" He settled back into his chair. "And there's a couple of brokers I want to talk to while I'm here." He gave a casual shrug. "Might as well, you know. Since I'm here."

Like most successful Australian businessmen born on the right side of the tracks, Mason cultivated an air of down-to-earth nonchalance, dropping the egalitarian "mate" all over the place as compensation for his taste for designer suits and European cars. Being seen to be "up yourself" wasn't good for business in Australia.

The waiter returned with their drinks on a gleaming silver tray. Lucy raised her glass. "To the Twilight Club!" They all echoed the toast. Lucy tugged back into place a straying shoestring strap of her hot-pink beaded camisole. "Now, don't you all go getting smashed," she said firmly. "We've got business to discuss later."

Jeremy groaned. "Do we have to, darling? We know you do a super job looking after the accounts. We don't need to actually see them, do we?"

Lucy looked put out. Since she was the only one without a paying job, she did all the hands-on financial work for the Twilights. Once Angelique received Danni's list of proposals every three months, she and Siow Lian marked their preferences, then e-mailed the list on to Lucy. She approved the cases based on what they could afford, then forwarded the funds.

"'Course we want to see the books," Siow Lian said, sliding an arm around Lucy's shoulders.

"And I've got something interesting for you to think about, Lucy," Angelique said. "When I was in Jakarta, Danni told me about an interesting business idea that might be good for us to support."

"Interesting, Angel?" Jeremy asked doubtfully, one eyebrow raised. He drew on his cigarette. "Not another souvenir shop? Market garden?"

Angelique grinned. "Banana fiber." Jeremy groaned, the others chuckled. She turned back to Lucy. "This small Australian company has developed the technology to make paper and building materials from the waste fiber of banana plants. There's no shortage of that in Asia, of course, and it's usually burned. And the process is chemical-free, apparently."

"Would be worth something to farmers, not to mention the employment opportunities," Lucy said. Then she narrowed her dark eyes. "But how do they plan to do it? It's not so great if the Australian company's going to take all the goddamn profits."

Angelique sipped her drink. "Franchising's the idea, I think. Danni's got the details. She's really keen on it."

"I'll get in touch with her."

Siow Lian gave Lucy a teasing grin. "You still having dramas with that new girlfriend of yours?"

Lucy shook her head in exasperation. Her black curls tumbled around her shoulders. "Gita's making me crazy! You know what she did? She wanted to move in with me." She shrugged. "So she moves in. Don't get me wrong. I wanted it too. But then she starts on me. She says we're like married now, and it's time I came out to my parents!" The others chuckled. "So, you know what? I ran out of excuses, and I did it!"

"God..." Angelique breathed. Lucy was in her mid-thirties and had said that she had never wanted or felt the slightest need to discuss her sexuality with her doting parents.

Lucy poked at her drink with the straw. "I'm over at their apartment one night, right? They're showing me photos of their vacation in the Bahamas. Stayed on a gorgeous yacht. Daddy was pointing at this picture of an amazing sunset. 'Will you take a look at that?' he said. 'Have you ever seen anything like it?'" Lucy drew deeply on her cigarette. "And I suddenly blurt out, 'I'm a lesbian!'" She looked at them all, her eyes wide as if reliving the horror. They burst out laughing. "There was this frozen moment that felt like a goddamn hour. Then my mother starts! She does this gasping thing and clutches at her chest. 'Did you hear what she said? Did you hear what your daughter said?' Daddy goes over to help her because she's gone all fainty, you know. 'What are you trying to do?' he yells at me. 'Are you trying to kill your mother, already? Is that what you want to do? Kill your own mother?'" Angelique and the others were in fits of laughter. Lucy paused to drain her glass. "So, I took it back."

Still laughing, Angelique managed to ask, "What do you mean, you took it back?"

"I told them I'd just made it up. To see how they'd react, you know." Lucy shrugged. "They mumbled about how it wasn't very goddamn funny and then went back to the photos. Never mentioned it again." She shook her head. "Gita was pissed, though."

The waiter came over. "Your table in the dining room will be ready soon, sir," he said, addressing Jeremy. "Would you like more drinks?" Everyone nodded, so Jeremy ordered another round of Singapore Slings.

Mason glanced at his watch. "Eight thirty! No wonder I'm bloody starving."

Jeremy elegantly crossed his legs and smoothed the lapel of his dark suit. "You're my guests tonight. And I've ordered a proper British dinner. They do that rather well here. Roast rib of beef with horseradish sauce and Yorkshire pudding."

"Mate," Mason said, rolling his eyes. "Right now I could eat a farmer's arse through a privet hedge."

Jeremy smiled. "Mmm...that sounds good too, I must say."

"Speaking of asses," Lucy said. "It seems you're not going to get yours on a seat in the House of Lords now they've changed the laws about hereditary peers."

"Quite right too." Jeremy grinned. "But I must say, I was rather looking forward to the fun and games in the House."

"Do those stuffy old Lords devote much time to the job?" Siow Lian asked. "Do they attend sittings for everything?"

"God, no!" Jeremy sipped his drink. "Most of the time they're at lunch, darling. Or working in the city, which, of course, is the same thing. They're not interested in debating legislation about government schools, public transport or anything of that sort. Most of them only turn up when there's something before the House that affects them personally or really interests them."

He paused, took a cigarette from his gold cigarette case and slowly, carefully, inserted it into his long, gold cigarette holder. "Like buggery, for instance." The others erupted with laughter. He lit his cigarette, relaxed in his chair, draping an arm over the back. "I remember when a bit of legislation was presented about lowering the age of consent for homosexual males. Well, darlings, they were all there for that one! I was watching from the public gallery, of course, along with every queen in London, bar Her Majesty. My father was there, naturally, tut-tutting along with all the other old duffers. It was passed eventually, but they rejected it at that first reading, despite the fact that many of them would've had a jolly good time as young boys at boarding school playing hide-the-sausage as soon as matron turned out the lights."

The waiter came over again. "Your table's ready, sir." They got up and headed through the bar for the dining room upstairs.

One of three semiprivate rooms, their dining room was small. Diners at the four other tables stole discreet glances over crystal glasses at Angelique's party as they were ushered to their table. Silver cutlery reflected the red-shaded brass lamps on the walls. A large fireplace topped with an oak mantelpiece dominated one wall. Was it resolute pomposity, Angelique wondered, or romantic sentimentality that had influenced the hotel's British architect a hundred years ago to include fireplaces? Perhaps he had simply thought it impossible for a chap to properly enjoy his after-dinner port without a mantelpiece to support his tweedy elbow. With the unsettling view of palms and cart-pushing coolies obscured by heavy lace curtains, an English gentleman might have almost felt at home. A solid oak table leg at your knee and starched white damask under your fingers may have allowed you to forget, for a while, the heat heaving in the stone walls and oozing in dark patches like sweat through the red flocked wallpaper.

"Couldn't face chow mein, darlings," Jeremy said with a grimace, allowing a waiter to help him off with his jacket and whisk it away. They all sat down, waiters moved in to shake out the crisp white napkins.

"Chow mein," Siow Lian muttered. "What the hell's that?" She shook her head. "Honestly, you Brits know nothing about food."

A waiter headed over pushing a trolley. With a flourish, he lifted the domed silver cover off a platter of roast beef. Glancing at it, Jeremy nodded approvingly. The waiter began to carve, another filled their glasses with Grange Hermitage.

Angelique took a sip. "Gorgeous wine, Jeremy," she said. "Your dinners are always excellent."

Jeremy beamed happily. He loved playing the generous host.

"By the way, Mason," Angelique said. "I had a meeting on Thursday with a new client, and I wondered if you knew anything about him." A waiter placed some fresh asparagus on Angelique's plate and drizzled it with hollandaise. "An Australian. Andrew Nolan from Pacific Holdings?"

"Bloody hell!" Mason spluttered, almost choking. "I went to school with that bastard. I wouldn't be doing any kind of business with him if I were you."

"Not overly fond of him, then, darling?" Jeremy interjected dryly.

Mason put down his glass. "At school he was a sneaky little cheat. No one liked him. He never did any work, and in the end he didn't even graduate. But his father was wealthy. He was into logging in Malaysia and Indonesia. You know, old-growth rainforests. I heard he took Andrew into the business, then later Andrew started up a forestry company of his own." He shook his head. "Can't see him having the brains, to be honest."

"You don't have to be Einstein to chop down goddamn trees," Lucy quipped, helping herself to golden squash from a silver dish.

Mason nodded. "Probably suit him, come to think of it. I wouldn't trust him as far as I could spit."

"Yeah, well, he was unimpressive, I must say. But my problem is that he's told me what he's up to in Seragana, and I feel I can't just ignore it."

Jeremy's head jerked up. "Seragana?"

"Where's Seragana?" Lucy asked.

"It's an independent island nation," Siow Lian replied. "In the South China Sea."

"Sounds to me like he's wrecking the place," Angelique continued. "And ripping them off in the process. The king he was dealing with died, and his niece who's taken over wants to get rid of him, it seems."

"Kira!" Jeremy blurted, his eyes shining.

Angelique was taken aback. "You know her?"

Jeremy chuckled. "Know her! Angel, she had a fling with my cousin, Cecilia. She's almost family, darling." Siow Lian and Lucy edged forward in their seats, their eyes trained on Jeremy.

"She's gay?" Angelique smiled. That could have compounded Nolan's personal dislike of Kira. His winning smile, undoubtedly persuasive with many women, would have had little currency with her.

"Indeed!" Jeremy smiled. "She and Cecilia got together for a minute when they were down at Oxford together. I first met her then. We moved in the same circles, ran into each other quite often. We had a few fascinating dinner conversations about her country. The last time I saw her, a year or so ago, she told me that her uncle had died and she had to go home. There was no one else, apparently. No other heirs." He sighed, shaking his head. "Poor girl. Raised in England since the age of five or something. She was English to the core. Since I'm in this part of the world it's a shame I don't have time to pop over and see her. Promised I would, one of these days. Got a big meeting in London on Monday, unfortunately."

"Royalty..." Lucy breathed. "A princess! Wow! What's she like?"

Jeremy paused, looking thoughtful. "Charming, bright, sophisticated." Angelique chuckled, watching Lucy almost swoon. "She's Melanesian."

"I would've thought in that part of the world they'd be Malays," Mason said.

"They're quite an interesting mixture, I understand. Malays, Polynesians, Melanesians," Jeremy said. "Their history goes back several thousand years, but according to Kira, the Melanesians came first. They seemed to run the place, anyway, before the British arrived. Of course, these days, there's Chinese and Indians too."

Lucy was breathless. "I'll bet she's glamorous, right? And beautiful?" A pink strap slowly slid off one shoulder.

"Well, the fact that she's royalty gave her a certain amount of glamour status in London's gay society. You can just imagine, I'm sure, how some of those young queens hovered around her, hanging off her every word." He gave a shrug. "Even though no one had ever heard of Seragana. And beautiful? Not the pretty little thing that you're probably fantasizing about, Lucy. She's more..." He paused, sipped his wine. "More the tailored type." He grinned mischievously. "More Angel's cup of tea, I'd say."

Angelique raised an eyebrow. "Would you, now?"

With a sigh, Lucy slumped back in her chair. She yanked her shoulder strap back into place, grabbed her glass and drained it at a gulp. The others chuckled.

"What else did Kira tell you about the country?" Angelique asked.

"Well, it was once divided into three kingdoms that governed separate provinces. Kira's family was originally one of those ruling kingdoms. When the British turned up, around 1860, they found that negotiating with three rulers with different interests was too messy." He shrugged. "So they engineered a showdown between them. A war, in other words. They brought in troops that were stationed in Malaya to bring about the result they wanted. They favored the Na Murgha family. Apparently they were more compliant than the others with British plans for the country's future. So, at the end of the only serious bloodbath in Seragana's history, the Na Murgha family emerged as sole rulers. But as puppets of the British, of course."

"Bastards," Siow Lian muttered.

Jeremy grinned. "Don't be so cross, Little Lotus Flower. Those were our glory days. We were still building the empire." Siow Lian wrinkled her nose at him, as much for his reference to the Empire, no doubt, as the English translation of her name, which she hated.

"Yeah, well, your glory days are behind you now, sweetie," Lucy teased. "Sitting in the backseat now, aren't you."

Jeremy chuckled. "All empires have their day in the sun, Lucy dear. You colonials over there in the good ole US of A should enjoy it while it lasts. Just like we did, darling."

Lucy tossed her curls, gave a dismissive snort of laughter.

Three waiters moved in and cleared the table. A fourth brought another bottle of wine and topped up their glasses. Jeremy had obviously told them to keep it coming. Angelique leaned closer to him. "So, after the war, what happened then?"

"Oh, well, the British settled in and tried to make the place work for them." He took a sip of wine. "Outside the town, though, things were pretty grim for most of the population. They had their land taken away so the British could install plantations, and except for those who were employed to work them, there was no place for many in the new commercial environment."

"Nolan gave me the impression that the Brits didn't stay long."

"Only fifty, sixty years. I gather it was a failed experiment, and eventually the powers-that-be in London got tired of pouring money into an unprofitable venture. So they all went home."

Gazing across the room, Angelique fiddled with the jade beads at her throat. "Well, from what Nolan told me, it sounds like he's picked up where the Brits left off."

"That'd be right," Mason said, shrugging off his jacket. "Cunning as a shit-house rat." A waiter appeared out of nowhere and quietly took the jacket away.

Jeremy nodded. "She mentioned that she was very concerned about some awful deal her uncle had with a logging company. The first thing she was going to do, she said, was get the company out of there."

"Well, she's having trouble doing that. Nolan complained that Kira's making things hard for him, but he's digging in. I couldn't believe it when he told me he actually owned half the island." Angelique paused, sipped her wine.

Jeremy looked amazed. "When I spoke to her, I'm sure she wasn't aware that he owned any land. She thought she'd just cancel his contract or whatever."

"Are you going to talk to her, hon?" Siow Lian asked. "See if she needs a hand sorting out this company?"

Angelique nodded. "I was hoping to. What do you think, Jeremy? Do you think she'd want to discuss this with me?"

"Darling, she'd be thrilled!" He sighed. "I wish I'd bloody known all this sooner. I had no idea she was in trouble." He drew deeply on his cigarette. "I'll call her tomorrow. She'll adore you." He gulped the last mouthful of his Grange. "And after a year in the wilds she's probably sex-starved too, poor girl." Everyone laughed.

"Her sex life isn't our concern, sweetie," Angelique said, smiling. "You've got a one-track mind."

Jeremy grinned behind his smoke screen. "Well, if Kira doesn't have you slipping off the rails, my dear Angelique, I'll be very surprised."

Angelique rolled her eyes. "You're hopeless."

A waiter set out fresh wineglasses. Another arrived with the dessert trolley. A sweet fruity-caramel aroma spun around the table as he lifted the lid on a large steaming date pudding.

"She's got a nice little plane, Angel," Jeremy went on. He was distracted by a waiter showing him a bottle of dessert wine.

"Lovely, darling," Jeremy murmured to him, then turned back to Angelique. "The country's dirt poor, but her uncle set himself up very comfortably, Kira told me. Bit of a naughty old thing, I believe." The waiter poured the viscous sweet wine. "No doubt she'll send her plane over here to whisk you off to paradise. And I want to know everything that happens." He leaned forward, his glass held high. "Everything!"

CHAPTER FOUR

Stephanie put down her pen, and pushed aside the case notes she'd been reviewing. She rubbed her eyes. It was six o'clock on Monday evening. Her meeting with Houlihan was in half an hour. First, she wanted to drop in on Dave and see how things were progressing with the investigation into the latest warehouse break-in on Saturday night. They'd had a tip-off from an informer that Williams was involved, confirming their suspicions. They were planning a search of Williams's flat.

She got up from her desk, took her jacket from the door, pulled it on. She gave the white cuffs of her pinstriped shirt a tug, straightened the white collar. From her desk she grabbed the folder containing her report, then crossed the corridor to the operations room.

Dave was perched on the edge of his desk, giving instructions to Jenny and four others standing around sipping coffee. Stephanie waited in the doorway, leaning against the doorjamb. "Now, we bloody know that Williams and his mates did over this joint," Dave said. "And I want something on him. I don't give a stuff if you tear his flat apart, just get me something that puts him at that fucking warehouse." He snatched up a folded document and handed it to the senior officer. "Here's your warrant, now get going."

Stephanie moved inside as the officers trooped out past her. "Might get lucky," Dave said to her with a little shrug.

"If we can nail this one on Williams, I've got a feeling we might clean up every file on these break-ins," she said. "He talks when he's scared enough."

Dave slid off his desk and plopped down in his chair. "Yeah. Looks like he's found himself some new friends. It used to be petty theft as a sideline to his dealing. This informer reckons they carry guns, this crew. But I don't know."

He drew a pack of gum from his pocket and tossed a couple of pellets into his mouth. "He's a bastard, Williams, but I don't reckon he'd know what to do with a gun. Except scratch his arse with it." He shrugged. "He'd gone quiet for a while. We had a good cleanup rate in trafficking down by the beach last year. Thought he'd moved on. Instead, he's expanded his repertoire." He grinned, leaning back in his chair. "Still, that's when we get 'em. When they get greedy."

Stephanie smiled, nodding. It amused her that what cops referred to disparagingly as greed in a criminal was praised as ambition in anyone else. Criminals were scum when they were losers, greedy when they got a bit clever.

"Well, he's stymied us with the Burzomi case," Stephanie said. Williams had an alibi for the night of the car theft. He'd been in the countryside north of Melbourne all that night and the day before.

Dave nodded. "Yeah, I'm pissed off about that. I haven't got a clue, now, who pinched that bloody car."

"You got the drug report on those pink pills yet?"

Dave sprang forward in his chair. "Shit, yeah! Just an hour ago, meant to bring it in to you..." He rifled through a mass of papers on his desk. A bulging folder slithered off a pile and knocked his coffee cup. He caught it just before its cold, milky contents sloshed over the desk. "Here it is." He passed her the document.

"Yaa Baa pills..." she murmured. Her friend Sam who worked mainly on drug cases had mentioned them once. They were widespread in Thailand and other parts of Asia but rarely found elsewhere. A cheap derivative of heroin, they had an effect that was unpredictable and dangerous. She looked up at Dave. "So when we know who's selling these, we've got our car thief and the person responsible for Brittany Burzomi's death." She handed back the report. "You'd better pass that on to the drug investigators. And we need to have another chat with the Burzomi girls. Andrea, anyway. Their mouthpiece. I think they're being a bit creative with the truth." Dave nodded, chewing madly. "I've got a meeting. I'll see you later."

On the third floor, Houlihan's secretary glanced up from her typing as Stephanie approached. She gave a friendly smile. "Go on in, Stephanie. He's expecting you."

"Thanks, Joan." A knot began curling in her stomach as she stood at his door. She raked her fingers through her hair, took a deep breath and knocked.

"Yep!" He was sitting at his desk, a pile of papers before him. He glanced up, his face expressionless. "Come in, Stephanie. Take a seat." He was moderately angry. It was "Steph" when he was pleased, and "Inspector" when he was furious, which to date had been seldom. She sat in the large leather chair in front of his desk. He resumed his signing of letters; she gazed at the window. It was dark outside. His bald head shone in the light from his desk lamp, reflecting like a moon on the window behind him.

Finally he put down his pen and shoved the papers aside. He leaned back in his chair and fixed her with steel-blue eyes. "Dropped the ball, haven't you, Stephanie?"

"No, sir. It was an unfortunate incident that was outside my control." She took her file from her lap and placed it on the desk. "The explanation's in my report."

With a sigh he stood up, turned his back to her and gazed outside. "How old are you, Stephanie?"

She rolled her eyes. He knew her age exactly. "Thirty-seven."

"Do you know how many detective inspectors there are in this state under forty?"

"Very few, sir."

He swung around. "And the others are all blokes!" he snapped. "You were made an inspector at only thirty-six because you were bloody talented and because you didn't let things happen outside your control!" He slid an agitated hand over his glazed head. "And all in spite of other things..." he continued more calmly. "People talk. You know that. All your superiors knew you were a...you know...whatsaname..."

"Lesbian, sir."

"Yeah," he mumbled, gazing off across the room. "And they supported GALPA because they believed it delivered a positive message. They trusted your advice and trusted you to keep it in perspective. You played everything by the book." He leaned forward, his hands on the desk. "That's why I always supported you. See?"

He turned back to the window. "Last year I defended you when others would've liked to revoke your promotion, when you..." He broke off. Stephanie inwardly shuddered. He cleared his throat. "When you, you know, had the whatsaname..." He gave an embarrassed cough. "Breakdown."

Stephanie sprang to her feet, her heart pounding. "I didn't have a breakdown!" she hissed. She knew she would never live down that show of weakness. She had known all along that someday that past failure would return to haunt her.

Late last winter there had been an unprecedented spate of violent crimes culminating in a mass shooting by a crazed teenage boy in a public park. Part of a task force of detectives working all hours to deal with the mayhem, she had also been studying for her inspector's exams. Then just after her promotion, her close friend, Deb, was shot in cold blood during a routine investigation. Stephanie had lost it. As if standing outside herself, she had watched herself unravel. She'd spent six weeks at home on leave.

It didn't matter that everyone was nice about it. It didn't matter that she intellectually comprehended the effects of stress and grief. What scared her then and scared her still was discovering her emotional strength had limits. Shoulders to cry on were soothing, but in the end you only had yourself. You liked to think that you, at least, would never fall over.

Houlihan was still staring outside. "My friend," Stephanie continued softly, "had just had her brains blown out. I was a bit upset, all right?"

Houlihan turned to face her. "Sit down, Steph," he said gently. He pulled out his own chair and sat. Willing her racing pulse to calm, Stephanie returned to her chair. "Anyway, the problem now is that it looks like you've lost perspective. You know damned well that you can't make public comments about any aspects of the police force without express permission." He reached into the pocket of his jacket hanging on the back of his chair and pulled out a pack of cigarettes. He lit one, then whipped open the bottom drawer of his desk and drew out a chipped china ashtray decorated with pink carnations. "So, what the hell happened?" He looked at her searchingly.

"You know as well as I do that GALPA would never have been sanctioned without someone of my rank behind it. Naturally it was positive news for the community. So I was approached to talk about it. And a lot of good has come of it after only a few months. I've had dozens of young gay and lesbian cops come to me and say things have improved for them."

"Jesus..." he muttered. "You didn't have a damned GALPA to wet nurse you. You got on all right on your own. No one gave you a hard time, did they? Wouldn't have bloody dared."

Stephanie stared at the floor. Early in her career she was running so fast she wouldn't have noticed. She was racing to get to the top where if someone pointed a finger at her it would be too late to hurt. Back then, an out dyke cop with a criminal father in the closet and a disappointed mother on her conscience had a lot to prove in a hurry.

"Why's this lot such a pack of namby...whatsanames?"

"Pambies?" She shrugged. "The world has changed. People aren't prepared, these days, to accept prejudice like they did in the past. Rather than being namby-pambies, I'd say they had guts to come out and join GALPA."

He sighed wearily. "Yeah, yeah, I know. But you can take it from me that any public comments are scrutinized carefully. Whatever the subject, you've got no damned place doing unplanned interviews with anyone." He leaned forward, lowered his voice. "And let's be honest, the world hasn't changed that much. The public doesn't want to think they've got a bunch of queers protecting hearth and home."

Stephanie knew there was truth in that.

"Jesus." He shook his head. "What next? 'The Chardonnay-Sipping Opera Lovers Police Association'?" He ground out his cigarette on a blowzy carnation. "So, give me the bloody details," he said.

Stephanie explained how her TVQ interview found its way onto national television. "I've spoken with the management down there, and the person responsible has been removed." She had felt some gratification at hearing that Sage Jaspar had been fired.

"Oh, well, that's all right, then!" Houlihan blurted sarcastically. "That'll be a great weight off the Chief Commissioner's mind. Jesus! A chat to a community group or two is one thing. But doing it on TV left you wide open. And why all the negative stuff, criticizing us?"

"I also praised management for its support and foresight, but they cut out that part." Stephanie raked back her hair. "I often go on TVQ. It's good PR. I couldn't foresee they had an idiot in charge."

"Of course they cut out the positive bits! And our PR department's been working overtime." He rolled his eyes. "The mums and dads sitting watching TV with their kiddies don't like seeing inspectors wearing jeans and T-shirts making critical comments about their police force to girlie-looking boys in glittery bloody...whatsanames." Stephanie gazed at the window behind him. Houlihan tapped his chest. "What was that shirt he was wearing?"

"Lamé, sir. Gold lamé."

He shook his head slowly. He tore a large sheet of paper off a notepad, emptied the ashtray onto it, wrapped the ashes carefully, then tossed the parcel into the rubbish bin. He replaced the ashtray in his drawer.

"Well, that's it. No more media appearances for you. Anywhere, about anything. You've got to be seen to be toeing the line. I know you want to go all the way up, Stephanie, so you've got to keep your head down." His voice was low, he had averted his eyes. Stephanie knew there was worse to come. "I have to take disciplinary action, you understand. An unauthorized public statement, well..." He cleared his throat. "You'll receive a Chastisement."

Stephanie caught her breath. A Chastisement was a serious blot on her record; it would seriously hinder further promotion. She felt her throat tighten. Houlihan was biting his lip, staring down at the desk. There was no point in trying to talk him around. She swallowed. "I'm sorry for any embarrassment caused, sir." She stood. So did he.

"It's the way it goes," he said quietly. "In the end we're responsible, whether or not something was within our control. We're supposed to cover all the bases." He looked at her, she held his gaze. "That's all." He sat back down. She nodded and left.

CHAPTER FIVE

Just over a week had passed since the Twilight dinner. Late on Monday afternoon Angelique was in a taxi heading for Seletar Airfield in Singapore's north. A military airbase, it was used by noncommercial aircraft. Kira Na Murgha had sent a plane for her. Phoning from London a few days earlier, Jeremy had reported that Kira was keen to discuss her Pacific Holdings problem. She had invited Angelique to dinner tonight and would fly her home to Singapore tomorrow.

The taxi turned off the freeway into the airbase. An immigration desk was at the security gate. Angelique completed a departure card and her passport was stamped. Then she was directed to the departure terminal. Armed security officers watched from every corner. Following a security check, an officer ticked her off a flight list. Then, with a jerk of his chin, he signaled to someone in the departure area.

A young man smiled at Angelique and hurried over. His turquoise-colored silk blazer dazzled against his dark skin. "Miss Devine? My name is Tahu. I am your steward." He gave a polite bow of his head. "Please, I will carry your luggage, miss." He reached for the overnight bag in her hand. "The plane is waiting. This way."

Expecting a tiny plane, she was surprised to see Tahu approach a twelve-seater Lear Jet on the runway. At the foot of the aircraft's steps two tall, dark soldiers stood at attention. Striking uniforms of turquoise topped with yellow berets gave an exotic air to their formidable bearing. Tahu handed Angelique's bag to one of the soldiers before climbing aboard. At the doorway Angelique stole a glance over her shoulder. The soldier, clearly not satisfied with Singapore's security measures, was rifling quickly through her bag. A bulky shape under his arm suggested he was armed.

The only passenger, Angelique chose a seat by a window. The importance of coming up with a solution for the princess suddenly weighed heavily. Kira had gone to a lot of trouble and expense and no doubt expected more than a sympathetic ear from her guest. The soldiers boarded the plane. One closed the door, the other wordlessly placed Angelique's bag under the seat beside her. The engines rolled up to a higher pitch. "What would you like to drink, miss?" Tahu asked. "I will bring it after takeoff."

Angelique snapped on her seatbelt. "Oh...a gin and tonic would be nice. Thanks." He nodded, went and sat down, and the plane took off.

Absorbed in a book an hour later, Angelique became aware that the plane was descending. She looked out of the window.

"God..." she breathed. In shades of jade, the island of Seragana was floating on a sapphire sea. A dozen or so tiny islands clustered around the mainland, their blue harbors like daubs in a painting. Ribbons of gold from the setting sun streamed across the sky.

"We are nearly there." Angelique turned to Tahu. Smiling, he pointed at the window. "My country." He chuckled. "You will like it so much, you will never want to leave." Angelique smiled. He took her empty glass and strolled back down the aisle.

Dropping lower, the plane shifted to the south. Then suddenly, through the island's dense green canopy, gaping wounds appeared. Meandering through one side of the island, the ridge of a mountain range was laid bare. Black earth, like flesh, lay shriveling in the hot sun. Coursing through the hills and around the valleys, blue veins of rivers made their way to the sea. Dotting the hillsides, black smoke curled from fires devouring Pacific Holdings' scrubby leftovers.

A tiny airport with one runway came into view. The plane scooped low over the sea, threatening to skim the curling waves heaving onto a white beach. The plane landed and came to a stop near a large thatch-roofed terminal building. Four soldiers guarded its entrance.

As Angelique made her way down the aircraft steps a woman came out of the building. Her long sarong, in turquoise matching Tahu's jacket, was draped and knotted over one shoulder like a sari. Her black hair tumbled down her back. She greeted Angelique with a warm smile, then almost apologetically asked for her passport. "Must put stamp," she said. She hurried inside, returning with it moments later. The soldiers from the plane strode over to an open-topped Jeep where a driver sat waiting.

A white Mercedes was parked nearby. Tahu placed Angelique's bag in the trunk. He whisked open a rear door. "Your car, miss." As she got in, a Chinese driver gave her a formal nod. The car drove out of the airport, the military vehicle following close behind.

A narrow coast road gradually began to climb into the hills. Gazing down at the ocean, Angelique spotted roofs of grass thatch peeking through trees. Red hibiscus blazed in the cool shadows. In lagoons, houses stood high on bamboo stilts. Hung out to dry, fishing nets cascaded from midair verandahs. Boats tied to the stilts tugged at their ropes.

Suddenly a chocolaty scent rushed through the open windows. Wrapped in rainforest, a cacao plantation emerged. Between neat rows of trees dripping with flowers and cocoa beans, masses of ferny undergrowth fought for light. At the plantation borders, creepers and vines whipped at the invading trees, some taking a stranglehold in the treetops.

The ocean view was momentarily blocked by high rock walls as they drove through a slice cut into the mountain. Then they emerged and began their descent back to the coast. Soon they entered the town of Ngali. Boats and cruisers were anchored at a recreational wharf. Yachts drifted on Victoria Harbor. In the far distance, beyond the harbor's protective reef, Angelique spotted cranes and barges at an industrial wharf. No doubt the departure point for Andrew Nolan's mahogany exports.

The driver turned into the town's main street. A wide boulevard, it was lined with magnificent palms. Huge colonial houses were set back from the road behind stone walls. The imposing courthouse was ornate with Romanesque columns, its windows shuttered. Incongruously interspersed with fine colonial buildings were simple shops. Doors flung open, they displayed their wares on the sidewalk. Fruit, vegetables, tins of cooking oil were piled outside some of them; drums of kerosene, sacks of seeds outside others. There were some less basic shops too, Angelique noticed, that obviously catered to the relatively well-off town dwellers and the port's recreational visitors. A telephone shop caught her eye. Signage shouted the attributes of a Malaysian service provider that sold mobile phones, broadband Internet accounts and devices. There was a surf shop, a sprinkling of Malaysian, and Chinese-style cafés, and on the waterfront, an impressive restaurant and bar built from a converted colonial mansion. People lounged on its broad verandahs sipping cold beer, watching their yachts bob on the water.

Chinese and Indians in shorts and T-shirts sauntered along the sidewalk, unhurried in the steamy heat. A few tired-looking cars were parked along the street. Bicycles leaned against trees. Scratched out between buildings, narrow dirt roads sprang off the main street. Lean-to wooden houses battled for ground with wild bamboo. Chickens and children scampered in the dust.

Facing the harbor at the top of the boulevard was a grand white building with wide graduating steps leading to its entrance. A plaque out front identified the government administration departments. Next to it, past an expanse of tropical parkland, were high ornate iron gates. In gold, "Royal Palace" was woven into the ironwork.

Angelique's car stopped, the army Jeep still at its tail. Two soldiers opened the gates as two others holding M-16s looked on. The high military presence seemed excessive for a peaceful country. Perhaps it was partly for show. Angelique had seen similar, apparently unnecessary, displays of military muscle in other Asian countries. On the other hand, maybe the threat from pretenders to the seat of power was more serious than Nolan had implied.

Angelique was relieved that their military entourage left them once they were inside the gates. The car proceeded slowly along a wide road sweeping through lawns planted with coconut palms and red-flowering tamarinds. A man chipping weeds from the stone border at the side of the road gave the driver a smile. On thick bushes pink hibiscus flowers trumpeted. Peacocks sashayed between frangipani trees, their plumage dragging behind them like brilliant satin gowns. The air was sweetly perfumed. In a clearing, tall, carved mahogany pillars held up the pagoda-shaped roof of a pavilion. A woman, barefoot, was sweeping pink blossoms from the tiled floor. The car crossed an arched bridge over a small lake.

Then, around another bend, the road ended at a cobblestoned forecourt in front of the palace. A sprawling lofty stone structure, it was divided into sections by arched laneways. Armed soldiers guarded each entrance. Angelique's driver entered one of the lanes, emerging into a spacious courtyard.

A man and a woman dressed in sarongs came out of the palace as the driver opened Angelique's door. "Good evening, miss," they both said, smiling. The man took Angelique's bag from the car. "Please come this way," the woman said.

The entrance was a cavernous octagonal vestibule with a high wooden ceiling and a glassy, polished stone floor. It was refreshingly cool. On pedestals against four of the walls stood porcelain urns brimming with yellow orchids. The slapping of the man's bare feet echoed as he disappeared down one of the four wide hallways branching off the foyer. "He take your bag to your room, miss," the woman said. "Come, please. The princess is waiting."

Her feet clad in silken slippers, the woman's footsteps whispered sedately down the long stone hallway. Angelique was hotly self-conscious of her black high heels hitting the floor with an ear-splitting crack that bounced off the walls like gunshots.

They came to double doors of polished mahogany. A soldier on guard threw Angelique a penetrating glare before resuming a mid-distance gaze. She had expected security, some pomp and ritual, but finding soldiers at every turn was making her jumpy. The woman knocked and opened the door, and they went inside.

At the opposite end of a large room, folded-back latticed doors opened the entire wall to a stone terrace and garden. Surrounding the terrace, massed plumbago shrubs rose in a blue mist; late sun beamed through the doors and splashed across the glossy parquetry floor. There was a movement on the terrace, and in silhouette a woman appeared in the doorway.

"Angelique," she said. She crossed the room, extending her hand. "I'm Kira. It's so good of you to come." She was taller than average, around Angelique's height. Her dark eyes quickly perused Angelique, her smile, small, polite, white against her dark skin.

"A pleasure," Angelique said, taking her hand. "It's fortunate we have Jeremy's friendship in common."

"Delightful man."

"He was able to give me a brief rundown on Seragana's history, but I'm ashamed to admit that before last week I knew virtually nothing about this country."

Kira nodded. "All my life in England I got tired of telling people I was from Seragana, only to have them look puzzled, asking, 'Where the hell's that?' Anyway, thankfully, you know about us now, and who would believe that I have Andrew Nolan to thank for that!" Her manner was amiable yet reserved. "How about a drink before dinner? Like to try one of my Seragana

Sunsets?" She smiled a little more warmly. "I doubt it would win any awards, but I'm rather addicted to them at the moment. Freshly pressed pineapple juice—they grow wild all over the place here—in a long glass with tons of ice and a decent splash of vodka. Lots of vitamin C. A health drink, really."

A glimmer of humor was encouraging. "Sounds perfect," Angelique said, smiling.

Kira turned to the woman still waiting in the doorway. "Thank you, Dala." Dala nodded and left. "Please, come and sit down." The clipped angles, the rolling hollows of her cultured London accent clashed with the Oriental antiquity.

She led the way to a nook of sofas, plush in a colorful tapestry of silk. Overlooking the terrace and garden, they were grouped around a black-lacquered low table. They sat down. Kira wore an air of formality that was at odds with her casually chic white cotton pants and sleeveless shirt. Perhaps, to some degree, it had been cultivated to accommodate her office. Angelique pictured her in a not-so-distant past, relaxed, laughing and chatting with Jeremy in some fashionable Knightsbridge café, sipping a latté.

Glancing outside, Angelique caught sight of another armed soldier patrolling the garden's walled perimeter. Maybe it was simply tension that Kira wore like a shield. Being constantly surrounded by military with guns at the ready would more likely engender a subliminal fear than a sense of security.

"After the trouble you've taken to bring me here, I hope I can be of some help," Angelique said. "Jeremy didn't make any big promises, I hope."

"Well, he told me about your background, what you do. Which is rather impressive, I must say. Just your concern about what's going on here is a relief to me." Her gaze flickered almost imperceptibly over Angelique before she averted her eyes. Her glances were fleeting, yet her eyes revealed a piercing intelligence that suggested she didn't miss much.

Angelique relaxed against the deep soft cushions. "You've been here for little over a year, I understand. Were you prepared for all this? After London, it must've been hard to adjust."

"It's been difficult, I must say. Although my parents always expected me to return to Seragana after my education was completed, even on a part-time basis, and make some contribution, it was never foreseen that I'd find myself in this position. Like most royal families, our hereditary system has always been patriarchal. You wouldn't normally have a ruling female unless there were no males left the line. My uncle was my father's only sibling. He became king after my father's death and died leaving no heirs." She paused, smiling. "'Giles,' he called himself. Thought it made him sound sophisticated, apparently."

Angelique chuckled. Kira seemed anxious to establish a social context to their meeting, to deflect business overtones.

"Anyway, I was an only child, perhaps because after my mother and I went to live in England, my parents rarely saw each other. So I was the only one left." She shrugged. "Of course, for some time, as each year went by without Giles taking a wife, I'd had to face the possibility that I might one day have to assume this responsibility. Since I won't be having any children, this is the end of the line. When Giles died last year of a heart attack, I got a desperate call from the king's chief adviser, Onbulu. He naturally expected me to take over."

"You're called a princess, but aren't you actually the queen now?" Angelique asked.

"I'm the crown princess. In due course there'll be a formal coronation, but that's the least of my concerns at the moment. It makes no difference to my authority, anyway." Kira gave a small sigh. "Unfortunately, since I was never really trained for the job, I have to rely heavily on my advisers." She ran a hand through her short wavy hair. "Onbulu's a very kind and wise old man. He advised my grandfather, then my father, then Giles. I trust his advice. He explained there'd be terrible instability if I didn't return. My other advisers are clan chiefs, and their positions too are hereditary. While their knowledge of village administrative matters is essential for me, I'm also aware of great pressure to protect their personal interests."

She paused, cast a glance outside. Two soldiers were chatting in the shade of a jacaranda. "There are a great many interests to juggle," Kira added quietly.

There was a knock at the door. Dala came in with a tray. She placed on the table a large glass jug of Seragana Sunset, two long glasses filled with ice and a large shallow brass dish of what looked like orange-colored chips.

Kira poured the drinks and handed Angelique a glass. "Try the chips. They're a popular local snack. Made from some type of yam."

Nibbling on the sweet and peppery snack, Angelique took in the room. The ceiling, at least thirty feet high, was domed. Glass panels let in shafts of golden-pinkish light from the setting sun. The walls, a glossy duck-egg blue were trimmed in cream and gold. She recognized a tall, beautifully carved statue on a sideboard. "I've seen that deity before," she said, gesturing toward it. "In Andrew Nolan's office."

Kira nodded. "The mountain tribes—our indigenous people—make them. I believe they're paid a few cents for them and someone exports them. She's Matawa, the most important of Seragana's traditional gods. Matawa is also the Seraganian word for mother, life and love." She smiled, her expression suddenly warm. "I like the sound of that, don't you?" She was thawing out.

"Surely the Brits brought Christian missionaries with them. They would've done a bit of damage to Matawa's status, wouldn't they?"

"Of course they tried. But the locals didn't take to it very well." She chuckled. "It was no fun, you see. They stood to lose all their special feast days, rituals and ceremonies. So, just to cover all possibilities, many of them simply added Jesus to their list of gods." Angelique laughed. "Anyway, there's so much to do here, so much I'm determined to change. Politically, my plans will be difficult enough to achieve. But without money I can't begin to create any wealth, and while we're virtual slaves to Pacific Holdings, it's impossible to plan a progressive future."

"It's disastrous that Nolan actually owns half the island. It gives him rights he shouldn't have."

"My uncle was a greedy fool," Kira said with a sigh. "To put things into context, I should take you back a bit. After my family became sole rulers, the British left the other two kingdoms with only a tiny portion of their original lands. The British, in the name of the Na Murghas, seized the rest for plantations. Many of the villagers who had traditionally farmed or fished or hunted—depending on their province—were deprived of a living. Their old way of trading too, bartering, was also finished. The British introduced the Seraganian pound." Kira grinned. An attractive dimple appeared in one cheek when she smiled. "It's worth so little these days that there's a flourishing business in illegal currency exchange. People will hand over a ton of pounds for a few Singapore dollars." She paused and sipped her drink. "So, the kings no longer received a living from the fruits of their subjects' labors, and they also established plantations."

Kira refilled their glasses. The Seragana Sunsets went down very easily. She went on to explain that the families of the other kings began to disintegrate, and many of them drifted out of the country. Their palaces, once protected for posterity by Kira's father, had fallen to ruin under Giles's leadership.

"All the ancient temples are still looked after, though," Kira said, staring into her glass. "Many of them are still in use." She looked up, the expression in her dark eyes suddenly intimate. "If you have more time on your next visit, I'd love to show them to you."

So, her guarded glances had been leading somewhere after all. Kira was flirting. And peeping out from behind her cool exterior was a warmth that was decidedly appealing. As if reading Angelique's thoughts, Kira dropped a sexy half-smile.

"I'd like that."

They held each other's gaze long enough to secure an understanding. Kira got up, went over to the sideboard and picked up a small wooden box. Returning, she opened the box and offered Angelique a long, thin cigarette wrapped in coarse-looking creamy paper. "They make these in the mountains. One of the crops the British played around with was tobacco. The leaf used for these is a feral form of those old plants. They mix it with cloves and God knows what else and wrap it in sugary paper. I enjoy them occasionally. Would you like one?"

"No, but you go ahead."

Kira lit her cigarette. It had an enticing aroma. Kira smiled. "Cloves. It numbs your lips."

They both turned to the open doors as a cacophony of

tropical birdsong suddenly erupted in the garden. It was almost dark. A teenage boy holding a torch of fire ambled around the garden lighting torch lamps on tall bamboo poles. Kira reached over to a side table and switched on a lamp.

Kira exhaled a stream of fragrant smoke. "My grandfather had just become king when the British pulled out. He'd grown up during their occupation, so although he didn't receive any formal Western education, he was a convert to their system. He believed Seragana's future lay in having an organized, Western-style economy, that the days of subsistence were over. As you can imagine, the discontentment of the people, spurred on by the old ruling families, rose to the surface again. He calmed things down by returning many of the British plantations to the descendants of the other royal families."

"Some of them would've done quite well."

"Yes, but it was an uneasy peace. Nothing had changed for the general population—the plantation employers had changed, that was all. And the ex-royal families wanted power. All of it. There was jealousy and distrust between the two families, on top of their desire to depose my grandfather."

Kira paused, looking thoughtful. Perhaps she had difficulty at times placing herself into a history only slightly less foreign to her than to Angelique. The responsibility she faced was awesome.

With a knock on the door, Dala appeared again. "Dinner will be served when you ready, Madam."

"Thank you, Dala. We'll be right along." Dala gave a quick bow of her head and closed the door. Kira stood. "I arranged a selection of Asian-style dishes. We have a wonderful Thai chef." She grinned. "I doubted that you'd want British fare."

Angelique got up from the sofa. "Well, I was rather hoping it wouldn't be brown Windsor soup and toad-in-the-hole."

Kira laughed. "Quite."

They left the room and strolled some distance down the hallway to an intersection. As they took a turn Angelique caught a flash of turquoise and yellow as a soldier slid out of sight.

"I thought we'd dine outside," Kira said. "It's the usual thing here." They passed full-length latticed windows. Through them Angelique glimpsed the sea.

Angelique commented on the beauty of the palace. Kira nodded. "My grandfather extended the original palace; later my father added some modern improvements. The new economy provided cash in the form of taxes and export duties. My father was able to provide Ngali with some infrastructure, which in turn encouraged the establishment of more businesses. There weren't the funds to go beyond Ngali, though. There still isn't the money for that. There are no schools, proper roads, electricity or telecommunications in the provinces where most people live."

They swung into another hallway, and suddenly ahead of them was a breathtaking ocean view. On the lawn was a magnificent pavilion. It stood high, its curved roof tiled in rich blue, its carved mahogany pillars painted red and gold. "The Royal Pavilion," Kira said. "Used on special occasions." Attendants were busy fussing around a table set with silver, lit by candles in glass holders.

Attendants held their chairs as they sat down. One of them took a bottle of wine from an ice bucket and filled their glasses. The birds had quieted, and the only sound was the ocean rolling in, crashing over the rocks below the garden wall.

Angelique was becoming distracted by the surroundings and, increasingly, by Kira. She hauled her thoughts back to the point of her visit. "I guess the reality is that Pacific Holdings contributes to the revenue that keeps your government operational."

"Certainly. He pays some royalties for the timber, although it's a token, really. And there's the employment of hundreds of workers. They're poorly paid, though, and their working conditions are shocking. There are lots of dreadful accidents too. But he's the biggest employer in the country, so he sets the standards. Those workers have no choice if they want a job." She shrugged. "I guess he's no different from big employers everywhere who have a market to themselves."

An attendant arrived at the table with a large white soup terrine. He lifted the lid and Angelique smelled lemon grass. He ladled the clear soup into small, brightly decorated bowls, then added a few succulent prawns and a garland of coriander.

"So, if you could get rid of him, what would you replace him with?"

Kira looked at her for a long moment. She seemed to be cautiously considering her reply.

"You would've seen the damage he's done as you were flying in. He has no regeneration program and refuses to implement one. Some of the estuaries to the major rivers are so badly silted up now that there's flooding in some places. Fresh water supplies to some areas have dried up, and much of the river fish and bird life has been destroyed. That can't go on just for the sake of some jobs. This is a rich and beautiful country. We could have a profitable eco-tourism industry. With better infrastructure we could encourage a food processing industry, instead of cheaply exporting raw spices, sugar, cocoa and coffee. I'd go along with forestry too, as long as it was self-sustaining, properly managed. She shook her head. "Lots of things could happen if we got back the other half of our country that he's exploiting purely for his own benefit. It's theft, pure and simple." Kira lapsed into silence, sipping her wine.

"You've sought legal advice, no doubt. Regarding the validity of his title and his negligence?"

Kira confirmed that she had. The advice had been that his title seemed legal as it had been signed by the king and that taking action for damages would be futile. It would cost a fortune, and even if a case succeeded, Nolan would only be fined or ordered to make reparations that he'd be unlikely to carry out. She had presented Nolan with new regulations in all matters, and he had ignored them. He had simply offered her money to drop her demands, suggesting that it might be invested privately in her name. That kind of arrangement had apparently worked well with Uncle Giles.

The table was cleared and more food served. There was crispy chicken, a curry of beef and okra, a seafood salad, sweet noodles and spicy rice. Angelique complimented Kira on the excellent dinner. "I'll pass that on to Kim, the chef," Kira said with a grin. "He'll be pleased. He was very excited about having a guest to cook for. Half the time I only want scrambled eggs on toast." Their glasses were refilled, and they were left alone again.

"Why not try going in harder? Nolan told me you're slowing him down at the mills and the wharves, but why not completely stop him at the wharves? Starve him out." He could try to fight Kira with the law, Angelique thought, but he'd have trouble forcing the nation's ruler to back off. Giles had granted him the status of a citizen, but that wasn't worth much. This wasn't a democracy.

Kira stared down into her glass. "Because it's dangerous," she said flatly. "It's complicated." She was holding something back.

"Do you mean there'd be social unrest because of the loss of jobs?"

"Yes. But not only that. During my father's time the social instability continued. His English education was cut short when his father died, and he took over when he was only nineteen. It was thanks to old Onbulu that he coped. Matters were made worse when he married my mother. She was from one of those other royal families. They were furious, as you can imagine, that she would marry a hated Na Murgha. But faced with it, they decided that the union should at least give them special privileges and a share of the power. It was clearly impossible to grant those things. The country needed strong guidance into a secure economic future. It couldn't be divided up again. By the time I was five, things had become so volatile, my father was afraid for the safety of my mother and me. He sent us to England." Kira gazed out to sea. "There were a number of nasty skirmishes that he put down quickly, thanks to the loyalty of the Royal Guards. They act as both police and army." She scanned the shadowy garden, and lowered her voice. "That's dangerous too. Their power. Something else I want to change eventually."

"Nolan told me you have relatives who still want power."

"Yes, and twenty years ago, when I was sixteen, they nearly got it. They led a coup that saw my father assassinated."

Angelique was taken aback. "I had no idea…" she murmured. Nolan's association with Kira's power-hungry cousin suddenly looked less than benign.

"The Guards held them back, though. Giles took over. He handed out some more candy in the form of land and carried on. When Andrew Nolan popped up ten years ago, Giles jumped on him. In some ways I can't blame Giles for that. He might have thought that Pacific Holdings would aid stability by providing employment and revenue." She sighed. "Of course, it made Giles personally a rich man. The income from Nolan is trifling for a government, but it's a lot when most ends up in the pocket of one man. Giles had a gambling habit. He spent much of his time out of the country, in Macau mostly."

"So, if you tipped Nolan out, you'd be setting off another power struggle."

"Exactly. Unless I could provide wealth from some other source." Kira leaned her elbows on the table. There was fear in her eyes. "If I get too heavy with him, he'll whistle in the wolves to help him. He's friendly with a cousin of mine who heads up the push for a takeover."

"Mbulo. Nolan mentioned him."

"If the climate were right, he'd make a move. The clan chiefs would shift their loyalty to him if he offered privileges and financial security that I wouldn't or couldn't give. Everyone belongs to a clan. The Royal Guards too could be influenced." Kira paused, gulped down some wine. "In the course of a couple of our unpleasant discussions, Nolan has casually dropped Mbulo's name, which I've taken as a subtle threat." She rubbed her forehead wearily. "I'm not suggesting that Nolan would want any part in a coup attempt. But I know he will protect his interests. He's cunning enough to realize that my relatives can kill, and killers don't make good partners. I'm a thorn in his side, yet I'm straight with him. But if I were to block him completely, I'm certain he would turn to Mbulo rather than walk away from his fortune. So, you see, putting pressure on him won't work in the long-term. I have to be more clever than that."

As the complexity of the situation grew clearer to her, Angelique grew tense. She had understood that Nolan would prefer to deal with a more amenable ruler. But he hadn't explained that his business interests were inextricably enmeshed with the ongoing power struggle. She was out of her depth. She'd been focused on how to push Nolan out of Seragana, but this was obviously not the wisest approach.

"I had no idea." she murmured. "I'm not feeling very clever right now myself."

Kira smiled warmly. "I'm just glad there are people who give a damn about what's happening here. As far as the rest of the world is concerned, Seragana is nothing. We're powerless, we have no voice."

An attendant appeared.

"Would you like dessert? Kira asked. "Fruit? Or just coffee? The local coffee's very good, by the way." Angelique went for the coffee. Kira stood, and wandered across the emerald tessellated tiles and gazed off into the garden.

"Do you get lonely?" Angelique asked quietly, as they waited for the coffee to appear.

"Sometimes. During the day, it's usually okay. I'm so busy. And I e-mail friends in London, phone them... It's at night mostly, that I can get lonely."

Angelique was curious to know if there was a lover in Kira's life. She took a sip of her wine. Adopting a casual tone she asked, "There's no one special in London you had to leave behind?"

Kira turned to Angelique, rested her back against the pillar. "No one."

Angelique grinned. "And I guess there's not exactly a gay scene here."

Kira chuckled. "Not a scene, no. They're here, of course, but as an ordinary part of the community. There's no need for a subculture. The missionaries, it seemed, didn't notice the gays. Or if they did, any attempts to demonize them apparently failed."

"So no one local has shown an interest?" Angelique chuckled. "The princess would be a good catch."

"Not that I know of," Kira said, laughing. "I really think it would be most inappropriate on my part. Besides, I'd have very little in common with anyone here." She gave a half-smile. "Of course, if I cast the net a little wider, it could take in Singapore. You could be considered a local, especially if you dropped by regularly."

Angelique smiled. "Is that an invitation?"

"It certainly is." Kira's voice was seductively low. Angelique smiled. Jeremy would be pleased.

The coffee arrived with a selection of liqueurs. Kira resumed her seat. The attendant poured the thick, aromatic brew, then vanished across the darkened forecourt. Stirring sugar into her coffee, her brow furrowed, Kira seemed once again absorbed with her problems.

Angelique couldn't bear to leave tomorrow without offering Kira some hope of a solution. "I'm sure we'll come up with an idea to deal with Andrew Nolan," she said. "Together with my friends, Jeremy and others, we've come up with solutions to a few tricky problems. In aid, we often had to work around political tangles." Kira looked at her hopefully. "We can't create a sudden void in business and employment, but maybe I can lure Nolan away with other opportunities. At the same time, I could look around for business ventures that would suit Seragana. Without his domination, we might be able to attract others."

"But he'd never give up ownership of his land."

Angelique sighed. "And I must admit, the changeover would take years to effect. The best we could hope for is a major decline in Nolan's logging activities or some improvement in his methods through your constant badgering."

Kira stared into the mid-distance. Not surprisingly she looked unsatisfied with Angelique's suggestion of compromise. Then suddenly she turned to Angelique, her expression intense.

"There's something I haven't told you." Her voice was almost a whisper. "Something that puts a different complexion on the whole situation." Angelique felt her pulse begin to quicken. "You'll appreciate that I had to have complete confidence in you before revealing potentially dangerous information. Over the past few days, awaiting your visit, I've given the matter a great deal of thought. No one but me knows what I'm about to tell you. In the wrong hands this knowledge would be deadly, literally." She paused, took a deep breath. "Yet if I don't put my trust in someone who may know how to use it, this information will be of no benefit either."

Angelique felt responsibility settle on her like a shroud. "You can trust my discretion," she said.

"I have a document you must see. It's locked in my study." Kira got up, excused herself, left the pavilion and vanished across the forecourt.

When she returned a few minutes later, she was tense and

breathless. She sat down, drew a glossy bound document from a plastic folder and placed it carefully before Angelique. She shot a quick glance into the shadows, then whispered, "Oil. Millions of barrels of oil!"

Out of the balmy night something cold seemed to brush against Angelique's skin. Staring at the document, she slowly opened its cover. Colorful graphs and aerial photos danced before her eyes.

"Seragana," Kira said quietly, "lies in an oil-rich region. It occurred to me some months ago that maybe there was oil here. So I decided it was worth spending some money to find out. I wanted someone from outside our region to take a look. I got an American exploration company over here and had them sign a confidentiality agreement about their findings."

Angelique turned another page. The technical data was detailed and complex, beyond her comprehension. But the text summary was clear enough. There were two major reservoirs, and the estimate of their value was huge.

"The geologist's first impression was that there was probably oil in a few different areas," Kira went on, "so I had a two-dimensional seismic exploration carried out. That showed there were only two accumulations big enough to be worth exploiting. And the geologist suspected they were large. The only way to be sure, though, was to drill and have a look."

Angelique was staring at a full-page map showing the two oil reserves in the north. "It's all in the east side," she murmured. She looked up at Kira sharply. "Nolan's side."

Kira nodded. "Therein lies my problem. Anyway, I had to know what I was dealing with, so despite the expense I got them to sink a couple of wildcats."

"Wildcats?"

"Small exploration wells. They can do it very neatly nowadays, causing a minimum of disturbance. They used a heli-rig. There's no other easy way into those wild places, anyway. Much of the cost was due to my employing the option of green exploratory procedures. The company fully restored the areas of the drilling locations, so it's almost impossible to see where they were. No one knew what I was up to. No one took any interest in the arrival of men and equipment. They had my customs clearance, and it was assumed they were connected with Nolan's normal operations. The drilling areas are a long way from Nolan's logging activities. He and his people were unaware of it." She poured herself another cognac. "Needless to say, the wildcats confirmed the geologist's expectations."

Angelique grabbed her glass and gulped down the rest of her liqueur. If only the oil had been on the other side, the country's poverty would soon be no more than a bad memory. Kira could afford to pay Nolan anything for his land to get rid of him, then begin to regenerate, rebuild. But if Nolan were to learn of the riches beneath his mahogany forests, his power and influence would be unsurpassable.

"Thank God he hasn't thought about oil himself," Kira said.

"Not yet. And perhaps he won't," Angelique said. "Besides, just because there's oil in the general region, doesn't mean it's everywhere. You took a long shot." Kira nodded. "But you can't just leave the oil in the ground," Angelique added.

Kira sighed. "I know. I'm blocked into a corner. I've thought about getting some big oil conglomerate in here, forming a partnership and just moving onto his land. After all, oil's a national resource that the government can lay claim to. But although I run the country, an oil company would have great concern about Nolan's land title. They could waste a lot of time and money if Nolan were to put up a fight. What if he didn't want to accept a fat check to leave? What if he argued that he could profitably exploit the oil? If a prospective oil partner wasn't scared off, I might lose them to him." Kira paused, lighting another cigarette.

"And then there's my cousin. Nolan would certainly turn to him for help. Mbulo wouldn't hesitate to move to against me. Word would go around that I was thwarting everyone's chances of getting rich." She gave a wry smile. "People would believe that. The chiefs and military too. Of course, under Mbulo's rule, he and Nolan would be the only ones getting rich. Like my uncle, who years ago paid Mbulo to leave Seragana, Mbulo has no interest in the development of the country and its people."

This sort of instability was precisely why legitimate foreign investment was virtually impossible to get in countries like Seragana. Despite her earlier suggestion, Angelique would have found it difficult to find businesses willing to risk their investment in this volatile environment. Yet giving up the oil to Nolan was out of the question. She gazed distractedly into the bowl of flowers on the table. Captured in tiny pools of nectar in the flesh-colored orchids, insects squirmed. Some were desperately trying to escape their sticky tomb, hopelessly clawing at the slippery petal walls. Others floated, glistening, spent or drowned. A formless idea drifted through her mind. Her heartbeat quickened.

"We could trap him," she suddenly blurted. She looked up at Kira. "Lure him to the oil. I don't know…involve him somehow…get him out of his depth."

"Drown him in it?" Kira smiled, then rose. "It's getting late. Let's sleep on it."

Angelique suddenly realized how tired she was. It was probably why she was getting crazy ideas. Nolan and millions of barrels of oil were suddenly tomorrow's problem.

"See that latticed porch over there?" Kira said. She pointed to the far end of the palace where a lattice pergola covered a stone terrace. "That's the garden entrance to your suite of rooms. I'll walk you over."

Kira grabbed her folder off the table and they strolled out of the pavilion. Dala appeared on the forecourt. "Thank you, Dala," Kira said. "That'll be all for tonight."

CHAPTER SIX

Stephanie struggled to focus on the monthly budget report. The spate of break-ins over the past couple of months had cost her department a fortune in overtime. Unless she could find a way to stretch some of the expenses into next month, she would blow her budget for the second month in a row.

But her thoughts kept drifting to the letter delivered to her a half hour ago. With a resigned sigh, she shoved the overtime sheets to one side, snatched up the letter and read it again. The police logo loomed large at the top, the signature of the chief commissioner scrawled heavily on the bottom. It was the official notification of her Chastisement. Unlike every other document she had received bearing that autograph, this one made her squirm with humiliation.

She stuffed the letter back into its envelope. She wasn't going to dissociate herself from GALPA, though. She was guest speaker at a Women's Business Association dinner in six weeks' time, and GALPA was integral to the speech she planned. She would just have to watch her back more carefully in the future.

She checked her watch. Two thirty. Dave should be back from his morning in court by now. This afternoon they were going around to pay another visit to the Burzomis. It was ten days since baby Brittany had been found dead. The coroner had made a finding of death from exposure caused by the actions of a person or persons unknown. It was up to Stephanie to establish a case of either homicide or culpable negligence. And the pressure was mounting. The daily papers bristled with horror stories about baby killers and the inadequacy of the police force to protect life and property. Houlihan, uneasy about her performance, was breathing down her neck for a result. Since Don Williams had been ruled out as the car thief, no other suspects had emerged. A drug investigation of the Yaa Baa pills hadn't led anywhere either.

She got up, grabbed her coat and went over to the operations room.

His back to the door, Dave was at the coffee-making counter. From the doorway Stephanie glimpsed the usual puddles of coffee and milk and trails of spilled sugar on the blue laminate. Pouring water from the kettle into a mug, Dave was talking with a young uniformed constable. They were discussing a recently discovered racket in stolen prestige cars. Stephanie dropped her coat over a chair beside Dave's desk and sat down.

"But, Sarge," the constable said, "that bloke that runs Presto Motors must be the one organizing the thefts. I mean, we already found this Mercedes in his workshop with the engine number half scrubbed off and the plates changed." Dave nodded, stirred sugar into his mug. "He reckons some customer brought it in for a spray job. But when we tried to contact the customer, no one had ever heard of him." He shrugged. "'Course, the bloke says it's not his fault if customers bring him pinched cars. Swears he's innocent. But it's not the first time, Sarge, and it's bloody suspicious, don't you reckon?"

"Suspicious?" Dave snatched up the milk carton. "Listen, son, every bloody thing's suspicious." He cautiously sniffed the milk. "Even this milk." He poured some into his coffee and peered into the mug. Apparently satisfied with its appearance, he gave it a stir and turned to the constable. "Of course that bugger's suspicious. Ever come across a motor mechanic who's not dodgy?" He took a gulp of his coffee, then winced. "Jesus! This bloody milk is off."

He slammed the mug down on the counter in disgust. He slid his chewing gum pack from his shirt pocket and jammed a couple of pieces into his mouth. "You find me a motor mechanic who's not dodgy, son, and I'll swim upstream in a river of shit with my mouth open."

The constable chuckled. Stephanie shook her head. "Of course he's the bastard doing the ID changes," Dave continued. "But he'd only be a bit player in this scam. Hasn't got the brains to organize a racket like this." He shook his head dismissively. "Couldn't organize a shag in a brothel." He caught sight of Stephanie. "Oh! Be right with you." She nodded. "You boys keep on his back, right?" Dave went on. "Keep paying him little visits. Know what I mean? Make him jumpy. Meantime we'll follow up some other leads."

The constable nodded and made for the door. "Ma'am," he murmured respectfully to Stephanie as he passed. Dave strode over and sank down in his chair.

"How'd you go in court?" Stephanie asked.

Dave sighed wearily. "Got off, the prick." They'd charged a man with torching his own shoe factory for the insurance payout. "He might've been on the verge of bloody bankruptcy, but he had enough cash tucked away somewhere to hire a shit-hot Queen's Counsel."

"Our case had holes in it. But it was the best we had. Can't win 'em all."

Munching on his gum, Dave nodded grimly. "So, we going around to the Burzomis' place? I thought it might be better to get them back in here for questioning. Andrea, anyway. Make her see we mean business."

Stephanie shook her head. "Andrea's too savvy for that. She knows the routine. She'll refuse to come in, believe me, unless we arrest her. And without a charge we can't manage that."

Dave shoved back his chair. "Oh, well, let's go."

Twenty minutes later Dave veered the squad car into the driveway of the public housing estate. Six identical cold-gray twenty-story blocks of flats rose out of a white concrete desert like monuments to misery. The symmetrical towers were separated by alleys of washing lines and garbage bins. Identifying your own underwear flapping around in one of those icy wind tunnels, Stephanie thought, would be the easiest way to recognize which faceless building was yours. The sixties, when this estate had been constructed, wasn't an era admired for fine architecture. Even so, it must have taken some determined, hard-hearted collaboration between bureaucrats and architects to come up with this design that crushed your spirit at a single glance.

Dave parked the car outside Block B. "Hope she's home," he said."

"Usually is during the day. Andrea's a bit of a night owl."

A brown dog shot out from a tumble of garbage bins, yapping, its teeth bared. On a patch of grass a short distance away, a group of young kids who should have been in school took a break from their football game to shout, "Oink! Oink!"

The foyer was gloomy. Although the lights placed high on the concrete walls were caged in steel mesh, someone had managed, doubtless with great difficulty, to smash four of the six fluorescent tubes. As she hit the button to call the elevator, Stephanie found herself wondering how the job had been done. Everyone enjoyed a challenge, and, for lack of other opportunities to explore your ingenuity, vandalism must provide some illusion of achievement.

The elevator arrived, and Dave pressed the button for the fifteenth floor. Using an indelible black marker, someone had decorated the stainless steel walls with a series of penises. In various stages of arousal they, were casually interspersed with brief scribblings about various girls who had reputedly "done it."

Dave kicked away a half-eaten Big Mac, then stuffed his hands into his coat pockets. "Quite an artist they've got round here."

"Good renditions, are they?" Stephanie said with a wry smile. The doors opened and they stepped out onto the concrete balcony. Clutching their coats tightly, they hurried down the blustery balcony toward flat number 1520. The pale sun pasted onto an icy sky offered no respite from the clawing wind.

Stephanie rang the doorbell. Dave was gazing through the steel mesh that enclosed the gap between the four-foot balcony wall and the balcony floor above. The housing department had installed the barriers years ago after residents developed the embarrassing habit of using the balcony ledges to jump to their deaths. "Great view," Dave said.

Stephanie glanced out at the bay in the distance. She could just make out billowing sails on yachts as small as seagulls flitting over the royal blue sea. Her eyes shifted focus to the rusty mesh confining them like monkeys in a zoo. "Envious, are you?"

Dave rolled his eyes. "Won't be sticking my name on the waiting list. Let's put it that way."

The door opened a crack, Andrea peered out. "Yeah? What d'ya want?"

"A chat," Stephanie said.

"I'm busy." Andrea looked drawn.

"So am I. So don't waste my time. These questions will go on until we get some sensible answers. You know that."

Andrea scratched her ear, her eyes narrowed. "You can come in, but not him." She tossed Dave a contemptuous glare.

Stephanie placed her hand firmly on the door. "DS Ryan doesn't bite," she said flatly.

The heat in the living room was stifling. A smell of burned toast overlaid that of the cigarette smoke drifting from the ashtray. Stephanie removed her coat, draped it over the back of the floral sofa and sat down. Dave unbuttoned his coat and remained standing, his hands in his pockets. Andrea leaned against the window ledge, facing them, her arms crossed.

"Where's Kylie?" Stephanie asked.

"Stayin' at me auntie's." Andrea clenched the cuffs of her oversized red track top in balled fists. Raising one fleecy-lined paw, she rubbed her nose. Beside her, in a shiny walnut-veneered cabinet, a new-looking widescreen plasma was switched on, its volume low. Dave was eyeing a sophisticated surround-sound system. This was just the sort of gear that had been disappearing from warehouses lately. But Stephanie didn't want to be distracted from the matter in hand.

She leaned forward, her elbows on her knees. "Got any more to tell me about those drugs found in the car?"

Andrea shook her head. "Told those drug cops the same as I told you. The bloke who swiped the car left 'em."

Stephanie held her gaze intensely. "I think it's time you stopped pissing us around, Andrea," she said quietly. Andrea averted her eyes, stared at the floor. "I know that you know everyone around this area. So does Kylie. You'd know the guy who took the car."

Andrea shook her head. She stomped over to the coffee table and grabbed her cigarette from the ashtray.

"There was no man in the car park was there?" Stephanie asked firmly. Andrea swung around, staring wide-eyed. Dave jerked his head up, looking puzzled. Stephanie was cruising on instinct. She couldn't figure why the girls would protect the person responsible for Brittany's death. They knew it wasn't Williams. Even if they were involved in some kind of drug deal and had been threatened into silence, there would've been some reprisal by now. One of George Burzomi's mates would've somehow avenged the baby's death. But nothing like that had happened, and no one seemed to know a damned thing about the matter.

Andrea perched on the arm of a chair. "Kylie never got a good look at him. How many fuckin' times do I have to tell ya?"

"For all your faults, I've never known you to lie so consistently."

Andrea blinked at Stephanie, then drew on her cigarette.

"What are you girls doing with drugs? You started dealing? Or developed a habit?" Andrea was biting her lip. Stephanie goaded her. "Maybe Kylie's the one with the habit, and she was out that night working the streets to support it."

Andrea jumped to her feet. "You think I'd let her do that?" she shouted, her eyes flashing. When enraged, Andrea often blurted the truth despite herself. She stomped over to the table and mashed her cigarette out in the ashtray. "You stupid fuckin' bitch."

"Watch your mouth, kid!" Dave snapped.

"Get fucked, arsehole!" Andrea shouted, her face crimson.

"Settle down, Andrea," Stephanie ordered. She gave Dave a meaningful look, inclined her head toward the kitchen. With an impatient grunt he left the room.

Stephanie relaxed back in her seat. "Sit down."

Tears glinting in her eyes, Andrea slumped down in the chair.

"I know," Stephanie continued gently, "that you feel you have to protect Kylie. And you've done a pretty good job of that over the years too." A tear rolled slowly down Andrea's face. Skinny, her scalp pink through her mousy hair, she suddenly looked painfully fragile.

A memory flashed into Stephanie's mind of herself close to Andrea's age. A class captain at her private girls' school, star of the netball team. Straight A's, which she managed much of the time, earned her a little nod of approval and a tired, yet satisfied smile from her mother. Stephanie knew it was up to her to compensate for her father's shortcomings.

But a rival had discovered Stephanie's shame. On a morning just after practice, Nina Anderson told the girls about Stephanie's jailed father. In the gym changing room, her hair dripping from the shower, dying inside, Stephanie had probably not appeared as exposed as Andrea did at this moment. But her heart had kicked against her ribs just as violently as Andrea's heart must be pounding now.

She could have told the open-mouthed gaggle of girls how much she loved her father and that he'd only made a stupid mistake. But holding back her tears with an iron will, she had shrugged. He was a lawyer, she told them with a dismissive air. There was some mix-up over investments or something. Soothed, the girls quickly lost interest in the story. White-collar crimes were a different thing altogether. After all, tax avoidance was a crime, yet they were taught the rudiments of that in economics class.

Andrea scraped the tear off her face with her shoulder.

Stephanie cleared her throat. "Okay. Who was actually driving the car that night? You or Kylie?"

"Kylie."

"And she left the car in the supermarket car park while she went to buy something for Brittany. Is that right?"

Suddenly Andrea covered her eyes with one hand, her shoulders slumped. "Those bloody pills," she murmured. "Our dad fixed it. I went to visit him. I told him we needed money." She looked up, tears creeping down her face. "Me brothers are still in school. Supposed to be, anyway, when they're not sneakin' off. They need things that sometimes I can't get money for. I don't want 'em pinchin' things, you know."

She wiped her nose on her sleeve, then reached over for another cigarette. "Dad said he'd sort it out. Said he'd get a bloke to come round with some stuff. A bloke Dad always used to get stuff off."

She lit her cigarette, then got to her feet, paced up and down the room. "I don't know who he is." Andrea threw Stephanie a challenging glare. "So don't ask." Stephanie nodded. She'd send someone down to the prison later to lean on George. "He turns up a few weeks ago and gives me these pink pills. He reckoned they'd be easy to move 'cause they're cheap. Only charge five dollars each, he said, and give him three. He'd come back in a month and get his money."

Andrea went to the window and stared out at the steel barrier. "So, that Thursday night, when I'm out, Kylie takes it into her stupid head to do a bit of business. Bundles up Brittany, sticks her in the back of the car and takes off down to the beach to sell these pills." Andrea paused, fingering the six silver studs in her left earlobe.

Over Andrea's shoulder, Stephanie noticed a wooden carving on a laminated sideboard. Richly colored, glinting with gold paint, the statue was of a dark Oriental woman. Her head tilted back, her arms behind her head, she seemed in a state of surrender or prayer. Mysterious and beautiful, the statue was entirely out of place amid walnut veneer, laminate and floral chintz. A movement in the crack of the kitchen door caught her eye. Dave had his ear to the door.

"Go on," Stephanie prompted.

Andrea sighed. "Kylie reckons it was about six thirty when

she met some friends down there. They were all headin' into a pub. Since having the baby, well, she never hangs out with her friends anymore. So she got all excited. Went with 'em. She can pass for eighteen with her makeup on, easy."

Andrea took a ragged breath, ran her hand over her cropped hair. "She goes and leaves Brittany in the back of the car in the supermarket car park. A block away." She turned to Stephanie with a look of horror. "She's only eight bloody weeks old!" Her voice cracked and she swung back to the window. "Kylie'd got some cash from about half the pills. You found what was left. And she spent it all on rum and Coke. Drank herself under the table, forgot about Brittany. For nearly four hours, she left her. In zero degrees with a bunny rug and no food." Covering her face with her hands, she broke down.

Stephanie got up and went to her. Putting her arm around Andrea's shoulders, she said gently, "Kylie's only a kid herself."

Forgetting herself for a moment, Andrea rested her head on Stephanie's shoulder. She was shaking. "It's my fault. I'm the eldest," she gasped. "Kylie didn't mean it. She loved Brittany. We all did. I just got her some new stuff. Jumpsuits and a dress. Bought 'em, too." She wiped her eyes with the back of her hand. "Anyway, Kylie comes and finds me and tells me, and I fuckin' freak, you know? Dumping the car and the story about it getting pinched. That was my idea. Brittany was dead. Stone cold." She gave a helpless shrug. "Didn't know what else to do."

"You've done the right thing now, telling the truth," Stephanie said. "Things will get easier from now on." Now she was lying. The legal tangle that lay ahead for them would only make their lives harder.

Her tears dried up, Andrea's old belligerence returned. She roughly shook off Stephanie's arm and ambled back to her chair. Dragging a crumpled tissue from her pocket she gouged at her eyes. "Snitching on your family's not the bloody right thing! Ya don't drop your family in it. Me dad will kill me."

Dave came back into the room. He took a notebook and a pen from his coat pocket. "What's your aunt's address?" he asked quietly. Without looking up, Andrea gave the address.

Dave scribbled it down, then pulled his mobile phone from his pocket.

Stephanie stepped over to the sofa, picked up her coat. "Grab a jacket," she said to Andrea. "We've got to go down to the station and take your statement." Her movements leaden, Andrea got up and went into an adjoining room.

Dave was arranging Kylie's arrest. "She's just a kid, right? Send Jenny down there with Sue or Kath to pick her up. Not one of you big brutes. No need to scare the little bugger out of her wits." Stephanie admired Dave's softness when it counted. With his free hand, he crammed some fresh gum into his mouth. "Yeah." He nodded. "Manslaughter." He hung up.

Andrea reappeared in a denim jacket. "Me brothers will probably be home soon," she mumbled. Aged twelve and thirteen, the boys were already starting to make a name for themselves with the police.

Stephanie slipped her coat on. "We'll get your aunt or a policewoman around here to keep an eye on them till you get back."

Andrea marched in front of them as they headed back down the balcony to the elevator. Stephanie glanced at Dave. "I'll arrange for you to make a media statement tonight. At this stage we'll just say that an arrest has been made. It'll calm down things down a bit."

"Me?" Looking surprised, Dave turned up his collar against the wind. Stephanie was normally the one to face the press.

Stephanie gave a weak smile. "My public image is lacking a bit of cred at the moment. Houlihan has banned me from making media statements."

"No worries."

It was close to eight thirty when Stephanie finally finished for the day. Fog curled around lights in the car park as she headed for her car. It had taken hours to process the Burzomis. Their relatives, who at other times showed little interest in the girls, had poured in like storm troopers, abusive, indignant that the police had dared to stick their noses into private family matters. Hovering at the edge of the battlefield, the child welfare people, with set mouths and mountains of paper, argued with the relatives, argued with the police. Floundering in the trenches well out of his depth was the legal aid lawyer who looked all of fifteen himself. And through it all Kylie wailed and Andrea hissed. Stephanie's head was splitting.

Shivering beneath her coat, she got into the car. She rubbed her breath from the windshield with the back of her hand. Her headlights beaming onto a white wall of fog, she carefully drove out into the traffic. Her apartment was in the city center a kilometer away.

By the time she got to the third set of traffic lights, the heater had cut in. The steam on the windshield peeled away, and the muscles in her face began to thaw. Inching across the bridge she gazed down at the Yarra River. The warmth of the city's heart had nudged the fog higher. Glowing in the lights of restaurants and bars, the Southgate Promenade bustled with people. Towering behind the complex, overlooking the city, the tops of luxury apartment buildings were lost in swirling mist.

The traffic surged forward. Stephanie put her foot down and shot through the next intersection, whizzing for half a block past leafless plane trees dazzling with fairy lights.

Dave had made a press statement an hour ago. There would be an en masse sigh of relief. The public would console itself with the comfortable conviction that this latest horror, like all society's ills, was down to dole cheats, drug pushers, teenage girls with babies living-it-up on welfare. Houlihan was pleased. All in all, if you didn't count the Chastisement notice, it had been a successful day.

But as was often the case, Stephanie felt no joy in the success. Just a flat satisfaction that a difficult task had been completed. Although her job was to protect the status quo, she often found herself out of step with people who had normal careers. When Charlotte had a successful day, a stock market win for an already wealthy client, it was celebrated with champagne. Stephanie usually preferred to wipe out her successes with a few scotches slammed down fast. She could murder one right now. She rubbed at her throbbing temple with gloved fingers. Of course, that was why most cops kept to themselves. But she had never dated a cop, afraid she'd be swallowed up in a one-dimensional world where experiences were commonly hard, ugly. She needed other perspectives and the gentler connection with the world of relative privilege in which she'd been raised.

Hunger gnawed. She would grab dinner at Giovanni's, the bistro downstairs from her apartment. Some fresh pasta, home-baked focaccia, and, after a settling scotch, a half bottle of red. The lights turned green, and she turned into Collins Street. The Regent Theater was ablaze with lights. Most of the shops were still open, and there were a lot of people around for a Monday night. The Singapore Inn, one of her favorite restaurants, was doing a good trade. Taxis cruised like whores, competing for a pick-up. Opposite her apartment near the top of the hill, tourists poured in and out of The Grand Hyatt. The warmth and coffee-drenched aroma of Giovanni's beckoned as she inched up the hill.

She wished Charlotte was at home waiting for her. Charlotte's job as an investment banker brought her to Melbourne at least one day a week. She could often arrange her appointments for a Friday or a Monday so they could spend a few days in a row together. The bank provided Charlotte with a small apartment, but she never used it, always stayed with Stephanie. She had left last night after arriving on Friday. They'd spent the whole weekend together. After their rocky patch, the last two weekends had reflected the excitement of their best times. It had been hard saying goodbye to her last night.

Stephanie sighed. Even if Charlotte could be with her tonight, there was no guarantee that all would be sweet and rosy. These days, you could never be sure that when Charlotte trotted through the door in a cloud of perfume, her beige leather suitcase clutched in one manicured hand, Donna Karan swinging on a hanger in the other, that a dark shadow of discontent wouldn't slink in behind her.

Giovanni's was a car length away, on the corner of the lane leading to her garage behind the shops. The café's warmth spilled onto the pavement. It was busy as usual, but Tony always reserved a small table or two for regulars. She glimpsed him behind his glittering espresso machine, that ubiquitous checkered tea towel slung over one shoulder. After a good dinner, pleasantly accompanied by a bit of opera delivered in Tony's excellent baritone, she would have an early night.

CHAPTER SEVEN

Still half asleep, Angelique stirred. A warm breeze tickled her feet. Feathery light kissed her all over. She sighed, and stretched across the white sheet. The ocean murmured at the fraying edge of a dream. Her senses were awash with the scent of frangipani. Then a peacock shrieked. With a start she opened her eyes.

A gentle breeze wafted through the French doors. The sun bled through the bougainvillea's crimson bracts spilling from the lattice over the porch. Leaning on one elbow, Angelique reached over to check her watch on the bedside table. It was seven o'clock. After a quick breakfast she had to leave for a client meeting early in the afternoon. With a sigh she got out of bed.

Silk rugs decorated the stone walls and floors. Opposite the bed, double doors opened into a sitting room. Another door led to a white marble bathroom. She grabbed some clothes and headed for the shower. Her idea for Pacific Holdings seemed to have taken some form while she slept. It was outrageous, but it could work. She only hoped, that as she discussed it over breakfast, Kira wouldn't choke.

Shortly after eight Angelique left her room. From her terrace she gazed out to sea. Down the coast she glimpsed the marina she had passed coming into Ngali. Seragana's wealthy merchants had their yachts out for an early morning cruise.

Dala appeared and smiled. "Good morning, miss. Breakfast is in pavilion." They crossed the lawn together. Looking laid-back and sexy in comfortable jeans, Kira was seated at the table engrossed in a newspaper. She looked up at Angelique and beamed a smile. Dala placed a glass jug of fruit juice on the table.

"It's a pity you have to leave so soon," Kira said as Angeligue sat down. She pushed the *Straits Times* aside and lifted a linen cloth off a wicker basket. "Croissant?" she asked. "Or would you prefer something else?" She smiled. "We do excellent bacon and eggs here, of course."

"A croissant's fine, thanks." Kira poured guava juice for them both as Angelique drizzled her croissant with honey.

"I've given more thought to the idea that came to me last night after dinner," Angelique said. Kira nodded, buttering some toast. "The way I see it, doing nothing about the oil isn't an option. It's a valuable resource your country needs to utilize. And there's a good chance Nolan will discover it in due course, anyway. I think instead of taking a defensive line, it would be better to expose Nolan to the oil riches, but control events, control the outcome."

Kira looked bewildered. Angelique took a deep breath. "The only thing is, my plan's not exactly legal."

Kira shrugged. "The law cannot protect my people's rights. We're out in the cold, outside the justice system that protects Andrew Nolan. It stands to reason a solution to our problems lies outside the law. Your law, that is."

Angelique continued. "He knows I was intending to meet with you. I can tell him that we hit it off pretty well." Kira chuckled. "And reveal that in the course of our discussions you showed me the oil exploration report. I'll tell him you weren't keen at all about forming a partnership with him. But you were open to further discussion about any fair and lucrative deals that I could suggest. So, you let me take a copy of the report away to think it over."

"I'm not exactly with you so far."

Dala arrived with a pot of coffee. "Thanks," Kira said to her. "I'll pour it." Dala took some empty dishes and left.

Angelique passed her cup. "I've brought the report straight to Nolan, right? The oil's on his land. I'm telling him that he's potentially a billionaire. He's going to grab it with both hands, and he'll want to leave you completely out of it. The thing is, of course, that the report I show him will be false. We'll have a copy made that shows the oil in the southeast portion of it instead of the north. Change the maps and the applicable data."

"So, he'll initially drill for oil in the wrong place," Kira said. "But it wouldn't take his engineers long to locate the correct area." She stirred sugar into her coffee. "Apart from wasting his time and money, I don't see the point."

Angelique shook her head. "He hasn't got that sort of money to waste. He'll need to raise venture capital." She explained that she would advise Nolan to float a company on the stock market to raise the funds. She reasoned that in the current depressed market, the initial public offer of stock for a solid commodity like oil would be snapped up.

Angelique finished her coffee. "I've got no direct experience in the oil business, but I know that, like all commodities, quality varies, and so does its value." Kira refilled their cups. She looked keenly interested. "Your report will only assess the size of the reserve. Adequate information for a prospectus, to get a float up and running. But investors will demand to see the quality of the oil to know the real value of the find."

"Nolan would have to do some testing," Kira said. "He'd have to sink a couple of small wells."

Angelique smiled. "And they'll be dry. The market will go mad. There'll be a massive sell-off. The stock value will crash. Hundreds of millions will be invested in a company that's worth a fraction of that. Relatively speaking, his forestry business is worth peanuts. Naturally Pacific Holdings will be liquidated.

Shareholders, hoping to recover some of their losses, would demand it. Nolan will be bankrupted."

Kira slumped back in her chair. "God... But what about the investors who lose money?"

Angelique said she hoped the brokers would go for a restricted share issue, open only to managed funds and institutions. They'd suffer but could cope with losses.

"And what about us?" Kira asked incredulously. "How are you planning on keeping out of jail?"

Angelique chuckled. "If I thought there was the slightest chance of that, I wouldn't have suggested it." She leaned forward. "Look at the facts. There'll be an investigation for sure, but any breach of the law will be impossible to prove. You showed me an oil report that turned out to be utter rubbish. But you only showed it to me. You were non-committal, open to discussion. You didn't induce Nolan or anyone else to invest money. On the contrary, he will have used your report without your permission and with the intention of squeezing you out of any share in the spoils."

She shrugged. "Of course, later, after all the fuss dies away, things will come out about Nolan's activities here and your attitude toward him. And in due course you'll be in the oil business yourself, proving there was oil here after all. People may guess you set him a trap. But they'll never prove it. As for me, well, like everyone else along the line, I innocently and reasonably believed the report to be genuine."

She paused and sipped her coffee. Kira gazed at the ocean.

"Nolan might face some charges of negligence or of not showing due diligence or something. He'll be financially ruined, although he'll look more like a fool than a criminal. He'll be gone from here forever." Angelique grinned. "And I'll bet there'll be half an island going at a fire-sale price."

Kira shook her head. "You're amazing." She stood, wandered to the edge of the pavilion. Leaning a shoulder against the pillar, she asked, "Do you really think it's all possible?"

"Not absolutely. Not until I talk to my friend, Mason. He's a share-trader and knows all about this sort of thing."

Kira suddenly looked anxious.

"You can trust him," Angelique reassured her. She told Kira about the Twilight Club. Under the circumstances, she knew her friends would approve.

Kira was impressed. "How fabulous!"

"I'll want their agreement and support before we proceed," Angelique said. Mason was in Melbourne at the moment, visiting his family. It would be easier to discuss this with him face to face. She would phone him later and ask him to meet with her in Singapore this week on his way home to Italy.

"Well, if you all decide it's feasible, I'll play along as you advise," Kira said. "I don't have a moral problem about committing fraud to end Nolan's destruction of Seragana when I have no other options. But you're not to take any personal risks."

Angelique nodded. "Wouldn't do it otherwise."

Kira stepped over to the table, bent down and kissed Angelique's cheek. "When will I see you again?" she asked softly.

"I wish I could say it would be soon. But if we go ahead with this, we can't have any contact until it's over. A trail of phone calls or visits would point to a conspiracy."

Kira's expression darkened. For a moment this powerful woman looked vulnerable. Suddenly sensitive to Kira's loneliness and the fear she lived with daily, Angelique wanted to comfort her, reassure her. Angelique looked away across the lawn and took a deep breath. There was an attraction simmering between them that she hadn't been prepared for. She was going to miss Kira. She cleared her throat. "I hope your staff are discreet," she said gently. "If questions are ever asked."

Kira nodded. "Don't worry about that."

Dala crossed the forecourt. "The airport phoned, Madam," she said to Kira. "They are ready and have clearance for Singapore." To Angelique she added, "The car is waiting, miss." Kira thanked her and Dala retreated.

Angelique stood. Kira stepped over to her. She seemed about to embrace Angelique but hesitated. She stroked Angelique's arm and took her hand. "Think it through very carefully," Kira said softly. Her tacit approval gave the idea the razor edge of reality.

Angelique squeezed Kira's hand. "Take care of yourself," she said.

Two days later Angelique was threading her way through the lunchtime crowd in Chinatown. Mason had been happy to make a stop in Singapore to discuss Angelique's proposal. They were meeting for lunch at Siow Lian's coffee shop. She stepped around a group of workers squatting at the edge of the pavement. Grabbing a quick lunch, they slurped at bowls of noodles. She dodged a man with a sack of rice on his shoulders lurching across her path.

At last the bright red awning of Paradise Gardens came into view. A typical Singaporean coffee shop, it had a café at the front that led into a small food hall. Siow Lian ran the café and one of the kitchens in the food hall. She was paid rent by the other independent operators in the food hall who prepared all kinds of delicacies in their tiny kitchens.

Angelique pushed open the glass door. The air conditioning was a relief. The tables in the café and food hall were full, customers jostling at the counters. Siow Lian's staff were busy serving sandwiches and ice cream sundaes. Slick and efficient, the place was a study in glass, white tiles and stainless steel. On her first visit years ago, Angelique asked Siow Lian why her mother had named the business Paradise Gardens. Even a single potted palm might have lent support to the exotic name. Siow Lian hadn't seen the irony, though. She simply replied, "It sounded nice."

Angelique headed into the crowded food hall. Chong's, Siow Lian's kitchen, was the first counter. Siow Lian caught sight of her. "Hi, honey!" she called.

Removing her sunglasses, Angelique leaned over the counter and kissed her cheek. "Can you stop for lunch?"

"No problem." In Mandarin she issued instructions to the young man draining noodles beside her. "Let's sit down. Mason should be here any minute." She pulled off her apron, and they sat at a table she had reserved by the window. "I told Chong you were coming. I assumed you'd want chicken curry today." One of Siow Lian's innumerable cousins, Chong was her cook. His famous curry was superb.

Angelique smiled. "I dreamed about Chong's curry when I was away in Jakarta." The young man from the coffee counter arrived with cups and a pot of jasmine tea.

Siow Lian poured the tea. "So, tell me about Kira Na Murgha. What's she like?"

"Well, she's everything Jeremy said she was." Siow Lian looked at her searchingly. Angelique grinned. "Very attractive."

Siow Lian chuckled. "Well, he is a good judge of these things."

"You'll like her." Angelique sipped her tea. "You'll get to meet her after we've sorted out her problem with Andrew Nolan."

Siow Lian pursed her lips. "You were strangely mysterious about that on the phone."

Angelique saw Mason striding toward the shop, his mobile phone clamped to his ear. The jacket of his cream linen suit flapped open in the breeze, his yellow tie wagged over one shoulder. He pushed through the door and stood looking around. Angelique waved him over.

"G'day," he said, smiling, bending to kiss them both. "Bloody hot, isn't it?" He slipped off his jacket, dropped it over the back of his chair. Loosening his tie, he sat down with a sigh.

"The usual, honey," Siow Lian said. "You've just left a Melbourne winter."

"Yeah, but after a couple of years in Europe, those winters make me laugh now. You know, my family were all complaining about the cold snap, and it was only about fourteen degrees."

Angelique frowned trying to translate that. It was a long time since she'd thought in Celsius.

"Close to sixty Fahrenheit," Mason prompted.

Siow Lian shuddered. "Freezing!" The others chuckled. "Tea?" she asked him. "Or a San Miguel?"

"I'll go for the beer, thanks, mate."

Siow Lian turned and signaled to one of her staff. "And what do you feel like for lunch? We're both having Chong's chicken curry."

"Sounds good," Mason said. The waiter brought the beer, then Siow Lian sent him off to the kitchen. Mason poured his beer and gulped down half of it in one go. "So, Angel, what's this idea you've got?"

Angelique told them all she knew about Seragana and Pacific Holdings' activities there. She paused as their lunch was brought to the table. Large bowls brimmed with the fragrant curry. Rosy with chili oil, creamy with coconut milk, it was spiked with crispy snow peas, chicken and egg noodles. "Kira's got a solution to the country's poverty, but she has to get Nolan out of there before she can proceed." Reaching down into her briefcase she drew out a color photocopy of the oil report. She opened it out on the table and told them about Kira's oil discovery.

"Jesus!" Siow Lian's food dropped back into her bowl with a splash. "It could be as rich as Brunei."

"If Nolan gets a whiff of that she's stuck with him forever," Mason said with a shake of his head. "He'll milk them dry."

"It depends on whether he gets a whiff of the oil or only thinks he does. My plan is to lead him to oil, but let him find water." The others looked at her blankly. Angelique drew a deep breath. "I'm thinking about fraud." Siow Lian gave a nervous laugh.

Mason nodded slowly. He picked up his glass, drained it. "Yeah? How?" He was hard to shock. Aid work did that to you. The hopeful, naive enthusiasm that you started with soon became encrusted in cynicism. At first you couldn't believe what people could do to each other. Then, after a while, you could believe anything. Respect for authority became optional. You judged situations in terms of justice first; the law was secondary.

She detailed her plan.

Mason dabbed his mouth with his napkin, then pushed his empty bowl aside. "Nolan will jump at the oil. No doubt about that. He'll think you're a bloody genius for getting hold of that report. And of course, he'll have to raise a company float to get the money. He'll think he's hit the big time and he'll want to rely on you, his clever business adviser, to hold his hand all the way along."

"But there'll be others who have a say," Siow Lian said. "Lawyers, brokers. They might be smart enough to know it's all a bit suspicious."

"How would they know that?" Mason wiped the sweat off his brow with the back of his hand. "You've got to understand how the market works. Do you think these brokers, underwriters, lawyers or whoever go around inspecting factories, crawling around in mine shafts? Do you think they're going to all pile onto a plane, go out to Seragana and inspect the bloody oil sites? Poke around in the rocks with a stick?" Angelique laughed. "They scrutinize figures, weigh up expected outcomes, costs. They examine the data, estimate the risks." He flipped over the pages of the report. "This report was professionally prepared. Anyone would accept this genuine version. And they'll accept one that's been carefully altered." He looked up at Angelique. "But the Australian Stock Exchange has requirements before a company can be floated. For something like this, they'll want a report from an independent expert."

"I knew it," Siow Lian said, slumping back in her chair.

Mason shook his head. "An expert only has to check that this data is reasonable and all necessary tests to support the claims have been carried out properly. He signs a bit of paper and gets a check for a grand or two. Easy."

Siow Lian sighed. "There's just the little problem of the company that carried out this exploration. You know? Someone might phone them to check a few details."

"We have to invent an exploration company," Angelique said. "Give them a nice name and logo."

"Yeah," Mason said. "And an office and a phone number."

"You're both mad!" Siow Lian blurted. Waving over her waiter, she ordered more tea and beer.

"It'd only be for a brief time, a couple of months at most," Angelique said. "Just until the prospectus is prepared and the ASX reports arranged."

"It's a remote chance, anyway," Mason said, "that anyone would phone this exploration company." He shrugged. "A really diligent expert might check their credentials. But that's easily fixed. I'll register a company in the Cayman Islands." He rolled his eyes. "No questions asked in the bloody Caymans. We'll need to spend a bit of the Twilight funds, though, to do all this."

Angelique reminded him that Lucy had recently shown them a healthy bank balance.

"Right," Mason went on. "You two can get busy creating some lovely credentials for this company to attach to the fake report. Vague stuff, of course, that sounds good but can't be checked."

Siow Lian's eyes lit up. "How about Global Explorations for a name?"

Mason grinned. "Bloody beautiful. But it should be an American company, so we'd better sling Inc. on the end."

"But it better not be in Texas," Siow Lian said. "Too obvious."

"How about New York City?" Angelique suggested. "It sounds respectable, and Lucy can oversee things." Lucy could rent a cheap office for a short time and get the phone connected. She couldn't sit by a phone all day, so they'd get a mobile account too and redirect the office phone to it.

"If anyone rings," Mason said, grinning, "Lucy can play receptionist and say the chief engineer will call back. They'll expect a bloke, of course, so, in my excellent New York accent, I'll return the call and tell the poor bugger whatever he wants to hear." They couldn't help laughing.

Their drinks arrived. Mason twisted off the top of his beer and filled his glass, Siow Lian poured the fresh tea.

"But will investors really fall for it?" Siow Lian asked.

"Yep," Mason said. "You know it's a dud so you find it hard to accept that others will believe it. But remember that gold scam in Canada years ago? All they'd found were trace elements of gold. But they made the technical data look good and waved around a few nuggets of gold for good measure. People invested something like one hundred million in the stock. Angel's right. With the market jittery at the moment, with the Middle East problems, interest rates rising, bank stocks wobbly, investors—especially institutional ones—will devour something real like oil stocks. If I didn't know better, I'd sink heaps into an oil find like this. Like everyone else, I know it's an oil-rich part of the world."

He gulped down some cold beer. "Even at the most conservative level, share investment is educated gambling. It's about guesswork, gut instinct. Stock in anything is only worth what the market on any day says it's worth. Prices move according to hopes, fears and whispers. So, even before Nolan has to publish the results of those dry test wells, we'll spook the market with rumors of a scam. Jeremy, with his influence in London—where there'll be interest, too—will get tongues wagging." Mason gave them a grin. "Extra insurance, you see, that the stock is totally dumped."

Angelique sipped her tea. She looked at Mason. "It can work, can't it? Do you think we should do it?"

"We'll check the legal angles with Jeremy, but I think it can work. It'll be hard for you, though," he said. "Obviously Nolan will want you in Melbourne, and you'll need balls to face all the people you'll have to work with."

"Ovaries," Siow Lian snapped, crossing her arms.

Mason rolled his eyes and went on. "But I've no doubt that when you tell Jeremy and Lucy, they'll get behind the plan, too. Between us, we've got some connections. We'd never let you get into any trouble."

Angelique turned to Siow Lian. "What do you think?"

Siow Lian sighed. "It scares me to death. But if you feel you can pull it off, I'm all for it. A few million Seraganians are going to have a free and secure future if it all works out. But I'm going to be worried sick while you're away."

Angelique asked her to take care of communications with Kira. Siow Lian agreed.

Mason checked his watch. "I've got to go. My plane leaves in an hour and a half."

Angelique was suddenly gripped with dread. "We haven't lost perspective, have we?" She looked anxiously from one to the other. "Are we being as unscrupulous as Nolan?"

"How many times," Mason said with a sigh, "have we seen this all before? Tiny Third World countries that most people haven't even heard of who can't get up off their knees because of greed, abuse and corruption. Our standards and laws have no currency in these places. Because of Kira, and you, this little country has got a serious chance of moving into the twenty-first century." Mason's eyes flashed. He was passionate about this stuff. "There's a chance their kids will get an education, get First World healthcare, get an economy." He sighed. "The law be damned. Nolan's got to go."

Angelique noticed that her paper napkin was a tight damp ball in her hand. She dropped it on the table. "I'll call Jeremy and Lucy as soon as I get home," she said. "I'll wake them, but we haven't got time to waste." She ran a hand through her hair. "Then I'll phone Nolan."

"It's a shame, you know..." Mason murmured. He gazed through the window, a dreamy expression in his blue eyes. "If we had some serious money to invest, it'd make all the difference. By investing at the bottom, then selling before the bust, we could make a stack of money out of this float for Seragana. Selling off a stack of shares at the time we spread the negative rumors would add a nice kick to the downswing that will throttle Pacific Holdings."

Siow Lian threw up her hands. "No, that would only add to the risk. Anyway, we haven't got that kind of money, and you know it."

Angelique locked eyes with Mason. For a radiant split second they shared one lucid thought. Even if everything went according to plan it would be a long time before Seragana could benefit from the oil. In the interim, several million desperately needed dollars could be put to excellent use. It was indeed a shame they couldn't manage to cash in. It would be the crowning glory.

CHAPTER EIGHT

Two routine weeks had passed since the arrest of Kylie Burzomi. It was a black cold evening as Stephanie drove through back streets heading for the Wharf. There were no houses around. The trucks that during the day hauled goods between the wharves and storage bays had deserted the area hours ago. Her headlights caught the cyclone fence enclosing the cargo wharf. Petrified thistles clogged the grimy wasteland behind it. She turned into the entrance to the wharf. Some distance down river, against the dark sky, she made out the black profiles of cranes at the loading dock. She parked in front of a wire fence bordering the river.

Switching off the motor she sat for a moment. An eerie quiet always hung over this place at night. Through the fence, lights glinted on boats moored at the dock. Small boats dipped up and down in the current, tugging at their ropes. A battered wire gate twisted in the wind, its single hinge shrieking. She checked her watch. She was meeting Charlotte in the city for dinner in an hour and a half, so she'd better make this quick.

She got out of the car. Pulling on her overcoat she climbed the few steps and went through the gate. Crying, a lone seagull circled a beam of light on a tall pole.

Her breath came in gusty clouds as she strode down the dock. Through the bright windows of a luxury cruiser she glimpsed people around a table. A little further along, a kerosene lantern glowed on the tiny deck of a canvas-covered boat. Probably an illegal squatter. Some boat owners obtained permission to anchor temporarily at the wharf, paying fees for connection to fresh water and power. A few boats, like the one she was headed for, were permanent. Most, though, just turned up and propped until they were chased away by the port authorities. Then at night, the owners, having no other place to go in their shabby floating homes, would slide back in. In the distance, beyond the river's end and beyond the bay, the city quivered with lights, rising into the sky.

She came at last to the high solid steel bow of an old pearler. Perched high on top, the glassed-in cabin glowed in a soft light. Approaching the ladder that led up to the deck, Stephanie heard voices and hesitated. There was a clink of glasses. A snively sort of chuckle was followed by a nasal voice, "Won't say no to another one, thanks, mate."

Stephanie stepped back to get a better look. The owner of the voice struck a match to light a cigarette. It was Tom Dorkins, a creep well known to police. Catching her movement, he peered over the side. He froze for a moment under Stephanie's icy glare. "You got a visitor, Jim," he said. "See ya' later." He scuttled down the ladder, shot Stephanie one last furtive glance, then disappeared into the darkness.

James Tyler looked down with a smile. "Hello, love," he said in his warm deep voice.

Stephanie climbed the ladder. The cabin threw a subtle light across the varnished hardwood deck. The sides of the boat were above waist height. Standing at the bow, his elbows resting on the wide ledge, her father gazed downriver. His dark hair, salted with gray, ruffled in the wind, and his long oilskin coat flapped around his ankles. "It's been months," he said.

"Been a busy time," she replied. Reaching down, he flipped open a cupboard built into the point of the bow and took out a clean glass. Grabbing the bottle off the ledge, he poured her a scotch.

"You okay?" she asked.

"Can't complain." He took a cigarette from a pack next to the bottle and turned his back to the wind to light it.

"What's Dorkins doing here?"

"Just turned up," he said, squinting against the smoke. "Staying on a boat down there somewhere." He inclined his head toward the bay. "He's called in for a chat a few times. I said I'd give him a hand to sort out his accounts and things."

Stephanie gave a dry laugh. "What bloody accounts? He's absolute trash. He'd be checking what you've got here. Planning to rob you, no doubt."

"Well, he said he'd been in trouble but that he'd changed."

Stephanie looked at her father in disbelief. He was truly one of life's innocents. Even after everything he'd been through, he still didn't know shit from strawberry jam. "Last time he was put away," she said, "it was for rounding up homeless kids and prostituting them down near the passenger docks. Underage girls, mostly, and a few young boys." She gulped down her scotch.

"Oh," James said flatly, staring down into his glass. "You learn not to ask questions once you've been inside." He shrugged. "I thought he was slow-witted, but harmless enough. Says he's got a job at some pub."

"Well, I hope they lock up the silver."

He laughed, lighting up his face. The handsome face and smile that Stephanie's mother claimed had swept her off her feet. "Some people can't take responsibility for their actions," he said. "Tom reckons the forces of darkness made him take a few wrong turns. But now he says, he's found religion, gone on the straight and narrow."

Stephanie shook her head dismissively. "Bullshit," she

muttered. In some people behavior could be modified, controlled to some degree. But a person's intrinsic nature was unalterable. Creatures like Dorkins who profited from the misery and misfortune of others were beyond redemption as far as she was concerned.

Her father swirled the ice in his glass. "I've got a nice casserole in the oven," he said. "Beef and mushrooms in red wine. Thought I'd toss a fresh salad. Got a good bottle of burgundy too." He shrugged. "Stay for dinner if you like." His carefree tone was betrayed by the obvious longing in his green eyes.

Stephanie looked away. A lump the size of a fist suddenly blocked her throat. How the hell did he always do this to her? Why did she let him? Their relationship, such as it was, had only been revived seven years ago after years of her living perfectly happily without him. Yet it seemed his love for her had never changed. It reached out at unexpected moments, in his words or through his eyes, tentatively touching the white dry bones of her love for him buried long ago.

She cleared her throat. "Can't. I'm meeting someone for dinner."

Nodding slowly, he gazed at the river. They were silent for a few minutes. "From here I can almost see the building where I used to work," he said. "Weren't nearly as many office towers then. From my office, right up the top, I could see out over the bay. Almost all the way down here." He drained his glass. "Back then, when you were little, I saw a wonderful world when I stared out that window. I was a bright young lawyer then. Great prospects. Could never have guessed that I was looking down on my future."

Stephanie drained her glass. "Wasn't a great career move, embezzlement," she said dryly.

He unscrewed the top of the bottle and refilled their glasses. "They called it that because I stuffed up. I know it was wrong, let alone stupid, but the sad reality is that if my investment had paid off, I would've been promoted. They would've called it creative accounting."

He'd said that before, many times. There was little point in arguing the semantics of right and wrong, since she suspected his assessment was correct. He resumed his position leaning on the boat's ledge. Well over six foot, he was her height when bent over slightly.

"It was a bubble that was bound to burst, of course," he said. "I always had ambitions that my family considered beyond me. A lawyer? No one in the family had ever been anything like that. You never met them because your mother didn't think they'd be good influence on you. A bit common, she said." He shrugged and gave a wry smile. "They were, I suppose. I used to drop in on them often, though."

Stephanie listened patiently to the reminiscences that increasingly preoccupied him. "But your mother, she was something else. I was only about twenty when I met her. I'd landed a job at a respectable firm, made the right friends. Christ, she was ravishing. Had this enticing quality, you know...all the more so because she was kind of aloof. You're a lot like her..." his voice trailed off, and he smoked his cigarette in silence.

Stephanie was uncomfortable with the likeness he was fond of drawing between her mother and herself. There was a physical resemblance but not a character one. At least, she certainly hoped not. It amazed her that he still thought of his wife in glowing terms, when in his position Stephanie would have become decidedly bitter. There was no question that his crime had devastated her mother, ruined their marriage. Yet her reaction—cutting him off for dead, whisking Stephanie away from their home, her school, her friends, and starting a new life elsewhere without him—seemed to Stephanie, even as a young girl, to be frighteningly cold-hearted.

"I wanted to give you both the world," he continued, "but I only ended up breaking her heart. And as for you, well, I gave you nothing..."

Unwanted, childhood memories flooded Stephanie's mind. On hot summer nights they would lie side by side on the lawn gazing at the stars and he would tell her about sweet candy-pink otherworlds way up there. Often he would burst in through the door at night and scoop Stephanie's mother into his arms. He'd whip off her apron and turn off the stove. "We're going out!" he'd declare. Stephanie would laugh and he would pick her up and kiss her and tickle her until she squealed. After a restaurant dinner, maybe a concert too, he would carry her up to her room while she half-slept on his shoulder and tuck her into bed.

Stephanie shivered in the chill air. It would be nice if she occasionally mentioned those memories to him. But later ones, memories of discovering her adorable father was a thief, was going to jail, continued to block the path of benevolence. None of it mattered anymore, she had told herself many times. She was a grown woman, not a disappointed little girl. But whenever she came here, some bloody thing jammed in her throat, prevented her from offering him any more than her fleeting presence.

She took a mouthful of the good scotch and rolled it around her mouth. What drew her here? Guilt, because she had cut him off too? Or love that refused to go away? It wasn't the hate, at least, that had burned in her as a teenager. You didn't come out of your way on a cold night when you had other things to do and drink his whisky and talk about fuck all when you hated him, did you?

"Charlotte, is it?" he asked.

"What?" She was disoriented.

"Who you're having dinner with."

"Of course it's Charlotte," she said, suddenly irritated. He and Charlotte had met once, at Charlotte's insistence. Early in their relationship they came here for a drink one night. James had turned this old pearling vessel he'd bought into a nice home. On the deck, near the cabin at the stern, there were cane chairs around a table. A rainproof striped awning could be rolled out across the deck in minutes. The cabin was his office—he made a reasonable living from bookkeeping. Below decks was a well-equipped galley, a comfortable living room, a bedroom and bathroom. It was compact, basic, but Stephanie was impressed with what he'd made of it. Charlotte considered it all a bit tacky and the wharf a miserable address.

Charlotte and James didn't hit it off, to say the least. He was a charming host, but, displaying his caustic wit, he picked up on and bit right through Charlotte's minor pretensions. Stephanie drained her glass. Considering his inability to distinguish between Tom Dorkins and Mother Theresa, James's pronounced dislike of Charlotte was annoying.

He chuckled. "She's a clever one, that girl. Knows she's onto a good thing. I could see she had big plans for you both."

"She was just talking." Stephanie glanced at her watch. Having come here straight from the station, she wanted to drop in at home to freshen up on her way to the restaurant. She was going to be late. "I have to go."

He strolled over with her to the ladder. "I heard about that GALPA thing you set up," he said. "Sounds good. You must've kicked a bit of arse to get that organized."

She smiled. "I had a lot of help and support." The only arse that had been kicked was her own. "I'll see you later, okay?"

He said goodbye. She climbed down to the dock and hurried back to her car.

As she neared the gate, a movement in the darkness made her stop. But for the gurgle of the river and the clang of a steel rope against a yacht mast, all was quiet. Holding her breath, she peered into the shadows. Then she caught sight of Dorkins skulking around the side of a boat. "What the hell are you doing?" she hissed.

He stepped out onto the path. "Nothin'."

She took in his greasy track pants and stained red-checked coat. His breath reeked of alcohol. "What's this job you're supposed to have? What pub would employ you?"

He squinted his bloodshot eyes. "Come on, Inspector," he whined. "Don't you go stuffin' it up for me. It's a proper job. Cleaning up the tables and that."

"Crawling under them looking for fallen wallets, more like."

He shoved his hands into his coat pockets, jutted out his pointy chin like an accusing finger. "Found God, me. Changed me ways."

"Crap. Last I heard, you were picked up trying to pass stolen credit cards."

"Got off, but didn't I?" He gouged a finger into his ear. "Lack of evidence. Anyway," he added, squaring his shoulders. "I found out he's your old man, Jim Tyler." His smug grin showed great pride in the knowledge. That he knew this came as no great surprise. Although it was rarely alluded to, she was aware that people knew about her father. "You should get off your high horse, you should," he added, a touch of superiority in his tone. "Come down a peg or two. What with your daddy bein' an ex-con, and you bein'...you know..." He paused to sniff noisily. "Well, you being kinky, and that."

A bomb went off in Stephanie's head. She lunged at him, snatching hold of his coat lapel. "Listen, you scum!" she hissed through clenched teeth.

Blinking and gulping like a snared rat, he tried to step back, but her grip was like a vise.

"You watch your filthy mouth! You hear me? And get the hell off this wharf! Permanently, right? Get out and don't come back."

"But it's me mate's boat," he whimpered, his arrogance evaporated. "Said I could stay there."

"I don't give a flying fuck if God said you could stay there. I'm telling you to clear off. By tomorrow. I'll be checking." He wriggled, and she shook him. "And if you go anywhere near my father again, I'll have you! If I just see your fucking face again, Dorkins, I'll have you! Got that?" He nodded.

With a rough shove, she released him. He stumbled back a few steps, then shot off into the shadows. Her heart pounding, she swept through the gate, down the steps, and leapt into her car. Tires screeched on the concrete as she swung her car around.

At ten past eight, Stephanie pushed open the glass and chrome door of Centro. Scanning the crowd of diners perched on chrome and black leather at travertine-topped tables, Stephanie spotted Charlotte. Her hair in a French braid, she was leaning back in her chair. Her legs crossed, the tight red skirt of her business suit revealed a nice thigh. She was alone; her friends were running late too.

Winding her way through the packed tables, Stephanie went over. Charlotte had arrived from Sydney this morning after Stephanie had left for work. As usual she had first gone to Stephanie's apartment to put away her things before going to her office. The apartment had smelled of her perfume when Stephanie got home earlier. Her clothes were hanging on the bedroom door, her cosmetics neatly stacked on the bathroom shelf.

"Hi, gorgeous," Stephanie said, bending to kiss her before sitting down beside her. Charlotte's eyes darted around to see if anyone had caught the illicit kiss on her mouth. "Sorry I'm late. Got held up." Stephanie slipped off her coat. "Another G and T?" Charlotte's glass was nearly empty. She nodded. Waving over a waiter Stephanie ordered the drink and a beer for herself. Reaching under the table, she gave Charlotte's thigh a quick stroke.

Charlotte smiled. "Missed me, have you?"

Stephanie admitted she had, privately wishing they didn't have to kick off their weekend together in the company of Charlotte's friends, Mandy and Carol. Ex-Sydney, they also worked in merchant banking, and for some inexplicable reason Charlotte was enamored with the couple.

"I've been looking forward to tonight. I love this bistro," Charlotte said.

Stephanie glanced around. The aroma of fresh coffee and good food hadn't yet eliminated the stench of Tom Dorkins. It took awhile, sometimes, to drag her mind out of the grime of the streets and fully appreciate the splendors of chrome and leather and quality glassware. She nodded, smiling.

The waiter brought their drinks, pouring Stephanie's beer into a long frosty glass. Gazing around, Charlotte fidgeted with the fine gold chain at her throat. An almost imperceptible tension pinched the corners of her mouth. Sipping her drink, Stephanie watched Charlotte as you might watch a crystal glass inching dangerously toward a table edge. She reached out to catch it before it crashed. "Something on your mind, darling?"

Charlotte turned to her. "Yes." She took a deep breath. "You didn't tell me you were in trouble at work. You mentioned the TV interview, but not that you'd gotten into trouble for it." Stephanie averted her eyes. It wasn't something worth bothering Charlotte about. It was over and done with, anyway. "I saw the letter on top of some books beside the sofa," Charlotte added defensively. "I wasn't snooping."

No, Stephanie thought, prickling slightly, but you took a letter out of an envelope addressed to me. Stephanie had pulled it out of her briefcase last night and thoughtlessly dumped it there. "They weren't too happy, but it's nothing, really," she said. "Just official jargon, you know." Charlotte looked doubtful. "Sounds worse than it is."

Damage control was the issue at this stage. It wasn't lying, exactly. This telling each other about every little thing was part of the intimacy that Charlotte expected of their relationship. In turn came an expectancy of commitment. To keep their affair within comfortable bounds, Stephanie doled out intimacy in measured increments. "I'm sorry, honey. I should've told you." She shrugged. "I forgot." Appeased for the time being, Charlotte gave a little smile. Stephanie swiftly changed the subject, asking Charlotte about her day.

Minutes later, Mandy and Carol sashayed over. Stephanie stood to greet them. Smiling, she glanced from one to the other, willing herself to tell them apart. Unsure, she settled on a safe "Nice to see you, sweetie," for them both, while kisses all round wrapped her in a sticky-sweet mist of Mandy-Carol perfume. They wore the same fragrance. While they chatted with Charlotte about money, Stephanie perused the wine list.

"Merlot?" Stephanie asked in a break. Charlotte thought it sounded like a nice choice, but Mandy and Carol preferred mineral water. It was healthier. The waiter came and took their orders.

While the others chatted about work, Stephanie gulped down her drink, watching them with a perverse fascination. She had to be careful. She was feeling like a wound-up spring tonight. The mineral water thing had almost set her off. Don't you two ever do anything that just feels good? she'd wanted to ask. Do you have any bloody spontaneity at all? She tipped the last of her beer into her glass. Mandy and Carol had identical medium-length blond messy hairstyles. Their laugh was the same, shrill, their lipstick matte beige. Stephanie drained her glass.

"Stephanie?"

She jerked her head up.

"I was saying," Mandy said. She was the one with the lisp.

"It must be a great relief to you to have that baby killer behind bars."

Stephanie leaned back, slowly combed her fingers through her hair. "She's not behind bars. She's not a baby killer. And, no, I don't feel what I'd call relief. The girls involved do their best to survive according to the rules they've been taught. Not surprisingly, they screw everything up. The whole thing's a tragedy."

"They survive, according to the papers," Carol said indignantly, "by selling drugs."

"Yeah," Mandy added, crossing her arms over her black angora breasts. "And the taxpayer."

Stephanie forced a smile. "Well, you wouldn't want us to get rid of every drug dealer, would you? How would your friends get hold of their designer party drugs?" Mandy and Carol averted their eyes. Charlotte shot her a warning glance. Just at the right moment, their dinner arrived.

Stephanie and Charlotte were sharing a dish of fried calamari and a plate of mixed pasta. The others were sharing a small platter of antipasto. Stephanie took a sip of her wine. It was rich and soft and soothing. She would feel more relaxed after a few glasses of this. She tasted the calamari. "This food's nearly as good as Giovanni's," she commented, feeling better already.

"Oh, come on, darling," Charlotte muttered in an admonishing tone. "Giovanni's is just an ordinary little café."

Gulping down her wine, Stephanie suppressed the urge to argue that despite its having quaint gingham tablecloths and light fittings a bit on the kitsch side, Giovanni's food was unquestionably superior.

"And what's more," Mandy said, "the newspaper report claimed that the father of those girls supplied them with the drugs to sell."

Stephanie suddenly yearned for a cigarette. She had quit a few years ago, but there were odd moments when a craving just shot out of nowhere. The urge this time, she suspected, was a desire to annoy Carol and Mandy. They despised smokers.

She went to top up Charlotte's glass, but Charlotte shook her head. Wouldn't want her friends to think she was overdoing it. Stephanie refilled her own glass.

"Well, George Burzomi's an idiot," she began, determined to adopt a chatty tone. "Given that he's uneducated, ignorant and has a total disdain for the law, he cares for his children as best he can. He's never been abusive with them, and except for his regular sojourns in prison, he's never abandoned them, unlike their mother." She paused to gulp down some more wine. A warm fluffy blanket was settling on her scratchy nerves. "Being inside, George couldn't help his kids with the money they needed, so he came up with an idea to solve the immediate problem. Selling drugs, for people like him, is like selling shares for people like you."

Above the matching black sweaters opposite, lips pursed, Revlon-tinted shutters slammed down.

Stephanie smiled to herself. "Until it all blew up, ended in tears, I've no doubt that George was very pleased with himself." She leaned back in her chair, crossed her legs. "He was probably sitting there in his cell wondering which concrete wall he would stick his father-of-the-year award onto."

Mandy and Carol toyed with two halves of an artichoke heart. Charlotte gave a small sigh, nudged her plate aside. Stephanie was privately amused. Her tone implied that she considered George Burzomi a terrific bloke, despite a few faults, and if not for his unfortunate internment she'd invite him over for dinner.

"I forgot to mention, Charlotte," Carol said, clearly keen to change the subject. "I did a terrific trade today in US shares." Charlotte perked up. "I snapped up a swag of massively underpriced stock." She went on to detail her purchase on behalf of a client.

Stephanie tuned in. "There was a story about that company recently on a current affairs program."

"Yeah," Carol said. "It's put a temporary hole in their stock value. But it'll climb back within weeks. Bad publicity's soon forgotten. My client stands to make a killing."

"It was a pretty damning report. They're marketing their baby formula to mothers in Third World countries, convincing them it's better than breast milk. Babies are dying, it said, because the formula often gets mixed with disease-carrying water. In a lot of places that's all there is, and the company knows it."

Carol rolled her eyes. "Dirty water is hardly the company's responsibility."

"Be realistic, honey," Charlotte added gently. "You can't expect private business to do the work of governments." In a reassuring gesture she caressed Stephanie's leg with the toe of a patent-leather high heel.

The wine bottle was empty, unfortunately. The waiter cleared the table. They ordered coffee.

Mandy gave Stephanie a challenging grin. "And when are you two finally going to tie the knot?"

Stephanie tossed Charlotte a pleading glance. There was no way she was going to discuss their relationship with Mandy and Carol.

"We haven't made any decisions yet," Charlotte said.

Right after coffee they'd leave, Stephanie decided. As soon as she got home with Charlotte, once they were alone, everything would be fine. They wouldn't talk any more tonight. All she wanted was to hold Charlotte naked, bury herself in the taste and smell of her.

"You look great together." Mandy wasn't finished. "You could do extremely well if you pooled your resources."

Stephanie bit her lip and gazed outside. Diners were at tables on the front terrace under gas heaters, smoking. Mandy and Carol would dart past them quickly on their way out, terrified of the fumes. You had to laugh, really, Stephanie thought. They both lived and worked in the city. You could scrape enough diesel out of their lungs to power a semi-trailer for a week, yet they'd fret over a waft from a Stuyvesant.

Suddenly, Stephanie's mobile rang. Glad of the distraction, she whipped it out of her coat pocket. It was Dave. A department store warehouse had been done over, and this time a guard had been shot. "Send a car to pick me up," Stephanie said. She gave him Centro's address. "I'll be waiting out front." She hung up. "Sorry, honey," she said. "I really have to go." Charlotte nodded. Stephanie got up, slipped her coat on. She kissed Charlotte's cheek. "See you at home." Apologizing to the others, she said goodnight.

Stopping at the desk on the way out, she paid for everyone's dinner. It was the least she could do. She hadn't been exactly scintillating company. She stepped outside and took a deep breath of cold, fresh air. A siren wailed in the distance. She focused on the crest of the hill, watching for the flashing blue light.

CHAPTER NINE

Angelique looked up from *The Australian* newspaper, swallowing to make her ears pop as the Singapore Airlines A380 slowly descended. Through the window she saw the darkness below had transformed into a carpet of lights. It was early August. It would be cold down there. Fortunately in a visit to Tokyo last year she'd bought some new winter clothes. A black overcoat was folded in the locker overhead.

The voice of the captain cut in: "We'll be landing in Melbourne in twenty minutes. Please reset your watches to eight p.m. Australian Eastern Standard Time. The report is that we have clear weather, and the current ground temperature is eight degrees Celsius. Around forty-six Fahrenheit..."

Angelique folded the newspaper and tucked it into the pouch of the seat in front of her. Throughout most of the flight from

Singapore she'd managed to push her fears to the back of her mind. But now her stomach was beginning to knot. She put her books away in the bag by her feet. Fastening her seatbelt, she leaned back and stared through the window.

Six frantic weeks had passed since her meeting with Siow Lian and Mason. Late that afternoon she had called Jeremy and Lucy. They not only fully supported the plan, they were passionate about it. Jeremy had been appalled to learn of Kira's disastrous problems.

When she phoned Andrew Nolan, he was predictably thrilled. Without hesitation, he set about cutting Kira and Seragana out of the deal. He had no qualms. "It's my land," he emphasized. He would pay some royalties, although no more than he paid for his timber. A token amount. It was his oil. As expected, he retained Angelique's services to coordinate a float to get the funds required and help to organize a team of contracted experts. And they'd better hurry too, he'd said. Before Kira got wind of their plans and screwed things up.

It had taken less than twenty-fours hours to create a good-as-new fake oil exploration report. Working through the night she and Siow Lian altered the text and data by shifting the well location coordinates and seismic line references. Searching the Internet for suitable information, they created a company profile for Global Explorations Inc. Early the next morning, one of Siow Lian's cousins, a graphic artist and printer, put it all together. By lunchtime two copies of the glossy color document were ready. Angelique e-mailed a scan to Nolan. Then there was no turning back. Within another day or so, Mason had registered Global Explorations Inc., and Lucy soon had an office and phone arranged. Fortunately, but unsurprisingly, no one had phoned Global Explorations. It wasn't normally something you did in business, phoning a company just to see if it existed. If people were always that fastidious, oversights, not to mention cons, would occur far less often.

The engines shrieked as the plane slowed. In the lights below she could make out roads, even cars. She expected to stay in Melbourne about ten days. Nolan had insisted that she arrive in time for the final meeting of all parties concerned, set for tomorrow morning—Monday.

Angelique was dreading it. Her stay might be easier if she were going to be busy all that time, but most of her preparatory work was done. She had organized the brokers and underwriters a few weeks ago and advised Nolan of his company's responsibilities to meet public company regulations. The underwriters had valued the float at four hundred and fifty million and set the price of the initial public offer at five dollars per share. The prospectus had been issued a week ago, and following the broker's energetic marketing to private clients—big companies and investment fund managers—there had been overwhelming interest formally lodged from Australia and abroad. The company was scheduled to float two weeks from tomorrow.

Angelique was relieved at the speed things were moving. The sooner it was all over, the better. In line with the schedule she had plotted with Nolan, she had organized a drilling company to move into Seragana next week and set up for the test drilling operation. She would be safely back in Singapore just as the share price would hopefully be going through the roof. Then, less than a week after listing, the shock test results would be made public.

She twisted her shoulders, stretching her back. During these past weeks her dealings with Nolan and the others had been conducted impersonally over the phone and via e-mail. Maintaining an unflinching deception would be harder to do face-to-face.

Sometimes she felt guilty about Nolan. He wasn't difficult to deal with. And it wasn't as though he were a particularly bad guy. If he were, her conscience wouldn't be jumping at every shadow. He was, in fact, quite ordinary. The business procedures that had impacted so devastatingly on a people and their environment were purely profit-driven. Nothing personal. What he was doing in Seragana was no worse than what a million other companies were doing all over the globe.

But she was in a position to make a difference in Seragana, she told herself. She had to single-mindedly focus on that. The healthy and wealthy future of three million Seraganians stacked up pretty well against Nolan and a handful of rich investors.

And, of course, Kira would be ecstatic when it was all over.

Angelique thought of her often. Her last contact with Kira had been to confirm the plan was going ahead, five weeks ago. Siow Lian had since confirmed that Kira was fine and feeling confident.

The plane touched down. Angelique sighed. She would try to enjoy her stay. Melbourne was famous for its shopping and its food and she was looking forward to indulging in both. And she was glad to be catching up with Bianca.

She couldn't help feeling some sadness too. This city, her real home, was the place where she had fallen in love. It had never happened again. One of those once-in-a-lifetime things, she'd come to believe. For six magical months she had been happier than at any other time in her life.

Then she blew it by taking the Jakarta job. She'd been insane to think they could sustain their love while living in different countries. But she'd had no previous experience of how difficult that was—or of the pain and loss that would follow.

Mind you, there had been fault on both sides. They had both been ambitious. Neither of them had been prepared or had the courage to compromise. She thought now, as she had many times over the years, how good it would be just to see her. The idea was ridiculous, of course. She would have a whole other life, someone who adored her—she was easy to love—and a fabulous career. Stephanie was a high-achiever. She wouldn't harbor Angelique's futile regrets.

The plane came to a stop. Passengers leapt from their seats, crammed into the aisles and surged toward the exit. Angelique slipped her feet into high-heeled ankle boots, zipped them up. She grabbed her coat from the locker, pulled it on. Nolan was sending his secretary to collect her and take her to an apartment he owned in the center of the city.

Having passed through customs, Angelique looked around at the crowd in the arrivals lounge. Then she saw "Angelique Devine" printed in large black letters on a sheet of paper held high by a blond woman. Angelique went over and introduced herself.

The woman, in her early twenties, gave a friendly smile. "G'day, I'm Gloria." Her broad Australian accent impacted like a whack with a flat paddle. Angelique almost reeled. Gloria's hair was straight and long, almost reaching her waist. She gave it a casual toss, her blue eyes scrutinizing Angelique. "Jeez, you're all right," she announced. "I was expecting some old bat." Angelique smiled. After years negotiating Asian subtlety, she was going to find Gloria's candor a refreshing challenge.

At eight forty-five the next morning, Angelique was picking over clothes she'd laid out on the bed. Time was slipping away while she agonized over what to wear to the meeting at nine thirty. Her stomach was beginning to churn. She had to leave in fifteen minutes. Grabbing her cup of lukewarm coffee from the dressing table, she wandered over to the window.

On the twelfth floor of a tower on Southbank, her spacious apartment overlooked the city skyline. The Southgate shopping and restaurant complex spread out below her. Fronting the complex, the wide promenade edging the Yarra River was swarming with people. The sky was a clear blue and bright sunshine glinted on the water. The footbridge arching across the river was alive with pedestrians and bicycles. Skimming beneath it, small motorboats transported commuters from riverside suburbs.

She fingered a fine gold chain at her throat. This fussing over what to wear was only a delaying tactic. Normally, even if a little nervous, she approached business meetings with enthusiasm. But today she wasn't going to stride into that boardroom and dazzle with some brilliant commercial strategy. She was going to be a prop supporting an illusion. An important prop, of course, since the personal impression she created might mean the difference between approving smiles all round or pointed ego-challenged questions. She glanced at her watch. Time had run out.

Dangling from under the tangle of dresses, pants and jackets was the sleeve of a royal blue suit. She snatched up the pencil skirt and cropped jacket and determinedly put them on. The suit was elegant, conservative, made no statement other than quiet good taste. She pulled on her overcoat, grabbed her laptop and briefcase and left the apartment to find a taxi.

Twenty minutes later Angelique stepped from the elevator on the twentieth floor into a vast reception area. Stretching out before her, the marble floor glistened like an ice rink. Down lights spiked like pins from a dark indeterminate ceiling. Beside the elevator two crimson deco-styled sofas curled like lips around a marble coffee table. At either end of the foyer, mirrored walls took the whole scene spinning off into infinity. Nolan's decorator was clearly a devotee of thirties Hollywood movies.

To maintain her bearings Angelique focused on the long mahogany reception desk directly ahead. Perched on one end, gilded and exotic, a match to the statue in the Singapore office, Matawa raised her face heavenward. Suddenly Angelique's heel slithered on the icy marble. "Shit," she muttered, just saving herself from a fall. Perhaps Nolan had designed his foyer with confounding mirrors and a slithery floor to deliberately throw people off balance. It would have to be near impossible to hammer home a hard bargain against him after you'd landed on your arse in reception.

"Hi, Angelique!" Gloria, in a short black skirt and tight leopard-print top, had somehow materialized out of a mirror and was standing by the desk.

Angelique was glad to see a familiar face. "Hi, Gloria."

Gloria introduced her to Debbie, the receptionist. Long, blond hair was apparently a prerequisite for a job at Pacific Holdings. Debbie gave a friendly hello.

"Debbie will take your coat and computer around to your office," Gloria said. "I'll take you to the boardroom. The others have all arrived."

Angelique groaned inwardly. She would have preferred to not make a special entrance. She handed her coat to Debbie.

"Love your outfit," Gloria said brightly, heading for a set of double doors beyond the desk. She tiptoed in a peculiar crab-like fashion. Realizing it was a well-practiced anti-slither technique, Angelique followed her lead.

"I've just taken in some coffee," Gloria said outside the doors.

"But I can bring you some peppermint tea, if you want. Good for nervy tummies." Angelique worried that her anxiety must be showing. "They can be a bit off-putting," Gloria added. "All sitting up at the table like penguins in their suits." She rolled her eyes and grinned. "Make you want to laugh, don't they?"

Angelique nodded, smiling. "Thanks, the coffee will be fine." Gloria knocked and opened the door. The first thing Angelique registered with relief was the boardroom's thick non-slip carpet.

Nolan got up from the long table. "Angelique!" They shook hands. "Here she is, gentlemen," he announced. "My brilliant consultant, Angelique Devine." The others all stood for the introductions.

Simon Nelson was the on-staff accountant. Nolan had outsourced an accounting firm to handle the complexities of the expansion. But Simon would continue to look after the forestry side and day-to-day accounting matters. Friendly, in his twenties, he had the bright-eyed air of a bouncy puppy. His jacket was draped casually on the back of his chair, its Armani label poking out like a tongue.

She greeted Max Drummond, Nolan's lawyer. She had spoken with him a few times, mainly about the delicate situation with Ms. Na Murgha. He was expecting Kira to give them some serious headaches down the track. He'd been impressed by Angelique's assurances that as long as his offer was reasonable, she was confident of successfully negotiating with the princess down the track. Weeks ago she'd found it amusing. It didn't seem so funny today.

Donald Monk, whom she'd talked to frequently, was the senior man from the brokerage firm. Gray and portly, he shook her hand gravely. She accepted a limp handshake from Philip Smyth from the firm of underwriters. Monk and Smyth had each brought along a junior man whose function, as far as Angelique could tell, was to shuffle papers and try unsuccessfully to look important.

The last man at the table was the only unknown quantity. Roger Ashen was the consultant geologist the underwriters had commissioned to examine and review the oil exploration report.

His written assessment was one of only a few documents yet to be forwarded to the ASX. Since the float arrangements had generally met with regulations, submitting these documents was a mere formality. The prospectus had contained information lifted straight from the exploration report. In principle, the data had satisfied all concerned. If Ashen had any problems he would've mentioned them before the prospectus was issued. But until they had his written statement it was in his power to bring the whole operation to a deadly halt.

Angelique poured herself a coffee. A half hour passed while dry legal details and matters of expenditure were discussed.

Then Philip Smyth called upon Angelique to clarify the proposed production schedule. "I'm questioning, Ms. Devine, the need to drill test wells so early," he said. "You've scheduled the results of those tests to come through only days after trading begins. What's the hurry? You've yet to request tenders from companies interested in taking up the production contract."

Angelique's heart raced. She opened her folder of notes. "I realize it's an expensive process," she said, looking directly into Smyth's watery eyes. "But since the discovery wells were not tested, we're obliged to conduct appraisal drilling at some stage prior to commencement of production." She hoped Roger Ashen wouldn't disagree with her. She had put in hours reading tedious reports issued by various oil companies, familiarizing herself with the technical basics. But she wouldn't survive a challenging argument from an engineer. She felt his steel-gray scrutiny. "We've yet to confirm reservoir deliverability and oil properties. Of course, the expectation is for outcomes to be excellent, so I feel that the sooner they're disclosed, the better."

Nolan nodded. Smyth was rubbing his chin thoughtfully.

"We already know how much interest our imminent listing has created. But highly valuable investors are still watching from the sidelines. If they don't take advantage of the initial stock offer, we want to be confident they'll buy in later. And we know that following initial excitement about a new stock, investor attention can flag. We don't want people selling out early, making the stock seem less attractive."

The minutiae of the share market was also outside her

area of expertise, and here, among experts, she was winging it dangerously. An opportunistic thought popped into her head. She adopted a smile neither overly confident nor self-deprecating. "Of course, I could be wrong," she said gently. "But I felt that having a reputable company like Mr. Ashen's, for example, drilling the test wells early, showing the world some quality oil, would create a resurgence of investor confidence." Roger Ashen averted his eyes, flicked through the pages of his report. Any doubts he might harbor about her timing were soothed by his benefiting from it. Encouraged, Angelique added, "The funds are already available, so why hold off?"

"I don't have a problem with that," Donald Monk said. "Investor confidence is crucial. And it won't affect the choice Mr. Nolan makes about the company he ultimately contracts for production."

Smyth nodded. "Fair enough." A wave of relief swept through her. Angelique gulped down some coffee. "Now, Roger," he said. "Your expert report on this exploration data is the last item on the agenda." Angelique held her breath.

Roger Ashen was fifty-ish. Above the gray pencil line of his mouth, a rocky nose divided his face like a dry-stone wall. He squared his narrow shoulders. This was his moment and he was making the most of it. All eyes were on him as he slowly opened his file. He cleared his throat. "Everything seems in order," he said in the tired tone of a person who really had more interesting things to do. Angelique masked her relief by feigning some notetaking.

"'Course it does, Roger!" Nolan boomed across the table. "Angelique dots her i's and crosses her t's, doesn't she, eh?" Angelique cringed inwardly.

Ashen's mouth disappeared entirely for a second. He cleared his throat again. "This company, Global Explorations Incorporated," he went on, "seems sound, judging by the credentials of its chief engineers and its past long experience." He paused to glance at his watch. "The seismic data is thorough, the geologic interpretation and reservoir mapping impressive." His jerked his head up, narrowing his eyes at Nolan. "At Oceania Resource Services, we dot our i's and cross our t's too, Mr.

Nolan," he hissed. Thank god that was a lie. Angelique had braced herself for a comment about the US company's registration in the Cayman Islands. It might have seemed odd to Ashen if he'd checked.

Nolan laughed too loudly. "'Course you do, Roger! Never had any doubts about that. No doubts at all." Angelique forced a smile, and a few mouths twitched reticently around the table.

At last the meeting came to a close. The smiles, goodbyes and handshakes were a gray blur as the men poured out into the foyer.

As the elevator doors closed, Nolan smiled. "That went pretty well." Angelique congratulated him. Suddenly craving some recovery time alone, she wondered where to find her office.

"Andrew?" Gloria called out. She was sitting at a desk in a small office at the end of a mirrored wall. "Bettina just e-mailed through some consignment papers for you to check. Some bloke in Tokyo's got the shits about his timber delivery. Reckons it's the wrong stuff or something."

"Jesus Christ," Nolan hissed through clenched teeth. "You've got to do every bloody thing yourself." He marched over to Gloria and snatched the copies from her hand. He swung around to Angelique. "We'll talk later. Gloria will look after you." Then he vanished into an office next to Gloria's and closed the door.

Gloria crab-walked over to Angelique. She tossed her hair and rolled her eyes. "Mr. Important," she said in a loud stage whisper. Debbie giggled. "Come on, Angelique, I'll take you to your office."

They crossed the foyer toward the other mirrored wall, where Gloria turned into a gray-carpeted corridor. "Do you get called Angie?" Gloria asked.

Angelique shook her head. "Angel, sometimes."

Gloria nodded in approval. "I'll call you Angel, then. It's quicker." Privately amused, Angelique wondered what Gloria was planning to do with all the time she would save by dropping a syllable. And certainly had her name been a quick and easy one like Jane, Gloria would have extended it to Janie without a care in the world for all the time she would squander. The

Australian habit of corrupting names was outwardly a friendly gesture, but subliminally it was a determined class leveler. "How come your eyes are blue?"

"Sorry?"

"Well, your skin's pretty brown."

"Oh. My dad had blue eyes, and my mother's Mauritian."

"Mmm..." Gloria sounded uncertain. Perhaps she hadn't heard of Mauritius. "Jeez, I'd kill for your color. Even if I sunbaked for weeks, I'd never get that tanned. I'm too fair." She sighed. "Can't do it anymore, anyway." Rolling her eyes, she added, "They reckon you get skin cancer." Angelique smiled, giving a sympathetic shrug. They stopped at the first door off the corridor. "This is Simon's office."

Simon looked up from his computer. "I'm restructuring our accounts system," he said. "With all the changes coming up, I thought I'd simplify things."

"Good idea," Angelique said.

"Would you mind looking over what I've done?"

"Not at all." Angelique smiled. "We can go through it together tomorrow."

Next door was her office. Her coat was hanging on the back of the door. Her laptop was on a large mahogany desk. It seemed that half the Seraganian rainforest had made its way into Nolan's offices. Gloria went to the window and pulled up the venetian blind. Sunshine spilled into the narrow spaces between office towers. It was a beautiful day.

"You'd be able to see the bay if those buildings weren't there," Gloria said.

Angelique sat at her desk and switched on her computer. She wanted to check her e-mail and send a progress report to Siow Lian. The Twilights had all decided the safest means of communication would be on Facebook using fake identities. They were to confine contact to essential matters only and under no circumstances use real addresses, phone numbers, names of people or places. Jeremy, who was discreetly acting as Kira's legal adviser, would pass on updates to Kira as required.

Gloria trotted back to the door. "If you need anything, just press six on the phone. That's me."

"Actually, Gloria. If you wouldn't mind, I'd love a cup of that peppermint tea you mentioned earlier."

Gloria grinned. "No worries."

CHAPTER TEN

On Friday evening Stephanie parked her car behind her apartment, then hurried up the lane to the blazing lights of Collins Street. A biting wind slapped her coat around her legs. On the corner, Giovanni's was packed. Through its steamy windows she glimpsed Tony tugging at the cork of a bottle of Chianti. Connie, his elderly mother, in her long white apron, was chatting with a table of customers.

Next to the café was the steel security gate to Stephanie's apartment. The gate was flanked on the other side by an exclusive boutique. "Madame Cuvellier. Couturier. Established 1928" swept in gold across the shop's display window. Stephanie's apartment was over the shop. She unlocked the gate and climbed two flights of worn-smooth bluestone steps.

The automatic central heating had warmed the apartment.

In the entrance foyer she switched on a standard lamp beside the black marble fireplace. She tossed her coat onto the maroon chaise lounge, and dumped her briefcase on the floor. Polished parquetry led to the living room through a double-width doorway. White architraves a foot wide were intricately carved in sharp stepped ridges. The small apartment's opulent deco features had seduced Stephanie into buying the place five years ago.

She went through the living room into the main bedroom. She switched on a bedside lamp, then dropped the blind. It was almost seven o'clock. Charlotte had phoned Stephanie's mobile twenty minutes ago. She was in a taxi on her way from the airport. Tonight Stephanie was giving her talk at the Women's Business Association's dinner. She wasn't bothered about missing the pre-dinner drinks scheduled for seven. But she wanted to be on time for dinner at eight. She undressed and headed into the bathroom for a shower.

Fifteen minutes later she had finished drying her hair. She raked it back from her forehead with her fingers, splashed on some fragrance and returned to the bedroom. As she finished dressing she heard the key in the lock.

Charlotte erupted through the door juggling a suitcase, briefcase, and hangers of clothes in zipped-up covers. "God!" she blurted. "That bloody traffic." Stephanie took the luggage from her arms, laying the hangers on the chaise lounge. "Don't leave them there," Charlotte said. "My clothes will crush."

Stephanie smiled. "No, they won't." She slid her arms around Charlotte's waist. Breathing in her tuberose scent, she pulled Charlotte close and kissed her. A sexy heat moved in her body like smoke curling in still air. Charlotte gave a little moan. She trailed her fingers over the shoulders of Stephanie's charcoal-gray suit jacket.

"You look fabulous, darling," she said, giving the white shirt collar a little tug. "You should wear formal suits more often." Then she turned and darted off toward the bedroom. "I'll be ready in a second," she called out.

Stephanie sighed. "You're fine!" Charlotte always looked immaculate. "We've got to go!"

Charlotte's voice echoed back from the bathroom. "I'm fixing my face. You kissed my lipstick off."

Stepping over to the fireplace, Stephanie checked her reflection in the gilt-framed mirror over the mantelpiece. Her lips glistened in Geisha Red. She grabbed a tissue and wiped it off.

Charlotte came bustling back. "Ready?" Stephanie asked, patting her pockets, checking for her wallet and the notes for her speech.

"Yes, and I'm starving to death."

Stephanie grabbed her keys off the mantelpiece.

Angelique clutched her coat tightly against the chill wind whipping up the hill outside Pacific Holdings' office. The street was teeming with taxis, but being Friday night each one that passed was occupied. It was nine thirty. With difficulty she'd managed to extricate herself from yet another of Andrew Nolan's marketing functions, and she was anxious to get well away from the place. She spotted a vacant taxi, stepped out and flagged it down.

"St. Kilda, please," she said. She gave the driver the name of the restaurant. As the taxi glided off she tried to relax. She was meeting Bianca, and for the first time in days she could really be herself. Bianca had invited her to a dinner function, insisting it wasn't a problem that Angelique had to work late and miss the dinner itself. She could join them all for drinks afterward and meet some of Bianca's friends.

Her first week had been busier than expected. Nolan and his brokers had to constantly nurture their existing shareholders and woo those institutions that hadn't yet taken the plunge. Angelique was expected to attend with Nolan the round of lunch presentations and sales seminars where Pacific Holdings' brokers encouraged fund managers to dump financial stocks in favor of good solid oil. Their PR company was hard at it too. Editorials in respected business magazines had given valuable weight to Pacific Holdings Australasia's profile. Big investors were buying up commodities, and Pacific Holdings' oil was fast becoming the stock of the moment. Siow Lian had reported that the company had attracted media attention in Singapore. Lucy and Jeremy confirmed the same in New York and London.

This evening Nolan was giving a cocktail party for his influential Melbourne investors. These power get-togethers always carried a contingent of networking socialites and on-the-make politicians. Nolan had developed a habit of flaunting Angelique like a trophy. "My personal business consultant, Angelique Devine," he had announced tonight to a gaggle of fund managers. "She's a marvel. I'd been sitting on a bloody fortune all those years and never had a clue." Keeping her nerve and keeping up the small talk was hard going.

The taxi squeezed out of the city center and crossed the river toward St. Kilda. Over recent days Angelique had often felt isolated. Constantly justifying her actions to herself had kept her focused, but sometimes the effort of maintaining her deceit made her feel disconnected from reality. Contacting Siow Lian and the others always grounded her.

Staring out the window she gnawed her lip. When she talked with Siow Lian on Facebook last night she hadn't mentioned a new development that could put a hazardous spin on their endeavors.

She'd met with Simon on Tuesday afternoon to look over his account restructure. The old system that he and Nolan had managed between them was complicated, audit trails unclear. No doubt the outsourced accounting team had ordered a cleanup. "You've done a good job," Angelique said.

"I've consolidated our bank accounts too," Simon said, taking a binder filled with statements from a shelf. "We had banks and accounts coming out our ears." Angelique flicked through the statements. Nolan's cash flow might have slowed in recent times, but Seragana's mahogany still provided quite buoyant credit balances. "Of course, we've got this tucked away," Simon added. From the back of the binder he drew out a slim folder. He opened it with a conspiratorial smirk. "No one knows about this little nest egg."

Angelique's eyes widened. The nest egg, in the name of

Matawa Limited, was held with a bank in Gibraltar, another popular tax haven. Like the other accounts, it was accessible online. A glance through a year's statements showed the last deposit had been made ten months ago. There'd been no withdrawals in that time. The balance was a cool eighteen and a half million. Angelique's mind began to spin. "Where did these funds come from?" she asked.

Simon gave a casual shrug. "Oh, you know. Cash transactions, here and there. Customers are often happy to oblige with cash in return for a fat discount. Can't tell the taxman everything, can you? You'd go bloody broke." Angelique's mind drifted, recalling Mason's wistful regret that they lacked funds to cash in on the float.

"Simon?" Gloria was at the door. "A bloke called Rod Jenkins is out in reception to see you."

Simon jumped to his feet. "Great! He's brought back the Porsche. He's been doing some rebuilding on it." He turned to Angelique. "You don't mind if I go and have a word?"

"That's fine. We're done, anyway."

Simon bounced past Gloria out into the corridor.

Gloria sighed, gave Angelique a roll of her eyes. "Porsche!" she hissed disdainfully. "What a wanker!" With a toss of her hair, she left.

Angelique looked back at the documents. Her pulse quickened. This money of Nolan's was stolen in tax avoidance. If she could lay her hands on the numbers to access the account online, Mason perhaps could siphon out some money and grab a bundle of shares at the initial price while they were still available. Icy perspiration prickled her skin. Donald Monk said a tenfold increase in value wasn't out of the question. If Mason snatched even half a million dollars, one hundred thousand shares could possibly turn into five million dollars within a few days. They would only be borrowing the money. Mason in a past life had worked in bank security. If he knew how to transfer the funds out, he'd know how to put them back. The profits wouldn't amount to a fortune for a nation, but it would come in handy for the cash-strapped government of Seragana.

She heard laughter coming from reception. Gloria's voice

ricocheted off the marble. "You know, Simon, don't you? Only underendowed men drive cars like that. They're a penis substitute." Debbie yelped in amusement. Angelique thumbed through the thick binder of bank statements. It was a logical place to keep identification numbers and passwords. He wouldn't have them in his head.

"Oh, you reckon?" Simon replied. "Well, I just might give you the ride of your life, one of these days, Gloria." There was more laughter.

"Keep him talking, Gloria," Angelique muttered under her breath. She scanned the pages for a note, a bit of scribble somewhere. She was starting to panic. If he walked back in, how would she explain herself?

"Not in that wanky little car, you won't," Gloria said. Angelique was about to give up as she riffled impatiently through the last pages. Then she found a yellow dog-eared sticky note stuck inside the back cover. Next to all the bank and account names, ID numbers and passwords were scrawled in pencil. A rush of adrenaline made her shaky. Tearing a sheet off a notepad, she began to write down the details for the Gibraltar account.

Simon's voice boomed closer. He was coming up the corridor. "Who said I was talking about a ride in the car, babe?" he yelled. Gloria and Debbie howled with laughter. Angelique stood and stuffed the note up her sleeve. Simon was chuckling, strolling back to his office, his car keys tinkling in his hand. He looked up at Angelique standing in his doorway.

Smiling, she had held up her pen. "Forgot this," she said brightly.

That night, covering her tracks like a criminal, she called Mason from a public phone. He was excited about the information. He would have to set up some bogus accounts for the transfers, and there was no guarantee he could manage it in time. But it was worth a go, he reckoned. When Angelique expressed misgivings about what amounted to theft, not to mention the risks, he laughed. "You're up to your neck in a multimillion dollar fraud, mate," he said. "And you're jumpy about this little misappropriation?" It was all in Seragana's cause, he reminded her. If they could hand Kira a tidy sum on top of eliminating Pacific Holdings, why wouldn't they?

"Well, don't mention it to Siow Lian," Angelique said. "She and Kira would have a fit if they knew."

"Stop worrying," Mason had replied. "You concentrate on the main game and leave this job to me. If it can be done, I'll do it."

Angelique gazed through the taxi window. They were on the Beach Road. A trickle of moonlight rippled on the bay. The waterfront restaurant, a little way ahead, was lit up brightly. It had once been one of her favorite haunts, and it was soothing to know it still existed.

The taxi drew up outside the restaurant. Angelique's mood brightened as she headed up the steps to the entrance. She needed to relax tonight. And she was dying for a drink. She only hoped, as she pushed through the revolving glass door, that her timing wasn't off. Bianca said there was to be an after-dinner speaker, and she didn't want to rudely burst in on her.

CHAPTER ELEVEN

At the podium Stephanie paused in her speech, allowed the laughter to subside. She rearranged her notes on the stand. About one hundred women were grouped around tables in the private function room. The lights were dimmed except for the one illuminating the podium. She could make out a few faces at the back tables, plus waiters gliding around discreetly serving coffee. She was nearing the end of her address. The audience had been warm and receptive. She had enjoyed herself. Checking her watch, she saw it was close to ten.

"I'm really happy with the overall response to GALPA. The existence of the association officially concedes that in some harmful pockets, prejudice still exists, and the police force is not prepared to accept that. I chose to talk about GALPA tonight because it demonstrates that we can all give something, make a positive difference to people. We only have to be determined and make the time in our busy schedules to do what we think really matters."

A murmur of approval rippled through the audience. At the back of the room a bright wedge of light suddenly appeared as the door was opened. In silhouette a woman removed her coat, handed it to a waiter. Tallish, she was wearing a long-sleeved clingy dress. The door closed and the woman was swallowed by the darkness.

"You read all the time, these days, about the helplessness that people feel about society's rapid changes. Problems seem too huge to tackle. The environment's suffering, they're doing strange things to our food. Globalization is concentrating wealth and power in the hands of a few, and opportunities for many seem to be dwindling. We look to governments to fix these problems, but increasingly they seem to be struggling too. Perhaps our leaders simply lack the courage to identify right from wrong. Or worse, perhaps they've lost the wisdom to know the difference." Stephanie looked up. "You're educated professionals. You're in the thick of things. So, what are you going to do about it?"

There was an outburst of applause. At a table to the left of the podium, a woman gave a wave to the new arrival who was wending her way between the tables. Only her legs had caught the light. Great legs.

Stephanie paused, her mind momentarily seized with a wisp of a memory that she couldn't quite grasp.

Stephanie glanced back at her notes. "Just being swept along, struggling with your sixty hours a week, hanging onto a job that a merger might snatch away anyway, isn't enough. Within your workplaces you can influence change, alter the culture. Encouraging profitable outcomes in tandem with fair practice is not an unreasonable ambition."

There was a murmur of approval. From the corner of her eye Stephanie saw the latecomer take her seat, saw her exchange a quick kiss with her companion. Unable to resist, Stephanie stole a longer look. Then she froze. The rest of the room became a black void. Angelique was staring back at Stephanie in shocked disbelief. Those stunning blue eyes, that face that had lingered in the shadows of Stephanie's mind every day for years.

Her memory spun with that awful scene from almost six years ago. The smell of lavender. Thick hedges of flowers oozed their fragrance into the hot night air. Soft music filtered down from the patio; Angelique's mother was playing the piano. On a patch of lawn Stephanie stood gazing down across sand dunes to the sea. She needed to be alone for a while to collect her thoughts. She and Angelique were ending a three-day break together with a visit to Angelique's mother. It had been more than a year since Angelique had left Australia, and this was only the third time they had seen each other in all that time. There had been phone calls every day, romantic exchanges of gifts, but for Stephanie it just wasn't working. It was hell living without Angelique. She had become like some kind of addict, her focus all day being the moment she could talk to Angelique. And the agony when she couldn't get her fix; when Angelique was in transit between cities or countries.

The audience was muttering. A chair leg scraped the floor as someone shifted. Stephanie rearranged the papers on the podium, struggling to pull her thoughts together.

Angelique had come out to find her, wandering through the shrubs, the strains of piano music merging with the sound of the waves smashing on the rocks below. Stephanie had swept her into her arms, kissed her with a desperate passion. Fighting back tears, she told Angelique how much she loved her, but their relationship was over.

Stephanie picked up the glass of water beside her and took a large gulp. A subtle glance to her right caught Charlotte staring at Angelique with a curious fascination. Jan was scrutinizing Angelique too but looking pleased to see her again. A few people cleared their throats.

"Umm..." Stephanie raked her fingers through her hair, took a deep breath. "So don't wait for others to solve problems that affect your life. If your job supports or reinforces practices that you know to be damaging or unfair, discuss, argue, lobby for change. Don't be intimidated. In all things, use your head and follow your heart." She gathered up her notes. "Thank you for inviting me to speak tonight." There was resounding applause.

The room lights came up slowly. Avoiding looking in Angelique's direction, she stepped down from the podium and returned to her table. "That was wonderful, darling," Charlotte said. Jan grinned, nodding in agreement.

"Seemed to go okay." Stephanie folded her notes and slid them into her jacket pocket. She desperately wanted to speak to Angelique, but how? She needed to do it casually, without inviting an interrogation from Charlotte.

Angelique stared vacantly into the mid-distance. When she entered the room and heard Stephanie's voice she had almost turned and fled. She was in shock, lost in time. Thoughts tipped out of her head like the contents of an upturned drawer. She hadn't heard a word from Stephanie since she'd told Angelique they were finished. Angelique had collapsed in tears. She had begged Stephanie to reconsider, but Stephanie, with her iron will, had not backed down. You'll learn to be happy without me, she said. You'll have a wonderful life. She removed herself from Angelique's arms and said, "Don't call me, don't write to me. Please, if you love me, do that for me." Then she left. Angelique had stood in the dark garden, in disbelief, as she listened to Stephanie's car tires crunch down the driveway and disappear.

Bianca nudged her arm. "Angelique?" She looked anxious. "I had no idea the speaker was Stephanie till I arrived. I called your mobile to warn you, but it went to voice mail." She poured Angelique a glass of wine. "Are you okay? You don't look too good."

The room was buzzing with conversation. Women were wandering from table to table, chatting.

"I'm fine." Angelique managed a wan smile. "I was bound to run into her some day." Trying to compose herself she leaned back in her chair, took a sip of her wine. She gazed over at the table where Stephanie had rejoined her group.

She looked fabulous. If she was feeling anything like

Angelique's upheaval she was hiding it well. But that was Stephanie—cool, strong, unflappable. Angelique felt her throat tighten as Stephanie raked her beautiful long dark hair away from her face, a gesture that had once been as familiar to Angelique as breathing.

Bianca leaned in close. "She's done pretty well for herself. She was introduced tonight as Detective Inspector."

Angelique smiled and nodded. Stephanie had been a senior sergeant when they were together. Her success came as no surprise at all.

"I guess that's her girlfriend," Bianca added. "The blondish one in the blue jacket."

Angelique felt a small twinge that had to be jealousy. She inwardly kicked herself. Grow up, she hissed silently. She had wished for a chance to see Stephanie again, talk to her, and here it was. This was probably just the thing to rid herself of those lurking old demons of guilt and regret. She took a deep breath. "She's a nice-looking woman," she said.

"Mmm…maybe a bit too much makeup," Bianca observed.

Another woman at Stephanie's table turned toward Angelique. It was Stephanie's friend Jan. She smiled and waved. Angelique waved back. She had good memories of Jan. Then Stephanie turned around.

Bianca grabbed her glass and put it to her lips. "Brace yourself. She's coming over," she muttered under her breath.

In spite of her determination to be calm and sensible, Angelique felt her heart begin to race. She stood.

Stephanie arrived, beaming a broad smile. "Angelique," she said softly. She had a gorgeous throaty voice. "It's great to see you again." She reached out and took Angelique's hand with both her own. A familiar warmth curled through Angelique's body.

Angelique smiled. "It's a lovely surprise to run into you." She gave a little shrug. "It's a wonder it hasn't happened before this."

"You look wonderful." Stephanie's tone was low, a touch intimate. Angelique felt her composure begin to crack. Stephanie gently released her hand. "You're here on business, I presume?"

"Yes, for another week or so."

Stephanie turned to Bianca, who still had her nose buried in her wineglass. "Bianca, isn't it?"

"Yeah," Bianca replied. "Nice to see you again. I haven't seen you since you both…" Her voice trailed off and she bit her lip. Just then Jan arrived.

"Angelique, you're a sight for sore eyes." Jan gave her a friendly hug. "Asia must suit you. You look a million bucks." Angelique chuckled and greeted Jan warmly. "Must be off," she said, with a quick look at Stephanie. "Got an early start tomorrow. Hope to see you again before you leave."

As Jan left, Stephanie subtly took Angelique's arm and moved her a step away from the table. "I'd like to see you before you go." Her voice was little more than a whisper. Angelique felt herself unravel slightly. It was becoming obvious to her that her feelings for Stephanie hadn't fundamentally changed. And Stephanie's tone suggested an interest that was more than merely friendly.

"I'd really like that." Angelique replied softly.

Stephanie seemed to be in a hurry. "Monday. How about dinner?" Angelique nodded. "How can I contact you?"

Angelique grabbed her purse and took out a business card. "Here's my mobile and the number at Pacific Holdings Australasia, where I'm working."

Stephanie perused the card. "Interesting. They've been in the financial news lately, haven't they? Found some oil?" She pulled a card from her pocket and handed it over. "In case you need to reach me."

At that moment the blondish woman appeared. She slipped her arm inside Stephanie's and smiled confidently. "Aren't you going to introduce us, darling?"

A barely discernible unease flittered across Stephanie's cool classic features. "Of course. This is Angelique Devine. A friend I haven't seen in years." Her diplomatic reply was delivered with relaxed charm. She gave the woman's arm a little squeeze. "And this is Charlotte Regan." No qualification of Charlotte's status was given. Then Stephanie snatched a glance at her watch. "Well, we must go, I'm afraid. It was good to see you again."

Angelique said goodbye and watched them, hand in hand,

make their way to the door. Angelique sank down in her chair.

Bianca leaned close. "Did I overhear her making a date with you?" Angelique gulped down the rest of her wine. "Just the two of you?"

"Apparently," Angelique replied.

Bianca scratched her head. "Bit odd, isn't it? Charlotte seemed like Stephanie's partner, not a date for the night. Bet she wouldn't be too pleased that Stephanie was out for dinner with her ex-lover."

Angelique shrugged, affecting an air of nonchalance. "I don't know any more than you about Stephanie's personal life. I'm looking forward to catching up with all her news."

Bianca looked skeptical. Before she could pursue the topic, though, a friend wandered over. "Hey, Sandy," Bianca said. "Sit down. Meet my friend, Angelique from Singapore." Sandy joined them. Angelique attracted a passing waiter, ordered coffee and liqueurs and settled in to enjoy the next couple of hours.

CHAPTER TWELVE

On Monday evening at seven thirty Stephanie left her apartment. Brightly lit trams whizzed past, and she considered jumping on one to take her the next couple of blocks. But the walk to Southbank would do her good. Give her a chance to collect her thoughts before meeting Angelique at eight. She wrapped her scarf more tightly around her throat, plunged her gloved hands into the pockets of her overcoat and headed down Collins Street hill.

All weekend she'd looked forward to tonight. If she were entirely honest with herself, she'd been waiting for it for years. Seeing Angelique again had shunted Stephanie's priorities in a new direction, abruptly, like switching points wrenching a train at full-speed onto another track.

Angelique had seemed pleased to see her too, although she

was probably just as flustered. It was a huge relief to discover that Angelique hadn't grown to hate her over time. Stephanie had relived their last meeting many times and it still upset her to remember how she had rejected Angelique so harshly, leaving her devastated.

Behind her excitement about tonight there was anxiety too. Why, exactly, was she doing this? She was interested in more than hearing about the interesting life Angelique had built for herself. She yearned to look at her, listen to her voice, feel her physical closeness. Her attraction to Angelique was still alive and well, it seemed. More complicated, though, was the impossibility of separating that from the passionate love they had shared. She might have a Pandora's box situation on her hands.

Stephanie raked her hair back from her face and stopped at the traffic lights. This situation could set her back years, back to the day she walked away from Angelique. If Angelique still wanted her too, how would they deal with that? On the other hand, what if Angelique had another partner these days, if her feelings for Stephanie were gone? That might be worse.

The traffic was piled up waiting for the lights. She crossed the street, zigzagging between idling cars. She squeezed past a queue outside the Regent Theater. At the end of the line a busker was playing guitar. His back to a wall pasted with tattered posters, he was singing "Blowing In The Wind." Beneath a green army greatcoat, his camouflage pants flapped in the cold wind. On the pavement in front of him, a combat helmet boasted four dollars. He was either an idiot or a genius of irony. Stephanie grabbed a few dollars in loose coins in her pocket and tossed them into his helmet.

The weekend with Charlotte had been difficult. She'd been especially sweet. Stephanie had done her best to disguise her preoccupation with Angelique, but Charlotte's attentiveness was unnerving. Stephanie had hidden herself in sex. With your mouth engaged making your lover happy, you can't talk. And if the lover in your mind wasn't the one in your arms, the pleasure you gave was the same.

Turning left she walked another block. Past the station she descended steps to a fern-lined path beside the river. Guilt about

Charlotte was creeping up on her. She was only having an innocent dinner with Angelique, but she'd been very damned careful not to mention it. She stepped onto the footbridge crossing the river. At night the river's earthy brown was transformed into shimmering color. The lighted domes of the station and lights from Southbank's shops and restaurants reflected on the glassy water.

She left the bridge and crossed the promenade. Captivated tourists watched two teenage boys playing didgeridoos, a fire-eater had attracted another crowd. Inside Southbank, Stephanie headed for the escalator. Angelique's apartment building was connected to the complex, and Stephanie had suggested they meet at a Japanese place on the third floor. Stephanie had booked a window table overlooking the river.

A waiter indicated Stephanie's table. Angelique hadn't yet arrived. Squeezing past chairs, dodging jutting elbows, she sat down and ordered a vodka tonic. With the furtive air she'd observed countless times in others, she cast a quick glance at the faces in the room. At the next table a woman sat alone. Twisting her napkin in her hands, she had her eyes trained on the door. There was something pathetic about people who waited with such undisguised longing. You saw them everywhere. Police stations, train stations, park benches. They craned their necks, jerked their heads up hopefully at every passerby. Stephanie snatched up the menu and began to study it. The waiter brought her drink. Resisting another glance at the doorway, she turned to the window.

"Hello, Stephanie."

Stephanie's body reacted like she'd been plunged into a warm bath. She swung around, stood up. Angelique was smiling. Light played on the sheen of her blue suit, an almost to the knee fitted skirt and jacket. She dazzled.

Stephanie smiled, asked Angelique how she was. Angelique placed a friendly kiss on her cheek and Stephanie almost reeled. She was a beautiful woman but what had struck Stephanie most when they first met, and hit her again now, was the kindness in Angelique's face. She held no conceit, though anyone would easily forgive her a little vanity. It was the kindness that glowed and had stolen Stephanie's heart.

Stephanie pulled out Angelique's chair and glimpsed those legs, black high heels as she sat down.

"This place was a good choice," Angelique said as Stephanie took her seat. "It's new, I think. I don't remember it from my last visit." She looked a lot more relaxed than Stephanie felt.

"Have you been back often over the years?"

Angelique shook her head. "Only once for two days since…" She averted her eyes. "Since we went our separate ways."

The waiter came for their order. They ordered a bottle of cold chardonnay. "I miss a lot of good Australian wines living in Singapore," Angelique said.

"You live in Singapore now?"

Angelique nodded. "For the last three years. Since I left the aid agency."

"So, you gave that up. I remember being concerned at the time that it would be pretty stressful. Did you suffer burnout?" The wine arrived and the waiter filled their glasses. They ordered their food and Angelique asked for fresh chilies on the side.

"You eat raw chili, these days?" Stephanie asked with a grin.

Angelique chuckled. "I grew to love it after a few years in Asia. It becomes addictive. My closest friend, Siow Lian, wouldn't dream of eating anything without it. And she knows about food. She owns a coffee shop, you remember those places, a food hall called Paradise Gardens."

Angelique explained how she had gotten started in her consultancy business. Stephanie wasn't surprised to learn of her success. She was talented.

Angelique grinned. "I guess I'm not a great team player. In aid work I couldn't do the things I believed were essential. It suits me better to work on my own." She took a sip of her wine.

Stephanie nodded. "You would've been too damned clever for them." She smiled. "Teamwork though is fundamental to a job like mine. Can't achieve much on your own."

"Must be easier for you now, though. You're a leader so the big decisions on cases would be yours, right?"

Stephanie chuckled. "It's much better being an inspector than a sergeant, let's put it that way."

"Still, in your talk the other night…the little bit I caught, that is, you seemed to be focusing on the responsibilities of the individual. You seemed to be saying that people should step away from the group when necessary and make a personal stand on things that really matter."

Angelique's eyes were distracting. Bluer-than-blue against those black lashes and golden brown skin. Stephanie had almost forgotten how mesmerizing they were. She looked down into her glass. "I just think many of us get so caught up in the minutiae of our daily lives that we ignore social issues around us. Most of us let ideals slide because we don't want to be fighting all the time."

Gazing at Stephanie over her glass, Angelique sipped her wine. "And, of course, some people have no ideals at all," she said. "I come across some of them in my work, and you would even more."

"I remember your explaining to me…" Stephanie hesitated, shot a glance down at the river, then pressed on. "When you first told me you were taking the aid job in Jakarta…" Angelique took in a sharp breath, toying with her glass. "You said you were keen to go into aid because you were fed up with the ruthlessness of the business world."

Angelique twisted her glass on the table. "Yes, I once had these grand ideas about the way businesses could be managed profitably and still be fair and responsible. I thought it was great when I got my first job with a big multinational company. That was before I met you, but I recall telling you about it." Stephanie nodded, remembering. "They were into everything, newspapers, TV networks, mining, breweries. But my job was far from the creative one I'd imagined." The waiter brought their dinner. Sushi, beef tataki, tempura, rice. "They acquired companies with great prospects but also vulnerabilities due to the financial climate, heavy debt, poor leadership or whatever. My job was to slice them up into saleable pieces. Destroy them, and figure out redundancy packages for the staff."

"That's right." Stephanie grinned. "They called your department 'The Wrecking Yard.'"

Angelique laughed. "You remember that!"

Stephanie offered the sushi plate to Angelique. "It's called asset stripping, as I recall." Charlotte often talked about the high profits that practice returned. The acquiring company's share price was boosted although nothing was actually produced.

Angelique put some wasabi onto her piece of sushi. "It's different now working for myself. I get to pick and choose my clients. For the most part they're decent people with honest intentions. Some of my jobs are very exciting."

"Well, your current job obviously would be. A new oil float is a pretty big venture to be involved with." Angelique bit into her sushi, seemingly uninterested in discussing the project. Stephanie pushed on. "That little country, Seragana, looks like it's really going places. Did you play any part in the oil discovery?"

Angelique gulped down some wine. "I just sort of pointed the company in the right direction," she said flatly.

It seemed she was holding something back, Stephanie thought. Perhaps there were issues of business confidentiality that Angelique had to honor.

Angelique put down her glass and trained her disturbing gaze directly into Stephanie's eyes. "And how are things with you?" she asked quietly. "Career-wise you've obviously achieved the success you always wanted. But apart from that, has life been good to you?"

Stephanie dropped her gaze. Her throat suddenly tightened. She had done nothing but focus on her job ever since their break-up. It was dreadful to realize, all of a sudden, that the happiest she had felt in the past six years was in the past hour sitting here with Angelique. They were both silent for too long. She swallowed, tried to compose herself. When she looked up, Angelique's eyes were glinting with tears.

"I'm so sorry, Stephanie," she said softly. "I ruined everything."

Stephanie reached out and took Angelique's hands in her own, caressing them gently. She could never stand to see Angelique upset. "Baby," she whispered. She shouldn't have said that. She had always called her baby, but it was inappropriate now. A glinting tear welled and trickled down Angelique's cheek. "It wasn't your fault," Stephanie said firmly. "You did nothing wrong." She took a tissue from her pocket and handed it to Angelique.

Angelique dabbed at her eyes, then took a deep breath. "It's just that you looked so sad. And I've spent a lot of time over those years thinking about how all that hurt might've been avoided."

Stephanie put on a brave smile. "What did we know then? Nothing." She gave a little shrug. "We couldn't see possibilities that we might have seen had we been older." She topped up Angelique's glass, then spooned some rice and beef onto her plate. "Eat something," she said.

Angelique ate some food. "It's good," she said with a watery smile. "I'm glad you brought me here."

Stephanie nodded, pleased that Angelique liked her choice. She bit into a tempura prawn and wondered if her next question would cause even more angst.

"So," she began, her voice oddly too loud. A man at a neighboring table glanced over. She cleared her throat. "A clever, gorgeous woman like you…has anyone snapped you up?" She'd tried to make the question casual, but her heart had started to thump. The last thing she wanted to hear was that Angelique was in another relationship, but she had to know.

Angelique shook her head. "No."

Stephanie felt a wave of relief. She wished she could hide her selfish pleasure in the information. "Are they completely stupid over there?" she asked with a broad smile.

Angelique chuckled. "Far from it. I'd love you to meet the friends I've made since I've been away." Stephanie poked at her rice with her chopsticks. Nice idea, she thought. But that wasn't likely to happen. "What about you?" Angelique asked. "Are things serious with Charlotte?"

Stephanie picked up her glass and gulped down the rest of her wine. "Not for me."

"For her, then? Does she love you?" Angelique looked troubled.

Stephanie sighed. "I don't believe so." With a start, she realized that Charlotte and Angelique were exact opposites. "Truth is, we both wish each other were quite different."

Angelique finished her food. She seemed to share Stephanie's relief, though the knowledge that they were both emotionally free was likely to cause them some headaches.

Angelique leaned back in her chair. "How's your dad?"

Stephanie felt a jolt. Angelique was the only person she knew who had ever bothered about James. Everyone else pretended he didn't exist. Before Angelique, Stephanie had been ashamed of him. His behavior had been a huge factor in her choosing a police career. He had been a lawyer, in charge of his firm's investments, clients' money, trust accounts. Not the perfect role for a gambling addict. Of course, his employers knew nothing about that.

The final straw was when a friend since childhood called on him to help buy a thoroughbred horse. It was a sure thing, James had been convinced. The friend was struggling, and James, from the same working-class background, felt he should help. The horse actually was a real champion with a terrific record, so James had told Stephanie. They thought it would only take a few good wins to get their investment back, then they'd be into profit. So James dipped into the clients' funds and helped himself to twenty-five grand, a lot of money in those days. He bought a two-thirds share in the horse in the company's name. He planned to return the money with interest before anyone noticed it was missing. Stephanie believed that. The judge didn't go for it, though, and James Tyler went to prison for five years.

Angelique had encouraged Stephanie to see more of him, to make her peace with him. She and James weren't exactly close these days, but it was thanks to Angelique that she kept in touch with him regularly.

Stephanie emptied the last of the wine into their glasses. "Oh, he's all right. Still frustrates me at times." She looked up with a grin. "He missed you terribly when you left."

Angelique smiled. "I wish I had time to see him, but I'm afraid I don't. Give him my regards, won't you?"

The waiter appeared and asked if they wanted dessert or coffee. Angelique shook her head and Stephanie asked for the bill.

"Let's go somewhere else for a coffee, maybe a nightcap," Angelique suggested. "There are heaps of places around here."

Stephanie signed the credit card bill and handed it to the waiter. She looked at Angelique with a grin. "I know where we should go. The Golden Horseshoe Hotel."

Angelique's eyes sparkled. "I'd forgotten all about that place. You still go there?"

Stephanie shrugged. "Rarely. But the girls from work go there quite often when they finish their shifts." It was an old-fashioned workers pub that, unlike most similar places, hadn't yet been gentrified and added to the trendy circuit of quaint city bars. In the old days, Angelique sometimes had met Stephanie and Jan there after work.

Angelique grabbed her purse and buttoned the jacket of her suit. The black silk camisole underneath shimmered. She straightened her delicate jade necklace. "Sounds good to me," she said. "Let's go."

CHAPTER THIRTEEN

It was close to eleven when their taxi drew up outside the red-brick hotel. On the other side of town, much of the street comprised trade supply shops. More than a hundred years ago, when the hotel was built, many businesses had been blacksmiths. Next door to the hotel was an old horse stable that had been fashioned into a home. Houses were interspersed with the businesses. Once tiny worker's cottages for the city's poor, they were these days shiny and renovated, many sporting a second story. Angelique had noticed how property prices had sky-rocketed in recent years, so that even the once less salubrious suburbs were now in high demand.

Angelique shuddered as they got out of the car. She had left her apartment and gone straight to the restaurant without having to go outside, so she hadn't brought a coat.

Stephanie glanced at the clear sky. "There'll be a frost tonight." She pulled open the pub door. Angelique felt her muscles uncoil in the warmth.

Wood fires crackled brightly at either side of the room. Soothing jazz was playing softly. Twenty or so women were sitting at the bar and around tables, half a dozen guys occupied a table down the back. An old man huddled in a tartan jacket, clutching a pot of beer, sat at a table just inside the door.

"Evening, Pete," Stephanie said brightly.

He looked up. "Inspector. Nippy enough for ya?"

What Angelique had always liked about this pub was that all types were welcome. There were gays, straights, a few down-and-outs, tradesmen, suited professionals. It was comfortable.

Stephanie pulled off her scarf, shook off her red-lined tailored black overcoat. Shoving it under one arm, she reached into the back pocket of her pinstriped pants and took out her wallet. "What can I get you?" she asked as they made for the bar.

There were two barstools free. Angelique sat on one, Stephanie dropped her coat over the back of the other. Angelique recognized the barman as he turned to them. Smiling at her he narrowed his eyes, as if in thought. "It's a French kind of name, isn't it?"

"Angelique," she replied. "How have you been, John?"

"Nothing wrong with your memory," he said with a laugh. "Where have you been all this time?"

"Mostly Singapore."

"Well, then. You'll be wanting a proper drink in a proper pub, I would think. What would you like? It's on the house."

Angelique chose a liqueur, Stephanie a vodka tonic. Angelique watched her as she nodded hello to a few people near the bar. It was a joy to be with her. She had a certain style that Angelique had never tired of observing. A stranger, catching a glimpse of Stephanie in repose, might notice her athletic shape, her classic features, her somewhat detached air. But to know Stephanie the way Angelique did you had to see the way she moved. She didn't walk, she strode. Her gestures were precise, her movements sure. While her manners were perfect, when she wanted a waiter's attention she got it. She didn't dodge around people, they seemed to glide out of her way.

John placed their drinks on the counter. They touched glasses. Stephanie rested one black ankle boot on the brass foot rail and took a sip of her drink. "Anything left like this in Singapore?" she asked.

"Actually, there are still a couple of them, left by the Brits." She took a sip of her drink and enjoyed the burning warmth in the back of her throat. "Not the same though. The Chinese have altered them a bit." Through a doorway Angelique glimpsed women wearing solemn expressions, pool cues in hand. In the music changeover she caught the clicks and thuds of a pool game. "There are even a few with pool tables," she said with a grin.

"Is there a favorite place you go with your friends?" Stephanie asked.

"There is one place I go to sometimes. It's mostly women who go there." Angelique chuckled. "Probably because it's called Venus Bar."

Stephanie grinned. "That'd put off more than a few guys."

"Actually, it's really nice if you go on a quiet night. Some nights it's given over to the dance crowd. Too noisy for me. I must be getting old."

Stephanie chuckled. "I like the sound of it," she said. "Maybe we'll meet there for a drink one of these days."

Their eyes locked. Stephanie's eyes were hazel-green. The color altered in different lights and with her changing moods. They had the sultry darkness now that Angelique had always seen before they kissed. She suddenly felt a shadow looming over her happiness. The end of the night was near. The end of her Melbourne visit was imminent. It was going to be disturbing, painful even, to simply say goodbye to Stephanie and return to Singapore.

Angelique sipped her drink. Stephanie shifted in her seat, deliberately resting her knee against Angelique's thigh. Desire stirred again in Angelique's body. This intimacy seemed the most natural thing in the world. In many ways it was as though they had simply picked up where they left off.

Avoiding Stephanie's gaze, Angelique stared into the fire. Orange embers leapt from the rolling flames. Up and down and around they danced before disappearing in the smoky vortex.

What a time for destiny to offer her a second chance with Stephanie. Just when she was heading up a fraud that would soon reverberate around the world.

The front door flew open. "Here comes the constabulary," Stephanie said.

Eight uniformed officers trooped in noisily. Their laughter, chatter and bulky blue boldness dominated the room. They congregated at a large table near the window. Scraping chairs over the polished concrete floor, they plonked down.

Before long Jan strolled over. She gave Angelique a hug. "Like old times, eh?"

Angelique beamed. It was good to see old friends. "You know, before tonight I thought I'd lost my place in Melbourne," she said. "But there are so many connections, and people remember me. It's wonderful."

"'Course they do," Jan said. "You're not easy to forget." She turned to Stephanie. "How's it going, Steph?" She clapped Stephanie on the shoulder as though congratulating her about something. Stephanie said she was fine and returned Jan's happy smile.

"All just finished a shift?" Stephanie asked.

"Yeah. Thought we'd meet up for a quick one before heading off home." Bottles of beer were placed on a tray and handed to her. "I'll leave you two in peace. Catch you later," Jan said.

Angelique watched Jan hand the drinks around to her colleagues. One by one they twisted around to steal a look at Angelique and Stephanie.

Stephanie shrugged. "The station will be jumping with gossip tomorrow."

"Does that embarrass you?"

"Of course not." She dropped an intimate half-smile. "How could anyone be embarrassed about being seen with you? They'll all be green with envy." Angelique just gazed into her eyes. "Another drink?" Stephanie asked.

Angelique nodded. Just one more. They could be together that bit longer. "Thanks."

If only she could confide in Stephanie. Tell her everything she was doing, just like she used to. Get her wise perspective, her support. She remembered how much they had shared and how much they had helped each other in all matters. Work, Stephanie's father, Angelique's lonely mother. When one had doubts, the other provided certainty.

But Angelique's business activity was one subject she could not drop into Stephanie's lap. While Stephanie would agree entirely with providing assistance to Kira Na Murgha and to finding a way to get rid of Pacific Holdings, she would never support the Twilight fraud plan. She might have even succeeded in talking Angelique out of getting involved in the first place. But it was too late for such thoughts now. Neither the plan nor Stephanie herself could be compromised.

"There you go." Stephanie handed her a glass. She searched Angelique's face. "You look a million miles away. You okay?"

"I'm fine." Angelique took a large gulp of her drink.

Suddenly, a young woman tumbled through the pool room door into the bar. She staggered, circled on the spot before she slowly regained her balance. Frayed cuffs of baggy jeans bunched under her track shoes, and her denim jacket hung off one shoulder. Facing the pool room, she yelled, "Yeah, well fuck youse, ya bitches!"

Stephanie groaned quietly and shook her head.

"You know her?" Angelique asked.

Stephanie nodded. "Andrea Burzomi. She shouldn't be here. She's underage."

Jan and her colleagues, like everyone else, had turned to stare at Andrea.

Jerking around, Andrea caught sight of the officers. She raised a hand in greeting. "Evenin' ladies!" she called out. "Nice night for it!"

"Christ," Stephanie muttered under her breath. "Anyone but Andrea would have the sense to quickly leave. But she always has to push until something gives." Jan and the others looked at Stephanie, as if waiting for her direction. Stephanie calmly sipped her drink as if hoping the problem would vanish.

Andrea swung around, swayed and stood blinking at Stephanie. Her young face was street-weary, Angelique noticed. Stephanie put down her glass and faced her. Andrea grinned.

"How are ya, Inspector?" Surprisingly sweet, her smile transformed her severe face. You could see the child in her, Angelique thought. "Let me buy you a drink." Andrea began digging around in her pocket.

"It's time you were going, Andrea," Stephanie said flatly. "You shouldn't be here drinking at all."

Andrea stepped closer. "Don't be like that." She noticed Angelique and gazed at her. "Knock-out girlfriend, Inspector! I wanna buy her a drink too."

Stephanie sighed.

Andrea leaned close to Angelique, grinning. "What's she like, eh? A tiger between the sheets? Or a pussycat?"

Angelique averted her eyes, knowing better than to engage in any type of conversation.

"That's enough!" Stephanie snapped. Getting off her stool, Stephanie looked down on Andrea. From the corner of her eye Angelique saw Jan rise to her feet, though she came no closer. Andrea slammed a handful of money down on the bar.

"I told ya!" Andrea hissed. "I gotta buy you a drink. I gotta thank you for lockin' up me little sister." She shot a fierce look at Angelique. "That's what your girlfriend done. Got her put into care! And I got the blame. From all of 'em." Angelique was taken aback by the desperation in the girl's voice.

Stephanie was staring at the wad of notes on the bar. "There's around eighty bucks here," she said. "Where'd you get it?"

Andrea shrugged, and rubbed her sleeve across her nose.

"Empty your pockets."

Andrea pulled out a pack of cigarettes. After a few clumsy attempts, she managed to light one. Stephanie took it from her mouth and handed it to John, who was staring at the scene. "There's no smoking in here, by the way," Stephanie said.

"Search me, why don't ya?" Andrea grinned. "Cuff me to the bar and give me a real going over." She broke into a bout of giggles. "Make my day!" She doubled over with laughter.

Stephanie raked back her hair. "Pockets," she said quietly. "Now."

Glowering at Stephanie, Andrea reached into a jacket pocket

and dragged out a small booklet. She slung it on the bar. "That what you're after?"

Stephanie picked it up. "The old raffle ticket scam, eh? Thought you'd given that one up."

"Haven't run a raffle for ages." Andrea grinned at Angelique. "It's a good one, too. Can win you a trip to Disneyland."

Stephanie turned to John. "How long's she been in here?"

"Honestly, Inspector, I didn't know she was here." He gave a helpless shrug. "The young ones sneak in sometimes, hide out the back and others buy their drinks." John looked shaken. Angelique felt for him. He ran a good bar, she remembered, and was not the type to allow underage drinking.

Stephanie nodded. "I understand. It's okay. Please just keep an eye out for her in the future. Maybe have someone check the back regularly, check ages more carefully." He nodded and returned to loading the glass washer. This wasn't the first time Angelique had seen something like this when in Stephanie's company. She couldn't help feeling some pride. Stephanie was always fair and always right as far as she was concerned.

Stephanie turned to Jan and gave her a nod. Jan immediately strode over. "You been naughty again, Andrea?" she said. Andrea threw her a hostile sidelong glance.

Stephanie handed Jan the half-empty book of raffle tickets. "Get one of the girls to go around with Andrea and find her customers. Give their money back." She handed Jan Andrea's wad. "Then see she gets home."

Jan flicked through the booklet. "What's the good cause this time?" she asked Andrea.

"Destitute lesbians of the Third World," Andrea slurred.

Jan rolled her eyes at Stephanie. Angelique suppressed a giggle. She was quite a character, this young girl.

"Well, come on." Jan grabbed hold of Andrea's sleeve. "Let's sort this out." She took Andrea to her table. She conferred with a constable who got up and steered Andrea to the pool room. "You're a bloody pest, Andrea," Angelique heard her hiss as they passed.

Stephanie sank down onto her barstool. "We didn't need that interruption, did we?"

"You're still a softie, I'm glad to see," Angelique said gently.

Stephanie straightened her shoulders a little. "I'm no softie," she said with a touch of defensiveness.

She was a total darling. Soft and strong rolled up into one sexy package. Before she could stop herself, Angelique leaned over and planted a long tender kiss on Stephanie's cheek. She felt Stephanie tremble just a little. She turned to Angelique and looked hard into her eyes. Then her gaze slowly moved to Angelique's mouth. She held that gaze way too long. If she didn't stop, Angelique thought, she might faint. Stephanie's eyes darkened and finally she shifted her gaze to the fire.

"You could have arrested her," Angelique prodded. "But you didn't."

"She's got enough problems, the poor girl," Stephanie said, quickly filling Angelique in on Andrea's background. "I don't know how she's going to fare once she's an adult though, unless she changes her ways." She took a gulp of her drink.

"What exactly was she doing?" Angelique asked.

"She buys these blank booklets," Stephanie explained, "then sells tickets for a couple of dollars each, telling people it's for some good cause or another. Tempts them with all manner of lovely prizes. People feel mean if they say no."

She shrugged. "It's incredible how easy it is. We've all bought raffle tickets that we never hear any more about. No one really expects to win. We don't ask questions about the draw, conditions, whatever. People just believe what they're told."

Angelique's thoughts suddenly shot to Mason and his identical advice. People believe what the papers tell them, what their stockbrokers say, what their friends mutter at the gym or whisper on the golf course. The Twilights were relying on that blind belief to make their scam work. Angelique twirled her glass on the counter. Motivation aside, when all was said and done, there was little technical difference between her crime and Andrea's.

"So, I know you would agree," Stephanie said. "Andrea deserves some help, right now."

Angelique nodded. "Of course. The letter of the law doesn't always line up with true justice. I think we both know that."

Stephanie tilted her head in a questioning manner. "You're a funny one," she said. "The things you come out with."

It would be a tremendous weight off her mind, Angelique thought, if she could achieve consensus on this point with Stephanie, at least in the abstract. "What I mean is, there are situations where personal judgment is called for. Where the rulebook can't help. Where the laws don't fit."

Stephanie's gaze moved over Angelique's face. Her eyes were soft, her scrutiny warm. "There are times, darling," she said quietly. "When personal judgment must take first place. Gut instinct about what's right and what's wrong should never be ignored."

Angelique gave a mental sigh of relief. No matter what followed over the next few precarious days, she would be able to cling to the thought that Stephanie, in her heart at least, might be on her side.

"But the law is there for good purpose," Stephanie added, "And if you flout it you do so at your peril."

Angelique averted her gaze. She hadn't needed to hear the last part. But what else could she expect? Personal judgment, kindness and wisdom aside, Stephanie's job was to uphold the law.

Angelique drained the last drops from her glass and put down her glass. Stephanie gently took her hand and caressed her fingers, one by one. "I know you have to go back to Singapore soon, but when can we get together again?"

Angelique's pulse quickened. After tonight there was little opportunity to be with Stephanie. It wasn't enough time.

"Tomorrow?" Stephanie prompted. "Wednesday?" She looked as anxious as Angelique felt.

Nolan had Angelique's schedule pretty full. The stock was to be listed in one week, a few days after Angelique's return to Singapore. "Wednesday. The company's got me booked up for investor meetings till then. That's my first free night. Is that okay?"

Stephanie smiled and rolled her eyes. "Any time is okay. Just wish it were tomorrow."

"Me too." Angelique's heart was still beating too fast. She desperately hoped that the night wasn't quite over yet. Could she get Stephanie to come back to her apartment? Should she even try? There was no doubt that Stephanie wanted her, but she had a cautious streak that Angelique knew well. "Maybe Thursday, too, with any luck. The plan is that I leave on Friday."

Stephanie smiled. "I'll take both." She stood and grabbed her coat. "It's late, we'd better go if you're ready."

Angelique picked up her purse and they headed for the door. They said goodbye to Jan and the others, then stepped out into the night.

"We'll have to walk to the corner and flag down a taxi," Stephanie said. Angelique shivered. "Come here," Stephanie murmured. She wrapped her coat around Angelique, helped her put her arms into the too-long sleeves. Stephanie drew her closer, turned up the collar. She was wonderfully close and gorgeously warm.

They strolled to the corner where the main road intersected with the street, then stopped. Stephanie turned to face her, slid her hands inside the coat and wrapped her arms around her. Angelique moved to kiss her mouth, but Stephanie, with a tiny groan, shifted her mouth to Angelique's throat. Every nerve in Angelique's body remembered Stephanie's every move, anticipated the particular pleasure that only Stephanie had given her.

Angelique felt herself slump a little in Stephanie's arms. "Come home with me, darling, please," Angelique managed to murmur.

Stephanie held her tighter and spoke over Angelique's shoulder. "You know I want to do that more than anything in the world. But I have a tiny shred of self-preservation left and I'm hanging onto it."

She leaned back and looked at Angelique. She ran a finger softly over her mouth. "I know those lips can melt a will of iron. I don't have the courage to kiss you." Angelique was faint with desire and could hardly comprehend what Stephanie was saying. "I have to know where this is heading before I take that step. Because once I take it there'll be no turning back for me."

A tear trickled down Angelique's cheek. In a tiny movement, a half kiss, Stephanie licked it away.

"No tears," she said. "You're going home for a good sleep. And I'm going to lie awake most of the night thinking about all this."

Angelique managed a half smile. "You always were a worrier."

Stephanie turned to the street as headlights approached. It was a taxi. She flagged it down, they got in and headed back to the city.

CHAPTER FOURTEEN

Stephanie strolled up the lane from her garage the following night. Angelique had a stranglehold on her mind. The old obsession, the addiction, was back with a vengeance. She'd been counting the hours till they would meet again. Reliving those final moments when she and Angelique had almost kissed. It had made it hard to concentrate at work, hard to even feel steady on her feet.

A gust of wind hit her as she turned the corner past Giovanni's. Laughter seeped through the windows. Her head bowed against the wind, she didn't glance in.

Maybe she should have just gone with the flow. Holding back hadn't helped much. Still, it gave them both a cool chance to think about what they were doing. Stephanie was determined to not repeat their old mistakes. Angelique had an impulsive element to her character, something that Stephanie had always found liberating. It meant that Stephanie had to be strong, logical, and figure things out with Angelique as if solving a case. What they still had, a love that was clearly as strong as ever, had to be protected this time around. It was just a matter of working out the logistics.

She arrived at her security gate. One thing had become perfectly clear since last night. Regardless of how things finally played out with Angelique, her relationship with Charlotte had to end. It was unsatisfying and unhappy for them both, more often than not. She pulled her keys from her pocket and unlocked the gate. At the landing she suddenly stopped. She stared up at the apartment door, her heart pounding. A sliver of light shone under the door. Maybe she'd forgotten to switch off the foyer lamp this morning. She climbed the final steps. At the door she listened before putting her key in the lock. Faintly she could hear the TV. She hadn't switched it on this morning. The only way into the secure apartment was with a key, and only one other person had one. She went inside.

The soft scent of tuberose wafted. Charlotte's coat was on the chaise lounge. The signature music that closed the seven o'clock news bounced from the living room.

"Is that you, honey?" Charlotte's voice rang out brightly. Stephanie dropped her coat beside Charlotte's. She wasn't expected until Friday night, and she never turned up unexpectedly. Charlotte disliked the disorder of the unplanned.

In the living room doorway Stephanie leaned a shoulder against the architrave. She forced a smile. "You scared the hell out of me."

Charlotte put her glass of champagne down on the side table and got up from the sofa. "I wanted to surprise you, darling," she said, sliding her arms around Stephanie's waist. As Stephanie lightly returned her kiss, she felt her irritation begin to dissolve. Instead, a strange sadness began to settle over her like cold ash.

"I flew down on impulse." Charlotte said. Her eyes searched Stephanie's face for a sign of approval. "You've often said I should abandon routine sometimes." She grinned, her expression playful. "Succumb to impulse."

Stephanie gently brushed a strand of hair from Charlotte's eyes. Charlotte went to the sideboard, took a bottle of champagne from the ice bucket. She filled a glass and brought it to Stephanie. "I started without you, but I didn't think you'd mind."

Charlotte's manner was weird, falsely cheerful. Stephanie suddenly felt a great need for a drink. She gulped down half the champagne.

Charlotte picked up her own glass and took a sip. "I haven't had any time off work for ages, so I just thought, what the hell! I decided to take a few days." She shrugged. "I'll do some shopping while you're at work. And cooking. I stopped at the market on the way here, and I'm going to cook us something nice for dinner."

Stephanie was bewildered. Cooking wasn't one of Charlotte's interests. Charlotte's smile faded as she held Stephanie's gaze. Then realization hit Stephanie like a blow across the head. Charlotte knew their relationship was all but over. The difference was, it seemed, that Charlotte had some plan to save the day.

Charlotte averted her eyes, gulped down some more champagne. "Well," she said. "I'd better start dinner or we won't eat till god knows when." She went into the kitchen.

The chopping board thudded onto the counter. There was a clang of utensils. Stephanie moved into the living room, put down her glass. She had to end this painful charade. She hadn't given a great deal of consideration to Charlotte during the day, though she had formed some vague idea of flying to Sydney on the weekend, after Angelique had left, and finishing things with her calmly and pleasantly. In those fleeting thoughts she had pictured Charlotte being in complete agreement and they'd part as friends. Stephanie sighed. But of course, life was never that damned simple. It wasn't going to be pleasant, after all.

"Charlotte," she called. Charlotte appeared in the kitchen doorway. "Don't cook dinner tonight, honey," she said gently. "We'll go down to Giovanni's. Have some wine. We've got to talk." Charlotte hesitated, but didn't argue.

The smell of baking focaccia underlaid the aroma of fresh coffee. The café was quieter than usual. Beside the wood-paneled wall at the kitchen end of the room, ten elderly Italian men sat playing cards. They often gathered there, sipping espressos and taking shots of Sambuca. Giovanni, Tony's father, nodded a greeting to Stephanie. At the counter Stephanie ordered a bottle of house red from Tony, then they went over to her usual table against the wall.

The light was comfortingly low. Stephanie felt herself relax a little. Saying what she had to say seemed easier on neutral territory.

Tony brought the wine, plonked down the glasses and filled them with a flourish. He grinned at Charlotte. "Good to see you, bella!" he said. Charlotte summoned a crooked smile.

Stephanie took off her coat. Charlotte kept hers on, her arms crossed. Maybe she wanted to be prepared for a quick escape.

Stephanie picked up her glass and took a sip. Her eyes downcast, Charlotte looked brittle. Guilt was turning acid in Stephanie's stomach. Regardless of how she did this, she was going to hurt Charlotte.

She could have spared Charlotte the suspense of this wine-washed, sweet-talking public farce. "We'll go down to Giovanni's," she had said, like an executioner slipping the mask over Charlotte's eyes. She could have told Charlotte upstairs that it was over, put up with some yelling, then escorted her to a taxi. It was ironic. Now, at the end, she was finding it desperately important to find the right words. Yet in the months leading to this moment words had been carefully avoided.

Charlotte took a tiny sip of wine. Her movements were stiff, her body rigid beneath the camel cashmere wrapping. Stephanie thought of all the occasions before this when she could have expressed her misgivings to Charlotte. But she had lacked the incentive to take a stand. She had let everything roll along without bothering to deal with the problems. And now, she castigated herself, now you are going to be sensitive, considerate, gentle. At the end. That way if Charlotte reacts badly, gets nasty, you can tell yourself that she was being unreasonable.

Tony burst into song, treating everyone to a few lines from *Tosca*. He came to their table with the menus. "Special today, chicken gnocchetti in brodo, roast lamb or fresh pesto with any pasta you like."

Stephanie gave him a smile. "Thanks. We'll order a bit later."

He strode back to the bar, grabbing empty plates along the way. Stephanie topped up their glasses. Charlotte was watching her, waiting for her to begin. Stephanie swirled the wine around her glass.

Charlotte's eyes suddenly hardened. "How long have you been sleeping with her?"

Stephanie's heart almost stopped. Charlotte had snatched the upper hand. How the hell could she even know that she had been out with Angelique? And why assume they were lovers? Stephanie cleared her throat. "What?"

"That woman, Angelique."

"I haven't slept with her." Stephanie was reeling.

"Oh, come on!" Charlotte hissed. "I saw the way you looked at her on Friday night. Everyone could see. And she looked at you like a lovesick puppy." She paused, swallowed. "So, how long?"

"She's been away. It's the first time I've seen her in years."

Charlotte looked incredulous. "Well, obviously you didn't fall in love with her on Friday night!"

Stephanie averted her eyes. It seemed incredible that the depth of her feeling for Angelique had been so obvious.

"You were lovers in the past. I've been asking around." Charlotte paused for effect. Stephanie gazed at her in amazement. "Who do you know who knows about my personal history?"

"You'd be surprised," Charlotte hissed. "I don't know the details, but I found out that you two were a serious item once."

Stephanie took a gulp of her wine. "Yes, we were together once. We were a couple. Then she went overseas and it ended." She gave a nonchalant shrug. She really didn't want to discuss Angelique with Charlotte. "We ran into each other again. So what?"

To her horror, Charlotte laughed. A humorless icy laugh that froze the conversation around them. A man and a woman at the next table glanced over. "Oh, Stephanie," she muttered. "I don't believe it. You've carried a torch for her all this time? You still love her? Clever, strong Inspector Tyler. The woman left you and you didn't take the hint?" She was smiling in cold amusement.

Her attempt to belittle Stephanie's feelings, to make her sound like an idiot was no doubt making her feel better.

"You don't know what you're talking about," Stephanie snapped.

"Why didn't you ever tell me about her?"

Stephanie shrugged. "What would've been the point?"

Charlotte slammed her glass down on the table. "The point would've been sharing things with me. I realize now there's a lot I don't know about your past, so much you've never told me."

"Never bothered you before."

"Have you always been like this? Did you use to tell her things?" Charlotte asked quietly.

Stephanie glanced away at the counter. Tony and his wife were deep in conversation in Italian, polishing glasses. She had been very different in those six happy months with Angelique. She had told her things. She'd told her everything. They had shared every thought, never stopped talking.

She turned back to Charlotte, who was biting her lip. "This isn't about Angelique. It's about you and me." Tears suddenly shimmered like cut glass in Charlotte's eyes. Stephanie continued quietly. "You know we're not going anywhere. You want a commitment. And I don't."

Charlotte quickly wiped a tear off her cheek. "I knew you were restless," she said. "But I thought we had something, you know?"

Stephanie touched her hand. "We do have something that's often really nice. But it's not enough. We see the world differently." She shook her head. "I think it's fair to say, Charlotte, that I'm not the person you really want me to be."

"At least what we have is real. It's not a fantasy." Charlotte was taking the no-nonsense line. "Sounds to me that with her you're chasing a dream." Charlotte drained her glass, grabbed the bottle, poured herself another. She was really putting it away.

"Do you want to order some food?" Stephanie asked.

"No." Charlotte drank half the glass in a gulp. "You've seen her since Friday?" Stephanie nodded. "But you didn't have sex?" Charlotte couldn't get past that.

"It doesn't bloody matter! But for the record, as I told you, no!"

Charlotte held her gaze. "Bullshit," she mouthed.

Stephanie felt a flash of anger. "For all my faults, I'm not a liar!" Charlotte downed even more wine. "And it's none of your damned business!" she hissed.

She watched her words hit Charlotte like a slap. She shouldn't have said that. Of course it was Charlotte's business if Stephanie had another lover. She couldn't stand any more of this. She focused on the red and white checks of the tablecloth. There were ten red blocks between her glass and the bottle, five and a half to the pepper grinder.

"Busy tonight, was she?" Charlotte's tone was catty.

Stephanie straightened up. "Can we stop this now?" she asked quietly.

Charlotte's eyes were tinged red. "Are you seeing her again?"

Stephanie raked her fingers through her hair. She had totally lost control of the situation. Charlotte was keeping her on the defensive. "Yes."

"Well, good!" Charlotte exploded. Her voice boomed around the room. Tony, at the counter, jerked his head up. The couple at the next table stared. The old men were hushed. "For god's sake!" Charlotte yelled. "Fuck her next time, will you? And get it over with!"

Stephanie froze. This couldn't be really happening. Charlotte was seething. A piece of cutlery hit the floor somewhere, and Stephanie jumped. Tony threw his espresso machine into action, filling the silence with its hiss and splutter.

Charlotte took a deep breath, collecting herself. "I'll go home tomorrow and give you the space," she said. "Get her out of your system. Call me when she's gone."

Stephanie couldn't believe it. What sort of person did Charlotte think she was? She was dismissing all this as a silly transgression on Stephanie's part, for which she was grandly prepared to endure some humiliation. Stephanie had always been conscious of Charlotte's pragmatism, but this cold and calculating attitude was appalling.

"For god's sake," Stephanie murmured.

Charlotte's shoulders slumped. Tears poured. Mascara underlined her eyes like soot. Her lipstick was gone.

Stephanie reached into her pocket for a tissue. "Mascara," Stephanie gently prompted, knowing how Charlotte would hate the smudges.

Charlotte took the tissue, dabbed her eyes. "I don't want to lose you."

Stephanie took a deep breath. "I'm sorry, Charlotte."

Charlotte suddenly set her jaw. She shoved back her chair. Its wooden legs screeched across the tiles. She stood up. Tony looked over. The old men fell silent again. The couple at the next table stared. Stephanie held her breath. Charlotte strode across the room, flung open the door and left.

Thank god for that, Stephanie thought. She refilled her glass and gulped it down. In a few moments conversation resumed around her. Tension began to slowly unknot in her stomach. Giovanni and his friends erupted in laughter and they all tossed down their cards. Connie tottered out of the kitchen with a huge platter of pasta which she placed on their table. Giovanni put his arm around his wife and gave her a hug. Tony took them plates and bread. Their voices were loud, happy.

Less than ten minutes later the café door swung open. The room fell silent again. Stephanie's heart nearly stopped. Charlotte was making an encore. Surrounded by luggage, frocks on hangers in plastic bags, laptop in hand, Charlotte stood in the doorway. Dramatically she raised one hand high above her head. Everyone in Stephanie's line of sight looked up. Then Charlotte threw something at Stephanie. It landed on the floor, reverberating like a round from a firing squad. It bounced three times before coming to rest meters out of Stephanie's reach. It was Charlotte's key to her apartment.

Stephanie gazed at her in shocked disbelief. She thought Charlotte would have a bit more class, more pride, at least. Charlotte gathered up her things and disappeared into the night.

Stephanie felt that she would choke in the silence that followed. She couldn't get up and fetch the key. She couldn't get up and leave. Covering her eyes with her hand, she stared down at the table. A few people whispered.

Before long a red apron appeared at her side. Tony placed a big steaming bowl of soup before her. Plump chicken gnocchetti tumbled in the clear broth. He put down a basket of hot focaccia. He released the key from his hand and with his index finger nudged it out of sight under the rim of her plate. Stephanie's throat closed up. In a voice loud enough for all to hear he said, "On the house, my friend. Enjoy!"

The old men turned back to their cards. The couple resumed their gazing into the mid-distance. General conversation wound up to its normal hum. And Tony, polishing his counter, was singing "Ave Maria."

CHAPTER FIFTEEN

Angelique's taxi crossed the river and headed north. She was meeting Stephanie at the restaurant at eight. The driver was taking a route she didn't recognize. The city had changed. Gentrification of the inner suburbs had spread, redefined by a network of new toll roads.

Stephanie had phoned Tuesday morning, sweet and concerned, to see how she was. She had been worried that she had disappointed Angelique at the end of the night on Monday. Angelique teasingly confirmed that she certainly had. "It's not like you to leave a girl in a state like that," she had purred into the phone. She'd heard a tiny groan at the other end of the line. "I'll make it up to you," Stephanie said in her throaty voice. Sitting in her office at Pacific Holdings Angelique had almost swooned. "After we've discussed some important arrangements,"

Stephanie added. Angelique had chuckled. "Business before pleasure, as usual."

Stephanie had called again today to reconfirm their date. She knew Angelique liked French food, she said, so she had booked somewhere special.

At least work with Pacific Holdings was proceeding to plan. She had talked to Siow Lian on Facebook last night and confirmed that all was well at their end. Kira was holding firm, waiting patiently.

Angelique dug around in her purse for her lipstick, then applied it. Things might be a bit tense with Kira once she returned. They had parted on a promise, more or less, that they would explore the attraction they'd felt for each other. With a sigh she stared out the window. She would have to carefully close that door and hope that the crown princess of Seragana wouldn't be too peeved.

She fought back the increasing urge to tell Stephanie what was she involved in. Now they were virtually reunited, a few technical details aside, like where they would live, it felt wrong to withhold something so important. But she wouldn't compromise Stephanie, so silence was imperative. Later, she would tell her every detail. Stephanie would have a fit, but Angelique could deal with that. Stephanie would understand in the end.

She had to smile, though, at the timing. It had to be right now, while she was involved in perpetrating a fraud, that she rekindled a love affair with an inspector of police.

The driver had the radio on. Angelique's attention was drawn to the eight o'clock news. "…And heading stock market news today, Pacific Holdings announced their initial public offer closed last Friday massively oversubscribed. The company is looking forward to brisk trading when the market opens next Monday. Financial commentators are tipping the stock could rise eight to—" The driver flicked the station over.

"Boring as hell, that crap, isn't it, love?" He eyed her in the rear vision mirror. She gave him a smile. "Stick on a bit of music, eh?" Some country music soon had him tapping the steering wheel happily.

She envied the rest of the Twilights, who hadn't had to

face Nolan day in and day out. He was excited that his small insignificant company had, in the space of a couple of months, become a major market force. But he was out of his depth. The business he had once directed single-handedly was swamped by lawyers, consultants, experts. Increasingly over the recent days he turned to Angelique for answers to his many questions, hanging on her every word.

Meanwhile, the drilling company had started work in Seragana. Nolan and the underwriters were anxious about the results, which were due on Friday of next week following the opening of trade on Monday. Nine days. She planned to be safely out of Nolan's reach before then. There was nothing personal in the entire Twilight plot; it would give her no pleasure to see Nolan's face when he learned that all they had drilled up was water.

Meanwhile Nolan was jumpy about Kira. His lawyer, Max, had contacted her at the time the prospectus was issued. Still in Singapore at the time, Angelique had heard both sides of that communication, from the anxious lawyer and from an amused Siow Lian. Kira had put on a good show, furiously claiming she'd been duped by Nolan and his crony, Angelique. To Nolan's great relief, the princess hadn't tried to prevent the test drillers from going in. But they couldn't start full-scale production without an agreement with the government about royalties and taxes, and she had yet to agree to terms. Nervous about which way Kira would jump, they wanted to bind her to a contract as soon as possible.

"Here we are, love." The driver pulled up outside an elegant two-story Victorian house. An illuminated sign set into the lawn identified it as Chez Jacques.

The lawn was manicured, the garden edged with leafless birch trees, silvery in the up lights. As she stepped onto the tiled portico, the door was opened by a head waiter. In the foyer a gas log fire burned brightly. He helped her out of her coat, then led her into the dining room.

Tall mirrors on high walls reflected subdued lamplight. Linen was white, starched. Roses spilled from vases. Stephanie was at a table at the end of the room, beside another fireplace.

She smiled and stood up to greet Angelique. She looked stunning in a charcoal pinstriped suit, an open-necked red shirt underneath.

She kissed Angelique's cheek. "You look beautiful," she whispered.

The waiter took a bottle from an ice bucket and filled crystal glasses with French champagne. Stephanie picked up her glass and touched it against Angelique's.

"You said we'd go somewhere special," Angelique said, smiling. "You weren't kidding."

Stephanie grinned. "I thought you'd like it."

A waiter came to take their order. They chose one of two set menus, though Angelique hadn't much appetite. They were both sparking, edgy.

"How's work going?" Stephanie asked.

Angelique shifted her gaze to the bubbles in her glass. "Oh, fine. The usual thing."

A frown flickered across Stephanie's brow. "You don't seem to want to talk about this job." She gave a little shrug. "You used to love telling me about your work, and I loved hearing it. It was so removed from my police work. I always found it fascinating."

Angelique squirmed. The last thing she wanted was to let Stephanie think she was excluding her. "Darling," she said gently. "This particular job is nothing like anything I've done before. It's difficult and complicated, and believe me, I would love to tell you all about it." Stephanie was looking perplexed. "But I can't discuss it until it's over." She smiled. "I'll explain everything then."

Stephanie didn't look satisfied. "Is someone putting pressure on you? Making things difficult for you? You only have to tell me, baby, and I'll help you. You know that."

Angelique gave Stephanie's hand a stroke. "I do know that. And nobody is causing me a problem. It's just the whole situation." She picked up her glass. "Please don't worry. It'll soon be over. Let's enjoy this champagne." She took a sip.

Stephanie obligingly sipped her drink, but she looked deep in thought. Angelique's explanation had sounded like rubbish, even to her. Stephanie clearly wasn't buying it either. But Stephanie wasn't one to nag, she was one to cogitate. She would let the subject drop for the time being, Angelique knew, but she wouldn't forget it.

"So, you're back to Singapore on Friday. What then? Will this job be over then?" Stephanie asked.

"I think there'll be a visit to Seragana soon after," Angelique said. "To finalize things." She beamed a smile. "I'd love you to go there with me at some stage. It's beautiful and virtually unspoiled. And you'd love the crown princess, Kira."

Stephanie grinned. "I guess she's a friend of yours. She must be pleased with the development you're assisting with."

"Not just me, friends of mine too." Angelique told Stephanie quickly about the Twilight Club and their private aid work and described their regular get-togethers. Stephanie looked enthralled.

"What a life you've made for yourself," she said. Her smile showed a hint of pride. "They sound like an interesting gang. I'd love to meet them."

"And so you will. We just have to figure out how." Angelique smiled over her glass.

Their first course, lobster soufflés with black truffles, was brought to the table. The waiter showed Stephanie a bottle of red wine. She gave him a nod and he opened it.

Angelique sliced her fork through the fluffy soufflé. "So have you figured out how we're to solve the tyranny of distance?" she asked.

Stephanie tasted the wine, nodded approval, and the waiter filled their glasses. "One of us will have to move house."

Angelique chuckled. "Oh, that's good. I seem to remember coming up with that idea seven years ago, only we couldn't decide who'd do the moving." Their plates were cleared. The soufflé was good, but they'd both only picked at it.

"Well, back then there was only one option, me moving with you to the new job. There's a big difference now. We're both at a senior level in our careers. That gives us more choices than back when we both getting a foothold on the ladder."

Angelique finished her champagne. A waiter whisked away

the glass. "I was thinking the same thing. With a business like mine I should be able to base it in Melbourne without too much trouble. I'd have to travel back and forth fairly often, but that's no big deal."

Stephanie looked pleased, gave a warm half-smile. "And I could look at a career change. Would probably be the making of me."

Angelique was taken aback. For Stephanie to make that suggestion was a huge show of commitment. She loved her job and had worked hard at it.

Angelique's expression must have reflected her surprise. Stephanie reached out and touched Angelique's cheek. "I'll do whatever it takes for us to be together. No job can be a substitute for a relationship as important as ours. It took too long for me to learn that."

Angelique felt tears pricking her eyes. "We'll have a ball. Be as free as the wind. It's a big world out there."

Stephanie nodded. "Where's your home in Singapore?"

Angelique found a business card in her purse and handed it across. "I rent a nice house. I run my business from home."

"I could come over with you, maybe quite often." Stephanie's eyes were gleaming with excitement. They looked bright green. "We could buy a little flat there. Or maybe there's work in that part of the world for someone with my background and organizational skills."

Their main course was brought to the table. The waiter served lamb fillets on a bed of baby spinach. He added buttered asparagus on the side. It looked delicious.

"I've no doubt about the opportunities for someone with your skills and experience," Angelique said. "It's just a shame we wasted so much time."

Stephanie firmly shook her head. "That's not the way to look at it. It simply wasn't our time, back then. But it's our time now. We should be grateful we got another chance."

That was Stephanie all over. While Angelique would turn over every little thing, analyzing tiny details, Stephanie could just put things into a nutshell.

Angelique helped herself to some asparagus. Their new plans

together were easy for her, whereas Stephanie had issues to deal with. "Have you figured out what to tell Charlotte?" she asked gently.

Stephanie's brow furrowed. She put down her fork. "Yeah, and I've already said it." She looked troubled, a little guilty. "Last night. She just turned up out of the blue. It was awful. I really hurt her and I didn't intend to." She looked up at Angelique with a helpless expression. "I tried to be nice. Really I did."

"It's never easy. You would've had some good times with her."

"Of course," Stephanie agreed. "But we never loved each other, so I didn't think she'd be so bothered." She took a gulp of her wine. "Anyway, it's done now."

Their path was cleared then. Angelique knew it was unreasonable, but she'd felt a pang of jealousy seeing Charlotte with Stephanie last Friday night. She'd spent the last three days trying to push from her mind the fact they'd gone home together, presumably spent the weekend together.

Stephanie toyed with her food. "This Kira, the princess..." she began. Angelique jerked her head up. Stephanie's instincts were astounding. "Most of the friends you mentioned, the Twilights, are gay. Is Kira gay too?"

"Yes, as a matter of fact, she is," Angelique replied, trying to sound casual.

Stephanie nodded. "Anything going on between you two?" She was scrutinizing Angelique with some intensity.

"A little frisson, that's all. Nothing to worry about." Stephanie didn't look satisfied. Angelique chuckled. "Don't start. If there was anything to tell you on that score I would have told you already."

Stephanie leaned back, threw up her hands in a gesture of innocence. "I just wondered if you'd slept with her, that's all."

Angelique burst out laughing. "No, lucky for you. Or she might have you sent to the dungeon!" Stephanie laughed too. She looked relieved though. "I guess I'd better not tell you about the hundreds, no thousands, of other affairs I've had over the years," Angelique added.

Stephanie gave her a wry grin. She got the point. The past

was the past, and they'd both had lives to live. "You're right. You'd better not."

They'd finished their meal. The waiter cleared their table and offered the dessert menu. Angelique gave Stephanie a meaningful look. "Do you think maybe it's time to go?"

Stephanie asked for the bill. She looked into Angelique's eyes, her gaze was sultry. "I seem to recall there was something I had to make up to you," she said in a low voice. A warm wash of desire momentarily took Angelique's breath. She nodded.

Stephanie took a deep breath. "My car's outside," she said. "Let's go home."

Stephanie's apartment was warm, the foyer softly lit. Angelique barely cast a glance around. She was looking at Stephanie. "You won't be needing this," Stephanie said. She removed Angelique's coat, dropped it onto the chaise lounge. Angelique slid her arms around Stephanie's shoulders, and they kissed.

An erotic charge almost unbalanced Stephanie. She tightened her arms around Angelique, kissed her hard. Angelique swayed a little. A groan from deep in her throat was like a tiny growl. That had always driven Stephanie mad with lust. Her heart thumping, Stephanie released her to slip out of her jacket. Angelique, a little unsteadily, leaned into the wall.

As Stephanie tossed her jacket down and Angelique moved back to her, she caught their image in the mirror. It was shadowy, surreal, projecting Stephanie's seasoned memories of Angelique. She was gripping Stephanie's shoulder with one hand while with the other she was caressing the skin beneath Stephanie's shirt. As her fingers pulled at the shirt to release it, her tongue teased Stephanie's neck.

Watching the gilt-framed replay, Stephanie reached down to Angelique's thigh, offered through a deep split in the black dress. She gently leaned Angelique against the wall, slid her hand behind her, unzipped the dress. She pulled it down to her waist. Angelique closed her eyes as Stephanie kissed her shoulders, then her breasts through her bra. Stephanie knelt down. Reaching under the dress she stripped Angelique of her underwear. Angelique stepped out of her high heels. Stephanie trailed her fingers along her inside thighs. Angelique spread her legs wider. Stephanie felt herself begin to shake as she pushed the dress up over Angelique's hips. She pulled Angelique closer, exposing her, then slid her tongue between her legs. Angelique groaned, knotting her hands in Stephanie's hair. Stephanie worked her tongue all over, then pushed it inside her. At once, tiny contractions told Stephanie it was time to withdraw. They had to get to the bedroom.

Naked on the bed, Angelique watched Stephanie undress. Her body was toned, just as Angelique remembered. A neon sign across the street pulsed behind the blinds. It washed the room in red, then green, then blue. Stephanie leaned over her, teasing her nipples with her tongue. She was composed, her actions controlled. As always, under her hands Angelique felt wonderfully helpless.

Easily, Stephanie turned her over onto her stomach. She kissed Angelique's shoulders, her neck. Her thigh found its way between Angelique's legs, spreading them wider. One hand crept up Angelique's thigh, the other slid beneath her to cup one breast. She squeezed the nipple. Stephanie's tongue began to travel down her spine. Warm, wet, it was like an electric current. Angelique began to shake. The hand climbing her thigh reached its mark. Angelique gripped the sheet. She was soaked in pleasure. There was nothing else in the world but this, this and Stephanie.

Stephanie shifted position and moved lower down the bed. Her tongue paused at Angelique's hip then continued traveling. Angelique shuddered as Stephanie's lips brushed her skin. Stephanie's fingers stroked faster. Her tongue swirled softly across her buttocks. Suddenly Angelique let her body go. Her mind switched off, silver light filled the space behind her closed eyes. She cried out. Only Stephanie's arms prevented her from floating through the ceiling.

Dimly, Angelique became aware that Stephanie was gently gathering her up. Leaning back on a stack of pillows, Stephanie was scooping up the watery, quivering pieces of her. She held Angelique securely against her. She was hot, sweaty, smiling. "Better now, baby?" she whispered.

Angelique kissed her mouth, her throat. Taking a nipple between her teeth she teased it with her tongue. Stephanie's breath came in short gasps as Angelique trailed her hand down across the firm plane of her stomach. But Stephanie caught it before Angelique's fingers reached between her legs.

"If you do that," Stephanie murmured, "I'll be finished." She rolled onto her side, leaned on one elbow. "We'll leave me till later."

She pressed Angelique onto her back, nestled between her legs. Neon colors played on her back and on her tousled hair. It trailed across Angelique's skin as Stephanie kissed her shoulders and breasts, and her fingers moved deep and slow inside her.

CHAPTER SIXTEEN

A sensual charge woke Angelique. Stephanie was softly kissing her mouth. She was kneeling beside the bed. Dressed in a white shirt, black jacket, and after little sleep, she still managed to look fresh, dynamic. "You taste of peppermint," Angelique murmured.

"You taste of sex." Stephanie kissed her again. Angelique slid an arm around her shoulders, drew her closer. Stephanie groaned. "I wish I didn't have to go. But I got a call while you were asleep." She kissed Angelique again. "I've got to go and catch a thief." She pointed to the bedside table. "I've brought you some coffee."

Angelique rubbed her eyes, looked at the clock. It was eight fifteen. She had to return to her own apartment and get ready for work herself. "I'll see you tonight?"

Stephanie smiled. "Nothing will get in the way of that. I'll call you later, arrange to pick you up after work." Angelique stroked Stephanie's cheek. Stephanie placed a key on the table. "That's for both the door and the gate. Help yourself to everything, baby. Take your time."

After Stephanie left, Angelique got up and opened the blind. Trams trundled past, bordered by cars stacked end to end. She watched Stephanie step outside, lock the gate. She turned at the little Italian café on the corner and disappeared down the lane.

Angelique shivered. She grabbed the cup and sipped her coffee. Life had taken a wonderful, albeit bizarre, turn. She wished the damned job was over so they could get on with their lives together.

The TV was on in the living room. A presenter was giving a rundown of the news. Pulling on a robe that Stephanie had hanging on the back of the door, she went in to listen.

"Last night saw overseas markets trading poorly again as the US dollar took another hit. The Australian dollar is currently trading at parity with the US which is having a detrimental effect on exports. Stocks exposed to export markets are continuing to fall. Commodities, though, were trading strongly in Hong Kong and Wall Street overnight. Pundits predict this bodes well for the local market. Excellent news for investors who committed early to Pacific Holdings Australasia's new oil stocks."

A familiar knot coiled up in Angelique's stomach. She comforted herself with the thought that small investors had been excluded from the initial stock offer. The only individuals able to afford to play the market when trading began on Monday would be very wealthy ones who could weather the loss. And she'd heard from Siow Lian that Kira had a remedy in mind for those left with worthless shares. Once she got her own float underway, in a year or two, she would offer discounted shares to those with small private holdings of worthless Pacific Holdings certificates.

She heard the familiar, but muted ring of her mobile. Racing to the foyer, she fumbled in her bag and snatched up the phone. It was Nolan.

"We've got a problem," he said, his tone cool. "Bloody

banks." He sighed. "I've got this offshore account." Angelique froze. "Simon mentioned it to you," he said.

"Oh, yes. Briefly. When we were going through his reorganization of the accounts."

"Yeah. Well, this bank in Gibraltar has made an error and they're blaming me for it. You won't believe this, but they've called in the Federal Police."

Angelique's heart pounded. Mason had taken the money. She cleared her throat, noting absently that the hand holding the phone was trembling. "What sort of mistake? I don't understand."

"There was close to eighteen and a half million there. The taxman doesn't know it exists. Know what I mean?"

"Uh-huh."

"Anyway, things have been going so well, I thought I'd invest in stock in my kids' names. Max and I set up a trust. After I transferred the cash into the trust account, the balance showed the account two and a half million short."

Angelique felt sick. Two and a half million? Why had Mason taken so much?

"It's clearly a stuff-up on the bank's part. They'll get around to figuring that out. But in the meantime I've got the bloody cops sniffing around. If any of this gets out it'll make the market jumpy as hell. Not to mention the tax office getting curious."

At least Nolan was blaming the bank for the time being. That wouldn't last long. She had to get out of Melbourne immediately. Angelique cleared her throat. "You're right, the bank will discover their mistake. It won't be a problem. You've spoken with the police?"

"Yeah, they've spoken with all of us. They want to talk to you too. They're coming back at ten o'clock. I said you'd be here by then."

"I'll be there. I don't know what I can contribute, though. I've been too busy with the IPO to pay attention to much of anything else." She took a deep breath, trying to calm herself. "Well, as you said, it's probably nothing. Computers, you know... online banking..." She swallowed. "It has its drawbacks."

"Well, once the bank sorts this out they'll have to kiss my arse to keep my business, I'm telling you!"

As soon as Nolan hung up, Angelique switched on her laptop and quickly searched airline departures to Singapore. Her chest felt like it had a ton-weight strapped to it. She could hardly breathe. She secured a seat on a Singapore Airlines flight leaving at one thirty that afternoon, then pulled on her clothes, raced into the bathroom, washed her face and combed her fingers through her hair. Snatching up the key Stephanie had left, she fled the apartment.

Locking the steel gate behind her, she hesitated. There would be no time to meet Stephanie before she left. She would have to phone her on the way to the airport. It was probably just as well. It would endanger Stephanie and ruin everything else. Face-to-face, she might even weaken, confess. She tucked the key into the back of her purse, then raced across the street and grabbed a taxi.

Forty-five minutes later Angelique, showered, dressed and slightly calmer, called Mason from the public phone downstairs from her apartment.

"Hello?" It was Gina. She sounded groggy. It was around midnight in Milan, Angelique realized. She apologized for waking her. "No, no. I just got up to feed the baby, anyway. And Mason..." she chuckled. "He's on his computer, looking at stock prices, you know how he is." Gina passed the phone over to Mason. Angelique filled him in.

"Bloody hell..." Mason muttered. "I took the damn money in two lots last week, shoved it into an account I set up in the Caymans and then quickly slid it into another account after that. I'd even figured out how to replace his funds after selling the shares."

"For god's sake, Mason! It's too late for that now. The police are waiting to talk to me. What am I supposed to say?" She felt like crying. "Why did you take so much?" Her voice cracked.

"Calm down, Angel," he said gently. "The amount doesn't make any difference now. But knowing how high the share price is expected to rise I decided I'd take a worthwhile sum. If we get up around the fifty-dollar mark, and that's looking seriously possible, we'll make a tidy amount for Kira." Mason's voice raised a little. "I don't give a damn about Nolan losing the money. It's not his anyway. He stole it. I won't be able to replace his funds now. The bank will close account access pending investigations. So, Kira gets to keep the profit and his capital, and that's fine by me. And I'd be happy to see the tax department investigate him."

Angelique tore a hand through her hair. She didn't need this. Mason should be as freaked out as she was. "I'm not bothered about principles right now. I'm bothered about being arrested."

"You'll be fine," he said. "You've got a ticket out today. Lucy has already gotten rid of our New York office for Global Explorations. They can't trace this money to me, so they can't trace it to any of us. Stay calm, get on the plane. It'll be over as soon as I sell the stock next week."

"Which better be damned fast."

"Within a day or two," Mason said. "I want a good price, mate."

"Jesus..." Angelique muttered under her breath. He had way too much nerve. "Can you contact Siow Lian? Tell her I'm coming home early. And tell her and the others what we've done. I'll have to lie low till after the stock crashes."

It was right on ten when Angelique stepped out of the elevator. She cultivated an air of confidence as she padded—her shoes safely resoled in rubber last week—across to the reception desk.

Gloria came out of her office, crab-walked up to the desk to meet her. "They're here to see you," she said with a disdainful eye roll. Two men were uncomfortably perched on the sofa's crimson mouthy curves. "Cops." Gloria hissed.

The men strode over. The older one in a gray suit lost his footing, sliding before he clumsily corrected his balance. Gloria giggled. He shot her a withering scowl.

"Ms. Devine? I'm Detective Sergeant Wakefield." Angelique

politely offered her hand. With some unease he accepted it, exposing the frayed cuff of a less-than-white shirt. "This is DC Brown," Wakefield added, introducing his younger sidekick. Brown drew back his shoulders, pulling himself up to his full height—which was a good few inches shorter than Angelique. He was less than thirty, and his hairline had receded prematurely. "You were expecting us, I understand," Wakefield said. His sharp blue eyes scrutinized her.

"Yes. Mr. Nolan said you were making some inquiries regarding a bank mix-up?" Wakefield and Brown exchanged a quick glance. "I don't know how I can help you, but I'm happy to try. Why don't we go into the boardroom?" Angelique said.

"Peppermint tea, Angel?" Gloria called out as Angelique showed the officers into the room.

Angelique gave her a smile. "Later."

Angelique placed her briefcase on the chair beside her and sat down. Side by side the men sat opposite her. Wakefield leaned his elbows on the table, clasped his hands. "We've been sent here to inquire on behalf of the Federal Police. They're providing assistance at this end with an alleged crime affecting the Europa Bank in Gibraltar."

Angelique gave a shrug. "I understand there's an accounting discrepancy. That happens sometimes, but it's usually corrected quite quickly. I really can't see what all the fuss is about."

"The fuss, Ms. Devine, is about a suspected case of Internet fraud involving close to two and a half million dollars." Wakefield's tone was flat. Angelique's stomach churned. Averting her eyes, she glanced at her watch.

"Holding you up, are we?" Brown asked with a smirk.

Feigning a lack of concern wasn't going to help, Angelique decided. They had nothing on her. She mustn't allow them to intimidate her.

"As a matter of fact, you are." She gazed steadily at Wakefield. "I understand you have your job to do, but I would appreciate your getting to the point. How can I help you?"

Wakefield cleared his throat. "Two online withdrawals were made from Mr. Nolan's account last week. The funds were paid into an account in the Cayman Islands. Due to their client confidentiality policies we can't ascertain the name of that account holder. Not at this stage, anyway. In any case, the funds were withdrawn within twenty-four hours, and the account closed."

Angelique felt a wave of relief. They were digging around in the dark. She leaned back in her chair, crossed her legs.

"The Europa account was logged into legitimately. Someone who knew the account information, passwords and the like, made this transfer. That's very few people, Ms. Devine. Mr. Nolan insists that he didn't make those withdrawals. His accountant, Simon Nelson, has had ample opportunity over the past two years to effect a theft of this nature, had he been so inclined. But it happened within days of your arrival, you see. So we think that you might have some idea of how this could be."

"Since my arrival I've been rather preoccupied with the final arrangements for Pacific Holdings' share market launch. Are you sure it wasn't hackers? It's what they do, figure out passwords, account numbers…It's well-documented that banks lose millions each year in fraudulent online activities. Perhaps there's a hole in the bank's security. Have you checked that Mr. Nolan's computer security is all it should be? If his passwords aren't changed regularly, it's possible for someone to access the information in his system via the Internet."

"We're well aware of those possibilities." Wakefield snapped. He yanked at his jacket cuffs. The sleeves were a bit short. "But I'm here to deal with this particular line of inquiry." Brown had discovered his breakfast on his suit and was scratching at it with a stubby fingernail. "You're familiar with Pacific Holdings' accounts, Mr. Nelson tells us."

"Simon asked me to look them over. But I'm a business adviser, Sergeant. Not an accountant. I'm not concerned with the company's banking arrangements." Wakefield stared at her in silence.

"Mr. Nolan has retained my services to assist with a specific business expansion," Angelique continued, pushing the point. "My time here is limited." She shrugged. "I really don't know why this discrepancy has occurred. It's most unfortunate, but it's more likely to be human error than anything else."

Wakefield nodded slowly. "Well, we'll let you get back to work, Ms. Devine. We'll see how the computer experts are getting along with their investigation. But I feel sure we'll have more questions for you later." The officers stood up. "You're in Melbourne for a couple more days, I'm told."

"That's the plan." Grabbing her briefcase, she stood and showed the officers to the door. She hadn't eaten, her heart was thudding, and the total effect was making her feel faint. In a week or so this investigation would probably dissolve, she told herself. In the aftermath of the company's crash, the missing money would be put down to Nolan's dishonesty or stupidity. The bank's obligation to prove the money was legitimately withdrawn would disappear. And so would their complaint. But if that assumption turned out to be wrong, she needed to get well away from Melbourne and Nolan.

Gloria leaned a miniskirted hip against the reception desk, where she and Debbie were chatting. They fell into silence as the officers made their way to the elevator. When the doors closed behind them Gloria gave her hair an indignant toss. "Got a bloody nerve, haven't they?"

Angelique breathed a sigh of relief. "Is Andrew in?"

"Yeah. Just got back from a meeting."

"I'll go and have a word. That tea would be great now if you've got time."

"No worries."

Nolan's door was open. He was sitting at his desk jabbing at his keyboard. At Angelique's knock he swung around. "Come in, Angelique." She sat down. "How'd you go with the police?"

"No problem. I reminded them that banks make mistakes, and also that it's not hard for hackers to obtain legitimate information to get into accounts. The bank would know that. It's up to them to find their security problem, instead of implying that your withdrawals must have slipped your mind."

"To tell the truth, I'm not all that worried about the money. They'll find it, no doubt. I'm more bothered about the fuss the bank is causing." Nolan rubbed his chin thoughtfully. "We're going to look damned dodgy if investors get the idea we can't manage a bank account. And there's the tax office. I've had it if they find out about this account. And then there's the wives." He groaned. "I've been socking cash away into this account for years. Gone through two divorces without anyone getting a whiff of it. If the wives hear of it they'll slam me back into court for a review of the bloody settlements."

Gloria came in with Angelique's tea. "I'll have a coffee, Gloria," Nolan said.

"You just had one. You want me spending all day going back and forth to the kitchen?"

He glared at her. "I want another one, all right?"

Gloria shifted her weight onto one foot, jutted out her hip. She crossed her arms, tossed her hair and stared at him. He fiddled with his computer. "A please wouldn't kill you," Gloria said. He threw her a dismissive glance. "Anyone would think I was a bloody servant."

Nolan's gaze was fixed on her long legs as she sashayed out the door. He grinned at Angelique. "If she wasn't so good to look at, I'd get rid of that girl."

Angelique sipped her tea. "I don't expect this inquiry to become public knowledge. It'll blow over in no time."

He shrugged. "Well, if it doesn't, it might be worth my while to tell the bank I did make the withdrawals. Or an employee did on my behalf, and we doubled up. Made a mistake. Just to shut them up. Kissing two-point-five million goodbye would be cheaper than facing the tax office or the wives."

She was tempted to encourage that move. But it would be odd advice from a caring business adviser. "Look, I wanted to talk to you about my leaving earlier than planned. Something's come up in Singapore that I need to attend to." He looked anxious. "It's another business matter that can't wait. But we've got things well under control here, and my leaving early might actually be to our advantage. I'd be in a better position to monitor the situation in Seragana. Sort out any problems the princess might have."

Nolan sighed. "There could be some fallout over this money drama over the weekend. I'd prefer you to be around to handle damage control in the event investors get wind of it. You've impressed people. If you're the one to tell them it's all a crock of shit, they'll buy it."

Angelique smiled. "Neither the bank nor the police will gain anything by publicizing the matter." Nolan chewed his lip, stared through the window. Over the course of the weekend, with more police badgering, she feared he might begin to share their suspicions. If she waited even a day she might find it difficult to leave.

"Yeah, you're right," he said. "At this point, I guess it's better that you're over there." He grinned. "By Friday next week we'll have our test results. Any glitches in the meantime will be quickly forgotten."

Angelique hid her face in her teacup. She hated these moments when Nolan showed excited anticipation of a rich and powerful future. It was easier when their conversations were confined to mundane objective details. "Has Max got a final contract ready to offer Ms. Na Murgha?"

"Yeah. I met with him about that this morning. In exchange for reasonable royalties, she has to agree to keep off my property and keep her nose out of the entire operation. She's been driving Max up the wall arguing with one proposal after another. We've come to the party as much as I'm prepared to go."

He leaned back in his chair, stroking his tie. "She'd be very unwise to knock-back this contract." His old cockiness had returned. "Her country will benefit nicely from this income. Heaps more than my forestry business offers. And there's a little something included for the princess personally that can be popped into a discreet account somewhere." He laughed. "But I won't be recommending she choose the Europa Bank in Gibraltar!"

Angelique managed a smile.

"Anyway, there'll be trouble if she doesn't cooperate..." Nolan continued. "I mentioned her cousin to you, the one who reckons it should be his backside on the throne. Mbulo would kill for the deal I'm offering. And I mean kill." He wrinkled his nose in distaste. "You know what these people are like. I hate violence, of course. But if Mbulo will do what she's too stubborn to do, then so be it. I can't afford to dance around forever with billions at stake."

Angelique gazed at him in disbelief. Her jumpy nerves

settled momentarily. Her troubled conscience felt washed clean. If push came to shove, Andrew Nolan was prepared to encourage bloodshed to get what he wanted. It was fortunate, in that case, that she was returning early. Kira may well find herself in physical danger.

Angelique took a gulp of her tea and resumed her role. "She'll accept a good offer when she sees it," she said. "I found her to be a very intelligent person."

"She's still pretty unhappy with you, remember." Nolan gave one of his glorious smiles. "You're the double-crossing bitch who brought me her exploration report."

Angelique managed another little smile to keep him happy.

"Still," Nolan went on, "it's all a fait accompli now. And she'd no doubt prefer to talk with you about the contract than Max." He edged forward on his seat. "You know, I've got an idea she might be a dyke." His tone was conspiratorial. "She's got a particular manner…a way about her. Know what I mean?"

Angelique looked at him impassively. "Yeah, I do."

He shook his head. "Shame. She's got something, you know? A change of attitude, a bit of lipstick…sexy dress. Bloody waste."

Angelique snatched up her cup and finished her tea. Many of her clients were aware of her sexuality. In Asia, particularly, people tended to note such things. Perhaps because Nolan was an outsider with the Asian business community, he hadn't picked up personal information about her. Good, she thought. There was nothing intimate that she wanted to share with him.

Nolan glanced at the door. Perhaps he was wondering where his coffee was. "Anyway, Max is sending her a revised contract. I'll get him to add in the covering letter that you'll be in touch to go over it with her. We've built in a bit of movement, you know. So she can score a few points that we don't care about. Max can e-mail you about that."

"Excellent." Angelique stood. "Well, I'm only a phone call away. I'll get back to you early next week. Hopefully by then I'll have Ms. Na Murgha's signature on the contract. I'd better go. The plane I want to catch leaves in just over two hours."

Nolan stood up and shook her hand. "Right. I'll let my

manager in Seragana know to expect to hear from you. Reg Thompson. He'll organize a chopper for you. Talk to Bettina, get her to sort out the details with Reg."

Angelique hurried around to her office to clear her desk. She said goodbye to Simon and Debbie, then thanked Gloria warmly for her help and support. She would miss her ingenuous humor. Despite her casual manner she was well organized and good at her job. When Pacific Holdings Australasia went into receivership Gloria would have no trouble finding a better job, one where she wouldn't be treated like a servant and wouldn't risk her neck crossing the foyer.

Angelique had packed at the apartment earlier and only had to drop by for her luggage on the way to the airport. But she still had to call Stephanie.

CHAPTER SEVENTEEN

"You're barkin' up the wrong tree, mate," Don Williams insisted, tossing Dave a sidelong glance. Smoke spiraled from the roll-up cigarette hanging from the corner of Williams' mouth. He jerked along, his spidery limbs splaying in all directions. Stephanie strolled behind them, accompanied by Jenny Saunders and another detective constable, Peter Meadows. They were heading down a narrow cobbled bluestone lane behind a row of rundown terrace houses. Between buckled stones, puddles gleamed dark and oily. From behind a gray bowed fence a dog started yapping.

Dave glanced around. "End of the lane, Inspector?"

"Yeah, so I'm told. Green wooden doors with 'Asians Out' spray-painted over them."

"Oh, well, there you are, then," Williams quipped over

his shoulder. "If I owned a bloody garage I wouldn't have that painted on me doors, would I? I like a nice Chinese takeout."

Stephanie smiled to herself. Plunging her gloved hands deep into her coat pockets, she glanced at the sky. This morning it was possible to imagine the lemony sun was offering some warmth from that washed-out sky. You didn't get perfect days like this often. When your body felt unfettered, easy. When you felt free and hopeful. When you pulsed with a secret sensuality. And to top it all off, an informer had come through with some vital information that could have her closing investigations into the warehouse burglaries and the attempted homicide of the security guard. She sidestepped a filthy pillow. Right after she'd finished this she would call Angelique. It was eleven forty-five, hours since she'd heard her sexy voice. She felt in her jacket pocket for her phone and realized she'd left it in the squad car outside Williams' flat.

"This looks like the one," Dave said, pointing to a garage in a row of four. The garages occupied tiny backyards. He gave the padlock a tug. "Open it up," he snapped at Williams.

Williams tossed his cigarette into a puddle. It spun in a whirlpool. "Told ya. It's not mine."

"Come on, Williams," Stephanie said. "Someone's dropped you in it. You went too far last time. Shooting people makes even the most loyal friends jumpy. Stop wasting our time."

"I never fuckin' shot anyone!" Williams spat on the ground. "You've been talking to liars."

Stephanie rolled her eyes. "You'd better unlock it, Dave."

Dave stepped back, braced himself, then gave the door a massive kick with the flat of his foot. The timber split away from the padlock with an ear-splitting crack. The doors gaped open. Dogs howled all around. Bright pink bristles of plastic hair rollers crept along the top of the fence next door. A grizzled face appeared. "Police!" Peter called out to the elderly woman. "Nothing to concern you." The face vanished instantly.

Dave pushed the doors wide open. Boxes were stacked neatly right up to the corrugated iron roof. TVs, DVD players, surround-sound systems, mobile phones, computers. At a glance the array of brand names linked the stockpile to every warehouse

job on the books. Stephanie smiled in satisfaction. "Beautiful..."
Dave nodded, chomping on his gum. Marks in the dirt on the
floor suggested a lot of stock had been removed. Already sold, no
doubt. Stephanie peered into a cardboard box on a stack of old
tires. She grabbed a rusty wood file hanging on the wall. Using
it to carefully poke around in the box, she found four black
balaclava masks, four black cotton sweaters, assorted gloves and
a couple of flashlights. "You're a good boy scout, Williams. All
packed and ready for the next job." He averted his eyes. "Where's
the gun?"

"I'm not sayin' nothing!"

Stephanie looked at Dave. "He's all yours. Break and enter,
aggravated burglary, attempted murder." Dave began to read
Williams his rights.

"Attempted murder?" At last Williams was panicking. "I'm
not wearin' that! I never shot anyone!"

Stephanie shrugged. "Well, on the way down to the station
you'd better try and remember who did. Otherwise we'll have
you for it. We don't mind." Dave slid the cuffs around Williams'
wrists and shoved him out into the lane.

Jenny stepped forward. "Will I call for some backup, ma'am?
To catalogue all this stuff and move it out?"

"Yes. And after they arrive, go around to the house and see
the owners of this garage. Find out who they rented it to. Maybe
they're involved." She turned to Peter. "You wait here with
Jenny. I'll head back with Dave." She picked up the cardboard
box. "Forensic will have a field day with this lot." Dave took the
box from her, and they went back up the lane to the car.

Dave pushed Williams into the backseat and climbed in
beside him. Stephanie got into the driver's seat and reached
under the dashboard for her phone. There were five messages.
She waited for a break in the traffic. The cars kept piling up, so
she flicked on the siren. Like the parting of the Red Sea, the
road opened. Planting her foot, she took off. Once the traffic had
thinned, she slowed down, turned off the siren. At the next red
light she flicked through her messages. The last one was from
Angelique.

"Darling, it's me." Her voice jolted Stephanie like an electric charge. "I've had to leave earlier than expected. Something urgent..." There was a vocal tremor, a sigh. She was obviously upset. "I've got no choice but to get back to Singapore today. I'm sorry I can't see you as we'd planned." Her voice sounded choked, as if she was holding back tears. There was another hesitation. "I'll call you as soon as I can. Might be a day or two. Don't try to call me, I'll be out of contact. Please don't worry, darling. Don't be angry. I'll explain everything later." Stephanie's mind was spinning, her heart pounding with worry. "I love you." Then she hung up.

What the hell was wrong? What could cause her to leave early and without warning? And why would she ask that Stephanie not phone? Stephanie swung off the road into the police station. "I'll have to leave you to process him, handle the questioning." She jumped out of the car.

"Sure," Dave said, getting out, dragging Williams behind him. "You got a problem?"

"Yes." Stephanie could feel herself beginning to unravel. "Sorry. I'll be back as soon as I can."

She ran to her car parked against the wall opposite, got in, then hit the recall button on her phone. Angelique's phone was switched off, and there was no voice mail connection. Pulling Angelique's business card from her wallet, she checked the office address, then took off for Pacific Holdings.

Ten minutes later, after dumping her car illegally in front of the building, Stephanie emerged from the elevator into a glassy glittery foyer. She went up to the reception desk. A young blond woman looked up. Out of habit Stephanie pulled her ID from her pocket, displayed it. "Is Angelique Devine available, please?"

"Sorry, she's gone. Returned to Singapore."

"When did she leave? What time's her flight?"

"She left about an hour ago and—" The phone rang. She turned away to answer it. Stephanie clenched her teeth in frustration. She glanced around. Her gaze fell on a large wooden statue at the end of the desk. Its gold paint glinted in the down lights, the robes draped around the dark kneeling woman were richly colored. She had seen a carving just like it before, but she couldn't think where.

The receptionist hung up. "Her flight leaves at one thirty."

Stephanie checked her watch. It was twelve twenty. If she was lucky she might just catch her at the airport. "What airline?"

"Singapore."

"Thanks." Stephanie hurried back to the elevator, hit the down button.

"But you people already questioned her this morning," the receptionist called out.

"What?" The elevator doors opened, Stephanie put out her hand to hold them.

"The police. They already talked to her about the missing money."

Stephanie's stomach curled up in a knot. What the hell was she talking about? "Oh, yes. Right." She got into the elevator.

When she got out front she discovered that her wheels had been clamped. "Fuck!" she muttered under her breath. That was the end of her car for the day. Soon it would be collected by a tow truck and impounded. She would have to deal with that trouble and expense tomorrow. She pulled her phone from her pocket and dialed Jan's mobile. "It's Stephanie. What are you doing? Are you in a squad car?"

"Yeah. I'm just heading back to the station. Why?"

"Have you been called out on anything else?"

"Nope. Not yet. I thought I might grab some lunch for a change."

"I need your help," Stephanie said. "A private matter, and it's urgent."

"Sure, hon. Where are you?"

Within minutes the squad car glided up the hill toward her. It pulled up and Stephanie jumped in.

"What's up?" Jan asked.

Stephanie gulped down her panic. "It's Angelique. She's in trouble. She's about to leave Melbourne, and I've got to catch her at the airport. We've got thirty, forty minutes at most."

Jan gazed at her in disbelief. "What sort of trouble?"

Stephanie willed herself to calm down. She was on the verge of hyperventilating, which was ridiculous after all the danger she had faced down over the years. "I don't know, but cops have been questioning her."

"Shit. Any idea why?"

Stephanie tried to find a clear space to think in her spinning cloudy brain. "It's to do with this job she's on. She refuses to tell me anything about it. There's something very wrong going on there."

"What job?"

Stephanie snapped impatiently. "The oil company job I told you about at work." Jan nodded. "She's been holding back some kind of secret. I bloody knew there was trouble."

"What stage are things at with you two? At the stage where she would normally tell you stuff like that?" Jan asked.

Stephanie raked back her hair. "At that stage, yes."

Jan beamed. "I'm so glad, Steph. She's such a great person, and perfect for you." She seemed to have forgotten the gravity of the situation. "Who would've thought, after all these years. What about Charlotte?"

"Forget all that!" Stephanie hadn't the patience to spell out the details. "There are others involved, supposedly her friends. And some damned princess." Jan shot her a confused sidelong glance. Stephanie gnawed at her lip, remembering the odd comments Angelique had made at the pub the other night. Stuff about justice and the law, and how they often conflicted. "Oh, fuck," she murmured as a horrible thought floated through her head. Angelique was altruistic and she was brave. She had the guts to do something less than legal if she considered there was no option. But surely she wouldn't be so naive.

Stephanie fought back tears. "Jan, what if she's broken the law, done something serious?"

"Are you joking?" Jan looked disgusted at the suggestion. "She spent years working in aid to help people, Steph. She's one of life's good ones."

"God, Jan. I know what kind of person she is. I'm not questioning her integrity, but her actions." She sighed. "I know what she's made of."

Jan shook her head. "If she's got caught up in some trouble it'll be down to someone else. Someone might be leaning on her."

Stephanie willed herself to remain objective. She watched the traffic moving along smoothly, other vehicles keeping a polite distance. They weren't moving fast enough for her liking. "Do you think you could step on it?" she asked.

Jan nodded. "Hold on tight." She flicked on the siren and planted her foot.

This was more like it. Stephanie turned to Jan. "How the hell will I be able to protect her?"

"Settle down, Steph. You're only guessing. Ask her yourself in a matter of minutes."

At ten past one they screeched to a halt outside the international terminal. They ran through the terminal, pushed past tour groups, shoved through queues. Leaping four steps at a time, Stephanie charged up the escalator, Jan right behind her. Pausing outside departures, Stephanie checked the flight list on the wall. A one thirty flight on Singapore Airlines was now boarding. "Gate Six," Stephanie said. They approached an official. Stephanie flashed her ID. "Got to grab a passenger," she said. He waved them through the security check. They ran to the gate lounge.

It was empty except for airline personnel and two men talking to someone beside the airline desk. You could pick them for cops a mile away. The one in a brown suit moved aside, and there was Angelique. Stephanie's insides did a slow somersault at the sight of her. "Who are those cops?" she asked quietly.

Jan shrugged. "Don't know them." They strode over.

"I really can't help you," Angelique was saying to the older man. "There's no point in my coming with you, I can't tell you anything more." She caught sight of Stephanie. Instantly tears glinted in her eyes. She looked cornered, vulnerable.

Stephanie focused her gaze on the older man, showed him her ID. "Is there a problem here?"

He looked her over with some hostility. "No problem at all, Inspector." He showed her his ID. Detective Sergeant Wakefield Stephanie read. He was from the fraud squad. "We're requesting that Ms. Devine comes with us to deal with some pressing questions."

Stephanie's tight chest was starting to actually hurt. "She's about to board a plane."

Wakefield sighed. "We have questions over a serious matter of missing bank funds. We're persuading her that she would be wise to cooperate with us."

"We thought she might leave," the younger cop announced smugly. "So we alerted airport security." He grinned, brimming with the impertinent arrogance of the stupid. "They called us as soon as she checked in."

Stephanie looked down on his balding head, glanced at his stained brown suit. "And you are?" she asked contemptuously.

"He's assisting me. Constable Brown," Wakefield said, tossing Brown a swift glare of warning.

"You obviously have nothing to charge her with," Stephanie said, winging it dangerously. "So I think you should let her get on with her business."

Wakefield sighed wearily. "With the greatest respect, Inspector, I think you should let us get on with our business."

"I have some questions for Ms. Devine, myself. I'd like a few moments with her in private." From the corner of her eye, Stephanie saw Jan pacing nervously.

Wakefield raised his eyebrows. "I beg your pardon, Inspector?"

Stephanie leaned closer to him. She was twitchy, getting angry. "Which bit didn't you understand, Sergeant?"

"You can't interfere with our investigations!" he hissed. "You've got no right!" His face reddened.

"Jesus..." Jan muttered off to the side.

"Excuse me." An airline attendant approached timidly. "If this passenger is traveling on flight 502, she must board now."

"She's not traveling!" Wakefield snapped.

Stephanie shot the attendant a sharp glance. "Three minutes, okay?"

Confused, the attendant retreated to his desk and picked up a phone. Angelique was blinking away tears and trembling. It took all of Stephanie's will not to grab her and hold her tight.

"Let me put it another way, Sergeant," Stephanie said. "Fuck off!" Wakefield drew back as though he'd been hit. He blinked in amazement. Then he stormed off to the side of the lounge, Brown trotting after him.

Stephanie took hold of Angelique's hands. They were ice cold. "Baby, what the hell's going on?" she asked quietly.

"I'm sorry, darling," Angelique said. Her voice faltered. She swallowed. "I don't want you to get involved in this. You'll get into trouble."

Stephanie scrutinized Angelique's terrified expression. "I face trouble every day of the week. I think I can deal with this. Just explain, for god's sake."

"I will. In a few days." Angelique's expression was pleading. "I know how bad this looks, but I'll be okay if I can get on the plane. I'll be safe. If you don't leave this alone, though, you won't be safe."

"Don't worry about me, I know how to deal with—"

Angelique interrupted her with a shake of her head. "I will not involve you!" Her eyes were brimming with tears, but her face was set with that sheer determination that Stephanie knew well. "Everything I've done is for the best. You must trust me. You've always trusted me. Don't stop believing in me now."

Stephanie bit her lip. Angelique wasn't going to budge. She was right, Stephanie trusted her, but everyone was capable of bad judgment. Anyone could be conned into doing things they shouldn't do.

"Sorry!" The airline attendant was snappy this time. "The pilot has informed me that the doors must be closed in two minutes. Traffic control won't let us wait any longer." Stephanie nodded. With a dramatic sigh he stomped off.

Angelique squeezed Stephanie's hands. "Don't be angry, please." Stephanie clenched her jaw. If she wasn't careful she would succumb to tears herself. "Don't get involved any more. Wait for my call." She released Stephanie's hands and quickly brushed her fingers over her cheek. She bent and picked up the bag beside her. "Love you," she whispered. Then she turned to the attendant who whisked her through the departure door.

Jan grabbed her arm. "Come on. Let's get out of here."

Wakefield and Brown stormed back. "You had no right to interfere, Inspector," Wakefield hissed. He was fuming. "You haven't heard the last of this." The two officers turned and marched off.

Jan was looking pale. "You're in serious trouble, Steph."

Stephanie felt shell-shocked. "I had to let her go. I don't know what'll be waiting for her at the other end, but I believe she would be in danger if she'd stayed."

"Yeah? Well, I doubt Houlihan will have much sympathy."

Minutes later they were speeding back up the freeway. Jan shot her a sidelong glance. "I hope you're getting a good story ready. Houlihan will know about this by now. If Angelique's caught up in something illegal, your actions make you look like a suspect yourself."

Stephanie noticed she was trembling. "In my shoes, what would you have done?" she asked.

"I would've encouraged Angelique to forget her bloody flight and go in for questioning." She swerved to avoid a truck that was changing lanes without signaling. "I'd rather deal with Australian police, if I were her, than Singaporean ones."

"It's an Australian matter, surely," Stephanie suggested hopefully. "Nothing to do with Singapore police."

"We have no bloody idea, do we?" Jan said flatly.

Stephanie gazed unseeing through the window. Another concern was swirling in her head. That wooden statue she had seen at Pacific Holdings kept hovering behind her thoughts. Where had she seen that before?

"Shit," she muttered out loud. She straightened in her seat. She suddenly remembered. "Drop me off at the public housing high-rise," she blurted. "I've got to talk to Andrea Burzomi." The statue was Asian, probably from Seragana where Pacific Holdings Australasia conducted its business. So what was Andrea Burzomi doing with a copy of it on her sideboard? Stephanie hadn't noticed them in shops. Besides, she couldn't picture Andrea perusing home-decor stores for an Oriental statue to stick next to her bowl of plastic fruit.

"Now? You've got more important things to deal with, haven't you?" Jan asked incredulously.

"There's something I have to follow up. It might be relevant to all this." She tore her fingers through her hair. "Don't know."

It was close to two o'clock when Jan deposited Stephanie outside the flats. Through Andrea's door Stephanie heard the babble of a TV game show host. She knocked loudly. Andrea opened the door a crack, looked Stephanie up and down. "What now?"

"Need a word."

Andrea poked her head out into the windy walkway, snatched a glance in both directions. "On your own?" She grinned. "Personal visit, is it? And here's me worried sick that you didn't fancy me."

"Don't mess me around, Andrea. Not today."

With a shrug Andrea swung the door open. Stephanie charged straight into the living room. Bathed in a sliver of sunlight that had squeezed through the balcony's mesh guards, the statue was still in place. Andrea skulked behind the sofa, lit a cigarette.

"That carving," Stephanie said, pointing. "Where'd you get it?"

"Can't remember." Andrea exhaled smoke at the ceiling.

Stephanie pulled a tissue from her pocket, covered the top of the carving and picked it up. It was a miniature of the version at Pacific Holdings, but still surprisingly light. She inspected its base. "Product of Seragana" was stamped there in green ink. But the wood had been cut, the letters of the words sliced. They didn't match up exactly. She gave the base a hard scratch, and a small plug of wood fell out. Grabbing Andrea's lighter off the table she illuminated a narrow cavity that ran the length of the statue. Caught in the rough splintery walls of the cavity was a pinkish-white powdery residue.

She turned to Andrea. "So this is the packaging the Yaa Baa pills came in?" Andrea nodded. "Is this the only one?"

"Yeah. I told ya, we only tried that once. Me dad put a stop to it after all that shit we went through. He thought the bloke was going to give me some Ecstasy tabs or something." She crossed her arms, scraped her chin on her shoulder. "Dad probably made sure that idiot got a proper kicking."

Fortunately for Andrea, the investigation into the pills hadn't led to charges against her. Sam, in the investigation team, had told Stephanie that a one-off possession of such a small quantity, coupled with his certainty that Andrea knew nothing of the drug's source, made charges a waste of time. Sam was leaning on George Burzomi instead, although to no avail, last Stephanie heard.

"Why did the delivery man give you the statue?"

Andrea sniffed. "He imports those carvings, he said. Suppose the pills are already in 'em when he gets 'em." She shrugged. "I dunno. He said he thought I'd like to keep the statue. Probably bein' nice because of me dad."

Stephanie groaned in frustration. "For Christ's sake! Why didn't you tell the drug investigators about this? It would've taken the pressure off you. Made you look good for being helpful."

"Would've taken it off me, that's why. And I like it."

"God..." Stephanie muttered. "Get me a plastic bag."

"What?"

"A large freezer bag, or something." Andrea stomped out to the kitchen.

Stephanie carefully replaced the wooden plug. This could lead directly to the importers and distributors of Yaa Baa pills. Maybe even more common and widespread Class A drugs as well. It was unlikely that a company like Pacific Holdings would be involved. But it had a connection with Seragana, a country that until recently Stephanie had never heard of. On the other hand, she had never heard of Pacific Holdings, either, until their oil find made the company famous. They could have been up to anything before that. Maybe in the course of her work Angelique had stumbled onto a skeleton in the company's closet. Maybe she'd been told to clear off, shut up, although she couldn't imagine Angelique putting up with that. Whatever it meant, she had to keep the statue from the drug guys until she discovered what Angelique was up to.

Andrea returned with a freezer bag. Stephanie slid the statue inside it. "I'm hanging on to this for a while." She went to the door, Andrea trailing behind her.

"Will I get it back?" Andrea asked with a petulant whine.

"Just keep quiet about it. You'll probably get it back at some stage." Stephanie hurried to the elevator.

Outside the building she was surprised to see Dave's car. He stuck his head out of the window and gave her a wave. With relief she slid into the passenger seat beside him. "Jan told me you were here," he said. "She thought you were in enough strife as it was, and maybe I should pop round and see if you needed a hand. Give you a lift back, at least."

"Thanks." Stephanie paused to take a few deep breaths. This was the day from hell and it was going to get worse. "I'm in a lot of trouble, Dave." He stopped chewing his gum and gazed at her with a furrowed brow. "I'm going to need your help." He nodded, resumed his chewing. "This carving that I just removed from Andrea's flat," she pulled it from inside her coat, "provides a lead on those Yaa Baa pills." Dave's eyes widened. "But I think it's also connected with another matter. A personal one."

"Shit," Dave murmured.

"I have to keep this out of sight for a few days, maybe weeks while I try to figure it all out." She handed the carving to him. "Lock this away safely. Don't breathe a word to a soul. As soon as possible I'll hand it over."

Dave took it from her, leaned over and placed it in a bag on the backseat. "No worries. You can rely on me. Make sure you let me know if there's anything else I can do."

"Thanks." Stephanie leaned back in her seat. It was damned lucky she had stumbled on this before the drugs team had. The connections looked grim. Pacific Holdings, Seragana, drugs, missing money, Angelique. She wouldn't have had a hope in hell of boarding that plane if this statue had been discovered.

"How did you go with Williams?" she asked.

Dave chuckled. "Bloody beautiful! He cracked. Gave us names, dates...I nearly broke down and wept. Best of all, we got the gun."

"You're kidding!" At least something had gone right today.

"We've already rounded up a couple of the others. One of them, that idiot, Rodriguez, had the gun in his pantry behind a jar of Tim Tams." Stephanie nodded, unable to raise a laugh. "Dumb as dog shit, half these blokes," Dave added.

"That's brilliant. Thanks for doing a great job. Sorry I abandoned you for those crucial few hours."

Dave gave a carefree shrug. "It's all thanks to that informer of yours, really." He turned into the station car park. "Look, I've gotta warn you. The shit's hit the fan back there. Houlihan's furious with you, apparently. They're saying you stuffed up something for the fraud squad."

"Yeah. I did. It was connected with that personal problem of mine."

Dave slung her a quizzical glance. He would be confused by this unprecedented entanglement of her personal and professional identities. She couldn't remember a time in the ten years they'd worked together when she'd ever referred mysteriously to "personal matters." She was changing. Perhaps subtle changes in her view of life generally had begun even before Angelique reappeared. Maybe that's why she'd been so emotionally open to her. But the last week had turned her world upside down. Angelique was once again her life's focus, and judging by today's events, building a life together was going to be quite a challenge.

She got out of the car. Only one thing seemed certain. The best days of her career were probably behind her.

It was three thirty when Stephanie knocked on Houlihan's door.

"Come!" he yelled.

He was standing with his back to the window, his hands in his trouser pockets. He didn't invite her to take a seat. "Where the hell have you been?" he snapped.

"After the airport, I had a couple of loose ends to tie up, sir. Sorry if I've kept you waiting." For a person who had worked hard to ensure she never had to make apologies, she'd cranked up a record number of them in recent times.

"Loose ends?" Houlihan rubbed his bald head impatiently. "I've had a superintendent from Fraud screaming his arse off about you pulling rank on his officers."

He ripped his chair out from under his desk and sat down heavily. "You've made me look like a damned idiot! What the hell did you think you were doing?" Houlihan's expression displayed a cold loss of respect. She had seventeen years of excellence behind her, but now it counted for nothing.

She decided to be as honest as she could afford to be. "It was wrong, I know. But it concerned a friend of mine. They only wanted to question her, and it seemed completely unreasonable to insist she miss her flight."

Houlihan planted his elbows on the desk and glared at her. "It was none of your business, Inspector." He shuffled through papers on his desk. "What have they written here? Oh, yes. You told this Wakefield to fuck off."

Stephanie felt a rush of embarrassment. She couldn't remember ever speaking to a fellow officer that way before. "I shouldn't have done that. Time was short, sir." She hesitated. "I was upset."

Houlihan drew a sharp breath. He glanced at his notes. "So you have a personal connection with this woman, Angelique Devine." He looked up sharply. "Doesn't look good. The fraud boys think she might be involved in the disappearance, the presumed theft, of two and a half million dollars!"

Stephanie gazed past him at the view outside. Two and a half million? That was quite a sum. Her mind detached from the scene for a moment. The sun was hitting the jutting wall of the office building next door. Low in the cloudless sky, on its last legs, the sun's rays were soft and lemony. Maybe spring would arrive early. She hauled her mind back. "I know she wouldn't have stolen any goddamned money."

Houlihan looked furious. "You know, do you? But can you conceive of the idea that she might know who did? That's why we question people, Inspector. They provide information, clues. Questions lead us to answers! Remember?" He sighed wearily. "You've stuffed things right up for them."

"Sir, they hadn't arrested her. They had no charge against her. Obviously it makes life easier for them if she's in town. But she had pressing reasons to go home."

"Tell me, Inspector," he said quietly, "that your relationship with this Ms. Devine is not the way this prick, Wakefield, reckons it looked." He gave a dry cough, stood up and turned to the window. "Wakefield reckons the two of you looked very close." He cleared his throat. "Holding hands, or something, he said."

"The nature of my relationship with Ms. Devine surely isn't the issue. I admit I went against procedure, but I was helping someone close to me who needed it." A sudden resentment swelled in her chest. "I'm sure, sir, that you would've stepped in for someone you cared about. What if it had been your wife, for example?"

He swung around, glared at her with undisguised astonishment. "This is beginner's stuff, Tyler. If it had been my wife I would have stepped right back." Stephanie squirmed. "I would've made sure that I didn't interfere." His words were textbook perfect but she didn't believe him. You had to be placed in that position to know how you'd react.

He gave an exhausted sigh, shoved the papers aside and plonked down in his chair. "A letter of apology first up. Then clear your desk. You're on three weeks leave as of tonight."

"What?" Stephanie felt faint. This was an overreaction. What good would it do to keep her from doing her job? There were the cases to prepare against Williams and his gang. The last thing in the world she wanted was leave. Here, she could start to do some digging around that might throw some light on Angelique's problems. She'd find a way to help her. Sitting at home, she'd be counting every nanosecond waiting on Angelique's call.

"You've got a ton of leave owing," he said flatly. "Use the time to get your life in order. Get your priorities right." He shook his head. "I don't know what's going on with you, Stephanie," he said quietly, "but you're skating on thin ice. I'll appease these blokes down at Fraud. The only thing saving you at the moment is that they had nothing concrete to hold her for. Just be glad I haven't made this a suspension. That would mean a formal inquiry, and that's the last bloody thing we need. Ryan will be Acting DI in your absence." He looked up. "Hand over everything to him and leave by the end of the day. That's all."

Stephanie nodded and strode out. After sorting out her files and clearing up her paperwork, she called Dave in and told him about her interview with Houlihan.

"Jesus," Dave muttered. "Bad timing, what with these cases

to organize. But look, don't worry about a thing. I'll keep in touch, let you know the latest." He toyed with the key to the filing cupboard. "And I'll keep that little trophy of yours safe till you come back or give me the word."

"I've let you down," Stephanie said softly. "All of you."

"No way!" Dave shook his head. "I won't have that. We all have our bad times. Remember a few years back, when I was having troubles?" He sighed sadly. "When my wife took off with the kids, went to her mother's place, and I was a hopeless bloody mess? You covered for me then. People had me in their sights because I wasn't performing, and you saved my arse."

"Of course."

"So, it works both ways." He shrugged. "You're the best, as far as I'm concerned. Upstairs, they can say what they like but I won't hear a word against you." Stephanie's throat tightened. His kindness was breaking down the strong façade she'd had up all afternoon.

"Make the best of the break," he advised. "Concentrate on those personal worries of yours. I'll guess I'll manage to keep the show on the road." He grinned. "But you'd better expect a pile of paperwork when you get back. I'm shithouse with admin stuff."

Stephanie managed a smile. This job had its satisfying side, but there were the horrors to face often. Many days were frustrating, downright miserable. It was only due to friends like Jan and loyal colleagues like Dave that she had managed to hold on, enjoy the good times and be successful. "Look after Jenny and the others. Give them opportunities, utilize their strengths. You're not a one-man band."

He nodded. "Yes, ma'am."

They said goodbye and Dave returned to the operations room.

She pulled on her coat. She would be calling on Dave, no doubt, to have him make discreet inquiries on her behalf. In the meantime she would wait for Angelique's call.

A night at Giovanni's felt like a good idea. She grabbed her briefcase. She would have to find a taxi to get home. At least a few boring hours could be filled in tomorrow while she picked up her car from wherever it was now impounded.

CHAPTER EIGHTEEN

It was almost eight p.m. local time when Angelique emerged from customs at Singapore's Changi Airport. It had been a miserable trip. Events of the morning had kept spinning in her mind. She'd tried to distract herself with a book but found it impossible to concentrate. Watching movies hadn't helped either; her thoughts kept drifting.

She and Mason had taken things too far. Their actions had placed them all at personal risk, possibly jeopardized their entire operation and, worse, created a terrible dilemma for Stephanie, who was completely innocent. She had learned enough about police procedure from Stephanie to know that her intervention at Melbourne airport would get her into serious trouble. And she knew that Stephanie would not quietly wait for her call as asked.

She would be panicking about the mess Angelique was in and starting to dig around trying to figure it all out.

As she approached the arrivals lounge her heart started thumping. For the past eight hours, she'd also been picturing being seized by the Singapore police as soon as she landed. The cops in Melbourne hadn't arrested her, but what if they'd changed their minds? Called in the local police to pick her up?

With relief she spotted Siow Lian squeezing through the crowd toward her. Siow Lian gave her a swift peck on the cheek, her eyes anxiously scanning the crowd. She was tense. "Come on," she snapped, grabbing a suitcase. "We've got to hurry."

Outside Siow Lian charged toward the car park. "I've got a car. Hurry, will you?" They both tossed the suitcases into the trunk and got into the car. Siow Lian's face looked drawn, she was a little breathless. Angelique's anxiety ramped up several notches.

"Are you and Mason mentally ill?" Siow Lian snapped as they headed out of the car park.

"It was a mistake, as it turns out." Angelique rubbed her tired eyes. "A case of bad timing. A day or two later and it probably wouldn't have been discovered before the share trading starts."

"Yeah, well you should've discussed your plan with the rest of us. Gotten some other views, like about the timing, for example." Siow Lian gave a frustrated sigh. "Down there, in the thick of things, you wouldn't be thinking too clearly, and as for Mason…" She rolled her eyes. "He's a bloody share trader. A complete risk-taker."

Angelique gazed out the window, gnawing at her lip. Her preoccupation with Stephanie wouldn't have helped her sense of perspective either. But this wasn't the time to mention that.

"I'm sorry," she said. "I should've just stuck to our plan." Siow Lian turned west onto the Pan Island Expressway. It wasn't the way home. "Where are we going?"

"Once Mason let us know cops were asking questions we spent yesterday working out what to do. We can't risk having cops sniffing around. You can't go home so you have to disappear till after the shares start trading and the test results are published."

"How can I disappear in Singapore for ten days? I just entered through immigration. I'm obviously here somewhere."

"So you're going to Seragana tonight."

Angelique felt like her head was stuffed with cotton wool. "Kira sends her plane over here, I get on it and nobody notices?"

Siow Lian shot her a withering glance. "You must be really tired. Officially using your passport to leave Singapore wouldn't achieve much, would it? You're being smuggled out. Kira's sent a boat."

"Oh my god," Angelique murmured. She swung around to Siow Lian. "I could get picked up by the Singapore border police! I'd be thrown in jail!"

Siow Lian nodded. "Tiny chance."

Angelique felt a rising panic. "This is riskier than my just going home and hoping for the best. Whose brilliant idea was this?"

"Jeremy's. He's a lawyer. He knows stuff." Siow Lian gave a shrug. "He told me where to take you to meet the boat. Kira did some asking around and found out the best places the smugglers from Malaysia use. The coast guard can't monitor them all."

Angelique felt a chill in the hot wind whisking through the open windows. This was all like a bad dream.

They veered onto the Tampines Expressway. "We've arranged a rendezvous," Siow Lian said, "at a point on Sungai Serangoon. An inlet off the Malaccan Straits."

They exited onto a quiet road that cut through open, undeveloped land. Sparsely populated, it was dark and quiet. A short distance down the road they came to a dead end. Down a grassy bank ahead of them was a low brick wall. Beyond the wall the inlet glistened in the ghostly light of a half moon.

"This is the spot," Siow Lian said, switching off the motor and headlights. They got out of the car. "The boat trip takes about six hours or so. You'll get there around dawn. But I'm sure Kira will be waiting up for you." The light from the trunk exposed Siow Lian's scowl as she hauled out the luggage. "She's been very bloody worried."

Angelique groaned inwardly. She wouldn't be too happy to hear about Stephanie either. Aside from the personal level, Kira might be seriously annoyed that Angelique had inadvertently drawn a senior police officer dangerously close to their covert activities.

They clambered down the embankment. A meter below the wall a narrow concrete path extended along the estuary. They jumped down onto the path, dragging the cases behind them. The water was still. There was no sign of a boat.

"We have to go up there." Siow Lian pointed north. "They couldn't moor the boat near any roads or houses." Watching their step in the darkness, they moved along silently. Clumps of wild palms hanging over the path loomed out of the darkness, swatting their faces.

Around a bend, Angelique caught a glint of something in the moonlight. "What's that?" she whispered. She clutched Siow Lian's arm.

"Shit!" Siow Lian hissed. "You scared me to death." She took a few tentative steps forward, peering into the shadows. Suddenly a man stepped out a few meters in front of them. They jumped back with a gasp.

"Siow Lian?" he whispered loudly.

She let out a sigh of relief. "Yeah?"

He came closer. His pants and T-shirt were dark like his skin. Angelique strained to see his expression. His body language furtive, he constantly glanced behind him. Dreadlocks flicked as he moved. "Matawa," he whispered, "the princess's boat. She up a ways." He jerked a thumb over his muscular shoulder. "You Miss Angelique?"

"Yes."

"My name is Tommy." As if it were weightless, he snatched up her luggage. "You go quick," he said to Siow Lian. "She be safe with me now."

Angelique hugged Siow Lian. "I'll call Kira tomorrow," Siow Lian said. "Make sure you got there safe and sound." She turned, scampered back down the path and quickly vanished.

Angelique followed Tommy around another bend in the path. A dinghy was tied at the water's edge. Matawa was moored way out in the deeper water. Dark and silent, it was an impressive size.

The dinghy pulled up beside the boat. Angelique wondered how something this large, this luxurious could go unnoticed.

"It's a bit obvious, isn't it?" she asked Tommy. "Won't the border police easily see us?" Two other men appeared on deck as Angelique and Tommy climbed aboard. They nodded in greeting, smiling shyly.

"They not come near a vessel like this, miss," Tommy replied. "Little boats, poor fishing boats, they carry illegal cargo." She glanced at him. Her expression must have conveyed her doubts. "I have papers, miss," he added with a confident smile. "This boat belong to Seragana royal family. They not dare come on board and search. Big country trouble."

Angelique assumed he meant that a search could cause a diplomatic incident. It made sense. Seragana might be insignificant on a world scale of influence, but it was officially recognized, and nations didn't go around upsetting peaceful neighboring national governments if they could avoid it. She felt a tiny tingle of confidence returning. Her illegal departure from Singapore wasn't worth a nasty standoff between Seragana and Singapore. Still, it might be another matter if Australian police called on Singapore authorities for assistance in investigating a matter of two and a half million stolen dollars. Seragana had to have some sort of diplomatic relationships with its neighbors, maybe even an extradition treaty with Singapore.

Tommy led Angelique through a door off the broad white deck, through a living room lit by a lamp. White shutters on the windows were closed. There were two silk-covered sofas, a TV, a bar. It was gorgeous. Angelique felt her tense shoulders relax. How could she not feel safe here? She couldn't stay in Seragana forever, she knew, but she could hope that their plans for the rest of the week would push her off the police radar, at least as far as that money was concerned.

A narrow corridor led past a dining room and two other rooms. Tommy went into a room at the end of the corridor. "Her Royal Highness gave instruction," he said, "you have the state room." He placed the suitcases down on the turquoise silk rug. An enormous mahogany bed was piled with plump tasseled cushions. These windows were also shuttered. "Bathroom there, miss," he said, indicating a white paneled door. "Bar there." He pointed at a cupboard flush with the wall. "We will stop in

Kuantan Port for fuel, but anyway, we be home by dawn. Please keep shutters closed." Angelique thanked him and Tommy left.

Angelique opened the bar, took some ice from the freezer and mixed herself a gin and tonic, pressing the cold tumbler to her throbbing forehead before downing a healthy gulp. She sat on one of two chairs at the small table by the window. Kira had a lonely and difficult life but there were compensations, she thought, looking around. Within minutes, she heard the low rumble of the engines and felt the boat moving off.

Clangs and thuds woke Angelique abruptly from a sound sleep. Blinking in the half-darkness, she felt for her watch on the bedside table. It was ten past five. She couldn't remember falling asleep. Exhaustion and perhaps that third gin and tonic must have done the trick. She got out of bed and carefully peeped through the shutters. Morning sun bounced off the water, dazzled her eyes. She glimpsed a jetty, but there was no indication where they were.

A knock on her door made her jump. "You awake, miss?" It was Tommy's voice. "We home now. Just tying up."

Angelique felt a rush of relief. They'd made it. She almost felt happy. "Great," she called back. "I won't be long."

She took a quick shower and fifteen minutes later arrived on deck. Tommy, all in white this morning and looking every inch the captain, was striding around checking ropes, snapping orders to his crew in Seraganian. He came over to Angelique, beaming a smile.

"You got us through safely," Angelique said. "Thank you."

"Matawa, miss." He raised his eyes heavenward. "She got us through." He meant Matawa the goddess, Angelique realized, not Matawa the boat.

Tommy sent one of his crew to collect her luggage while she disembarked. The white Mercedes was waiting for her at the quayside. A few soldiers stood by watching over the proceedings. Two others sat in a Jeep behind her car. She had the same driver as before. He touched his cap in greeting as he opened the door for her. They took off for the palace.

Dala came out to meet the car. "Nice to see you, miss," she said, smiling as if Angelique had casually dropped by for a visit on the off-chance. Seraganians were quite imperturbable. A palace attendant strolled down a cool corridor with Angelique's luggage, while Dala led Angelique to the dayroom.

At Dala's knock Kira whipped open the door. She gazed at Angelique almost in disbelief. "Thank you, Dala," she said, her voice a little choked. She closed the door and slid her arms around Angelique's waist, drawing her close. "Thank god you're safe." She moved to kiss Angelique's mouth. Angelique shifted her face slightly and landed a kiss on Kira's cheek. Kira stiffened slightly but for barely a second. Then she stood back, scrutinizing Angelique searchingly. "I've missed you, been worried…"

Angelique headed over to the coffee table where a jug of water and glasses were waiting. She poured two glasses and handed one to Kira. "We're almost done," she said. She took a long drink. "Sorry about this hitch with the money. Mason and I really thought it would be worth it to you."

Kira took her glass over to her usual position near her desk overlooking the garden. "It will be worth it to me," she said. "Unless the whole Twilight plan comes to a screaming halt because of it." Angelique stared at the floor. "But it won't," Kira said, grinning. She had been teasing. "We're too close now for it to hurt. It was a clever sideline for you both to consider." She gave a small shrug. "Aside from the obvious benefits to my people, it will convince the clan chiefs that I have access to money. They'll always be ready to compare whatever I can deliver against rumored promises from Mbulo's followers. Naturally, I'll have to somehow give priority to the provinces where there are difficult chiefs to deal with. Keep them on side."

"Sounds like politics anywhere." Angelique finished her water. She sank down in a feather-cushioned chair. "I still can't help feeling nervous about the police. They jumped on me pretty quickly for some reason. Ironically, Nolan was equally worried, afraid that their investigations would somehow be made public and screw everything up for the start of trading."

"The funds were undeclared earnings, right?" Kira sat down opposite her. Angelique nodded. "In that case he'd prefer to quash any inquiry. It'll cost him more to pay back the tax department and the fines. Then there would be his loss of reputation to deal with." She sipped her water. "In his mind two or so million will not even be worth considering within weeks."

"Yeah, he gave me that impression. But once he'd made the bank aware his balance was incorrect, the bank raised the alarm, not him. I don't think he can stop the inquiries even if he wants to."

"Unless they move incredibly fast their investigations won't impact on our plans. The big day—the dry well announcement—is only a week away." Kira leaned back in her chair and gave a smug smile. "Anyway, no police can get hold of you while you're here. Whether they're from Australia or Singapore I'll deal with them."

"No extradition agreement with Singapore?"

"Oh, yes," Kira said. "Or we'd have all their criminals pouring in here. We don't want that." She smiled. "But they don't know you're here, darling. No trail. That's the point. In any case, they can't just charge in here without permission. I'd stop them at immigration entry points. You forget, Angelique, that in Seragana the monarch controls everything."

Angelique gave a wry grin. "Lucky for me it's not a free country yet."

Kira nodded. "Quite."

"Still, I'd be happier to know the police have dropped the matter."

"Well, darling, Jeremy said they'd have to establish a connection between you and the account the money was transferred to in order to bring any charge. Obviously they can't do that."

Angelique felt a little calmer. At least Kira wasn't irritated and Jeremy wasn't too bothered.

"Come and have some breakfast," Kira said, getting up and heading out to the terrace.

A servant glided away from the table, vanished inside. The table was laid with pots of tea and coffee, a platter of rolls and pastries. "And I think Mason feels a little chastened by the reaction of the others," Kira continued as they sat down, "He phoned just after I spoke with Siow Lian. Lovely man. He wanted to reassure me he's planning to sell all our shares early. Do you know he's hoping to get around twelve million? Maybe more?" She rolled her eyes. "It's fabulous!" She poured some coffee for Angelique and a cup of tea for herself. Then she leaned back in her chair, watching Angelique.

Angelique focused on her bread roll, spreading it with butter and Harrods' raspberry jam. Kira's scrutiny was unnerving her. This reunion would have been happier if she and Kira had simply become firm friends at their first and last meeting. But their acknowledgment then of a mutual attraction meant there were expectations now that Angelique couldn't avoid.

"Tell me about what happened while you were away," Kira said.

Angelique began with her arrival at the office of Pacific Holdings, its ridiculous glossy floors, Gloria and the meeting with the men heading up the float arrangements.

"No, no," Kira said, interrupting her with a wave of her hand. "Something else happened. There's a change in you. Want to tell me about that?"

Kira topped up Angelique's coffee. A peacock on the lawn shrieked and brandished his shimmering feathers. "A personal matter came up," Angelique ventured finally. "Something that's changed my life." She added sugar to her coffee and stirred it, waiting for Kira to throw in a helpful comment. Kira remained silent and still.

Angelique hesitated, gazing past Kira at the garden. Green parrots clustered around the crimson fruits of a fishtail palm. Screeching, they fought over the choicest berries, gulped greedily and pecked at one another. Angelique cleared her throat. "Many years ago, about seven, I met the most wonderful woman I've ever known. We fell in love."

Kira brushed a few crumbs off the table onto the terrace giving the impression that she might quickly become bored with this story.

Angelique stood and strolled to the edge of the terrace. "I couldn't believe it was possible to be so happy. After six gorgeous months we had started planning the details of our future together. Then I wrecked everything by accepting a great career opportunity in Asia."

"So you left her."

Angelique swung around. "It wasn't that simple." She sighed. Naturally she couldn't expect any sympathy from Kira so she decided to get to the point. "We met again by chance when I was in Melbourne, picked up where we left off." She headed back to the table and sat down. "I know you and I imagined things between us might go somewhere...I'm sorry but my future has taken another course."

Kira lit one of her clove cigarettes. The early sun glowed yellow among the palms and was getting hotter. Cicadas began to wail. "What's her name?" Kira's tone was clipped.

"Stephanie."

"And how did you explain your untimely departure to the lovely Stephanie?"

Angelique shifted in her chair. This was where things got a bit delicate. There was no choice but to tell Kira of the chance that Stephanie might make inquiries, in Angelique's best interests, and cause some headaches.

"I don't want to worry you," she began, "but you need to know that Stephanie is a police officer. A rather senior one." With a thunderous scrape Kira pushed back her chair and got to her feet.

"You are joking, aren't you?" Kira's voice was dangerously low. She began pacing up and down the terrace. "She'll know about the missing money!"

"Yes, she knows about that. But nothing else. She knows I'm in some kind of trouble, but she trusts me."

Kira stormed back to the table and stood over Angelique. "If she's any kind of cop at all she'll start trying to piece things together. She could bring this whole operation down!" Her voice was raised.

Angelique suddenly felt a rush of indignation. She stood and glared back at Kira. "She can't hurt the operation, for god's sake, and she can't hurt you!" Kira stubbed out her cigarette. "She'll try to find a way to help me, protect me. But she's extremely intelligent."

Kira rolled her eyes and sighed, indicating that Stephanie's prowess, cerebral or otherwise, was of no interest whatsoever to her. "She's hardly going to share her discoveries with anyone, is she?" Angelique insisted. "While she protects me, she protects us all. And we're talking about a mere week or so."

Kira swiped up her glass of water from the table and headed inside. "It's too fucking hot out here," she muttered impatiently. Angelique sighed, took up her own glass and followed Kira inside.

Kira sat down heavily at her desk. "I don't have time to dwell on the absurdity of this situation. We have to focus on what the impacts may be." She lit another cigarette. She was clearly unnerved. "Will she set out to find you?"

"It's possible, but not immediately. I asked her to wait for my call."

"But you assumed you'd be in Singapore and could call her once the shares started trading in a few days, right?"

Angelique nodded. "I could've told her enough to put her mind at ease, then left the rest till after the test results. The crash."

"But now you're in hiding you can't call. So she's going to come looking."

Angelique moved to the sofa and plonked down. "Probably."

"Right," Kira muttered, as if to herself. "If she finds her way here, I'll let her in, talk to her. If I turn her away she might panic and call for support."

"Stephanie doesn't panic," Angelique threw in quietly.

"My dear Angelique," Kira said through clenched teeth. "Get your head out of the bloody clouds. Whether or not she's the love of your life, she's a senior police officer snooping around while we're committing a rather large fraud, darling!" Kira paused to exhale a stream of spicy smoke. "She could gather enough information to arrest you all!" Angelique kept her eyes averted. "Not to worry," Kira added. "Once she's here I can hold her as long as necessary. At least until we've completed our work."

Angelique's mind drifted to the comical remark she'd made to Stephanie about Kira throwing her into the dungeon. It was peculiar the way reality and providence could entwine.

A sudden knock at the door made them both jump. "Come!" said Kira.

A guard entered the room, bowed his head. "You wished to be advised, Madam. Customs at the airfield called to say Mr. Nolan arrived by chopper fifteen minutes ago, got into a car and has headed here to the palace. He is minutes away." Kira shot Angelique a disbelieving glance. Angelique felt herself pale.

"I'll see him when he arrives. Thank you." The guard gave another quick bow and left.

Angelique jumped to her feet. "That's impossible! I left him at his desk late morning yesterday. There was no mention of his leaving—"

"He's changed his mind, for some reason," Kira interrupted her. "Got a plane to Singapore late yesterday." Servants were out on the terrace clearing up the breakfast table. Kira rose and closed the door.

"His last words were that I was to try to contact you, meet with you and get you to sign the agreement," Angelique said. "His only worry was the business with the bank."

Kira took a deep breath, clearly trying to compose her thoughts. She fiddled with the complicated knot of her turquoise-colored sarong. "His test drilling team has been hard at work out at their site. My people report that a heap of equipment has been set up and quite a large camp for the team. Maybe Nolan just wants to touch base with the boys, so to speak."

"Why now?" Angelique asked. "I don't like—" Another knock at the door halted their speculation.

"Mr. Nolan has arrived, Madam," said Dala.

Kira sprang into action. "Right, take Miss Angelique next door. And grab that, that and that!" In quick succession she pointed to Angelique's purse on the sofa, sunglasses on the chest near the door and the water glass on the coffee table. Dala scooped up the items and opened the door to the adjoining room. Angelique threw Kira one last glance before entering the room with Dala.

Dala placed Angelique's things on a carved sideboard. Scurrying to the side of the room, she closed a series of French doors overlooking another garden. Its focus was a long and wide pergola dripping with purple bougainvillea. Wooden seats placed at intervals on either side of the pergola led one's gaze to the deep-green mountains in the distance.

"Don't go outside, please, miss." Dala looked anxious. "I go now and take Mr. Nolan to Madam." She left.

Angelique's heart was thumping again. Andrew Nolan had plenty of urgent matters to deal with in Melbourne. It was Friday, the last weekday to lock in financial and any remaining regulatory details before the opening of the market on Monday. And there was the final marketing function planned for tomorrow night that Angelique had originally been expected to attend. It was his last chance to charm the champions of business in the city. She gazed outside. Maybe he came here purely on impulse, was simply overexcited.

She heard a knock at the door to Kira's dayroom. Stepping silently up to the adjoining door, she heard Dala announce Nolan.

"Mr. Nolan," Kira had adopted a cool, clipped tone that suggested she was in no mood for a friendly chat.

"Madam," Nolan responded. "Hope you're well." Angelique was surprised to hear Nolan observing protocol in addressing Kira. He'd had so many confrontations with her and spoke about Kira with such casual disdain that she'd imagined him being less correct.

"What business brings you here?" Kira asked.

Angelique thought she heard a little snort or snigger from Nolan. She had to get a look at the proceedings, she decided. Judging from their voices, Kira was at her desk with Nolan facing her. That meant he would have his back to Angelique. Extremely slowly and gently she opened the adjoining door a crack. Fortunately, she was just outside the line of sight of a guard in the room. Nolan was standing in the middle of the room. He was wearing a smart gray suit with a crisp white shirt. Dala was standing near Kira, a few steps behind the desk. The ceiling fans were working at full spin in the high ceiling but were no match for the icy air-conditioning of Nolan's Singapore office. No doubt he'd love to rip off his jacket and sling it on the sofa.

"What brings me here? Well, let's see." Nolan gave his head

a little scratch. "Oh, yeah, a rather large oil venture comes to mind." It was early in the meeting for ego-boosted sarcasm. Kira glared at him, said nothing. "A number of things have suddenly given me cause for some last-minute concern. I thought you might be able to put my mind at ease." He gestured toward a water jug and glasses on a tray on the coffee table. Kira nodded, and he stepped over and filled a glass for himself. He drained the glass at a gulp.

Angelique wished she could see his face. He'd be tired from an overnight flight followed by a helicopter trip. His body language was tense, the set of his shoulders hostile

"First of all, Angelique Devine seems to have disappeared at a rather odd time." Kira gave a couldn't-care-less shrug. "Have you heard from her?" Kira shook her head. "She would've arrived in Singapore from Melbourne yesterday evening, a couple of hours before I left Melbourne. I can't raise her on her phone. I asked her to try to see you, and she's had time to make contact with you by now."

Kira sighed. "Can't help you with that little mystery. What else is on your mind?"

Nolan started to pace up and down, losing patience. "Some money went missing from an account of mine just before she had to urgently leave."

"Well, that's a surprise." Kira feigned a shocked expression. "She helps herself to money as well as confidential oil exploratory reports?"

"For god's sake!" Nolan snapped. "She's a well-respected businesswoman. It makes no sense that she's got anything to do with it unless she's been coerced in some way. Or been set up to look like she's involved. That would take someone with a damned lot of influence. Plenty of heavy-handed clout."

Kira glowered at him, a hint of warning in her voice. "I certainly hope, Mr. Nolan, you're not suggesting any impropriety on the part of the Seraganian government."

Nolan shifted his weight from one foot to the other. Did he really hope that Kira would confess, confide, assist? Angelique wondered. He was way out of his depth. He couldn't touch the crown princess.

"And I've had a call from my manager here. He's overseeing the test drilling operation. They're scheduled to get some oil out of there and tested in one week, but I'm told the geologist in the team has got some concerns." He tugged at his shirt collar as if trying to get a breeze down to his skin. "Very strange after all the rigorous examinations of the original reports to have this guy asking questions about rock formations, wouldn't you say?" His tone was accusing. He was poking around in the dark but seemed to sense that Kira Na Murgha knew more than he did about any number of things.

Angelique felt sweat trickle down her spine. They had all expected that problems with rocks, soil or other technicalities would be recognized at the same time they drilled up water. Discovery of problems prior to the start of trading hadn't been factored in.

"Rock formations?" Kira sounded decidedly bored. Angelique marveled at her bravado. She sat down at her desk. Dala moved forward and poured her some water.

Apparently Nolan had been waiting for Kira to take a seat. He stepped briskly to the sofa and plonked down heavily.

That set Kira off. "Did I invite you to sit?" she hissed. The guard at the door took a step forward. Nolan gave him a quick glance then grudgingly got to his feet. Angelique bit her lip. Nolan's personal contempt for Kira coupled with an Australian's natural abhorrence for kow-towing to anyone might push him over the edge.

"I've just about had it with you!" His voice was raised. The guard made a movement that Kira quelled with a look. "What about the bloody contract, the agreement between your government and my company? You seem remarkably ignorant of everything else but does the contract ring any bells for you?"

"I'll sign the agreement when I agree with it, Nolan!" she snapped.

"You know we can't start production till we have this signed off. And we can't delay production over a matter like this without the share price collapsing." Angelique allowed herself a tiny breath of relief. This was one worry he'd raised that didn't matter a damn.

"I have the future to consider." Kira rose to her feet. "You're talking about a highly valuable resource that belongs to this country." She'd lost her composure now. "It belongs to the people of Seragana! Who the hell do you think you are?" She took a step forward. She was livid. "You're the scum of the earth, Nolan. Everything you see that glitters you must take for your own. It doesn't matter a damn to you that people have lost homes, farmland, water sources, so you can grow rich from our forests—"

He cut her off. "I bloody pay! Taxes, wages!"

"Peanuts! That's what you pay! It's not enough to sustain the people who work for you, let alone enough to repair the damage. How is your business supporting progress in this country? We're worse off than before you set foot on our land."

"I pay the going rate! You can't blame me for your pathetic currency."

Angelique held her breath. Kira stood before him, her fists clenched by her sides. Angelique silently begged her to back off before she blurted out something she would regret. The guard's impervious mask shifted and Angelique glimpsed his hostility. She caught sight of Dala, still as a statue.

Kira took a deep breath, resumed her place beside her desk. She drank some water. Turning to Nolan she spoke more calmly. "I have received your amended contract. It's with my lawyer. We'll get back to you as soon as possible. You must understand, I'm taking a little more care with the terms than the king before me did. If he hadn't been so careless as to give away almost half the country, you and I wouldn't be having this unpleasant conversation."

"Your uncle didn't have an education like yours. He was a useless gambler who didn't have a clue how to get this country out of the past and probably didn't even care." Nolan was clearly unconcerned by the dressing down he'd received and was determined to have the last word. "I helped him become a businessman. Between us we got some enterprise going on here!" Kira clenched her jaw. She seemed to be willing herself not to take the bait.

"If you don't get your act together and do your bit to get this oil enterprise working, I'll have no choice but to turn to someone who will!"

Kira looked like she'd been slapped hard. Angelique imagined she heard her gasp.

"I've had a little chat with your dear cousin, Mbulo," Nolan said sliding his hands into his pockets. His shoulders looked more relaxed now that he'd played his last deadly card. "Mbulo's been following the news of the oil find closely. He's thrilled that his country has a chance to be rich. We discussed in detail, only in theory, you understand, how things might work if he were the crown prince right now. He seemed more than happy with the terms I proposed in my theoretical contract."

Kira's voice came out as a loud whisper. "You've actually discussed business proposals with him?"

"Yes, madam," he said, his hands still jammed casually into his pockets.

"You know the potential volatility here! For the sake of your own business interests you've always had the sense to keep away from Mbulo and his misguided thugs!" Kira was seething again. "You hated dealing with me, but for all your stupidity you seemed to comprehend it was a whole lot better than working with a double-dealing killer like Mbulo!"

"I'm running out of time!" Nolan yelled.

She shook her head in disbelief. "Do you want a bloodbath, Nolan? I couldn't stop that. It's a matter of clans, land, the past."

"It would hold things up a bit, I grant you," he replied. "But things would be settled at last, we could progress."

Kira's face was shocked and pained. Tears pricked at Angelique's eyes as she imagined the horror churning in Kira's mind.

"Look," Nolan added in a quieter voice. "I don't want any of that, obviously. I just wanted you to be aware there are options and to remind you of your obligations to enterprise in Seragana." He gave a little shrug. "Just want you to see sense."

Kira turned her back to him and gazed outside through the open doors. Her shoulders tensed. "You have threatened me, Nolan," she said. "You've openly threatened the state. Your political intrusion may have placed the population at risk." She swung around to face him, her face set like ice. "Crimes against the state are dealt with harshly in Seragana."

Nolan withdrew his hands from his pockets and held them up defensively. "No, no, you've got the wrong end of the stick," he said. He'd gone too far and it was good watching him squirm.

"Leave the country by tonight!" she snapped. She cast a small but obvious glance toward the guard who was glowering at Nolan with open hostility. "I'd consider leaving sooner, if I were you. Either way, you will not return until our business is concluded to my satisfaction."

"Madam," Nolan said in a conciliatory tone. He wasn't all that far from kow-towing from Angelique's point of view. "I'm a citizen of Seragana. You can't really prevent me coming and going as I please."

Kira's icy expression was unchanged. "I can do as I like. Now get out."

She sat down and shuffled some papers on her desk. Nolan seemed frozen to the spot. The guard opened the hallway door, preparing to deliver Nolan to another guard who was waiting outside. Nolan quietly left the room.

Kira spoke to her two staff, her voice measured. "Thank you, that will be all."

Angelique's pulse thumped loudly in her temple as she watched what followed. Kira's staff, in one crystallized moment, demonstrated the magnitude of her personal, political and cultural importance to the people of Seragana. Dala knelt beside her chair, her head bowed. "I stay here with you, Madam," she said, her voice choked with emotion.

The guard cleared his throat. "I stay too. Please, Madam." She turned to him and he dropped his head in a deep bow.

Kira stood. She gently touched Dala's arm, bringing her to her feet. "Thank you both. Everything is under control. Protection outside the rooms is sufficient," she said. The guard nodded. "Please arrange a meeting for this afternoon with the head of palace security. And see that an urgent message is sent to the chief adviser to come and see me." Angelique remembered Kira's mentioning Onbulu at their first meeting. He was wise and trustworthy, a powerful supporter of the Na Murgha family, someone she could rely on for help and advice.

"Yes, Madam." He bowed his head again, then headed out into the hallway.

Dala discreetly wiped at her eyes. She was clearly frightened for her princess. "Haven't we still got a guest next door?" Kira asked. "Please bring her in to see me. And perhaps some tea would be nice."

Dala's face looked a little brighter as she headed toward the adjoining door. She looked momentarily surprised when it opened and Angelique entered the dayroom. "It's okay," Angelique said. Dala nodded and went out to arrange the tea.

At her desk Kira sat with her head in her hands. Angelique hurried over to her. "Kira, I heard everything."

Kira got up. She looked and sounded suddenly exhausted. "And watched everything too, I noticed."

"Of course," Angelique said. Instinctively she put her arms around Kira and hugged her tightly. "Nolan's losing his nerve, for some reason. It's illogical that he'd call on Mbulo now, after all this time." Kira seemed soothed by the affection. Her rock-hard shoulders loosened a little. "Doesn't he see that political unrest would be as off-putting to investors as any other scandal?"

"Come and sit down." Kira led her to the sofa.

"What do you expect will happen?" Angelique asked.

Kira took a cigarette from the box on the table and lit it. In the noon silence the spices crackled softly as they burned. "I'm going to seek advice from Onbulu, but I expect Mbulo will begin to stir up some old discontent, perhaps mobilize some activists. Don't really know." She exhaled a white plume of smoke. "We'll need to reinforce security around the palace and public buildings."

There was a knock and Dala entered with a tray that she set down on the coffee table. There was a small pot of coffee, one of tea and a platter of tiny soft white cucumber sandwiches. "Lovely, Dala," Kira said.

Angelique ate a sandwich as she poured herself a coffee. "Obviously you'll go into hiding, right? Leave any skirmishes to your security people?"

Kira looked at her in amazement. "I can't go into hiding, Angelique. I'm in bloody charge!"

"But you have to be protected as the—"

Kira dismissed her comments with wave of her hand. "The palace is government headquarters. Like Parliament is elsewhere. It's also home to the monarch. This is where I have to be, this is where they'll look for me. Do I want violent people searching through the town and countryside for me, causing terror and mayhem?"

"The people revere you, they would want you safely away from any danger."

"I'm all they've got." Kira managed a humorless smile. "They revere me because they believe it's my birthright, my destiny and my duty to lead the country." She gave a tiny shrug. "Well, the vast majority do, anyway. Tribal chiefs manage day-to-day domestic matters in the villages, but otherwise, I'm it! I'm responsible for the economy, foreign affairs, education, health—" She stopped and bit her lip. She looked suddenly overwhelmed as if the burden of her situation was really hitting home.

Angelique gulped down some coffee. She willed herself to remain calm. In her aid-work days she'd witnessed the aftermath of social uprisings. But an imminent coup d'état was too much to even grasp.

Kira sighed. "Don't worry. I'll be fine. Nothing might come of it at all. Nolan could just be mouthing off." She finished her cup of tea. "Let's hope so, anyway."

"Seven days of peace and no further grumbles from Nolan about money, rocks or anything else and we can all relax." Angelique smiled. "All your problems, Mbulo included, will be solved forever."

Kira smiled too. "Quite." She stood up. "But in the meantime we need to move you to safety." Angelique's heart sank again. "I'm sending you to the Royal Villa."

"I'd rather stay here. Give you some support."

Kira shook her head. "Out of the question. No trouble-makers will go near the Villa; it's a vacation palace these days." She gazed at Angelique. "It's beautiful there. My father built it for my grandmother. Traditional architecture, breezy verandahs...

It's beside a protected atoll on the sea. Good for swimming."

Angelique rubbed her throbbing forehead. She was in no mood for a holiday.

Kira gave the bell on her desk a little shake. Dala appeared at the door. "Dala, you're to accompany Miss Angelique to the Royal Villa. You're to stay with her until I send for you both. Take three or four palace servants with you and Lim—" She turned to Angelique. "He's from Singapore, a wonderful cook." Angelique and Dala exchanged a wondering glance. Kira's consideration of such details at a time like this was bewildering. "Go now and collect Miss Angelique's luggage. And please send Haku to see me."

Dala left the room and the guard who had been present earlier entered. He bowed his head. "Haku, I want you to arrange transport to the Royal Villa for Miss Angelique. Use one of the old jeeps, not the limousine. Have the driver in plainclothes, not a uniform. Transport the staff and supplies separately and discreetly."

"Yes, madam."

"Arrange a squad of armed guards to protect all parts of the villa. I want them inside and outside, around the clock. Understood?"

"Yes, madam."

"No one enters or leaves the villa's grounds without my personal permission. And no one involved is to speak a word to anyone."

"Yes, madam."

"Thank you, that's all."

Kira turned to Angelique as Haku closed the door. Angelique was blinking back tears. She couldn't help believing she was partly responsible for the peril they all found themselves in.

"All we have to hope for now," Kira said dryly, "is that your Stephanie doesn't drop by for a visit."

"God…" Angelique murmured. Another day or so without word from Angelique and Stephanie would be itching to take some action. "When Siow Lian contacts you, tell her to phone Stephanie on her private number." She grabbed her purse and dug around for Stephanie's card. "Siow Lian's got to convince her that I'm safe and everything's fine. Persuade her to stay home and wait for me."

Kira turned the card over in her hand. An amused smile twitched at the corners of her mouth. "If I were in her position, that would be like a red rag to a bull."

"Well, if she does come to Seragana, don't let her in!" Angelique blurted. "I don't want her in physical danger."

"I have to let her in, as I've already explained. Better she gets some answers here than she takes her questions elsewhere." Kira sighed. "No one can be trusted right now. Not even her, I'm afraid."

Dala returned. "Everything ready, Madam. Jeep waiting with luggage."

Kira took Angelique's arm and briskly kissed her cheek. "I'll keep in touch."

"Take care of yourself," Angelique replied in a whisper.

CHAPTER NINETEEN

Stephanie put on her bathrobe and began toweling her wet hair. She headed out to the kitchen and poured a cup of tea. She ran her thumb over a tiny chip on the teapot's spout. It was a beautiful Chinese pot that she and Angelique had chosen on a shopping trip during Angelique's first year away. She hadn't been able to bring herself to throw it out. They would buy a new one soon, she told herself. She wandered into the living room, plonked down on the sofa and flicked on the TV. It was seven in the morning on Sunday.

Absentmindedly toweling her hair she focused on the current affairs show presenter. "All eyes this week will be on the world's newest oil stocks that will start trading at the opening of the market tomorrow."

The picture dissolved to an overhead shot of a large island.

Stephanie inched to the edge of her seat. "The tiny kingdom of Seragana, in the South China Sea," the presenter continued, "the location of the new discovery by Pacific Holdings Australasia, suddenly finds itself in the world's spotlight." The image cut to a shot tracking past the Royal Palace, followed by one of some extravagant colonial-style homes, then to a panoramic view of a bluer-than-blue harbor replete with yachts. "While some wealthy businesspeople, mostly from Singapore or Malaysia, call the capital, Ngali, their second home, the majority of the population live in poverty in the rural provinces. They stand to benefit greatly from the wealth to be generated by this investment by an Australian company." Shots followed of camera-shy families outside basic wooden huts with thatched roofs, kids shinnying up trees and knocking down coconuts, men tossing small fishing nets across the river.

Stephanie sipped her tea. It could be any one of a million geographically beautiful, poverty-stricken places on earth, she thought. And like most of them, the people's poverty and ignorance would be benefiting someone nicely. In independent countries like Seragana, it was usually the monarch, sultan or dictator, sometimes in cahoots with foreigners.

Stephanie sighed in exasperation. This was exactly the sort of place where Angelique's aid work had taken her. It seemed too much of a coincidence that she'd taken a job assisting a company to exploit oil in a dirt-poor country with so many problems. What had drawn her to Seragana in the first place? Stephanie wondered. Was it the money to be made or the poverty to be addressed? Angelique seemed to completely trust the princess, but she hadn't known her long. On the other hand Angelique's silence about the company and its activities telegraphed to Stephanie that she wasn't nearly so trusting of Andrew Nolan.

"Good morning, thank you for coming in." Stephanie jumped to her feet and stepped closer to the screen. The presenter was interviewing Andrew Nolan. "You've had business interests in Seragana for many years, I understand," the presenter said.

"Yes, my timber business there has been highly successful and I believe has been of great benefit to the general population."

Stephanie inwardly groaned. She knew that in an undeveloped

country covered in tropical rainforest, "timber business" meant old growth logging. So that locked one piece of information in place. There was no way Angelique would want to do business with this company. Something or someone was compelling her to work for this guy.

He had an annoying habit of sliding his expensive-looking tie through his fingers and flashing movie-star smiles at the drop of a hat. "I'm fortunate to enjoy an excellent business relationship with Crown Princess Kira," he went on, "and I'm looking forward to further assisting this beautiful country to progress toward a prosperous future."

"Further assist…" Stephanie muttered aloud contemptuously. Where were the shots of the hospitals, roads, bridges and schools that had been built with money generated by the activities of Pacific Holdings? But it was obvious this was a promotional interview. There would be no hard questions for Nolan while he was the latest stock market darling. A lot of people expected to make a lot of money, probably including the owner of this TV network.

The program cut to another story. Stephanie switched it off.

After blow-drying her hair she headed into her bedroom and put on jeans and a black sweater. Sitting on the side of the bed she pulled on a pair of black ankle boots, the same routine she'd followed on Friday morning and again yesterday, as if she had a clear plan for the day. Friday had left her seething with frustration. She'd spent much of the day on the landline to Dave, helping him prepare the cases, every nerve in her body primed to respond when Angelique made the promised call to her mobile. On top of that she'd had to fork out over five hundred dollars to collect her car from the impound yard.

Yesterday, the start of a weekend, was even worse. Angelique's call still did not eventuate. She felt an urge to charge out the door, resolve this mess immediately, get answers like she always did. But it was a lot harder to get answers when you couldn't ask questions for fear of making matters worse. It was as if she were tethered to some invisible pole, confined to movement in an endless circle.

She needed to get out, get some fresh air. A glance out the

window showed a clear sunny day. She pulled on her tweed overcoat, grabbed her wallet and her laptop. Tapping her jeans pocket, she made sure her mobile was there. She would do some investigating about Seragana on the net while she tried to enjoy a good breakfast. Then tomorrow when Dave was back at work she might have some sniffing around for him to do.

She locked up then headed down Collins Street to Federation Square. It was always teeming with people, there might be a music event on the public stage. A crowd would make her feel better, more connected to the real world.

Stephanie looked up from her computer screen and squinted into the sunshine filling the public space with some welcome winter warmth. She slid her sunglasses on and leaned back in her chair. A dance troupe from West Africa was giving a performance on the stage, their real-life movements dwarfed by the projection of the performance onto an enormous screen behind them. People lounged on deck chairs provided by the city and low plant-edged stone walls that defined the areas, spaces and levels.

She caught the attention of the waiter. "Another cappuccino, when you've got a moment."

It was getting on for eleven o'clock and she was feeling a lot more positive. Her breakfast bacon, eggs and pancakes had done her good. But even better, her Internet investigations had yielded something.

Seragana's government website didn't offer much of use to her, its focus being population figures, crop information and exports—mainly Nolan's timber, it seemed. But scraps of information from other sites had helped. She had come across a photo posted by a traveler of the carved statue that linked Pacific Holdings and Andrea Burzomi. The traveler explained it was an image of Matawa, a goddess central to Seraganian religious beliefs, yet it had been purchased in southern Thailand. Stephanie hadn't been able to discover how the carving came to be there or where else, outside Seragana, they could be purchased.

That provided another firm link to the carvings and

Thailand's Yaa Baa pills. But who was exporting the carvings from Seragana? It seemed highly unlikely that a big, about to be huge, company like Pacific Holdings Australasia would bother with such a tiny enterprise. And it seemed at least as unlikely that the company had anything to do with drug smuggling. Still, Angelique was tangled in these connections somehow and that gave Stephanie more reason to worry.

Her coffee arrived. Stephanie spooned sugar into the cup and stirred it distractedly, studying the list she'd made of tasks to attend to tomorrow morning. They included a call to Pacific Holdings' office in Singapore. That was closer to the target than their Melbourne office. Their website was brimming with information about the oil and how to invest and sales advice about their timber. Nothing about handicrafts, but maybe their sales manager could throw some light on the subject.

Sipping her coffee, she gazed at the giant TV screen. The rhythmic music and sensual dancing soothed her nerves. Research about Seragana's exact location and how to get there had put things into perspective a little. Stephanie was prepared to bet that if Angelique wasn't in Singapore, she'd be in Seragana.

Stephanie flicked her computer screen back on. Commercial airlines didn't fly to Seragana. Private craft required a pre-clearance at the airport. But there was a passenger terminal near their industrial wharf. The Port of Singapore international terminal would be the place to head for if she needed to get to Seragana.

Suddenly her phone rang. Shock and anticipation sent her body into meltdown. She fumbled to get the phone from her jeans pocket. She glanced at the phone to see the number. It showed, "Withheld."

"Stephanie Tyler." There was an echo, a few beeps. Her heart started to thump. It was an overseas caller.

"Hello, Stephanie." The woman had a Chinese accent. "I'm calling for Angelique."

"Where is she? How is she?"

"She's fine, no problem. She's safe but can't talk to you now. She says you are to wait at home till she can phone you. And she said you are not to worry."

Stephanie willed herself to calm down. "You're a friend of Angelique's? Can you tell me your name?"

"No need for names. She's my best friend."

"Siow Lian?" Stephanie asked hopefully. At least knowing that Angelique had friends close by offered some comfort.

After a long hesitation, the woman affirmed her identity. She was being cautious but not hostile. "Angelique told me about you years ago. I know she would be very happy now you're together again. But…" she paused, "the timing is not so good."

"You haven't spoken to her yourself?"

"No. I got a message to call you."

"Who from?" Stephanie blurted. She heard the woman take a ragged breath. Clearly, Stephanie's questions were spooking her. She didn't want the woman to hang up. "Sorry, it's just that I'm worried half to death. Please tell me, why is Angelique in hiding?"

"Not so much in hiding. More being very discreet right now." That was an interesting take on the situation, Stephanie observed. "You're a police officer, you know that sometimes it's important to keep your head down. Angelique can't afford communication trails at the moment."

"Is she in Singapore?" Another long hesitation at the other end.

"Moving around a bit. Unless there are any holdups, she'll call you on Saturday." Saturday was a long way off, and what did Siow Lian mean by "holdups"?

"I've gotta go," Siow Lian said. "I look forward to seeing you in Singapore when everything is back to normal."

"Please give me your number—" The call ended. Stephanie sat staring at the phone in disbelief. There had never been an investigation in her life as important as this one, yet her one live lead had just slipped from her grasp.

A gust of wind off the sea blew the *Tribune* onto the terrace floor. Angelique bent down, gathered it up and set it back on the polished bamboo table. She held it in place with the water jug.

She got up and wandered to the edge of the wide stone terrace where flame-red hibiscus and a tangle of palms spilled down the rocks toward the beach. In the pale sky a shimmer of tangerine signaled the beginning of sunset. Angelique raised her face to the clean salty wind and closed her eyes. It had been a long, hot day.

It was Sunday. She hadn't heard anything from Kira since they parted on Friday, but she knew Dala was in constant contact with the palace. Many times in the past forty-eight hours she had asked her if there was any news. Dala had answered no with a reserved but calm expression, so Angelique was at least confident there had been no violence and Kira was still safely in charge. There was no way of knowing, though, if Nolan was pushing ahead as planned in spite of money and rock mysteries or if something else had cropped up to cause him concern.

Angelique slowly walked across the terrace. On the other side, beyond an expanse of lawn, two guards stood near the high stone wall surrounding the villa. Another guard was lighting bamboo torch lamps around the garden's perimeter.

She stepped through the open doorway and entered one of the villa's vast sitting rooms. She switched on a lamp and sat down on a silk-covered sofa, its design of multicolored tropical fish dominated by the turquoise of Seragana's seas. Saturday's *Straits Times* and Ngali's city paper had arrived after lunch today. Angelique had scrutinized the papers for any hint of negative news about Pacific Holdings. There had only been a mention in the Singapore paper of the float's first day of trade tomorrow. There was no mention in the Ngali *Tribune*. She picked up the TV remote and switched on the TV. The one Malaysian provider of the mobile phone and broadband network had blessed Ngali with cable TV too. Angelique was so relieved to have it that she wasn't even going to dwell on the lack of competition. She flicked through the stations looking for anything that might mention the share market or Seragana. Nolan had woken the sleeping dragon, Mbulo, and he might sabotage the oil float just to cause problems for Kira.

Suddenly the screen flickered and cut to black. The lamp went out too. The electricity supply was unreliable, especially at this time of day, she had learned. The palace would have backup generators, no doubt, but it was oil lamps and candles at the villa.

She got up and lit an oil lamp. She was edgy, restless. She kept reminding herself that if there were news that mattered it would reach her. Silence at this time was no bad thing. They only had to get through to ten a.m. tomorrow Melbourne time and they'd be reasonably safe on all fronts.

Thoughts of Stephanie scratched constantly at the back of her mind. Wondering what she was planning, worrying about how she was coping. She wanted to contact Siow Lian to see if she had spoken to her. But until she had Internet access she remained cut off from the outside world and the Twilights. There was no connection at the villa. Needing anonymous access she had asked Dala yesterday to send for a prepaid mobile USB modem for her laptop, from Ngali. It hadn't shown up yet.

A servant lit oil lamps down the long hallway outside the sitting room, exchanging greetings with the guard, Haku, who had spent much of his time in that hallway since Angelique's arrival. It was only six p.m.; she had showered and dressed following an afternoon swim, and dinner was still a ways off. She decided to head off to the kitchen. Maybe Lim, the cook, was there and would like a fellow Singapore resident to talk to.

"Miss," Haku said in greeting as she passed.

There were so many corridors. As she passed through them, making her way toward where she thought the kitchen was, guards watched her every move. Eventually kitchen-type clangs drew her into a large space with a glossy polished stone floor and matching counters. Oil lamps added a magical tone to the rustic room, illuminating counters piled with baskets of mangoes, papayas, cabbages and beans. A woman in a headscarf was energetically grating a coconut. A young man was peeling chunks of ginger.

"Hi there," a voice rang out. Over by a newer section of stainless steel counters stood a young Chinese guy. He was smiling, wiping his hands on a towel. "I hear you're from Singapore."

"Hi, you must be Lim. I'm Angelique."

"Any requests for dinner?" he asked. "I'm thinking of glass noodles in sweet soy, tossed in minced chicken and chili." He grinned. "And maybe Hainanese chicken rice."

Angelique swooned at the mention of chicken rice. "Heaven!" she said. It was the favorite dish of virtually everyone in Singapore. She nestled onto a high stool at the counter. Behind Lim, propane-powered gas jets had pots and woks simmering. The air was fragrant with galangal and garlic. "That's a huge pot of rice you've got there," she said, pointing.

"I've got the staff to feed too," Lim explained. "The household and thirty guards."

"That many?"

"In and around the villa and at points along the road. They come in for dinner in shifts." He lifted off the lid carefully and forked out a sample. Satisfied it was cooked he turned off the heat. He poured two cups of jasmine tea and handed one to Angelique. "They grow amazing rice here, you know," he said. "Nutty, a touch of sweetness. Asians would go mad for it. They should export it."

"Well, they could do with some local entrepreneurs," Angelique said. "With some education, some money, a lot could change here."

"And their cloth too," he added. "Brilliant quality cotton fabrics, unique prints." He shrugged. "I've got half a mind to quit cooking and start a trading business here." Lim leaned across to direct a kitchen hand to slice some chicken paper thin.

"What's stopping you?"

He took a sip of his tea. "Well, I wouldn't be confident in a country like this. The place needs organizing, you know? A proper workforce with proper rules. You feel like anything can go wrong here. I mean, it's not a democracy, is it?"

Angelique took his point but couldn't help feeling inwardly amused. "Singapore's not exactly a democracy either," she said. "They say it is, but it's not. The opposition is only a prop."

"Yeah, let them find out you voted for the other guy and they cut off your water!" They both chuckled. "But it looks like one," Lim added. He cast a glance out the window at a cluster of guards. "Anyway," he continued, "there's trouble brewing here. Something about the oil I thought, but the guards say it's politics." He shrugged. "That's why I wouldn't start a business. Why I probably won't stay long." A kitchen hand signaled to him. "Got to hurry now," Lim said to her. "The first crew's in for dinner."

"Miss! There you are! I look for you. I have thing you want." Dala bustled into the kitchen and handed Angelique a small package. It was the Internet connector. Angelique felt almost dizzy with relief. She thanked Dala, resisting the urge to hug her, and hurried back to her sitting room terrace and her laptop.

It was two hours before Angelique got her connection working. Haku had noticed her muttering and cursing earlier and offered some advice. "It's the clouds, miss," he said. "Storms behind mountains." He shrugged. "Internet not work. Have to wait."

So she had waited. The natural world would not be ignored in Seragana. It wasn't shoved behind tall buildings or smothered in concrete. You felt it, heard it, scrutinized and smelt it all day, and despite technical frustrations Angelique had begun to find that reassuring.

The power came back on while she was waiting, so she watched some TV while having dinner. Lim's chicken rice was sublime. Eating off a tray while settled on the silken sofa watching Discovery was almost as cozy as a night at home having takeout.

"Yes!" Angelique murmured to herself in delight. She had finally connected to Facebook using her identity, "Blue." Chat showed Siow Lian was online. Angelique sighed with relief. She clicked on Siow Lian's identity and typed:

I've missed you, Lotus. How are you?

All good here, Blue. Concerned about tension at your end. Should be okay, at least till after we are done.

Did you call S?

Yes. Very worried. Told her you said to wait till end week. Sounds nice.

Was she convinced? Will she stay there?

Probably not but who knows? You know what she does for a job.
Had a lot of questions. You okay?

Yes, but scared. Haven't heard from K. Want to finish this soon.

Will be soon. Enjoy a holiday. <g>

They signed off and Angelique checked through her messages. There was one from "Lord," Jeremy's guise.

Blue, darling. You did a brilliant job! I hear you're jumpy about the fund-raising methods of a colleague, but relax. No trails to find. They may as well question the cleaner! Will land on HIS head later. Lotus told me about S! Hope she stays put. Look forward to meeting her, but sad there'll be no Royal Wedding! Hugs and kisses!

Angelique allowed herself a smile of satisfaction. Contact with her friends had improved her perspective. Life was bubbling along as usual in London, Milan, New York and Singapore. Jeremy had the comforting ability to reduce a complicated problem to a minor irritation in just a few words.

Suddenly her screen froze. Her connection was lost. She sighed in resignation. Checking her business e-mails would have to wait until tomorrow. She had given Jeremy access to her e-mail account so he could keep a sharp eye on communications from Nolan that might require attention. No doubt he'd already waded through a swamp of vitriol. But she wouldn't mind seeing if there were other business inquiries to attend to when this project was safely behind her.

"More coffee, miss?" Dala was holding the coffeepot. Angelique accepted another cup. After she left, Angelique gazed at the dark sea. A tiny flash in the sky caught her eye. Then another larger one illuminated the clouds for a second, followed by a distant rumble. Feeling calmer than she had in days, she decided to have an early night.

Stephanie paused to switch off the TV before placing her teacup on the small dining table under the window. It was early afternoon on Monday, and it seemed that all she had heard from the TV all morning was about the surging price of Pacific

Holdings' shares. In just a few hours they'd already increased in value up to forty percent. She assumed Angelique would be happy about that, at least, regardless of whatever had sent her into hiding.

It was ten a.m. in Singapore. She picked up her phone and dialed the number for Pacific Holdings. It was answered after a few rings by a pleasant, efficient young woman.

"Can I speak with your sales manager in relation to exports from Seragana?" Stephanie asked. There was a click before the phone was picked up again.

"Bettina Chan speaking. How may I help you?"

Stephanie gave a story about wanting to import handicrafts from Seragana for a new home décor business. "I'm particularly interested in the carvings produced there of Matawa. I'm hoping to develop a theme around that image in fabrics and so forth."

There was a tiny sigh at the end of the line. "We're a rather large company with broad business interests. Here in this office we deal with the export of quality raw and dressed timbers from Seragana, but not handicrafts, I'm afraid."

"There's not a lot of information available about trade there," Stephanie continued. "Perhaps you could direct me to a person or business who could help?"

"Perhaps you should call their department of trade and industry," Bettina Chan suggested. "Although that can be a slow process. They won't be there on a Monday."

Stephanie was feeling reassured already that Pacific Holdings had no connection to the carvings or the drugs. That reduced one area of danger where Angelique was concerned. She gently prodded Bettina for more information.

"There's a business in Ngali," Bettina added helpfully, "that imports and exports. They handle all kinds of items. I have their number somewhere…" After a short delay she gave Stephanie a name and a phone number.

Satisfied so far, Stephanie took a gulp of her tea. She focused on drops of rain clinging to her window. A glance at the street below showed people wrapped in coats, holding umbrellas. The sky was split into gray and blue segments, as if it couldn't decide on what sort of day to be.

She picked up her phone again. Dave was due to call soon, and it would be ideal to have her information about the carvings ready for him.

She dialed the number Bettina had given her and heard the ring signal alter, indicating the phone number was being forwarded to another line. "Yah, hello?" The line was scratchy, obviously a mobile with poor coverage. The man's voice had a Malaysian accent.

Stephanie explained her business, asked if he could supply carvings and other works.

"You need to place an order," he said. "But it would need to be big or else not worth it." He explained he was in Kuala Lumpur and went to Seragana periodically to deal with shipments in or out. "I pack and ship out carvings when the guy in Seragana sends them down to me."

"What guy?" Stephanie absentmindedly doodled circles on her notepad.

"He live up in the hills, on an old plantation. Been there for years. He knows the locals and the hill tribes and he buys some of their handicrafts."

Stephanie felt a tingle of success. Sounds like my man, she thought. She asked for the man's name and number.

"Reg Thompson. I give you his mobile but he be pretty busy right now with this oil business. He work for Pacific Holdings. You heard of them? Big in news."

Stephanie took down the number, thanked him and hung up. A connection to Pacific Holdings existed after all, but not one that bothered Stephanie too much. Angelique was working for Andrew Nolan, not his foreman in the hills. She pictured Reg Thompson. Middle-aged, well-paid, with a native wife living in a Third-World rich man's paradise. He didn't fit the pattern of the type to deal in drugs, but you could never be sure till you knew the stakes being played. The carvings could be a side interest for him. Either way, Reg and the exporter between them would be able to provide Dave and the drug crew with the information they needed to trace the Yaa Baa drugs into Australia.

She got up and headed back to the kitchen with her cup. Her phone rang. It was Dave at last. She had asked him to see what he could sniff out from Fraud about that money and their interest in Angelique.

"I got onto my mate, down there," he said. "Told him we had an interest in that bank in Gibraltar. Some other complaint a while back...I was vague. He didn't care."

Stephanie found herself gripping the phone too tightly. The question of misappropriation hanging over Angelique was a constant black cloud in Stephanie's mind. While she was confident she could sort out problems where other parties might be making life difficult for Angelique, there was little Stephanie could do to protect her if the cops produced evidence of grand theft. "What's the story?"

"They've dropped it. Closed the inquiry."

Stephanie thought she'd faint with relief. "Why?"

"Story is, the bank made the complaint to authorities because the account holder, Andrew Nolan, raised an alarm about his balance. Apparently, he has since revised his story. Told the bank the withdrawal was legitimate and had been overlooked. So the bank has gone away happy."

"Two and a half million had been overlooked?"

"Yeah. Sounds unlikely, doesn't it," Dave said. Stephanie could hear him chewing in the pauses. "The bank must've thought so too. Told him to take his business elsewhere, apparently. Of course, the Fraud guys know he's covering something because his company's in the news. Wouldn't want bad publicity."

"Well, it's his money," Stephanie said.

"Exactly. Anyway, point is, there's no further interest in Angelique Devine." Tension began to uncoil in Stephanie's shoulders. At least Angelique was in the clear as far as the law was concerned. But Nolan was obviously up to something, and Stephanie still had to know how that impacted on Angelique. One tiny step after another seemed to place Angelique closer to safety, yet she was in hiding till Saturday. What was happening in the meantime?

"You're brilliant, Dave," she said, a smile tugging at her mouth. "And as a reward I've got some information you can use to make yourself look pretty good."

"This should be quite straightforward," she said, after enlightening him on the procurement and export of Matawa carvings and giving him the names and numbers she'd collected. "They only originate in one place, and one of them is sitting in your locked filing cabinet." Dave was thrilled. "There's only one proviso on this. Wait till next Monday to pass on the information. Not a word before then." Dave agreed and they finished their call.

By Monday, Stephanie reassured herself, she would have spoken to Angelique one way or another. In the meantime, she had to balance her fears for Angelique's safety with regard for her wishes. She could have any number of reasons, even shady ones, to be playing this waiting game. All Stephanie knew for certain was that Angelique's motives would be pure. If Stephanie barged in like an elephant she could ruin something delicate that had taken Angelique an age to set up.

On the other hand, Angelique's plan could be full of flaws, or she could be surrounded by double-dealers. If she hadn't called by Saturday, as Siow Lian promised, Stephanie was going over there to find her.

Angelique stirred, then woke up. Had she really heard a noise? Or had it been a dream? She gazed for a while at light flickering on the wall from a flame torch in the garden. Crickets continued their song undaunted. There was the occasional chirrup of a frog. Her eyes began to close.

Then she bolted upright, her heart pounding. There was no mistaking the noise this time. It was gunfire in the distance. Dala burst into her room. "Miss, stay calm!" She was holding an oil lamp.

Angelique jumped out of bed and grabbed her bathrobe. Snatching up her watch, she saw it was three a.m., Wednesday. She flicked at the switch of a lamp a few times, but the power was out. "What the hell's going on?" she asked.

"They say it Mbulo's men. They outside Ngali," Dala replied.

Angelique felt faint. "Heading to the palace? Is the princess there?" she asked in a half-whisper.

"Yes, miss."

Angelique pushed open one of the French doors to a long vaulted verandah beside a lawn. Guards in pairs charged along the garden perimeter wall, guns in hand. There was some shouting, in Seraganian, probably of orders. "Do you know where the rebels are exactly?" Angelique asked.

"Haku say they miles from villa and not at palace yet. He say not worry. Too many guard, not many rebel. He say for you to stay inside and calm. Please go to sitting room, miss, and I bring you tea,"

Trembling, Angelique headed down the gloomy corridor, past the flickering oil lamps and nervous-looking guards, into the sitting room. Another burst of gunfire made her jump. It was a short volley and no closer than before. Dala knocked and entered with a tray.

Suddenly Angelique lost patience with the formality and protocol. She craved normality, especially against a backdrop of blazing guns. "Where is everyone?" she asked. "Lim and the others?"

"In the kitchen, miss," Dala replied.

"Right," Angelique said. She plucked the tray from Dala's hands and marched toward the corridor. "Let's go there."

Standing at the bathroom mirror on Wednesday morning, Stephanie brushed and blow-dried her hair. She was feeling more optimistic than she had in days, increasingly sure that a positive conclusion to Angelique's mysterious predicament was close. She'd also had a good day yesterday with her father.

Angelique's untimely departure and her own forced vacation had given Stephanie plenty of time and incentive to examine her personal life. She realized that since their relationship ended six years earlier, her heart had closed again, bit by bit. In their early days together, Angelique had encouraged Stephanie to take emotional chances, to venture beyond the walls she'd erected after her father's arrest and incarceration. Angelique, who took people as she found them, had never had any reservations about James. She'd helped Stephanie see that he was intelligent, warm, funny and, by that time, no longer a gambler.

The TV presenter's sing-song patter drifted into the kitchen as Stephanie poured boiling water into the teapot. After her breakup with Angelique, she had resumed much of her old caution with James, maintaining contact but on her terms and at arm's length. Her reunion with Angelique was a reawakening. It was time to move on, clean up personal messes, so she'd called James on Monday. When he mentioned he was having some improvements done on his boat the next day, she had offered her services to help move furniture.

James had a woman in his life, she had discovered, a retired lawyer who lived in Byron Bay. He seemed happy to have a chance to share the news with her and overjoyed to hear hers about Angelique. They had such a good afternoon, they continued into the evening. Stephanie had taken him to a Hutong dumpling place in Chinatown where they had slurped hot soupy dumplings and drank ice-cold Chablis until quite late.

Stephanie poured tea into her cup, then paused, straining to hear the TV. Had the presenter just mentioned Seragana? She went to the living room.

She froze as she took in the images on the screen. Outside the Royal Palace there were dozens of armed soldiers. A pan down the city center showed soldiers positioned at intersections and down near the harbor. The picture cut back to the presenter. "This outbreak of violence is expected to take a huge toll on Pacific Holdings' oils stocks when the market opens this morning. It's believed the outburst is directed at the crown princess. As king, her uncle oversaw a peaceful period in Seragana's history. But he took the throne only after the princess's father had been assassinated."

Stephanie began to shake. This turn of events was way beyond anything she had imagined. There was no way she could wait any longer. She raced to the dining table, powered up her computer and began searching for flights to Singapore. Within fifteen minutes she had bought a ticket on Singapore Airlines. The earliest flight with a free seat, it was due to depart at midnight.

Angelique was exhausted, but wired, jumpy. It was close to seven in the evening on Wednesday. She'd been assured that the violence of the early hours had been contained, that the princess was safe and well, but she would feel a lot happier when she heard that directly from Kira. Dala had brought a message that Kira would phone her this evening.

Seated at her bamboo table on the terrace, she picked at her dinner. Lim had cooked to order a perfect steak, fries and salad. She had eaten half of it but without appetite. Nothing seemed to have much flavor, including the glass of red wine that she had almost finished.

The day's newspapers were in a tangle on the table where she had left them. Seragana's troubles and the plight of Pacific Holdings' oil stocks were front page news in the *Straits Times* and Ngali *Tribune*. The shares had fallen to below their opening value as soon as the market had opened in Melbourne this morning. TV news throughout the day reported markets around the world had followed suit.

This was a major setback. The last thing Angelique and the Twilights wanted was for the shares to languish. The worst that could do would be to delay Nolan's move into production. It was only when the oil tests showed no oil at all that the stock would be completely wiped out. Those results were legally bound to be published on Friday before the close of the Australian Stock Exchange. But if Nolan was still harboring concerns, or his geologist was, this civil unrest could provide him the opportunity to obtain an exemption from that obligation for a time.

Angelique slid the *Straits Times* closer and re-read its report on the situation.

Palace spokesman, Mr. Onbulu offered reassurance to the people of Seragana, and the rest of the world, that a minor uprising overnight had been completely crushed, without loss of life. The Royal Guards quickly brought the matter under control, he said. Crown Princess Kira Na Murgha has requested that people resume their normal lives and business as usual.

Angelique's heart skipped a beat as the phone on the table rang. She snatched it up. "Kira? Are you all right?"

"Everything's fine," Kira replied. "There were about two dozen rebels, very disorganized, and they didn't get close to the palace. Two of my guards and eight of the rebels received gunshot wounds. No one was killed, I'm pleased to say."

Angelique was relieved. Listening to the bursts of gunfire last night she had visualized a small army on the attack. "What have you done with the rebels?" she asked.

"Most of them were caught, arrested and questioned till the early hours. They're all from villages in Mbulo's province and claim Mbulo suggested they make a bit of noise."

"Don't they understand that you're on the throne legally, that Mbulo has no legal claim? No right to interfere with the rule of law?"

Kira sighed. "These are ignorant men, related to Mbulo, who were given the idea they would benefit personally from Seragana's oil if they helped Mbulo move in. Interestingly, the chiefs in that province were not involved."

"They must've known about it," Angelique suggested. "Isn't it their job to keep the peace on a village level?"

"I think they adopted a wait-and-see attitude." Kira paused, Angelique caught the click of a lighter and the crackle of burning cloves. "Onbulu and I have called an emergency meeting for tomorrow with all Seragana's clan chiefs. I'm going to address them about changes coming to the country. Advise them that new laws will be drawn up and that, where I deem it useful, they'll be consulted about them. One of the first will be a ban on firearms throughout the country. They'll be reminded of their obligations under law, both Crown and traditional laws, to protect their monarch and keep the peace."

Angelique felt a tingle of excitement. She gulped down the rest of her wine. Kira was taking them on, and she wasn't going to stand for any nonsense. Real strength was essential for the future and Seragana's citizens had to know who was boss.

"Over time they'll be groomed for a democracy, and the role of the chief will become cultural only," Kira went on. "Ways will be found to accommodate traditions."

"In the meantime, how do you stop Mbulo?"

"His rebels have been charged with sedition. They'll face trial and if found guilty they'll be imprisoned." Kira paused for a draw on her cigarette. "A few slipped away. An urgent search is underway. We'll find them. Guards are posted everywhere and on high alert. As for Mbulo, we know he's in Singapore. There's a warrant out for his arrest on a charge of treason." Angelique gasped. Treason sounded like a step into medieval history. "We'll get him, with or without Singapore's assistance. If he's found guilty, we'll throw away the key."

"Who's organizing all these cases for the Crown?" Angelique asked, although she could guess.

"Jeremy, of course, darling. He's getting a team together that includes the palace legal advisers. He agrees with me that we have to take the hard line if we're to move forward."

"Well, no one will need be afraid they have a wimp for a monarch," Angelique said, a smile on her lips.

"Quite."

"That still leaves our problem with the stock price and our Friday test deadline."

"Yes," Kira agreed. "But I noticed on the news just before I called that there are dreadful problems in the Middle East. Real and justified uprisings that make ours look like a romp in the park. The market might decide our stock's not so bad after all."

They arranged to talk again on Friday, then said goodnight.

CHAPTER TWENTY

Stephanie stepped outside Changi Airport to grab a taxi. It was just seven in the morning, but already the day was as hot and steamy as a sauna. She had forgotten Singapore's relentless heat. There was a familiar perfume in the air too. Despite the fumes of a crammed and busy city, the scent of Asia somehow persisted.

Her first stop was the boutique hotel she had booked online. A renovated British colonial building on the edge of Chinatown it had agreed to an early check-in. At least she wasn't tired, she thought with relief as the taxi driver loaded her suitcase into the trunk. She had no trouble sleeping on planes, could sleep leaning against a post if she was tired enough. But she was desperate for a hot shower and a change of clothes.

It was just after midday by the time she began to thread her way through the packed streets of Chinatown. Finding places was never easy here, with businesses inside other businesses burrowed into the nooks and crannies of building after building. She'd had to ask repeatedly for directions. Finally, she stood outside a building that had been described to her and perused the store list out front. "Paradise Gardens" at last. Eager for some air conditioning she stepped through the automatic doors.

Past some coffee-drinkers in the front area she came to a food hall packed with people. She paused, wondering where she might find Siow Lian. People pushed past her to a counter just ahead. "Hey, Siow Lian," she heard a woman say. "Any of Chong's chicken curry left?"

"Of course, honey. Take a seat."

Stephanie scrutinized the woman who had replied. Lean but not skinny, her compact body was a study in coordinated efficiency. Almost quicker than the speed of light her hands lifted lids off steaming pots, poured soup into bowls, slid noodles onto plates, tossed food in a wok, and all the while she yelled instructions to her busy team. She had black spiky hair, dimples and a warm smile.

Stephanie stepped up to the counter. "What can I get you?" Siow Lian asked.

"Chicken curry, please, and some tea," Stephanie replied. Siow Lian gave her a second glance. Maybe it was her Australian accent. "I'm Stephanie," she added.

Siow Lian's mouth fell open. She gazed at Stephanie in amazement. "Sit over there," she instructed, pointing to a free table in a corner. "I'll come over."

Stephanie felt closer to Angelique just seeing Siow Lian. She was someone who had seen Angelique regularly in recent years, someone Angelique cared about. She sat down. Depending on what Siow Lian had to say, a trip to Seragana now seemed unavoidable. She'd gone to Angelique's house before coming to the coffee shop. She was pretty certain Angelique wouldn't be there, but she had to check. It was the cop in her, she supposed. After ringing the bell several times she had stood for ages just looking at the garden and up at the windows. It was a lovely Peranakan house. It had been easy to imagine Angelique in there cooking, working or sitting in the garden she had described at the back.

Siow Lian plonked down a tray containing a steaming bowl of curry, another of rice and two big cups of jasmine tea. Looking frazzled, she sat down and stared at Stephanie. "You and Angelique make a great pair," she said. "You're almost as stubborn as her."

The curry smelled appetizing, and Stephanie realized she was starving. She spooned up some curry and rice. It was as delicious as it looked. "Great curry," she said.

"Best in Singapore." Siow Lian crossed her arms. "Angelique isn't in Singapore."

Stephanie nodded. "So, she's in Seragana." Siow Lian looked down at the table. "Come on," Stephanie said gently. "Where else? Are you going to start pretending she's in Paris or something?"

Siow Lian took a gulp of her tea. "You can't go to Seragana."

"Why not?"

Siow Lian sighed. "Don't you read the papers? There's been some trouble there."

Stephanie had done some checking on the Internet and hadn't seen any suggestion that the country had closed its borders. "Don't you see? That's exactly why I have to go and find her. I can't keep simply believing she's safe when there's reason to think she's not."

"She's okay, really." Siow Lian looked anxious. "Just stay in Singapore a couple of days. You'll hear from her soon." She managed a watery smile. "I'll keep you company. We'll go somewhere for dinner, one of Angelique's favorite places, and you can tell me all about yourself. The plans you both have." She was a really nice woman. Stephanie didn't doubt that she genuinely believed what she was saying about Angelique's situation.

Stephanie dabbed her mouth with the napkin. "You know that I'm a cop, right?" Siow Lian nodded, looking a touch uncomfortable at the reminder. "I'm unable to accept your view about Angelique's safety, not because I mistrust you, but because I know that people make mistakes. Loyalty can make them blind. And people like Angelique..." She paused and took a deep breath. "She's very determined and convincing. She might

think she's safe, but she may be unwittingly caught in a trap."
She shrugged. "I won't know till I find her."

Siow Lian bit her lip. Clearly, just like Angelique, she was
hiding something big.

"I'm damned sure that something less than lawful is
going on," Stephanie continued, "but whether that may harm
Angelique, I don't know."

Siow Lian slumped back in her chair. Snatching up her cup
she gulped the rest of her tea. "Don't know how you'll get there,"
she mumbled. She sounded defeated. "There's no planes."

"Boat," Stephanie said.

Siow Lian's head jerked up, her expression suspicious. "Never
heard of that," she murmured. Stephanie pulled her wallet from
her jeans pocket. "No, you're welcome." Siow Lian waved away
the money. They both stood up. Siow Lian gripped Stephanie's
arm. Her expression was one of genuine concern. "You take care
of yourself," she said. "I'll see you again soon." Then she raced
back to her counter and a queue of waiting people.

An hour later Stephanie was standing at the bookings
counter at the International Passenger Terminal at the Port of
Singapore.

"Seragana?" The man at the counter twisted around and
scrutinized the large map on the wall behind him. It included
Singapore, Malaysia, Indonesia, a bit of Thailand, Seragana and
a sprinkling of islands. The map showed routes from one port to
another, and even she could see there was no spidery line joining
up Seragana with anywhere else. "You're the first person who's
ever asked." He sat down and clicked a few keys on his computer.
"Funny," he added. "till recently you never heard of Seragana,
now you hear it every day." He grinned. "The oil. The cruise
companies might soon have to add a route there." After a few
more clicks, he shook his head. "No ferries or cruise liners cover
it, I'm afraid."

Stephanie was starting to feel frustrated. "There's got to be
a way if planes don't fly there."

"Private planes would fly in," the man said. "They've got an airport of some sort." He shrugged. "You could go by private boat."

That was more like it. "How do I find one of those?"

He pointed through a window that overlooked a berthing dock. "Any of those private cruisers are registered to travel throughout those parts of the South China Sea. They're licensed to carry passengers. That is, they've got accredited crews, meet safety requirements, and provide adequate personal facilities. You'd have to find one who's happy to go there and make a private arrangement."

Stephanie nodded. "No visa required, I presume."

"You Australian?" She confirmed she was. "No visa, same as any of these countries." Stephanie thanked him and headed out to the wharf.

A number of private cruisers were lined up in a neat row. A few men that she assumed were crew were hanging around on decks chatting, some working on ropes or polishing timbers and windows. Stephanie caught sight of a small group of men who looked more senior, perhaps boat captains, chatting under an awning closer to the terminal building. They all wore shirts carrying the Port of Singapore logo. She wandered over to them.

They nodded at her politely. One said, "Are you looking for your boat? You have to embark from the building, via immigration."

Stephanie smiled at him. "Actually, I have to organize my trip first. I was advised to talk to a boat owner." They all paid her closer attention. "I need to get to Seragana." They gazed at her in silence for a beat, then began shaking their heads, stepping away.

One guy, taking pity on her, moved closer. "It's just that we work by getting small group bookings to go to a destination. We're an alternative to the cruise liners." Stephanie nodded her understanding. "If no one's got a group booked to go someplace, they won't go there for one person."

Even under the awning it was as hot as hell. The black silk tank top she was wearing allowed air through but it had started to stick to her skin. She raked her hair back from her face. It seemed ridiculous that there wasn't some traffic back and forth to Seragana. But perhaps those wealthy people she had seen on the TV news had their own cruisers or planes, and maybe everyone else in Seragana just stayed put.

"It would be a matter of money, I suppose," she ventured.

"Of course," he nodded somberly. "Isn't everything?"

"Which one's your boat?" she asked. He pointed to a fine-looking cruiser. Three or four crew members were up on deck. "Could you take me there?"

He gave an awkward laugh, then scratched his head. "I've got bookings for two trips around the Singapore islands this afternoon," he said. "Maybe later in the week…"

"What about tonight?" She slid off her sunglasses and gazed at him.

"Overnight…" he rubbed his chin. "It's about six hours, and I have to return, of course. A lot of fuel, a lot of crew overtime."

"How much?" she asked.

"Do you want a cabin?" She hesitated. "It's clean and comfortable. Three stars. There's a hot shower in there." He shrugged. "Cheaper if you want to sit up all night."

Stephanie was already concerned that this was going to be expensive. But there was no other way for her to get to Seragana, at least, not immediately. She might as well have the cabin, get some sleep, have a shower in the morning. The thought of turning up on Seragana tomorrow without those things was off-putting. She would need her wits about her, and looking disheveled wouldn't help. "I'd want a cabin," she said.

"Give me a minute," he said. "I'll talk to my crew."

She watched the crew gather around him, turn to look at her, then resume their discussion. He climbed down off the boat and returned. He gave her a price that almost gave her heart failure. She could fly to London and back for that money. She cleared her throat. "When could we leave?"

"Tonight, or actually, early in the morning. I'll have to get the trip logged, but two a.m. should be okay." Stephanie agreed. He beamed a smile. "I'm Jian." Stephanie shook his hand. "Come to the booking counter with me," he said, "and we'll book it all in and get you a ticket." They headed inside the terminal. Stephanie paid and was given a ticket by the man she had talked to earlier.

"Get back here by one a.m.," he said. "You'll board the boat from a gate once you're through immigration." He grinned. "Seragana, overnight, eh? You must have some urgent business up there."

Stephanie stepped out of the terminal back into the mid-afternoon sun. Her business was urgent all right, but she'd be a lot happier if she knew exactly what business it was.

She grabbed a taxi and headed back to her hotel. She decided to stay cool indoors for the rest of the afternoon. Maybe watch a movie to take her mind off things. There was a nice looking Beijing-style restaurant a few doors from her hotel, and she might head there for a late dinner before returning to the Port.

CHAPTER TWENTY-ONE

Stephanie's alarm woke her at seven the next morning. She sat up in her bunk and took a look through the tiny porthole. The sky was a dazzling blue, the sun glittered on a sea that was smooth and benign. No sign of land yet. She had climbed into her bunk within minutes of leaving Singapore, intending to read for a while. But instead of keeping her awake as she expected, the constant regular thrum of the boat's engines seemed to have lulled her to sleep.

She got up and squeezed into her tiny shower. At least the water was hot and the pressure good. She took her time getting ready, drying and brushing her hair carefully, then dressing in a charcoal-colored linen suit. She liked the suit because it said "business" without being overly formal and because it was lined in silver-colored silk that gave an unexpected flash of light when she moved. Her plain silk camisole underneath matched. She put on her watch, packed up her things and went up to the main cabin.

Jian came out to her. "We had a good trip, did you sleep?" Stephanie smiled and confirmed she had. "I'll send someone with your breakfast," he said. "Only cereal and fresh fruit, I'm afraid. Tea or coffee?" She asked for coffee, placed her jacket over the back of her chair and sat down to enjoy the view.

She had just finished her mango when she spotted land. Jian strolled over. "There she is," he said. "Seragana. Let's hope they're happy to receive visitors right now."

Her heart skipped a beat. There was that to consider, she thought. Although Angelique was her focus, in a place where guns had blazed in the street only two days ago she had better watch her step.

Standing at the rail Stephanie watched their approach. It was almost eight o'clock. She could see the wharf clearly now and some buildings that she assumed included the passenger terminal. Beyond the wharf was a tangled mass of palms and enormous bright red flowers. Hills rose in the distance, covered in rainforest. It was like a poster for a tropical holiday. As they drew closer she saw people on the wharf. They seemed to be marching or patrolling.

She became aware of Jian beside her, and they were soon joined by three crew members. One had a pair of binoculars trained on the wharf. "Soldiers, boss," he said. "Lots of them."

"Radio in," Jian snapped. "Let them know who we have on board. I want some kind of clearance." Jian and his crew dashed off. Stephanie felt a knot of tension in her stomach.

They slowly rolled up to a large jetty. It was attached to an enclosed walkway leading to a terminal building made of dark-stained timber with broad verandahs and a high thatched roof. They were close enough that she could see ceiling fans spinning inside its glass walls. Behind her Jian snapped orders to the crew, as four soldiers on the wharf marched toward the boat.

Jian appeared at her side. "All seems okay," he said. "The guy on the radio sounded friendly enough." He picked up her luggage and walked with her to the boarding ramp. "All the best of luck," he added, and they said goodbye.

Two soldiers came up to her as she stepped onto the wharf. While the uniforms were clearly military, they were predominantly turquoise in color. They looked fabulous, like a militarized version of some ceremonial dress. If not for the guns on the men's hips and the M-16s cradled in the arms of their colleagues further down the wharf, the men could have been a welcoming team for tourists.

"Good morning, miss," a soldier said. "Your passport, please." That was quick, she thought. She hadn't even entered the arrivals building. She noticed she was a little breathless as she fumbled for her passport. The soldier scrutinized it. "Thank you, miss. Come this way, please." His tone was clipped, but not especially hostile.

Wheeling her luggage behind her she followed the two into the terminal. She was given the usual arrivals card to complete, and her passport was stamped. She was given a thorough going-over with a metal detector, then her luggage was taken away.

She was directed through a gate to a car park. The soldier who had led the proceedings so far snapped his fingers and a car glided up. A Mercedes complete with uniformed chauffeur. The soldier barked some orders and another soldier tossed Stephanie's luggage into the trunk and opened the rear door for her. Stephanie knew she was not a wanted guest so the nice car and the personal service only increased her apprehension. She ventured a question. "Where am I being taken?"

"To the palace, miss," the solider replied coolly. She got into the car. A soldier hopped into the rear seat beside her and another took his post up front next to the driver. Her door was slammed closed and the car took off.

Stephanie glanced at the soldier beside her, but he unflinchingly kept his eyes on the road ahead. The knot in her stomach was turning into a rock. There was no way that Angelique could be safe in this place, she thought. It was another world, closed, cut-off from everywhere. Angelique—and now she too—could be held here indefinitely without anyone being able to do much about it. Australia had no consulate in Seragana and, for all she knew, no diplomatic relationship with it at all.

The car sped up into the hills. At each turn in the road, at the ends of small bridges over the river, in clearings on hillsides, she saw soldiers. Even though there were only two or four at each point, if their presence was intended to be a warning to anyone, Stephanie decided, it was working.

They emerged from a cutting through a mountain and began a sweep back down to the coast. She couldn't help but be distracted by the view. The hills on one side and the cliff face dropping down on the other were bursting with palms, vines and flowers. And the centerpiece of the spectacular sight was the bluer-than-blue harbor she had seen on TV.

As they powered along what was obviously the main boulevard of Ngali, they passed people on motorbikes, barefoot, hair streaming, baskets of goods strapped to their backs. Everyone on the street turned to look at Stephanie's car. Not because it was a Mercedes, she realized, but because the locals viewed a passing government vehicle with awe. Or perhaps it was fear.

Stephanie stepped out onto a stone-paved forecourt. Both soldiers jumped out of the vehicle and went to stand near the entrance. A man in a shirt and sarong appeared. Her suitcase was handed to him and he disappeared inside with it. Stephanie slipped her jacket on, straightened her watch, raked her hair back.

Another solider strode up to her. "Follow me, miss," he said. She followed him down a series of long stone corridors while another one marched behind her. They stopped finally at a pair of enormous, beautifully carved wooden doors, where the first soldier knocked. He entered the room, bowing his head. Hopefully no head-bowing would be expected of her, Stephanie thought. She doubted she could manage that. He quickly returned, ushered her into the room and left, closing the door carefully behind him.

Stephanie stood still, carefully scanning the room. Her heart thudded. Decorated with silken sofas and rugs, the vast room ended in a long wall of ornate French doors. A number of these were open, revealing a deep stone terrace replete with plumbago hedges and tall urns filled with flowering plants. She stilled her breath and listened. Close by, she heard the ocean heaving and crashing onto rocks. The ceiling fans overhead made a whirring sound like giant dragon flies. A tropical bird let out a shrill call.

Finally her eye caught something, a tiny wisp of smoke curling inside from the terrace. There was always something to find if you looked hard enough. She relaxed a little, knowing there was a person out there. And someone having a quiet smoke wasn't likely to be pointing a gun at you.

"Welcome to Seragana, Inspector Tyler." She jumped slightly at the sound of a voice. It was cool, low-pitched, the accent cultured British. It had to belong to Kira, the princess Angelique had spoken of with such high regard. But maybe Angelique's judgment had been way off, for once, because the princess's tone was anything but friendly. One thing was obvious, though. Stephanie's arrival had been expected. Siow Lian must have alerted them.

Suddenly the owner of the voice entered the room, revealing herself to be as tall as Stephanie, dark-skinned and wearing dark pants and a white shirt. She strode to a desk inside the doors and put out her cigarette. The smell of cloves wafted through the room. She stood side-on to Stephanie, shuffled some papers around her desk, while stealing subtle glances in her direction. Stephanie slid her hands into the pockets of her suit pants and shifted her gaze to a tapestry on a wall. Let her give me a good look over, she thought. From the corner of her eye she saw Kira twist her head and scrutinize her.

A phone rang. She picked it up and strode back outside. Stephanie's immediate fears for her safety began to give way to a growing irritability. Unused to being kept on the back foot, she wasn't happy about the prospect of standing in this room all day playing peek-a-boo with the princess. Spotting a tray holding glasses and a jug of iced water, she walked over and poured herself a glass, gulped it down then sat on the sofa.

Kira returned briskly. This time she sat at her desk, faced Stephanie, crossed her legs. "You've come at a difficult time, Inspector. What can I do for you?"

"I'm not here as a police officer," Stephanie said quietly. "Please call me Stephanie." Kira looked indifferent. "I have no doubt you're well aware that I've come to find Angelique."

Kira shrugged. "She's working for me at the moment on matters requiring great discretion. She'll return home soon."

Anger prickled Stephanie's neck. "I'm sick of being told she's busy, and it will be over soon. What kind of work demands such discretion that she can't call home? This country is off the bloody radar. For all I know she's being held here against her will."

Kira stood up, glaring at her. "And for all I know, you're here to cause trouble. The last thing we need right now is the interference of nosy cop."

That confirmed Angelique's business here was illegal, but Stephanie still couldn't grasp the connections. Kira looked angry, but maybe it was anxiety that Stephanie was seeing. She had to consider the personal side too. Kira would surely be aware of the relationship between Stephanie and Angelique, and maybe she resented that. After all, Angelique had mentioned their little frisson. Although what Angelique had seen in this glacial woman, Stephanie couldn't imagine.

She stood and returned Kira's hostile glare. "I'm not interested in anything other than Angelique. I know she's in this country, and I want to see her now."

"I don't give a damn about what you want!" Kira shouted. "I've got issues to deal with here that are bigger than you, bigger than Angelique. Many things, including the safety of the population, the future stability of the country, hang in the balance! You have no choice but to accept my advice that Angelique is safe!"

"I have no reason to trust you!" Icy perspiration trickled down Stephanie's spine. "And your political problems, the reported violence, soldiers everywhere, don't exactly give me a lot of confidence." She dragged her fingers through her hair, trying to regain some control.

"Why would I want to see Angelique in danger?" Kira paused for effect. "Why would I lie?"

Stephanie sighed. She took off her jacket. "Many years ago," she said, "I was called out to a domestic violence complaint. I questioned the woman who answered the door. She swore there was no problem, swore the call had been mistake. She seemed calm, reasonable, she even smiled." She paced back and forth a few steps, working off some nervous energy. "Meantime a couple of cops had got inside unnoticed. They found her deranged husband in a corner holding a carving knife at the throat of their newborn daughter. People lie for all kinds of reasons." She shrugged. "Maybe there's an invisible knife at your throat, and you'll say anything."

The phone rang again. Kira jumped, snatched it up and tore back out to the terrace. Stephanie suddenly pictured Angelique hurt, or worse, and agonized over the possibility that Kira was keeping that secret while she worried about her other problems hanging in the balance. She sank back down onto the sofa. She bristled in frustration.

When Kira burst back into the room, her cool, measured demeanor had been replaced by a feverish intensity. She picked up a remote, and a wide flat-screen TV on the wall flickered to life. Stephanie's pulse leapt. What the hell was she doing? Kira grabbed a cigarette from a carved box on her desk and lit it without taking her eyes off the screen. She seemed to have forgotten Stephanie's presence.

Stephanie turned to the TV as a news presenter, obviously in Singapore, started a report. "The latest news has caused shockwaves in share markets throughout the world. The eagerly awaited results of the oil testing by Pacific Holdings Australasia have revealed that their supposedly enormous oil reserves contain nothing but groundwater."

Stephanie glanced at Kira, anticipating a look of utter dismay, and saw with a jolt that she was beaming in delight. A tiny ball started rolling around in Stephanie's brain but couldn't find a slot to fall into. Why would it please Kira to learn that her country, instead of growing rich, was doomed to remain lying in the dirt?

"Rumors began circulating earlier today, causing mayhem as stockholders desperately tried to divest themselves of the stock." The image cut to footage shot outside Melbourne's stock exchange building. "Trading was halted by the Australian Stock Exchange by late morning pending discussions with Pacific Holdings Australasia and their technical team. Shortly afterward the senior geologist in the testing team confirmed that the results were undeniable."

The little squeal of delight from Kira didn't lessen Stephanie's unease one bit. Angelique had worked hard to get this whole project underway. It looked as if she may have been caught up in some double-dealing.

"There is expected to be further chaos when the markets open in London and Wall Street. Meanwhile the exchanges in Australia, Tokyo, Hong Kong and Singapore have de-listed the stock. The Australian Securities and Investment Commission is expected to begin a fraud investigation."

Kira flicked off the TV and turned to Stephanie, her eyes glistening. "Do you understand what you just saw, Stephanie?" she asked. Her tone had lost some of its icy edge.

"I think I just saw that you've been involved in a fraud. Which might explain why you're holding Angelique."

Kira took a deep slow breath. "What you just saw was freedom for my country." Her voice dropped to little more than a whisper. "We've been freed of chains that have bound us for one hundred and fifty years." Her intense gaze remained trained on Stephanie. "All our old masters are gone. You just saw the rebirth of a nation."

Stephanie stared back at her, disarmed by the tear rolling down Kira's cheek. "And we've got your beautiful Angelique to thank for that."

Stephanie froze. The ball rolling around in her brain fell into a slot. Angelique, it seemed, hadn't been a pawn, but instead was a key player in whatever had gone down. Her tension began to melt away. Legal tangles might lie ahead for Angelique, but she was alive and well, and that was all that mattered.

Kira strode over to her and extended her hand. "I don't think I introduced myself. I'm Kira."

Stephanie shook her hand. "The crown princess."

"Quite."

She marched back to her desk and grabbed her phone. "It's time to put you out of your agony, Stephanie." She headed for the door leading to the hallway. "Come with me. I've got some people for you to meet. They'll explain everything." In a half-daze, Stephanie picked up her jacket and followed her.

DENOUEMENT

Angelique flicked off the TV in the sitting room. She had been channel surfing all afternoon just for the joy of hearing the reports over and over again. An enormous load had been lifted from her. She felt like a feather blowing in a warm wind.

The latest reports indicated that Andrew Nolan was being questioned by authorities. Not that she gave a damn about his personal welfare, but to be fair, she was glad it would become clear before too long that his intentions to drill oil had been genuine and not fraudulent. The world would see him for what he was—an inept man whose greed for easy bounty and lack of due diligence wreaked havoc and finally brought him undone. Angelique got up and left the room.

Strolling to the edge of the terrace she gazed at the sea. She would be questioned too, of course, but she had no concerns about that. No one expected a business consultant to be able to understand the technicalities of oil exploration, let alone recognize a false report. It wouldn't hurt her business credibility one bit. It was also a great relief that Stephanie had accepted her need to lie low and had waited at home. If she had turned up during the uprising, Kira might not have been able to protect her. Angelique sighed happily. Tomorrow she would call Stephanie, and arrange to meet in Singapore or Melbourne—wherever she liked. She couldn't wait to see her. It would be an interesting reunion, though, where she explained her role in an international stock fraud.

She glanced at the sky, something she'd been doing increasingly lately to tell the time. A few ruby streaks told her it was around five. Kira had called late yesterday. Following a fantastic trading day where their stock price had shot back up again, they shared a cautious optimism. They'd talked about Kira's future plans pending this morning's outcome and had arranged dinner at the villa this evening, come triumph or defeat.

Earlier she'd paid a visit to Lim, shared a cup of tea. He'd expressed surprise that she was so happy in the wake of the news that Seragana wasn't going to be rich after all. She had suggested that the riches were more likely to have benefited the Australian company than Seragana, and that maybe he should hold tight for some better news to come. He had shrugged, and continued slicing shallots. He'd been vague when she asked what he was serving the princess tonight, which was odd, she thought. He loved talking about food.

Red hibiscus flowers dangled over the stone wall of the terrace. Absentmindedly she picked one, spun it around on its stalk. During the past week, hunkered down, stressed or terrified, scrutinizing reports about shares or Nolan or uprisings, the days had flitted by. But today had dragged. She'd tried to talk to the Twilights on Facebook a few times, but while they'd left her messages of congratulations, none of them were online. She had passed a few interesting hours, though, restlessly wandering around the villa, pushing open doors, prying into cupboards and musty bookshelves. She had come across a camphor chest filled with dozens of exquisite sarongs, all featuring turquoise and a glitter of gold thread. Dala said they were probably gifts to Kira's grandmother that had never been used. She had shown Angelique how to wear and tie the garment, a hybrid of a sari and a sarong that swept in one unbroken length over one shoulder while holding firm just above her breasts. It came to the ankle with a split down one side that made walking comfortable.

Traditional dress seemed like the perfect thing to wear for tonight's dinner, so after a soothing shower she had wrapped herself in a sarong, added a few of her favorite jade pieces, and, for the first time in days, put on a little makeup. She tossed the hibiscus flower over the wall, watched it flutter down to the sand. Surely Kira would arrive soon. The breeze had dropped. The heat intensified. All was still. It was that breathless time just before sunset.

Her heart leapt at the unmistakable crunch of tires on gravel. At last, she thought. Car doors slammed and then there was silence save for the shrieks of a few homeward-bound seagulls.

"Angelique."

Angelique froze for a second. She couldn't believe her ears. Then she went into meltdown. She turned and there was Stephanie, leaning against the villa's stone wall. Before she could move, Stephanie raced to her side and wrapped her arms around her. She had a second to register the happiness on Stephanie's face. Then they kissed. Angelique's mind stopped working as her body became as liquid as the sea.

Suddenly a loud bang made Angelique jump in alarm. Her heart thudded but Stephanie was still smiling.

"Champers, Angel, not a gun!" It was Jeremy. He rounded the corner of the villa onto the terrace brandishing a bottle of Bollinger. He was quickly followed by the rest of the Twilight Club, then Kira.

They exchanged hugs and kisses, the tension of the long arduous weeks evaporating as if it had been a dream. Angelique blinked away tears. They reminded Angelique of a pack of puppies all tumbling over and around each other.

She grabbed Stephanie's hand and gripped it tightly. It was

all too easy to imagine her vanishing as magically as she had appeared. "Have you all…I guess you've met—"

Jeremy was pouring champagne into flutes and handing them around. "Angel," he said. "We've spent hours with Stephanie. Hope you approve, darling. We've made her an official member of the Twilight Club." Angelique's head was spinning. What had they all been up to?

Stephanie was grinning. "An honor I've accepted with great pride."

"Are you proud that I've been part of a fraud of international proportions?" Angelique asked, relieved that the others had already done all the explaining.

"Immensely," Stephanie replied. "Once Kira filled me in on the background, I understood it was something you would have do. I'm just glad you had such clever friends to support you."

"A breeze, wasn't it, darlings?" Jeremy fanned his face with a silk handkerchief. Angelique groaned, the others laughed.

Kira raised her glass. "I think Angelique deserves a toast. She's the mastermind." They all raised their glasses and took a few gulps.

"Let's sit down," Kira suggested. "After today's emotional roller coaster I need to take the weight off my feet." She led them to a terrace on the other side of the villa where a table had been set up and laid for seven.

They moved to it and plonked down in relief, making themselves comfortable. All was well with the world, Angelique decided, studying her friends' ecstatic faces.

Kira beamed at them. "A small announcement. In recognition of your services to the Crown, I offer to the Twilights the gift of lifetime enjoyment of an entire wing of this villa. My grandmother loved this place, and she would want this too, I know."

Angelique's eyes widened. This place was immense. A huge suite of rooms for each of them would still leave rooms to spare.

Lucy chimed in. "That's very generous, sweetie. But I hope that leaves plenty over for our grand resort plans."

Kira waved away Lucy's concern. "Heaps, darling. The Twilight wing will be a small, entirely separate, part of all that."

Angelique shook her head. Obviously she had some catching up to do. "What resort?"

Stephanie laughed along with the others. "I think every detail of Seragana's future was discussed this afternoon. There's a lot of talent around this table, I learned today, and it'll be put to good use in the development of Seragana."

Siow Lian put down her glass. "The only thing I'm not sure of is what you'll say, Kira, if you're asked questions about the oil report."

Jeremy topped up their glasses. "She's the crown princess. She can tell authorities from other nations to fuck off, if she wants."

"I probably won't do that," Kira said with a wry smile. Chuckles rippled around the table. "I'll be charming and helpful. Good relationships with other countries and a good reputation in the business world will be necessary when we're ready to start our own oil production." She leaned back in her chair. "But this is a perfect example of what goes on in countries with autocratic rulers, despots. What happened here under Giles. The business of government is secret. No one knows the truth and no one dares to question anything."

"Off with their heads!" Jeremy threw in with a grin.

"I'm in that position now. I can give any explanation I like. Nobody but me actually knows the truth." She clicked a fingernail against her glass.

"What about the exploration company that created the original report?" Stephanie asked. "It's likely they'll come forward in an investigation."

"It doesn't matter," Mason said. "Any investigation is going to reveal that our exploration company is fictitious and that the report is a fake. But so what?" He shrugged. "Kira didn't give the report to Nolan, or induce him to use it. She made no claims about its authenticity."

"Exactly," Jeremy said. "And no one can prove that Kira knew it was fake. Perhaps it was prepared long ago, found among the king's papers. She found it in a drawer!" Everyone laughed. "She showed it to Nolan's business adviser, and Nolan ran off with it. One big misunderstanding!" He grinned. "Just as well you're an autocrat for a bit longer, Kira, darling."

Lucy reached for a cigarette from Jeremy's pack. "Pity that natural resources aren't such a great thing in the long term," she said.

Kira nodded. "I agree. But before we can move toward a democracy, we need organization, infrastructure, good medical and education services, and the bureaucracy required to manage it all. Our oil will allow us to pay for that. With money, we could, for example, finance a dedicated renewable energy university. Get the world's best brains on the job."

"What's happened with the money you made for Kira?" Lucy asked Mason.

"It's in the bank account she gave me."

Kira almost choked on her champagne. "Already?"

Mason nodded. "Yep, about twenty mill. We did okay."

"That much? Fabulous!" Kira exclaimed.

"You must've jumped in at the right moment, sweetie." Lucy took a drag of her cigarette. "That share price moved like a Mexican wave."

"Yeah. I sold late Tuesday. The price fell through the floor on Wednesday after the uprising, so I thought I'd done well," Mason said. "Then we were hit with the Middle East news, and the market decided our oil was okay after all." He shook his head. "I should've held off, sold yesterday. Would have done a lot better."

"I'm delighted, Mason," Kira said. "You did a brilliant job. I need to get a few urgent things underway."

"The regeneration project?" Stephanie asked. To Angelique's delight, she and Kira were talking like old friends. Stephanie was obviously well up on Kira's plans.

"Yes, reforestation, regeneration of damaged land and waterways. Nolan's land will be returned to the Crown."

"You've already sorted out Nolan's land ownership and citizenship issues?" Angelique asked.

"Paperwork's done, Angel," Jeremy said. "After this oil catastrophe, Nolan won't have a leg to stand on. No court anywhere is going to even listen to him." He smirked. "There was no naturalization process, no swearing allegiance to king and country, and all that, so we can revoke the citizenship. It's meaningless, anyway; the government could simply have him exiled." He relaxed in his chair, draped his arm over the back. "As for the rest, Pacific Holdings Australasia will go into receivership any day. His land and his logging business are separate assets. The land will be sold, and Kira will buy it back. Undeveloped, it wouldn't cost much. Anyway, if I can mount a case to show the land was acquired from the king through bribery or corruption, she might not have to pay anything at all."

"As for the logging, the government will refuse to issue any new permits," Kira added. "So that business becomes worthless. We'll look at sustainable options, down the track, with suitable partners. That's one of Angelique's areas."

Stephanie gave her a look of surprise. "I know people, expert consultants who have the green credentials," Angelique explained.

"You'll need more than twenty million," Mason said.

"Of course," Kira said. "But that sum will get things rolling. I'll need to compensate Nolan's workers too, in the medium term at least."

"Could be more social unrest, otherwise," Siow Lian suggested.

"Quite. Onbulu and I have decided to call a special meeting with the clan chiefs early next week to advise them of the plans for a new economy. That should settle any public anxiety and generate optimism for the future."

Two platters of honey and chili prawns were delivered to the table. "Lim's a wonder," Angelique said to Kira. "He's thinking of leaving Seragana, but he's just the sort of person you need to keep. He's not just a good cook, he's got ambitions, business ideas and he's smart."

"He's a fabulous cook," Siow Lian added, popping another prawn into her mouth.

"Well, you're the government's business adviser," Kira said. They had discussed that arrangement in general terms on the phone. "Find a way to encourage Lim, and others like him."

A surge of adrenaline had Angelique shifting in her seat. Kira was clearly offering her a broad canvas for her business initiatives. "I could work on some kind of government incentive scheme to encourage entrepreneurs."

"And there's something else," Kira said. "We'll need an expert on law enforcement and public safety. Eventually, the Royal Guards will cease to act as police officers and will act exclusively as a defense force. We'll need a proper police force." Stephanie's eyes were trained on Angelique. Biting her lip, she looked a little anxious but her eyes were shining. "Stephanie has agreed to take on the job as adviser to set it all up. Rules, procedures, training academies…"

"What do you think?" Stephanie asked Angelique.

Thrilled, Angelique leaned over and kissed Stephanie's cheek. That was the start of Stephanie's career change, right there. "Darling, I think it's the best news I've heard since this morning."

Smiling, Stephanie was clearly excited. "Solves the question of where we live." Angelique reached under the table and squeezed her hand.

"Well, wherever that is," Kira said, "You must visit a lot. I'll be wanting the company."

"The villa will get a good workout," Mason said. "We'll all be visiting a lot."

"And in the future, when Seragana freely elects its own government, what will become of you, Kira?" Siow Lian asked, her expression troubled.

"That's for the people to decide." Then Kira grinned mischievously. "Perhaps I'll have to return to London and find a job."

"Never!" Jeremy exclaimed with a dismissive flick of his handkerchief. "They'll always adore their monarch. Especially one who set them free. You'll be a constitutional monarch, of course, darling. Just like our dear old Queen Elizabeth in England."

Kira drained her glass. "I would expect so," she said. "In fact, now that the future looks bright, it's time I sat down with Onbulu and planned my coronation."

Lucy's shoulder strap slipped off. "Oh, my god…" she breathed, her eyes wide.

"The people have been waiting for their princess to be crowned. It's time," Kira continued. "It'll provide a sense of continuity, and will be a major boost to public morale. Naturally, you'll all be special guests."

"You'll have to wear a dress, darling!" Jeremy teased. "And a tiara!" Kira rolled her eyes and everyone laughed.

Angelique reached for her glass. "With so many plans to discuss," she said, "there's something we must do before the night slips away." Guessing what was coming, Jeremy grabbed the Bollinger and took care of refills.

"It's been a momentous day for Seragana and for each one of us," Angelique continued. "So I propose a very special toast." The others took up their glasses. "To the Twilight Club."

In unison they raised their glasses high. "To the Twilight Club."

Publications from
Bella Books, Inc.
Women. Books. Even Better Together.
P.O. Box 10543
Tallahassee, FL 32302
Phone: 800-729-4992
www.bellabooks.com

CALM BEFORE THE STORM by Peggy J. Herring. Colonel Marcel Robicheaux doesn't tell and so far no one official has asked, but the amorous pursuit by Jordan McGowen has her worried for both her career and her honor.
978-0-9677753-1-9

THE WILD ONE by Lyn Denison. Rachel Weston is busy keeping home and head together after the death of her husband. Her kids need her and what she doesn't need is the confusion that Quinn Farrelly creates in her body and heart.
978-0-9677753-4-0

LESSONS IN MURDER by Claire McNab. There's a corpse in the school with a neat hole in the head and a Black & Decker drill alongside. Which teacher should Inspector Carol Ashton suspect? Unfortunately, the alluring Sybil Quade is at the top of the list. First in this highly lauded series.
978-1-931513-65-4

WHEN AN ECHO RETURNS by Linda Kay Silva. The bayou where Echo Branson found her sanity has been swept clean by a hurricane—or at least they thought. Then an evil washed up by the storm comes looking for them all, one-by-one. Second in series.
978-1-59493-225-0

DEADLY INTERSECTIONS by Ann Roberts. Everyone is lying, including her own father and her girlfriend. Leaving matters to the professionals is supposed to be easier! Third in series with *PAID IN FULL* and *WHITE OFFERINGS*.
978-1-59493-224-3

SUBSTITUTE FOR LOVE by Karin Kallmaker. No substitutes, ever again! But then Holly's heart, body and soul are captured by Reyna... Reyna with no last name and a secret life that hides a terrible bargain, one written in family blood.
978-1-931513-62-3

MAKING UP FOR LOST TIME by Karin Kallmaker. Take one Next Home Network Star and add one Little White Lie to equal mayhem in little Mendocino and a recipe for sizzling romance. This lighthearted, steamy story is a feast for the senses in a kitchen that is way too hot.
978-1-931513-61-6

2ND FIDDLE by Kate Calloway. Cassidy James's first case left her with a broken heart. At least this new case is fighting the good fight, and she can throw all her passion and energy into it.
978-1-59493-200-7

HUNTING THE WITCH by Ellen Hart. The woman she loves — used to love — offers her help, and Jane Lawless finds it hard to say no. She needs TLC for recent injuries and who better than a doctor? But Julia's jittery demeanor awakens Jane's curiosity. And Jane has never been able to resist a mystery. #9 in series and Lammy-winner.
978-1-59493-206-9

FAÇADES by Alex Marcoux. Everything Anastasia ever wanted — she has it. Sidney is the woman who helped her get it. But keeping it will require a price — the unnamed passion that simmers between them.
978-1-59493-239-7

ELENA UNDONE by Nicole Conn. The risks. The passion. The devastating choices. The ultimate rewards. Nicole Conn rocked the lesbian cinema world with *Claire of the Moon* and has rocked it again with *Elena Undone*. This is the book that tells it all...
978-1-59493-254-0

WHISPERS IN THE WIND by Frankie J. Jones. It began as a camping trip, then a simple hike. Dixon Hayes and Elizabeth Colter uncover an intriguing cave on their hike, changing their world, perhaps irrevocably.
978-1-59493-037-9

WEDDING BELL BLUES by Julia Watts. She'll do anything to save what's left of her family. Anything. It didn't seem like a bad plan...at first. Hailed by readers as Lammy-winner Julia Watts' funniest novel.
978-1-59493-199-4

WILDFIRE by Lynn James. From the moment botanist Devon McKinney meets ranger Elaine Thomas the chemistry is undeniable. Sharing—and protecting—a mountain for the length of their short assignments leads to unexpected passion in this sizzling romance by newcomer Lynn James.
978-1-59493-191-8

LEAVING L.A. by Kate Christie. Eleanor Chapin is on the way to the rest of her life when Tessa Flanagan offers her a lucrative summer job caring for Tessa's daughter Laya. It's only temporary and everyone expects Eleanor to be leaving L.A...
978-1-59493-221-2

SOMETHING TO BELIEVE by Robbi McCoy. When Lauren and Cassie meet on a once-in-a-lifetime river journey through China their feelings are innocent...at first. Ten years later, nothing—and everything—has changed. From Golden Crown winner Robbi McCoy.
978-1-59493-214-4

DEVIL'S ROCK by Gerri Hill. Deputy Andrea Sullivan and Agent Cameron Ross vow to bring a killer to justice. The killer has other plans. Gerri Hill pens another intriguing blend of mystery and romance in this page-turning thriller.
978-1-59493-218-2

SHADOW POINT by Amy Briant. Madison McPeake has just been not-quite fired, told her brother is dead and discovered she has to pick up a five-year old niece she's never met. After she makes it to Shadow Point it seems like someone—or something —doesn't want her to leave. Romance sizzles in this ghost story from Amy Briant.
978-1-59493-216-8

JUKEBOX by Gina Daggett. Debutantes in love. With each other. Two young women chafe at the constraints of parents and society with a friendship that could be more, if they can break free. Gina Daggett is best known as "Lipstick" of the columnist duo Lipstick & Dipstick.
978-1-59493-212-0

BLIND BET by Tracey Richardson. The stakes are high when Ellen Turcotte and Courtney Langford meet at the blackjack tables. Lady Luck has been smiling on Courtney but Ellen is a wild card she may not be able to handle.
978-1-59493-211-3